# ANONYMOUS ACTS

## Christina C Jones
Warm Hues Publishing

# ONE.

Darkness surrounded me.

I preferred it that way at this time of night, between the point when sleeplessness had stolen the final chances of a good night's slumber, and when the sun would come up, bathing the house in light.

The sheets had lost the coolness that initially welcomed me to bed, contributing to my restless state. I flipped them back, kicking them away from my legs, and lay there for a few moments longer, considering my plight.

According to the time, I had four hours before I would need to get up and start preparing for the day ahead. I could take something to help me sleep, which may or may not work, but would definitely leave me lethargic afterward. There was also the option to not bother with sleep, and waste the next four hours on whatever was on TV at this time of night. But that would lead to the zombie feeling as well.

So… what was a girl to do?

I brought my hands up from my sides, slipping them underneath my soft cotton gown to cup my bare breasts. My nipples were already beaded into hard peaks. My fingers found them and squeezed until it hurt, sending a jolt of arousal through me that centered between my legs, making me clench my thighs together, tight. I pulled my lip into my mouth, gently scraping over it with my teeth as I made the decision to climb out of bed.

Carefully, I picked my way to the other side of my home in almost complete darkness, using two years of memories to avoid any obstacles. As I turned down the hall to my office, I willed myself not to get excited. There was always the chance of disappointment, the chance of a need left unresolved. And that would really, *really* be too bad.

The office was black. I closed the door behind me even though I was alone, and the only lights were the tiny dots on the computer tower, indicating that the power was connected, and the blinking from the router and modem. I sat down at my desk and jealously woke the computer from slumber. A few seconds later, it powered on, and the room was bathed in the grey-blue light from the screen.

First, I typed my password in, and waited for it to load. Once it was done, I pulled the expensive, high-definition webcam from the drawer in my desk, and plugged it in. I spent a few moments making sure it was focused well, and carefully positioned so that there was a full view of my body, but not my face. And then I turned it off.

I opened up a web browser and navigated to the website I needed. I logged in with an email I'd set up specifically for this purpose, and then made sure my status was set to "offline" before I double-clicked to open an ongoing chat between me and... him.

**SleeplessInSanDiego: you up?**

I held my breath after I hit send on the message, waiting for those three little bouncing dots to appear, letting me know my message had garnered a response. Willed those dots to appear, because I needed them to.

Because I needed *him.*

A relieved gasp escaped my throat when his tiny round profile icon appeared under my message, letting me know he'd seen it. I

8

swallowed hard, watching the screen, and then my shoulders sagged in relief as he began to type.

**NoRestForTheWicked: be a miracle if I wasn't. surprised to see you on a tuesday.**

I scoffed, letting out a dry chuckle as I scrubbed a hand over my face.

**SleeplessInSanDiego: it was a tough day.**

Some – lying ass – "customers" were claiming that *Vivid Vixen* – my cosmetic company – was releasing products that were a health hazard, which I knew was patently false. I employed my own team of chemists, used my own production facilities, was careful about the quality of my products. Still, at the unsubstantiated word of a few less than professional beauty "gurus", there was suddenly a social media backlash against my company, and it was gaining traction, despite my efforts to quell it.

**NoRestForTheWicked: I'm sorry. This "adulting" shit is for the birds sometimes.**

**SleeplessInSanDiego: Agreed. And of course I can't sleep. But that's not new.**

**NoRestForTheWicked: No, but still fucked up.**

**SleeplessInSanDiego: yeah.**

**NoRestForTheWicked: so...**

**NoRestForTheWicked: You need...?**

**SleeplessInSanDiego: PLEASE.**

A few minutes passed with no response, and then my computer chimed to let me know a video call was coming in. My hands were shaking with anticipation as I pulled on my wireless headphones, and then accepted the call.

Just like me, he had a high-definition camera, giving me a crisp, clear view of his body. His face was cut off, just outside of the frame, but enough of him was visible that when he moved, I caught glimpses of neatly groomed facial hair layered over his jaw and chin.

He was shirtless tonight, filling my screen with beautifully defined abs, coated in deep chocolate skin. Nice biceps, nice pecs, dotted with flat dark nipples that I desperately wanted to lick.

They weren't the only things of his I wanted to lick.

"You gonna let me see you tonight or not Sandy?" he asked, his voice a warm rumble through my headphones. "Sandy" wasn't my name – not even close. It was something he'd taken to calling me as a play on my username, and damn if the sound of it didn't send a shiver up my spine that landed right between my legs.

"Patience. Aren't I worth that to you?"

He chuckled. "That and a helluva lot more."

Warmth settled over me. And a feeling akin to… relief. I pulled open the drawer again, withdrawing a bottle of Creed cologne that I spritzed in the air, filling the room with the sensual, masculine scent. I inhaled a deep breath, and then let out a deep sigh.

"I wish I never told you what I cologne I wore, woman."

I could hear the smile in his voice, and smiled back. "Why is that? And how did you know?"

"Because you always make that same sexy little sound when you spray it. I'm jealous of your ability to set the mood. I only got a small bottle of your Tom Ford, and haven't replaced it yet."

I laughed, then bit my lip, buoyed by the visual of his dick getting harder. I'd done that to him… just my laugh. It had made him twitch, and now he was rising, and growing, right before my eyes.

"Sounds like a personal problem to me, Wick. Shouldn't be so damned cheap."

"Or maybe… your tastes shouldn't be so damned expensive."

This time, I rolled my eyes a little as I laughed. I didn't know very much at all about the man I referred to as "Wick", but one thing I knew was that money was no problem for him. Even though he would talk in slang, and drop a few 'g's' here and there, his grammar and diction spoke to being well-educated. High-quality camera, the expensive watch he was wearing on the days he was still dressed from work, and the gorgeous park view that came in little peeks from behind

10

him… whatever woman he had in his life – in his *real* life – was undoubtedly well taken care of.

My hand curved around my wireless mouse, and a few clicks later, I was live on screen. My nipples beaded all over again, responding to Wick's groan of approval.

"Perfect," he murmured, but the thickness of voice, and the way his hand moved down to grope his dick said much, much more. He'd never explicitly asked, but his reactions over time told me that he liked me in white, and that's what I was wearing. A simple cotton nightie that molded around my breasts, so thin that the deep chocolate of my nipples against my honey-toned skin showed through.

"You were already undressed," I whispered, cupping my breasts in my hands. "What were you doing?"

"Working, since I couldn't sleep. Let me see it."

My legs spread like they had a mind of their own, and the hem of my gown inched up my thighs. I lifted it up to my waist, scooting to the edge of my seat to give him a better view.

"Open for me."

My hands went between my legs. I was already wet, so my fingers slipped and slid as I parted my lips for him, so he could see all of me, like he always wanted.

"Get some of that sweetness on your fingers so you can play with it for me."

A little grunt of satisfaction escaped my lips, just at the instruction. Fatigue laid heavily on my body and mind, but I did as he said, dipping my middle finger into my opening for wetness, and then pressing it to my clit. A little jolt ran through me as soon as I touched myself, and Wick's hand closed tighter around his dick. I started moving my hand. Slow circles, heavy pressure, and I didn't hold back a single sound.

Every hiss, every moan, every contented sigh, he wanted to hear it, so I gave it to him. I smiled at *his* sharp intake of breath as I started rolling my hips to meet the pressure of my hand. I shifted, massaging my clit between my forefinger and thumb. I whimpered at the change in sensation, and Wick sat up a little straighter.

"Does that feel good for you?"

"*Mmmhmm.*"

"Show me those pretty nipples again. Give them some attention."

"*Mmmhmm.*"

With my free hand, I pushed the straps of my gown off my shoulders, and tugged the soft cups away from my breasts. I cupped one in my hand and squeezed, letting my thumb and forefinger follow the natural course of slipping over my areola and moving down to curve around my nipple.

"Do it harder."

"*Ahh,*" I cried softly as I rolled my nipple between my fingers, pinching and squeezing as pleasure spiked between my legs. I closed my eyes as my hand and hips moved in furious circles, faster and faster as pressure built in my core. Layer on layer, higher and higher, until it overflowed, and I came, with a high-pitched whimper of delight.

"There you go," Wick murmured in my headphones.

When I peeled my eyes open, I was rewarded with a sight I'd been craving since I sat down. He'd finally lowered his boxer briefs, and his dick was beautiful. Not massive, but long and mouthwateringly thick. The same gorgeous chocolate tone as the rest of him, nicely veined, and surrounded by a thick patch of neatly trimmed dark hair. He had his big left hand cupped around it – no ring, not even a tan line – and it was glistening in the glow of his screen as he stroked himself.

If I had a dick like that, I'd jack it off for strangers on the internet too.

My lips parted, and I moved closer to my screen, my fingers playing in the fresh wetness between my legs as I watched him move his hand over his dick.

"Hold on," I whispered.

Wick chuckled. He knew what I was about to do. I reached into my drawer, pulling out a relatively new purchase – a dildo I imagined

12

was the same size and girth as him. I rubbed coconut oil over it – he was using coconut oil as his lubricant too.

"Open your legs wide. I want to see this."

I giggled a little. "I bet you do."

My stomach muscles contracted as I pressed the dildo to my vagina and pushed it in. I moaned as it sank into me, stretching me, filling me up.

"Goddamn that looks good."

I grinned at the screen. Wick was right. The deep, dark brown against the pink of my pussy was an extremely erotic visual. I stared at the feed from my camera as I moved the dildo in and out, matching a sight with an incredible feeling. My body clenched and complained, trying to keep it in as I pulled it out, then stretched and welcomed, hugging it tight as I pushed it back in.

"Feels so *gooood*," I moaned, closing my eyes and leaning my head back as I pushed the dildo deeper, angling it toward the front of my vagina in search of a particularly sensitive spot. "I need to do it harder."

"Do it."

His permission had barely left his lips before I took advantage, fucking myself harder, and faster.

I opened my eyes so I could see him. He was keeping pace with me, his grunts and growls in my headphones making it feel like he was with me in the room. He had his hand gripped tight around his dick, pumping hard as he watched me. Every breath he let out, every groan, spurred my enthusiasm. Pressure started building in me again, but not like before.

This time, it started as a tingling all the way down in my toes, spreading over me. I couldn't even keep my mouth shut, stuck in a steady loop of *"Ahh, ahh, ahhhh, hell yes, ah, ah, yes"* as pleasure coiled around me, laying heavy on my skin.

"Switch to one hand, so you can play with your clit. I want to see you come. And I want to hear it."

I did it. I stroked myself as deep as I could with one hand, and pressed my fingers to my clit with the other, shaking it back and forth.

My toes tightened and curled, thighs clenched, eyes crossed, eyelids fluttered as the orgasm hit me, snatching away my breath.

In my dark, empty, office I screamed, vocalizing my pleasure as my pussy clasped and throbbed, trying in vain to milk the dildo. Wick was in my ears, his breathing hitched as he jacked himself off. I was still coming down from my own orgasms, still flinching as residual waves hit me, but I forced my eyes to stay open. I watched, enthralled, as Wick nearly raised up from his chair, grunting and groaning in my ear as he came.

I licked my lips as thick, translucent semen oozed from his closed hand over the tip of his dick. Neither of us moved for a few moments, just sat there trading contented sighs as our breathing leveled out. After a while, I watched through heavy-lidded eyes as Wick pulled a towel from his own drawer, and cleaned his hand and dick.

"You feel better?" he asked, his voice a little rougher now, but still sexy, raw from the sounds we'd made.

"Yeah," I whispered, hissing a little as I pulled the dildo out of me, wrapping it in a towel to take to the bathroom for cleaning. "Barely keeping my eyes open now."

"Good. I'm actually feeling it a little bit too. Sweet dreams, Sandy."

I smiled. "Yeah… you too. Thank you."

"You're welcome."

I blinked, and he wasn't on my screen or in my ears anymore.

I quickly logged out of the computer, and put everything away except what I needed to clean. I wiped down the chair, and closed the door to the office behind me before I made my way back through the dark to my bedroom.

There, I cleaned up, and then climbed into bed, relishing the feeling of cool sheets. I closed my eyes and turned onto my side, snuggling into my pillow.

Finally, I went to sleep.

The lack of sleep was getting to me.

I blinked hard, then rubbed my eyes before I leaned toward my computer screen, reading the same paragraph of email text for what had to be the third time. When the words started swimming together yet again, I gave up.

I clicked the button in my browser that would start my text-to-speech program. Reclining backward in my office chair, I closed my eyes, and let the program read the email to me. Apparently, my "Wicked Widow" collection was on thin ice after the "scandal" yesterday. Those posts claiming my products were ruining people's nails had more than gone viral. They were fucking pandemic by this point.

We *specialized* in beautiful hands. What had started as me mixing nail polishes together to create custom colors for my friends had turned into a real business. Hundreds of polish colors and formulations, hand creams, manicure tools. One of my favorite things to do was to walk into Target and see *my* brand, built from the ground up, on their shelves.

This shit felt like an attack on my dreams.

*Vivid Vixen* was a relatively small cosmetic company – big enough for our own production facility, investors, etc., but not enough that a few – supposedly – dissatisfied customers should be able to make this huge splash on social media. But people were acting like it was supposedly the beginning of the end. My PR team was already on the job, trying to turn this back into the non-issue it should have been for the public, but that didn't make it less of a headache on my end.

"Monica?"

I flinched at the sound of my name coming from the intercom on my desk phone. Opening my eyes, I sat forward, pressing down on the button to reply. "Yes Kim?"

"Your husband is here."

Those words sucked the air out of my lungs, and immediately my nostrils flared. The tension from the headache I was already battling multiplied and spread out, weighing me down with pressure.

*As if I weren't already tired enough.*

"You can send him in," I said dryly, and then pulled my body from the comfort of my office chair. I smoothed a hand over my hips, easing any wrinkles in the deep orange dress I wore as I stood. I tugged at the hem and sleeves of my tribal print blazer, making sure everything was perfectly in place before I walked to the front of my desk and crossed my arms, waiting for the snake I'd married to step into my office.

Years ago, I'd loved the hell out of Kellen Stuart. We met in college, and he pursued me hard, bending over backward for a chance with me. He was charming, fine, smart… it was easy to give him that chance, but I still made him work for it. And he did. By the time we were graduating, and Kellen put a ring on my finger, I knew unequivocally that he loved me.

And *now* I knew, unequivocally, that he did not.

Kellen walked into my office smelling like his whore, and I wondered how long ago he'd left her bed. He approached me with a smirk etched onto his handsome face, arms outstretched like he was about to pull me into a hug.

I took a step backward, not bothering to keep the disdain off of my face. "If you touch me, I swear to God I will dig your eyes out. What do you want?"

"A man can't come and check on his wife? I just wanted to see how you were doing. I saw you get slaughtered on social media… yet no tweetstorm from the *Vivid Vixen* herself. I know it has to be bothering you."

"*Mmm.*" I made that little sound in my throat, nodding as my gaze skipped over Kellen's face. To the casual observer, it probably looked as if he were being a good husband, concerned for my wellbeing. But I knew him a little better than that. I was fully aware of the amused glint in his eyes.

Once upon a time, my husband could make me melt with a single glance. He was tall, broad-shouldered, handsome… oozed the kind of

16

sex appeal that you could feel just standing in the same room with him. Today though? I just wanted to smack that stupid smirk off his face.

"How'd you sleep last night?"

My eyebrow twitched. I forced my features to remain in the cold expression I'd worn when he entered. "Not as well as you and Crystal in the condo I pay for, I'm sure."

His mouth spread into a grin, and so did mine, but neither of us had anything for the other except clear contempt. And I don't even know what the fuck *he* was so mad for. It's not like I was the one living off of him.

"Crystal is my *assistant*, Monica."

I rolled my eyes. "Oh please cut the bullshit. Since when did personal assistant duties include emptying your boss's balls with your mouth? And, pray tell, what the hell do you do that requires you to have an assistant? It's not like you do meaningful work, that, I don't know… pays a bill?"

Kellen's jaw went tight, eyes flashing, nostrils flared. "I am *so* damned sick of you disrespecting me."

Lifting an eyebrow, I drew my head back in disbelief. "Me, disrespecting you? Kellen… you have a lot of fucking nerve to say that to me when you know what you've done."

Shaking my head, I started to walk back to my seat, but Kellen caught me by the arm, pulling me against him. "What happened to you? You used to be sexy, and fun. Now you just walk around looking sour."

I snatched away from his grasp. "What happened? I went to *work* is what happened. At least one of us had to have a job to live, and it obviously wasn't going to be you. It's been four years, Kellen. Has your muse come up with anything?"

His eyes narrowed, and he advanced on me in a way that sent a tiny prickle of fear up my spine. Still, I crossed my arms and didn't back down from his glare, because after everything *else* I'd given this motherfucker, the knowledge that he had the power to scare me was something he would never, ever get.

"You are such a miserable bitch," he spat, with a derisive rake of his eyes. "It really bothers you that I actually have a passion for something that isn't you, doesn't it? To answer your question, yeah. My muse *is* back. Been back ever since I "hired" Crystal. She's a wonderful motivator."

I sneered. "How wonderful. Let's have our lawyers talk, so you can make her an honest woman."

"Oh we're just fine with life as it is," he smiled. "So very, very *happy*. And that bothers you doesn't it? To think of me, so happy, while you're miserable."

"It bothers me to think of your lazy, selfish ass at all. Crystal can have you. I have no use for a "man" who won't work to earn his keep."

"You don't have too many more goddamned times to imply I'm less than a man."

"Then you'd better see yourself out of my office, because I'm just getting started."

I shoved him away from me, rolling my eyes as I stomped to the other side of my desk and sat down. His eyes were still on me, and I shook my head. Just being in the same room with his ass made me sick to my stomach.

I snatched up the phone from my desk, pressing the button to connect me to Kim. "Please send security to get this man out of my office. And make a note that he is not allowed in my office, or even on the premises, again."

Kim agreed, and I shot an ugly look in Kellen's direction as he chuckled. "You are a trip, you know that right?"

"And you aren't worth the skin and brain matter it took to make you. You know *that*, right?"

"Whatever you have to tell yourself. You don't have to do all of that with your security and shit. I'll gladly leave. I just wanted to tell you the good news before you heard it elsewhere, that Crystal and I are expecting."

I snorted. "Expecting *what*? A penicillin shot for the STDs you're probably trading back and forth with each other?"

18

"Ha, ha. Very funny," he said, as the smirk crept back onto his face. He crossed the office to the door, and put his hand on the knob. "A baby. We're *finally* gonna have a baby, sweetheart. You might wanna get your PR team on it now."

If the length of the room hadn't been separating us, at that moment, there was a good chance I would have tried to kill him. He'd delivered those words with venom, and they had the desired effect, even though I didn't let him see.

"Congratulations," I managed to say, with an affect that I hoped sounded bored, and an expression I desperately willed to remain unbothered. His eyes narrowed at my lack of reaction, but security arrived to get his ass away from me, and their timing couldn't have possibly been better. As soon as I was alone again in my office, I locked the door and then went back to my desk, where I fell into my chair.

I tried my best to think of something else. Fanned my face, thought "happy" thoughts, but nothing worked. I *hated* Kellen, with such a passion that it made me ache. Knowing that he was getting something that he – *we* – had so badly wanted, was more than I could handle.

Hot tears sprang from between my tightly closed eyelids, despite my efforts to hold them back. I took several deep breaths, trying to calm my nerves before I finally reached for my phone to connect to Kim.

"Reschedule anything else I have down for the day," I told her, barely keeping my voice steady. "I'm going home."

# TWO.

The soothing spray of hot water blasted against my skin, helping to relieve some of the tension in my neck and shoulders. I'd come home and immediately popped a few tablets of guaranteed sleep and then climbed into bed and closed my eyes. Ten hours later, it was just after midnight, and I was aching from the apparently awkward position I'd passed out in. After my shower, I pulled on a tee-shirt, grabbed a pint of strawberry cheesecake gelato, and got right back into my bed.

I flipped the TV on, and then picked up my phone, which was blissfully free of the hundreds of social media notifications that had plagued me the night before. Chloe, PR guru and good friend, had made me disconnect all of the accounts, and she and her team were managing them for now. There was only one notification on the phone that I actually cared about – a message from Wick.

**NoRestForTheWicked: Hope today was better for you.**

I smiled, even though it definitely hadn't.

**SleeplessInSanDiego: No such luck ☹.**

**NoRestForTheWicked: ☹ Sorry. You need to talk?**

I stared at those words for a few moments before I responded.

**SleeplessInSanDiego: yes.**

The… friendship, I guess, between me and Wick had started innocently enough, on an online support forum for people who suffered from insomnia. Five years of late night ramblings had eventually turned us into good friends. What we'd done together last night was a relatively new development.

About two years ago, I'd kicked Kellen out. Technically he'd never moved in, but we chose this house together, as one of the last real attempts at repairing our marriage. After signing the papers, he'd insisted on going to his studio, saying he had some creative energy he needed to work out. Later that night, I showed up with dinner and wine, thinking that my spontaneous plans were romantic, and maybe we'd end up working some different energy out.

I walked in on Crystal sucking his dick.

So… yeah.

For me, that was the end of that.

I didn't make a scene, didn't curse them out. I didn't even let them know I'd seen, because what would have been the point? What would have changed?

Instead, I took my ass back to my dream house, with all the perfect finishings I'd chosen, and imagined living there alone… which wasn't very hard.

That realization was what brought the tears, and eventually, the phone call to Wick, that I still vividly remembered.

*"He hates me," I whispered into the phone to Wick, a few hours after yet another blatant betrayal, my voice raw from screaming and crying. "That's why he can do things like this, with no guilt, no remorse. I can't keep pretending otherwise."*

*On the other end of the line, Wick sighed. "Cheating can mean a lot of things, Sandy. Not necessarily that he hates you. He married you. Didn't you say you were college sweethearts?"*

*"Yeah. But who he is now, isn't who he was then. He lost that finance job, and just… became somebody else. He was charming, and dynamic, and driven, and he just… he had his shit together. After that job loss? All he wanted to do was sit around wearing a damn hole in my couch. And I let him – I didn't bother him, didn't push, because I wanted to give him space to feel whatever the fuck he needed to feel, but while he did that, I was grinding. Which… is part of the problem."*

*"Why would that be a problem?"*

*"Because I didn't need him. I paid the bills. I built my business, I got investors, and I didn't tread water, waiting for him to pull himself up. And... I thrived. I ignited, while he fizzled, and he resents me. I can feel it, even when he's pretending to be Mr. Wonderful. It's contrived. I um... my business... it got featured in a pretty important business magazine – a magazine he told me, back when were sophomores in college, that he wanted to be on the cover of."*

*"That sounds like something to be proud of, Sandy."*

*I let out a dry chuckle. "It is. I mean... for most men, it would be. But when I told him about it, all excited... he never even said congratulations. No, "that's amazing sweetie," nothing. He couldn't even pretend. That was almost a year ago, and he hasn't touched me since then. I've offered, he declines. And I'd been wondering, you know... how is this man willingly depriving himself of sex, for so long? And now I know... he wasn't depriving himself at all. Just me."*

*"I... wow."*

*"I'm sorry." I shook my head as I squeezed my eyes shut, silently cursing myself for heading down this line of conversation at all. But I was... exhausted. And hurt.*

*"Don't be." Wick's voice was authoritative, leaving no room for me to argue back. "We're friends. And if you can't go to your friends to vent your frustrations, where the hell could you go?"*

*I busted out laughing at his passing reference to a popular meme. "You're crazy," I told him, and then raised the bottle of wine I'd been drinking from for the past hour, draining the last drops down my throat.*

*"I'll be that, for the desired result – getting you to laugh. Do you feel better, now that you've talked it out?"*

*My laughter turned into a heavy sigh. "Yes and no? I'm exhausted now, and I have a headache from crying, but I already know sleep is not coming easily for me tonight. I need a good orgasm – the kind I haven't had in years. I bet that would put me right out."*

*"You should go for it. I know it helps me."*

23

*Another sigh.*

*"I'm not even in the right frame of mind. Besides, they're only so good alone."*

*"But you're not alone."*

*Maybe it was the wine. Maybe it was the time of night. Maybe it was the deep, sexy timbre of his voice, soothing my raw, frazzled edges. Maybe it was all of the above, plus some. Whatever it was, those words didn't sound crazy to my ears.*

*They sounded like respite.*

*I swallowed hard, then lifted my gaze to the mirror on the wall, taking in my disheveled, red-eyed appearance – a direct contradiction to what I always presented to the world. I didn't want to be the woman scorned, who was more committed to her business than her marriage, who hated the way her husband looked at her made her feel about herself.*

*I just wanted release.*

*"Talk me through it?"*

*"Yeah."*

*That response came easily.*

*"You sure your wife or girlfriend won't mind?"*

*He chuckled. "If I had either of those, this conversation wouldn't be where it is right now."*

*"Right."*

*I felt silly about it – maybe even pathetic – but that small declaration of fidelity actually turned me on.*

*"Why?" I asked, at risk of turning the conversation away from the path that would lead to my relief. "We've never talked about anything like this, hinted at it. You don't even know what I look like. Why now?"*

*"Because you and your late-night soul voice have talked me to sleep plenty of nights."*

*I giggled. "Late night soul? What does that even mean?"*

*"You know what it means. All soothing and sensual."*

"Wow," I said, heat rising to my cheeks. "Glad someone thinks so."

"Well, now you know. Now put your hand in your panties, and tell me how that pretty pussy feels on your fingertips."

Everything shifted. My breath hitched in my throat, thighs clenched, as a man who I'd long thought about in abstract terms, though we spoke often, became something else. Something... real.

I did what he said.

I was already wet, just from anticipation. I sucked in a breath as my fingers made contact with my slick, sensitive skin.

"Tell me how it feels. Tell me how wet you are."

I closed my eyes, moaning a little as I pushed my middle and index fingers through my wetness, letting them sink into me. "Dripping. It feels good."

"Just "good"? What can I do about that?"

"Just keep talking," I whispered, as I pulled out and sank in again, enjoying the way my body clenched around my fingers, trying to keep them in. "Your voice... it..."

"Ahhh," he chuckled. "I must have a little of that quiet storm action too, huh?"

I half-giggled, half-moaned as I stroked myself again. "Yeah," I breathed, and Wick groaned into the phone.

"You sound really fucking sexy right now, and I want to hear every filthy sound that pretty mouth makes, okay?"

"How do you know it's pretty? How do you know my pussy is pretty?"

"Has to be. With a mind like yours, and a voice like yours, it's the only logical deduction, Sandy. You have a mirror close by?"

I glanced up, at the mirror on the wall. "Yeah, but..."

"Take your panties off. Take everything off."

"But I'm holding the phone."

"Put in your earbuds."

No room for question. No room for rebuttal.

I did what he said.

*"Can you see yourself?"*

*"Not completely."*

*"Then get where you can."*

*Taking the phone with me, I moved to the front corner of the bed. From there, at that angle, I could see myself. But I didn't want to. Why would I, when my own husband didn't either?*

*"Open your legs, Sandy. Watch the way you look when your fingers sink in. It's beautiful, isn't it?"*

*I averted my gaze instead. "Um... yeah, I guess."*

*"Wrong answer. You must not be looking."*

*"I was."*

*"Then you're using the wrong set of eyes. So... close them. And just play."*

*Again, I did as I was told. Shutting my eyes allowed me to go back to the place I was in before, of feeling without thought. After a few minutes, he demanded I open my eyes, and this time...*

*Whoa.*

*"I'm guessing you see it now," came that warm rumble in my ear again, rife with amusement. "I bet you look so fucking good right now."*

*"I... do," I responded, sounding surprised even to my own ears. In the dim lamplight, my skin was like burnished gold, my bright blue manicured nails like sapphire as I played with my nipple with one hand, and stroked myself with the other. The hair I'd seen as disheveled read as sexy now – wild and free around my shoulders, the honey blonde at the ends making it resemble a lion's mane. The thick, curvy body that Kellen viewed with such disdain? Lush, and comfortable.*

*"Good," Wick crooned into my ear. "Now put those fingers between your* other *pretty lips, and tell me how you taste."*

*It was like he had me on puppet strings. There were no first, or second thoughts, just my fingers in mouth, tasting my own arousal.*

*"Like ecstasy."*

*"Yes," he growled. "That's what I want to hear. Get those fingers wet, and play with your clit. You're already playing with your nipples?"*

26

*"Yes."*

*"Pinch harder. Play harder. Make yourself cum. I want to hear it."*

*I let him.*

*By the time he gave me those instructions, my body was already humming, and that was just the permission I needed to push myself over the edge. With Wick's voice in my ear – grunts and groans that gave me fair certainty I wasn't the only one chasing an orgasm – I worked myself into a climax that snatched the breath from my lungs, leaving me panting as I collapsed back on the bed, thighs clenched tight, with my hand still between my legs.*

*When I could hear again, heavy, contented breathing in my ears assured me that Wick had reached the same phenomenal release as I had, and I let a big, exhausted smile spread over my face.*

*"Well... that was interesting," I told him, dragging myself up onto the bed so that my legs had room to stretch out.*

*Wick chuckled. "Yeah... I guess that's one way to put it. I hope my joining you wasn't too much of a creep move. You sounded so—"*

*"No, it's fine," I interrupted, suddenly feeling... embarrassed? "It actually made me feel like less of a creep myself... asking you to do something like that."*

*"It was more like I offered. So you shouldn't feel any kind of way, except good. Sated. Relaxed. Do you?"*

*I bit my lip to hide a smile he couldn't even see. "All of the above. Thank you."*

*"You're welcome. Glad I could help."*

And now here we were. I didn't "really" know him, and he didn't "really" know me. But he knew me better than almost anybody else.

When the phone chimed to let me know he was initiating a call, I pressed the button to answer and then put the phone to my ear.

"Who I gotta fuck up today?" Wick asked, and I laughed a little as I shook my head.

"While I appreciate the sentiment, that's not necessary. I got myself into this particular mess. And now... I guess I have to pay the price. I *chose* him."

"Ah. *That* motherfucker again. Your husband."

I grunted. "Well, I prefer not to call him that, even though everyone else does. He has a new title now anyway – baby's father."

There was silence on the line for a second, and then, "Wow. You're pregnant?"

"No."

Silence again. "Oh. I'm sorry."

"Don't be. Fuck him. I should be past the point where he can even still hurt me anyway, but... whatever. Soon enough, something is going to have to give. I... I can't live like this anymore."

Silence.

"Are you okay?"

"I..." my breath hitched in my throat as I tried with everything I had to make my mouth form the word *yes.*

"It's okay. You don't have to be."

Good. Because...

"I'm not."

After that, I couldn't hold back. One sob broke free from my throat, and then they all came pouring out until I was snot-nosed and red-eyed, and my neck hurt.

"Talk to me, Sandy," Wick said after a while, and I sniffled as I tried to calm myself down.

"Give me a second."

I climbed out of bed to get a cool towel for my face, cringing at my red-rimmed eyes in the mirror. I looked exactly how I felt – a fucking wreck. I took a few seconds to clean my face and calm down before I went back to the phone, hoping Wick hadn't hung up.

"Hello?"

28

"Yeah, I'm here," he rumbled in response, and a contented sigh escaped my lips.

"Sorry about that."

"No need to be sorry. Go get on your computer, so I can see you. See for myself that you're fine."

I scoffed. "I don't see how an orgasm would make me feel any better."

"Did I say anything about that? Come on. Don't even change, just show me you're alive and well… not hurting yourself. Nothing like that."

Inaudibly, I sucked in a breath.

"Okay."

A glance at the side of the bed told me my bag from work was still there, so instead of trekking down to my office, where I usually went, I got up and retrieved my laptop. It took me a second, since that specific computer was one I used for work, and had never connected to my home network before. But after a few minutes, I was on-screen from the chin down, looking at a similar view of Wick.

"*Hey*," he chuckled. "Blakewood is my alma mater. Not telling what year though, you already tease me about being old."

Even though he couldn't see me, I grinned at the screen, about to retort that I'd graduated from there over a decade ago too, but my screen name in the corner halted my tongue.

*SleeplessInSanDiego* had been created in the wee hours of the morning, after a particularly grueling thirty-two hours without sleep. I was, indeed, in San Diego at the time, on a trip, but I certainly didn't live there.

That was the impression Wick had though.

An impression that I let stand, in the same way I let him call me Sandy, and I called him Wick. Those weren't our names, and San Diego wasn't my city. We were friends, but we'd never seen each other's faces. He didn't know the name of my company or what I did, only that I was an entrepreneur. I'd never even mentioned Kellen's name either, as much as I'd revealed otherwise about that situation. It was all an effort

29

to maintain anonymity – something that honestly helped me value him even more as a friend.

He knew the real me, without knowing the real me.

It was refreshing.

"No, I'm not doing any teasing today. I might drink a whole bottle of bourbon though," I said, deflecting the possibility he might want to dig further into my Blakewood shirt. It was a popular enough HBCU that tons of people, not just alumni, wore them.

Wick chuckled. "Whew. Trust me, you're not going to find what you're looking for at the bottom of a bottle of brown liquor. Wick did that so you wouldn't have to go through that."

"Okay, because I was going to say, that sounds like experience talking."

"Too much experience," he confirmed. "Ten years sober."

My eyes went wide. "Wow. You've never told me that before."

"Never had cause. But, if you're thinking about hard liquor to self-medicate, beyond a couple of glasses… please allow me to steer you in a different direction. I started drinking to forget what I'd lost, and almost ended up losing the things I had left. That's not what you want. You're smart, successful, funny, beautiful. Don't let him make you lose sight of that."

I smiled again. "There you go with that again, calling me beautiful like you're so sure."

"Because I *am*," he insisted, swiping his chin. "I told you a while ago, a voice like that…"

"Oh whatever. You're just saying it… because it's true."

"*Finally*, she confirms it," Wick laughed, and I couldn't help joining in, before a bittersweet feeling settled in my chest. In another world, another place, another time… I could've married a man like *this*. Someone who made me laugh, and feel good about myself. Someone who was *still* the man that Kellen *used* to be.

"Hey, Sandy… are you… are you trying to access my computer?"

30

Wick's tone shifted, from laughing to something serious that made an uneasy feeling wash over me.

"What? I don't even know what that means."

"Hold on…"

My heart started beating a little faster as I heard the furious tapping of a keyboard from the other end of the line, punctuated every now and then by a low, *what the fuck?*

"Your computer," he said out loud, to me. "You have some type of hyper-aggressive security on it or something?"

I frowned. "Huh? This is my work computer, not the one I usually use, in my office. So… it has whatever my assistant put on there, I guess. Why?"

"Wait, you're using a different computer? Connected an outside computer to your network?" he asked, in a way that made it very clear there was something wrong with that.

"I… yeah. My laptop that usually stays at my office, but I don't understand—"

"*Sandy*," he interrupted sharply. "Is your mic on, on the laptop?"

"No, it's muted, since we're talking on the phone."

"*Maybe,*" he muttered, then pushed out a sigh. "Alright, listen to me. Turn off your laptop, *now*."

I was confused, but I did as he asked, even though my mind was overflowing with questions. "Okay, now what?"

"Now I need you to go in your office, and unplug your computer, your modem, your router, everything."

"My computer isn't even *on* right now though."

"Sandy, just *do it*," he demanded, and I sucked my teeth.

"I'm not doing anything until you tell me what the hell is going on!"

"You're being hacked," he shot back. "I'm watching it happen now, because whoever is doing it tried to access *my* computer while we were connected."

I shook my head. "What? What do mean you're watching it? We aren't connected anymore."

"Whoever tried it didn't know who they were fucking with," Wick answered, with an arrogant edge that made me frown. "I hacked their asses back, but they don't know. There was probably a trojan horse on your work computer. As soon as you gave it access to your home network, you gave access to everything."

"How do you even *know* this?!" I demanded. "Who the fuck are you?"

"We gotta get off the phone, Sandy. If you're on your home wifi, they're probably in that too. But listen - get a pen or something so you can write this down," he said, ignoring my question.

Still feeling flustered and confused, I grabbed a pen and a scrap of paper from the notepad I kept by the bed to jot down new polish names that I thought of in the middle of the night. I took down the business name and address he gave me, then stared at it for several long moments.

"Tomorrow," he told me, in a rushed tone. "Take all your stuff there, your laptop, your phone, your computer. He's an old colleague of mine, and I trust him. Tell him you need any spyware, keystroke loggers, all of that, gone. And depending on what kind of information was on your work computer, maybe the police."

"Who should I tell him sent me?" I asked, trying to stay calm. "What's your name?"

"You don't need that. Just tell him what you need to be done. We gotta get off this line, okay? And don't discuss anything sensitive on this phone until you've had it looked at, alright?"

I scoffed. "I don't know if this—"

"*Alright?*"

I let out a short huff. "Alright. Fine."

"Okay. And Sandy?"

"Yeah."

"… stay safe."

The total silence after that told me that he'd hung up the line, after delivering two words that left me feeling the exact opposite of the sentiment. I dropped the phone and looked around, suddenly feeling as if

I was being watched – a sensation that only intensified when I looked at the address he'd given me again.

It was in my city.

How the *fuck* did he know where I lived? And if he knew that, there was another question – how long had he known?

Suddenly, the security of my home felt nonexistent. I pushed everything out of my lap and raced to my bedroom door, flipping the flimsy lock. That was okay though – I just needed it to hold long enough to snatch a pair of yoga pants and sneakers on, then retrieve the loaded gun from the drawer in my bedside table.

My obsession with learning to shoot, insistence on having a gun since I was living alone suddenly seemed a little less paranoid.

With my cell phone in my pocket, and my gun at eye level, I left my room, heading straight for my office. The house was dark, but I didn't need light to make my way around. At the door to my office, I took a deep breath, not knowing what I'd find. I carefully turned the doorknob and pushed the door open slowly, stopping when I realized how much light was coming from inside.

The computer was on.

It wasn't supposed to be.

Throwing caution to the wind, I shoved the door open, pointing my gun directly at the chair behind my desk. To my relief, it was empty – the whole room was empty, but the computer was on, and when I peeked at the screen, it was filled with steadily running, nonsensical lines of code.

Remembering what Wick had said, I unplugged everything, pushing out a sigh as it powered down, blanketing the room in quiet and darkness.

But I didn't feel settled.

Who the hell would want to *hack* me, of all things? I made nail polish for a living, I didn't have state secrets, or bomb schematics. But for someone to have access to something that was mine, and use it to access my *home* computer, which was even more personal… it was a violation, of the deepest sort.

And then there was Wick… now, I suddenly felt a need to know who, *really*, this man was. Hacking a hacker back? What regular person had a skillset like that?

And there was still the question of how the hell he knew where I was.

My tee shirt wasn't nearly good enough.

Blowing out a sigh, I pulled the phone from my pocket and dialed a familiar number.

"Hey," I said, relieved when my call was answered. "I hope you're not busy?"

"No… but it's late," Chloe said, her voice thick like I'd woken her. "What's going on?"

"Well, for starters… I need somewhere to stay tonight. I don't feel safe at home."

# THREE

I woke up soaked in sweat, with no idea where I was.

As I sat up, images of a masked, gloved intruder kept playing in my head, holding the terror of my nightmares at the front of my mind, instead of dissipating when I opened my eyes.

*What the fuck is happening?*

I glanced around a room furnished as lavishly as any luxury hotel, and the events of last night came rushing back. My conversation with Wick, the hacking, the necessity of pulling out the gun I hoped I'd never have to use, and finally… calling Chloe to ask if I could stay the night with her.

It probably hadn't been my best idea.

I'd chosen Chloe because for years, it had just been her and her kids in the large, well-appointed condo she called home. She, though it wasn't curated that way, was my only friend who didn't live with a partner, which in my mind, made her the person to call for a place to lay my head if I needed it.

Only… her living situation had changed.

Now *I* was the only one with the lonely bed.

Shaking my head, I pulled myself from the covers, making a mental note to have Chloe send me a dry-cleaning bill. I grabbed the suitcase I'd brought with me, dragging it to the attached bathroom to take a much-needed shower before I started my day.

In the mirror afterward, I began the too-long process of doing my hair and makeup. A smarter, less vain woman would brush her sew-in weave into a ponytail and throw on some eyeliner and gloss and call it a day.

I… couldn't.

After so many years of stepping outside wearing beauty as an armor, with perfect hair, makeup, and clothes standing in the gap for the weight I'd long given up on losing… I wasn't about to start today.

*Especially* not today.

Not the day after my computer was hacked, after finding out that the man who was *very much* still my husband had impregnated his mistress, the day after the company I'd poured everything into was under attack on social media. I was drained, mentally, physically, and emotionally, but damn if I was going to look like it.

I carefully brushed edge control onto my hairline and tied it down, then plugged in my flat iron. While it was getting hot, I smoothed the primer for my makeup onto my face, giving that time to dry while I ironed away every hint of a curve, giving myself bone straight hair. After that, I went through my makeup, layer by layer, covering any trace of a blemish, concealing the bad and highlighting the good until an even more flawless Monica looked back at me in the mirror.

I cleaned up my supplies and got dressed, shoes and all. I'd taken up more than enough space and time in Chloe's home, and had no desire to overstay my welcome. I slung my bag over my shoulder and stepped out of the room, following the sound of voices down the hall to the kitchen, where I stopped in the doorway.

Chloe and I were friends, but from the time I'd known her, her interaction with men who were not family, friend, or client was basically nonexistent, as far as I knew. One of the things I loved about Chloe, as both a businesswoman and a friend, was that she was so steadfast. Not closedminded, or stubborn, but *consistent*. Very little surprised me with her.

But seeing her with a densely muscled arm wrapped around her, very clearly enjoying herself while her shirtless husband fed her strawberries from a bowl on the counter… that stopped me in my tracks. They were beautiful. And so obviously happy that it made a lump build in my throat, bringing to mind memories of when Kellen and I had been so in love, so into each other.

Just like that.

"Are you going to just watch, or are you going to say good morning, Monica?" Chloe asked, her voice still tinged with a British accent even though she'd lived in America so long. Embarrassed heat rushed to my face, and I averted my eyes.

"Sorry Chlo. Good morning. And good morning, Reggie," I said, giving him a nod as he chuckled.

"Good morning to you too," he told me, then gave Chloe a kiss on the side of her head, saying something into her ear before he released her from his hold.

Chloe nodded, giving him a lingering, smoldering look before he left the kitchen using the opposite doorway, grabbing a set of keys from the counter as he went. She watched him, lip pulled between her teeth, until he was gone, and then finally turned to me, with a smile.

"How is it that the last two days have been absolute personal and professional chaos for you, and yet you look photoshoot ready? On a fucking Thursday."

I grinned back, finally stepping into the kitchen and putting my bag down on the counter. "Lots of water, and a really expensive under-eye serum. Not that you need any tips – you could bottle and sell the glow that Reggie is giving you, and never have to work again."

"Uh-uh," she mused, taking a seat at the counter. "I am keeping that *all* to myself. I waited long enough, and feel no guilt about being absolutely selfish."

As she shouldn't. The man had spent twelve years in federal prison. After standing by through that, she *deserved* to indulge in him however she saw fit.

"Are you leaving already?" she asked, gesturing toward my bag. "It's early, and I could have sworn I encouraged you to take the day off."

"You did, but I still have things that need taking care of."

"*You* need taking care of," Chloe insisted. "A nice massage, a beautiful lunch, with wine and dessert, and a little something to help you sleep."

Internally, I cringed. As tired as I was, sleeping was the last thing I wanted to do while visions of masked intruders danced in my head, ridiculous or not.

"Maybe I'll try to get into something later, but for now… I need to figure out what's going on with my computer. Everything connects to my home network – my laptop, my desktop, my phone, my security system – hell, even my car connects."

Chloe nodded. "Yeah, we have to get that taken care of. You're sure there's nothing I need to know about on your phone, your computer, none of that? *Before* it gets out to the public," she said pointedly, because of course, that's where her mind would go. Friend or not, she handled the publicity for my brand, and by extension, me.

She wanted to know if she was about to have yet another fire to put out.

"No," I told her, shaking my head. "Or at least not easily. All of the important things for *Vivid Vixen* are password protected, encrypted all of that, but not *on* my computer. Still…"

"Right. You're lucky you noticed it was happening before it got too far. Do you have someone in mind?"

At first, my mind went to the name and address Wick had written down for me, but I shook my head. "No. Do you have a recommendation?"

There was *no* way I was using the person Wick had written down for me. Not until I had more time to figure out that situation.

Chloe's face spread into a smile. "Oh, yes ma'am I do. I'll send you to my personal favorite. I use them for everything. Even legal."

I frowned. "You... use a computer security firm for legal work?"

"No," Chloe laughed. "The people I use, they have like... a collective. A bunch of former law enforcement and government agents, in a whole suite downtown, with a tech store, a security firm, and a law firm. And a gym, interestingly enough. The gym came first though."

"Seriously?"

She nodded. "Seriously. Five Star Enterprises. I'll text you the address."

"And you said it's right downtown? Never heard of it."

"Because you *never* go anywhere," Chloe teased as she picked up her phone. "Perhaps if you did something other than work and go home..."

I sucked my teeth. "Whatever Chloe. I do other things... sometimes... on occasion."

"Of course you do, doll. That's why you're having dinner with me, Blake, Nubia, and Kora tomorrow night. No excuses. It's been too long."

I raised my hands in consent. "Fine. No excuses. As long as they have good wine, I'm there."

"Perfect. I'll text you the information for Five Star Tech."

"Actually," I sighed. "Write it down for me. I'm leaving my phone off, just in case, until I get it looked at."

"Ooh, probably smart. I can do that. And Monica... I'm *not* kidding about tomorrow night."

"I *know*," I told her, smiling. I was beyond grateful for friendship – my friends were the only thing keeping me human these days.

"You're sure? Because I'll drag you there myself, if I have to."

"Chloe, I will be there, I promise. There is *nothing* that will keep me from having dinner with my favorite women in the world tomorrow night."

*Damn. Maybe Chloe was right, and I* do *need to get out more.*

As I climbed out of my car, in the huge parking lot reserved for the block of businesses that encompassed *Five Star Enterprises*, I shook my head. I'd driven past this place what had to be a million times and never noticed it, but… it wasn't as if I spent much time noticing my surroundings.

I was always on the phone, always obsessing over this or that. A new marketing plan, new hand cream formula, fresh color lines, cute polish names. Sometimes I got from home to the *Vivid Vixen* offices with no recollection of even making the drive, because my mind was so occupied with everything else.

This was cool though.

The majority of the storefront space was taken up by a large gym, *Five Star Fitness*. Next to that was a door with a similar logo, only that one read *Five Star Security*. The next one was *Five Star Legal Services,* and finally, was the one I needed – *Five Star Technology*.

The whole "five-star" thing seemed a little corny, but Chloe didn't accept anything less than excellence. If they were good enough for her, they were good enough for me.

And, they weren't the ones Wick had tried to steer me toward, so I considered that a plus.

When I opened the door, I was surprised by the amount of space that sprawled in front of me. The front part of the store was obviously retail, but further in, there were glass-walled classrooms, and past that, workstations for repairs and customizations on one side, and desks for consultations on the other.

What caught my attention most was the classroom on the left – or rather, the teacher. The pupils were young – young enough to not be at school on a Thursday morning. Instead, they were soundlessly laughing and playing, bright blue electronic tablets in their hands as they chased bubble-shaped robots around the room.

The teacher though… *damn.*

He was wearing a dark blue tee shirt with *FIVE STAR TECH* printed in white across the front, and the edge of the short sleeves – I noticed it on the sleeves because of the way they fit over golden, tattooed biceps. One of the kids ran up to him, tears in her eyes as she shoved her tablet at him, obviously having a problem with it. He adjusted black-rimmed glasses on his face before he smiled at her, showing off perfect teeth before he bowed his tall, broad-shouldered frame down, kneeling at her level to help.

"Quite a sight, isn't it?"

I tore my eyes away from the classroom to see that I'd been joined in my voyeurism. The woman next to me had thick, glossy natural hair pulled into a bun, and was wearing a shirt like his, only hers was white, with the words in blue.

My lips quirked into a smile. "I bet it's hard to stay focused and work with something like that walking around, huh?"

"You have *no* idea," she said, moving her hand in a way that my eyes instinctively followed to a very round, very obviously pregnant belly that I hadn't registered at first.

Then I noticed the ring.

"Oh, God," I said, covering my mouth with my hand. "That's your husband, isn't it? And I'm standing here being a creep."

She laughed. "Don't sweat it. I'm just teasing you. Hell, I stand around and just look at him too. It's how I ended up with this one," – she pointed to her belly again – "and the one currently charming him with those crocodile tears. He's such a sucker."

When I looked again, he was hugging the little girl, who shared his green eyes, but had her mother's deep copper skin. I watched as he gently wiped her tears away with his thumbs, and then held the tablet out to her again, pointing at the screen as he patiently explained something to her.

Despite her teasing words, beside me, the woman was obviously very, very happy. Beaming with it. And I couldn't blame her. A gorgeous child, a gorgeous husband, and another baby on the way. The love in her eyes was so obvious that it made a lump build in my throat.

This was the kind of moment I'd only ever experience vicariously.

"You have a beautiful family," I told her, averting my gaze away from both visuals, toward the consultation area at the back. My grip tightened on the strap of the laptop bag slung over my shoulder. "I should um... probably get to the point of my visit though. My friend Chloe sent me, I need to talk to someone about a computer being hacked?"

She smiled. "Well, you're definitely in the right place. I'm Renata LaForte, one of the owners here at *FST*. You have the computer with you?"

"Yes," I nodded. "Well, one of them. I brought the laptop and my cell phone, but my desktop is at home. I figured we could fix these and then I can bring it."

"You think all three were compromised?"

"Well... maybe? My um... my friend, said something about my network?"

Renata gave a deep nod. "Ah, yes. If they were all connected to the same wireless network, that can definitely make them equally vulnerable. Let's go over here and you can tell me what happened."

I pulled the bag down from my shoulder as she led me to one of the consultation desks – basically smaller versions of the soundproofed classrooms. Inside, I handed her the laptop, and she put something into the side of it before she turned it on.

"What is that for?" I asked as I sat down across from her.

She smiled. "*That* is for me to hack you. Right now, we have no idea who hacked your computer, what they put on it, or what it was set to do when you turned it back on. The thumb drive I put in there automatically gives *me* the control. I can see everything, do anything. The computer won't run a single program I don't tell it to. Walk me

42

through exactly what happened. How did you know you were being hacked?"

"Well, I didn't. I was on the phone, and a video chat with a friend. He asked me if I was trying to access his computer, and I asked him... what the hell he was talking about. He told me that my computer was trying to access his, and that I must've been hacked. He had me turn off the laptop, and my phone, and then go check on my desktop. And... he was right. When I went to my office, it was running... some type of code. Something I'd never seen before. I completely unplugged it. That's what he said to do."

"Good. It was quick thinking. You can't hack something that's not turned on – well, unless it has its own power source, and... never mind, I won't bore you with all that. Your friend, does he work with computers? What does he do?"

My lips parted, but... "I... don't know, actually. We never..."

"*Oh!*" Renata grinned, eyes sparkling as she leaned in a bit. "I recognize that hesitation. A little computer love, huh? Quentin and I know *all* about that. It's how we met, when we were just kids." She let out a dreamy sigh when she finished. Those were *obviously* good memories for her.

I shook my head though. "Not *love*. Not like that. We were good friends though."

"Were?" Renata's eyebrow perked up. "Not anymore? Do you think he hacked you?"

"What? I... I don't know, actually. It all just happened last night, and I haven't talked to him since then. It just freaked me out really bad, mostly because I *don't* know."

She nodded. "Okay. I'm going to assume you don't know his real name?"

"No."

"I didn't think so. Okay... give me a second... this is a personal computer, or you use it for school or business?"

"Business," I answered. "I help build marketing campaigns on it, manage social media, communicate with my scientists, and production team, and keep up with financial records—"

"Okay whoa," Renata laughed. "I'm sorry, let's backtrack – what is your name, and what is that you do again?"

I returned her laugh. "Sorry, we did just dive right in, didn't we? I'm Monica Stuart, owner of *Vivid Vixen* Cosmetics."

"Seriously?!" she shrieked. "I use your Luxe Vixen hand cream – that stuff is amazing! And I'm wearing your polish on my nails right now, it's—"

"Jalapeno Face," I finished for her. "I noticed, actually. The green is beautiful on your skin."

"You cannot *ever* stop selling this color, okay?"

I laughed. "Scout's honor."

"Okay. Okay, enough fangirling," she said, taking a deep breath. "Now, as far as your computer, I can see exactly when the virus was introduced, directly on your machine. Do you always have this computer with you?"

I shook my head. "I *rarely* have it with me, unless I'm in my office at work. What does that mean though?"

"It means that, this type of virus... you don't get it by clicking the wrong link in an email, someone had access to your computer, and installed this. There's a keystroke logger – which would be used to capture passwords, a screen recorder, and crawlers, looking for specific keywords and anything connected to those keywords, on your computer. There's also a component that infects anything that you connect this computer to with the same virus, unless you had some pretty intense security, which most people don't."

I pushed out a sigh. "Wow. Um… can you see what files or whatever they're after?"

"I can. And… Monica… you should probably take this to the police."

I frowned. "The police? For what?"

"From what I can tell, there's a heavy interest in your business dealings, copies of your patent filings, chemical formulas... this could be the work of a rival company, either stealing from you or looking to sabotage you. Either way, I don't think this is a phishing scam from Russia, or some teenage hackers playing around. This is *criminal*."

"No, I don't think—"

"Monica," Renata interrupted. "Seriously. I... used to be in the FBI. Cybersecurity was my specialty. I know exactly what I'm looking at. You need to take this to the police, and you need to figure out who put this on your computer. It's been there since last year, and I bet that a whole lot of your company's sensitive information has gotten into the wrong hands between then and now."

For a second, I simply sat there, stunned. I didn't want to believe her, but the sincere urgency in her voice had my heart racing.

Someone I *knew* had hacked me?

Absently, I nodded, agreeing with Renata's words. "I...uh... yeah. Yeah. I'll do that."

"My friend Marcus is one of the guys in charge over at *Security*. He still has contacts in the police force here, I'll get him to set up a meeting with a detective for you, okay? Let me get your phone number and other information."

*Shit.*

"I... my phone. I haven't even turned it on again since last night."

Renata chewed at the side of her lip. "It was connected to the same network? Your Wi-Fi at home?"

"Yeah."

"Yeah, then probably so. Okay, we have phones, so I can get you one of those. And a laptop to use, because the police will probably want to keep yours, and the computer at your house, as evidence. But, you *cannot* connect either of them to your home network, not until the virus has been stripped. Right now, it's just waiting on something new to infect."

"Perfect," I blew out a sigh. "So... how do I get rid of it?"

Renata shook her head. "Don't worry. You're in the right place." She looked away from me, out into the open area. Suddenly, her eyes lit up. "You see him? That's Chad. Smartest guy in here – the *best* hacker we've got. We'll get you down on the schedule, and he's gonna come out and get your network cleaned up *and* protected, so this never happens to you again."

I followed her gaze to broad shoulders in a polo that I was sure was *FIVE STAR TECH* branded like Renata and Quentin's tee shirts. Only, "Chad"'s back was turned to me, so I couldn't see the logo – but I *could* see how perfectly tight and perfect and tight his ass was in his tailored gray khakis. He had biceps like Quentin's too, only his were coated in smooth mahogany skin. When he turned, I noted similar black-framed glasses and beautifully sculpted features, down to the neatly trimmed facial hair.

"What is this place, a damn sexy geek factory?" I muttered, and Renata laughed.

"Something like that. Chad is actually Quentin's cousin, and *he* is single. No small children. Tall, smart –"

"I'm married," I interrupted, and her mouth immediately stopped moving. But then, after a few seconds…

"My bad. I just—"

"No need to apologize. It's not… I don't even know why I still wear this," I said, without meaning to. "I'm sorry, that's not—"

"Uh-uh," Renata shook her head. "No need to apologize. But… I will say… and I hope I'm not overstepping… *Five Star Legal Services* could handle that for you, *if* it needs handling. Just saying."

I let out a dry laugh. "I… will keep that in mind."

Renata gave me a comforting smile as she stood, stepping out of the door to grab "Chad". I forced myself to look away, not wanting to be caught staring. Instead, I played with the tiny platinum cross that served as a constant fixture around my neck.

Until I felt eyes on me.

When I glanced up, he was looking right at me as he listened to Renata speak. Not wanting to be awkward, I smiled and gave him a little

46

wave – actions that ended up being awkward anyway, because he looked away as if I hadn't done anything.

A few minutes later, Renata breezed back in, with a still-boxed smartphone and an appointment card in her hand.

"Well, I got your phone, which we can setup now, but Chad is acting like he's too busy to come in and consult right now, so we'll get to that later. For now, I'm going to write down my contact information so we can set up a time and date, and I'll talk to Marcus for you about an appointment with the police, okay?"

I nodded. "Okay."

"Perfect," she smiled. "Now, let's get your phone set up, and you'll be back on the path to normalcy."

I sat back in my chair, thinking of everything that had transpired in the last two days. "Back on the path to normalcy sounds *great.*"

The simple act of pulling into the parking lot of the building that housed *Vivid Vixen* held a certain sense of fulfillment that never seemed to go away. I was no perfect wife, no perfect daughter, maybe not even a great friend, but when it came to this company, it could never be said that I hadn't put in the time.

Kellen had his mistress, and I had mine.

When I considered things in those terms – and I did, often – I could almost bring myself to sort of understand the way things so far south between us. Kellen's departure from Barker Financial had been sudden, and ugly. There were charges, indictments, search warrants, frozen financials, scrutiny from the FTC.

Kellen's *dream* job.

Here one day, and gone the next.

He struggled with it, mightily.

We used to stay up late at night, laying across the bed in our tiny off-campus apartment, daydreaming out loud about the future. For Kellen, it was always *Barker Financial* this, *Barker Financial* that. His singular focus worried me, but who was I to put a damper on what he obviously wanted so bad?

His focus paid off though. An internship right out of college, and then a low-level position. For ten years, he worked his way through the bullshit and office politics and landed himself a coveted senior financial advisor position. He was so, *so* happy.

But then he was so, so broken.

No one wanted to hire him.

Just him, out of all of the upper-level employees from *Barker.* Long after the public was done with the scandal and had moved on to something else, his name alone was tainted. It wasn't as if he could just leave it off his resume, because how in the world would he have explained a missing ten years?

So he stayed home, and I didn't mind.

He was finding himself, figuring out what he wanted. He bought a guitar he couldn't play, turned our garage into a wood-working shed where he discovered a supposed saw dust allergy, painted canvases that didn't sell, tried to be a podcaster, etc., etc., but nothing stuck.

And in the meantime?

The mortgage had to get paid.

So I was grinding.  In my mind, I was doing what I was supposed to – holding him down while he figured his shit out, and got it together. I hired corporate lawyers, took on investors, did what I had to do to build *Vivid Vixen* to a place where it didn't even matter if Kellen had an income.

But that was a mistake.

Because, while the money didn't matter, it *did* matter that the man I'd fallen in love with, the man I'd taken vows with, was a go-getter. He was handsome, athletic, funny, sure. To anyone who wasn't deaf and blind, Kellen was sexy. But his drive to be successful, his work ethic, his pursuit of prestige in his chosen field… *those* were the things

48

that set him apart, and really got my motor running. I didn't need Kellen to be rich, or powerful.

I just needed him to *do* something.

But he wouldn't.

Or maybe couldn't.

But the longer he "tried to find himself" the less interested I became. I threw myself into work to avoid being at home, and while my marriage withered... *Vivid Vixen* soared. That wasn't Kellen's fault – it was mine.

Maybe I should've worked less, spent more time rubbing his shoulders and telling him it would be okay. Spent days on the couch with him, figuring out a new dream to chase. But I wasn't wired for that, and again... it just wasn't the type of man I thought Kellen was.

But, I hadn't seen the pregnant mistress coming either.

Even though Crystal had been preceded by a long line of other women – some, the early ones, were only revealed through the marriage counseling attempt, others, he was blatant with – I somehow still held on to the notion that there was some part of him that still cared for me. Fourteen years of marriage had to mean *something*, right?

I shook my head as I climbed out of my car, clutching my brand-new phone and laptop. When it came down to it... no, fourteen years of marriage didn't mean a goddamn thing. *Vivid Vixen* was the love of my life, and I couldn't even bring myself to feel any sort of real regret over what my focus on it had done to my marriage. Guilt? Maybe.

But now... *Vivid Vixen* was all I had.

Inside the building, I made my way past security and up to my office on the third floor. The basement was our warehouse, where we kept merchandise stocked and ready to send out. The first floor was reserved for production, and the fourth floor – the most secure floor, for good reason – housed research and development.

Instead of taking the elevator straight to the third floor, I purposely got off on the second, and ignored lots of curious stares as I made my way past customer service, sales and marketing – I already knew, everybody wanted to see my reaction to the social media lies about the products. But they had their scripts and talking points, handcrafted by the *queen* of public relations – Chloe.

With any luck, they were the key to turning this whole thing around.

It was important, I thought, for them to see me looking breezy and unbothered by all of this, which was why I got off on two, and used the tempered glass staircase in the middle of the floor to make my way to the third.

I wanted to make an entrance.

As soon as she saw me, Kim jumped up from her desk, rushing to meet me as I entered the reception area that led to my office.

"Good morning, Mrs. Stuart," she greeted. "I wasn't expecting you today. Is that a new laptop?"

"It is," I nodded, putting the box into her hands. "I need you to set it up for me, without connecting to the company network. You can tether it to the internet from my phone."

One of Kim's neatly groomed eyebrows lifted. "Why wouldn't you want to use the company network?"

"Because it's hacked. So, I also need you to make sure that R&D stops any type of automatic syncing of research notes, anything like that. Until I've gotten someone in here to get it all cleaned up, everything needs to be kept locally. *No* internet connections. Shut it down."

Kim shook her head. "But we can't work without the internet. What about customer service, and—"

"Well, obviously not *that* department," I snapped, with more bite than I intended. "I don't want to shut down operations – everybody should work as usual, except for the fourth floor. I don't want to give them anything more than they already have."

"Who is *they*?"

I pushed out a sigh. "I don't know yet. I wish I did. I have a contact with the police who is working on getting someone to look into it, so we should know soon. And I'm sorry for snapping at you."

"I didn't take it personally," Kim said, offering me a sympathetic smile. "I know it's probably been a rough morning."

50

I frowned. "I... what do you mean?"

Kim's lips parted, and she took a tiny step backward. "Oh, I just um... I'm sorry. I assumed that because of the whole thing with Kellen this morning, you'd—"

"What thing with Kellen this morning?"

"Oh." She cringed. "You... didn't know."

"Didn't know *what*?"

She looked like she'd rather swallow razor blades than tell me, but she motioned for me to follow her to her desk. She put my new laptop down, and went to her own, where she typed in something in a search box that quickly pulled up what she'd assumed was causing me to have a bad day.

"I'm going to kill him."

Those words were out of my mouth before I could even fully process what I was seeing, and the next moment, my phone was in my hand, and I was dialing his number.

"I'm going to *kill you*," I hissed into the phone, as soon as he answered, sounding groggy and relaxed, as if he'd just woken up, even though it was almost eleven in the morning.

That only incensed me further.

"You lazy, pathetic, conniving, useless son of a bitch," I jeered. "You couldn't even give me twenty-four hours before you just *had* to go running to tell the press you knocked up your whore. I am sick of you, and sick of your bullshit, Kellen. I have tried, and tried, and tried again to simply fucking ignore you, and you just can't seem to let me have any peace. Well, I am *done*. I hope you enjoy this, because this is the last time you'll do something to hurt me, motherfucker. I promise you *that*."

I should have hung up.

I should have said what I needed to say, and hung up the phone, but no. I waited for his response. And he... laughed.

A long, hearty laugh, that only made my blood boil hotter.

"Oh, Monica, sweetie. We *both* know that's an empty threat. See, if you *could* get rid of me, you would've already done it. But you won't, because you know what I'm taking with me when I go – half of the only baby your bitter ass will ever have. So really, you aren't gonna do shit, but sit on the phone cry and take whatever the fuck I decide to do."

"We'll see about that."

Then, I did hang up, and only barely repressed the urge to launch the phone at the wall. I took a deep breath, then turned back to Kim.

"When did this news break?"

She shrugged. "I don't know. Maybe thirty minutes ago? Chloe called the office looking for you, said you weren't answering your cell phone."

"*Fuck*," I muttered under my breath. I'd left it silenced on the ride from FSE so that I could have some time to think and reflect without any interruptions, but apparently that wasn't in the cards for me today.

"Set up the laptop for me," I told Kim, then stalked into my office to call Chloe.

We had yet *another* crisis to figure out.

It would have been nice to talk to Wick.

No – I *needed* to talk to Wick.

This was our… thing. It had become something like a habit – Kellen shows his ass, I call Wick and complain about it. It was a wonder, honestly, that he hadn't simply stopped talking to me because he was sick of hearing me whine about my husband, but he always took it in stride. He served as the sounding board that I desperately needed – the male perspective that I wouldn't have considered otherwise.

He was the only reason I even remotely understood my own damned husband.

Understanding him didn't make me feel any better though.

In fact, I would have much preferred being confused by his current actions, than knowing for certain that his hatred of me ran so horribly deep.

But when I was talking to Wick – when it *wasn't* about Kellen – it was easy to completely forget him. And forgetting him… was exactly what I needed to do.

I couldn't make myself dial the number though. I couldn't make myself send that text, because everything was so all over the place, between Kellen's bullshit and the hacking and the social media scandal thing, my head was swimming with questions and mistrust and…

*Fuck!*

Out of sheer frustration, I smacked the steering wheel of my car, then immediately regretted it as pain radiated through my hands. I pushed out a sigh as I pulled away from the stop sign and into my neighborhood, navigating to my house. In my driveway, I put the car in park and turned it off, taking the time to gather up my things from work, and the two bottles of wine I'd stopped for on the way home.

I managed to maneuver my keys into my hands as I approached the walkway that wrapped around the house, but stopped in my tracks as soon as I turned the corner, putting the front door in my line of sight.

It was already open.

A quick glance around showed no strange vehicles on the street, and it was broad daylight. Surely there was a good explanation for this, something better than the current theories floating around in my head. It was really just a crack.

Hell… I'd left in such a hurry last night that it was possible I'd left it open myself.

With that in mind, I took a deep breath and shook off my unfounded alarm. I'd had enough craziness in two days to last a whole year – there was no use in inventing more.

I stepped inside and locked the door behind me, then headed straight for my kitchen, dumping the contents of my hands onto the counter. Grabbing the bottles of wine, I bent to put them in my coveted specialty cooler. When I straightened, I brought an already chilled bottle with me, to open and enjoy while I ran myself a bath.

It was going to be *glorious.*

But as soon as I took a step deeper into the kitchen, the pointed toe of my heels collided with something on the floor.

*Glass.*

My eyes went wide as I actually looked around the airy, bright kitchen, with all the open shelving I'd insisted on. I'd spent good money on pretty glass dishes and drinkware, special shelving for my beautiful custom wine glasses to hang. The shelves were empty.

It was all smashed on the floor.

I didn't waste time thinking – I just *moved.*

Straight to my bedroom, straight to my bedside drawer.

As soon as the gun was in my hands, I raised it to eye level, ready and willing to kill anything that moved. My stomach lurched as I surveyed my bedroom, realizing that *someone* had to have been in here too – my lingerie drawers were hanging out of the dresser, with their contents strewn haphazardly across the floor.

I swallowed hard as I eased open the bathroom door with my foot, checking there before I looked under the bed and in my closet, confirming that no one was there. Room by room, I checked the whole house, growing more and more agitated by the destruction I found.

Irreplaceable art ripped off the walls, priceless glassware smashed on the floor. In my office, the bookshelves had been destroyed, pages ripped from treasured signed copies of my favorite novels. In fact, as I looked around, it seemed that the only thing of value that *hadn't* been touched… was the computer.

My heart leaped into my throat as the doorbell sounded, and I tightened my grip on my gun. Carefully – *quietly*—I made my way back to the front of the house, then cautiously looked through the peephole.

There was no one there.

I switched positions to hold the gun with one hand as I reached for the deadbolt. Just as I was about to turn in, I noticed a tiny white envelope on the floor in front of the door. I furrowed my brow as I bent to grab it, maneuvering it open with one hand.

My frown deepened as I read the single line of typed text on the card.

There was no signature or anything to indicate who it was from, on the front of back of the card. A second look at the envelope made me realize it had come from a local florist, which only confused me more.

I dropped the card and envelope onto the table where I usually left my keys, then unlocked and opened the door.

A prickle of fear ran up my spine as I took in the huge bouquet of long-stem roses smashed on my doormat. The deep crimson blooms mingled with the mangled remains of a black vase and the water that had been keeping them fresh was already leeching color from the petals, almost making it look like my front step was covered in blood.

I couldn't slam the door closed fast enough.

My hands were shaking as I rushed to the kitchen to dig my cell phone out of my purse. I dialed 9-1-1 at first, but then cleared the numbers from my screen, shaking my head. It would probably be better to call Chloe first, since having my home taped off as a crime scene was sure to invite yet *another* scandal I didn't really need. Not to mention, just the thought of having police crawling all over my home felt like yet another violation.

I stared at the phone for a few seconds, trying to calm the thoughts racing at light speed through my head. After a moment, something clicked, and I dialed a number – a new number that I'd just gotten today.

Relief settled over my shoulders when Renata LaForte's chipper voice came over the line.

"Hi," I started, not realizing how shaken up I was until I heard the tremor in my own voice. "This is Monica Stuart, and um… you mentioned earlier, that you had connections, in the local police force?"

"Yes. Well, Marcus does. What's wrong? Are you okay?"

I let out a huff. "I… um… someone broke into my home, and I just… I would like to handle it with as little fuss as possible, because I have enough going on already, and—"

"Say no more. I'll talk to him, and he'll get somebody over there as soon as possible. Are you okay?" she asked again. "Are you there now? Are you sure they're not still in there?"

"Yes, I'm in the house, but no one else is. And I have a gun."

"You know how to use it?"

"Yes."

"Good. Keep your finger on the trigger until the police get there."

# FOUR

"So bitch... what you're saying is, you're cursed. I mean... that's really what this all boils down to," Nubia said, shaking her head before she picked up the wine in front of her and drained the glass.

I followed suit, emptying my glass down my throat, even shaking it to make sure I got *every* last drop.

God knows I needed it.

Across the table from me, Kora shot a glare in Nubia's direction, and must've kicked her under the table, based on the yelp that Nubia let out. "You realize you don't *have* to say every little thing that comes to mind, right? How is that helpful?"

"Uh, Monica appreciates my candor. Don't you, Mon?" Nubia asked.

I nodded. "Actually, Kora, I do. And hell... I agree. My entire world has tumbled upside down in a damned *week*. I'm just trying to figure out exactly what type of karma this is. Who did I fuck with in a past life that it's come down to *this*?"

"Will you cut it with the karma stuff?" Chloe asked, rolling her eyes. "You haven't done anything to anyone, and this is *not* karma."

I chuckled, then reached over our tapas plates for the bottle of wine in the middle of the table. "Fine. Voodoo then. Santeria. Witchcraft. *Something*. The ancestors or some-fucking-body with some magical mythical something are not pleased with me."

"It's just life," Blake said, shaking her head. "Just a valley."

"Well, can a bitch get an airlift out of here?" I asked, spurring laughter around the table. After a moment, I laughed too, giving in to the generally good vibe of being with my girlfriends.

It was *necessary.*

Even though I was semi-homeless at the moment, with my house being processed as a crime scene, I'd kept my word and come out on this "date" with my girls. I hadn't realized how much I needed it until we'd all sat down, passing around bottles of wine and plates of appetizers.

I needed it *bad.*

Because of whatever favor Renata called in, Detective Sam Turner and his partner, Tonya Velez, were the only law enforcement I'd actually had to interact with. They showed up in a plain car to take my statement, about the break-in and the hacking, and then gave me time to put together a bag and leave before the uniformed officers showed up to do whatever they needed to do.

It was a minor blessing, considering everything that was going on. And no matter what Kora or Blake or Chloe said, this didn't feel like "life happening". It felt insidious, and the shit was terrifying. Especially when I was helpless to stop it, because I had no idea what was going on.

"Seriously though," Nubia said, reaching to grab my hand. "I really hope the police figure all of this out for you, because it's nuts. I mean... the smashed flowers? That made my skin crawl."

I took a sip of my freshly poured wine. "Girl, who are you telling? I honestly feel like it's worse than the break-in. I'm allergic to roses. That shit was *personal.*"

"So... who do you think is doing this? And *why*?" Kora asked, leaning in.

I shrugged. "Who knows? Probably Kellen or one of his whores, or Kellen *and* one of his whores. I'm so fucking sick of that man. I wouldn't put it past him to concoct all of this, after I told him yesterday I was done with his ass."

"Really?" Chloe chimed in. "You're finally going to pursue the divorce?"

58

"What choice do I have?" I tipped my head back, staring up at the ceiling as I continued. "I can't keep letting him use me, my name, my connections, my money, while he blatantly disrespects me. It's time for it to stop."

Kora groaned. "So you're really going to give up half your business for that bastard?"

"Not if I can help it," I answered. "Before, I was told that there was no way around it, and I just… accepted it. I started the business after we were married, so if we divorce, he has a legal claim. As long as he just left me the hell alone and did his dirt quietly, I was content to ignore him, just for the sake of keeping the peace… and keeping my business. But now? Fuck that. I am going to hire the best, most ruthless lawyer that I can afford, and we are going to make it our mission to leave him with as close to *nothing* as possible."

Beside me, Nubia moaned. "Oh, please keep talking, I think I might cum."

"You're so damned silly," I laughed, slapping her hand when she raised it for a high five.

"Crudeness aside, Nubia is right," Kora said, and Chloe and Blake nodded.

"This is music to our ears. You deserve so much better than a man who sits back and lives on a woman's dime. It's shameful!"

I sucked my teeth. "Kellen lost his capacity for shame a *long* time ago. Probably right around the time he decided he hated my guts, but you know what? The feeling is mutual. Kellen is *nothing* to me. As far as I'm concerned – he's dead."

"I'll drink to that!" Nubia piped, grabbing a bottle of wine to pour herself a fresh glass. The bottle quickly got passed around, and then we all leaned forward. "To your newly minted status… as a widow," she said, grinning, and all five of us tapped glasses in agreement before we drank.

I was just putting my glass back down on the table when I heard a minor commotion happening behind us. I turned around just in time to see that four uniformed police officers had converged on the front of the restaurant, and the hostess at the podium was pointing directly at me.

My eyes went wide as they pulled their weapons, eliciting screams from a few other patrons, and a *"What the actual fuck?"* from Nubia.

Not knowing what else to do, I stood up when it was demanded of me by the first officer that reached the table.

"Are you Monica Stuart?" he barked, with his gun aimed right in my face.

"Y-yes," I stuttered. "What in the world is going on?"

I cringed as he grabbed my raised arms, twisting me to pin them behind my back before he locked me tight into a pair of handcuffs.

"Monica Stuart, you are under arrest for the murder of Kellen Stuart."

*The murder of Kellen Stuart.*
*The murder of Kellen Stuart.*
*Murder?*

*"This has to be a joke,"* I muttered to myself, looking around the sparse, dimly lit interrogation room. I'd never had occasion to be in one before, but I was struck by how remarkably similar it was to the ones on TV. The plain table, uncomfortable chair, the mirror they were undoubtedly watching me through, waiting for me to... I don't know... break?

But I wouldn't break, because I hadn't *done* anything. Not that they believed it, but the news of Kellen's death had struck me hard, in a way I didn't expect.

It... hurt.

As a matter of fact, as I sat there in that cold room alone, I forced myself to fight back tears that confused the hell out of me. Kellen despised me, and the feeling was mutual, but still... I'd been his wife for *fourteen* years of my life. I was having a hard time remembering why I hated him when memories of those early years – the good times – were swimming in my head. Suddenly, the joke I'd made about him being dead to me at the dinner table seemed so unnecessarily crass.

Maybe because now... I really *was* a widow.

And I had no idea how to process it.

"Mrs. Stuart."

I flinched as the door suddenly flung open and two men stepped in. Plainclothes officers or detectives, I didn't know, but I had a good idea about what was going to happen next.

One sat down across from me and dropped a file folder on the table, while the other leaned against the mirror, arms crossed. I pulled my sweater tighter around me, trying to hide my cleavage from the one who was closer, and seemed to be enjoying my breasts a little too much.

"I'm Detective Crowley, this is Detective Bauer," he said, smirking as he nodded toward his partner. "Why don't you go ahead and just make this night easier for all of us, and tell us why you did it?"

"I didn't do anything," was my immediate answer. "And I'd like to know why I wasn't notified before this about Kellen's death. One of those cops earlier – they told me his body was found this afternoon. I didn't know anything about it until you came and made a spectacle of arresting me at dinner with my friends. I am his *wife*. I should've been notified."

Crowley grinned. "Wow, you see that Bauer? She seems a little upset."

Bauer nodded. "Yeah, she does. Maybe it's because she doesn't understand that we tend to avoid notifying the spouse *too* soon... when they're the primary suspect."

"Don't talk about me like I'm not sitting here," I demanded. "Why the hell would *I* be your primary suspect? I didn't know it had happened!"

"*This*," Crowley said, flipping open the file and snatching out a picture that he slapped on the table in front me. "Is *why*, Mrs. Stuart."

Bile rose up in my throat as I took in the image in front of me, of a very bloody, very dead Kellen, tied to a chair. At first, I didn't understand why he was showing me this, but then my eyes landed on something written across his bare chest, in some sort of black substance.

*BY DEATH WE PART.*

I swallowed hard, trying to keep myself from puking at the table. I looked away as he spread out more pictures, close up shots of Kellen's injuries – deep gashes marring the beautiful golden-brown skin I'd always admired so much.

Including one across his throat.

"If I didn't know better, Mrs. Stuart, I'd think this was your first time seeing this. Here's something that should be pretty familiar," Crowley said, tossing a picture on top of all the others.

My eyes went wide at the sight of a bloody kitchen knife – one of my *Shun Kaji* knives, that I'd considered the perfect tools for my perfect kitchen.

Knives that were missing after yesterday's incident.

Across the room, Bauer cleared his throat. "You don't even have to ask whose fingerprints are all over this knife, do you?"

"Those were *stolen*," I insisted, looking right into his face. "Yesterday, someone broke into my home, I filed a police report and everything. That was one of the things they took!"

"More like the *only* thing they took," Crowley drawled. "Which I find mighty convenient. Don't you think it's a little *too* convenient Bauer?"

"Oh definitely. Just like the "hacking". Pretty damned well-timed, you supposedly get hacked, so your security system, all your cameras are offline. It all just seems… planned. Is that what this is, Mrs. Stuart? This was your plan?"

"I didn't need a plan, because I didn't *do* anything."

"Oh come off it," Crowley snapped. "You were upset because Kellen couldn't keep it in his pants, so you decided to send a message."

My face screwed into a scowl. "By *killing* him?! That doesn't even make any sense!"

"According to his girlfriend, you called Kellen yesterday morning, screaming that you were going to kill him. Today, he turns up dead, and your fingerprints are on the knife. This all makes *plenty* of sense to me."

Bauer nodded. "Kellen hasn't worked in what... four years? You've been paying all the bills, while he runs around like a single man, spending your money. You don't divorce him because you don't have any legal recourse to keep him from taking half of everything, or at least insisting on spousal support. That's enough to make anyone snap, right? Is that why you did it? To keep him from getting anything?"

*"I didn't do this."*

Crowley sat back in his chair, staring as if he was considering my words before he looked at his partner. "What do you think, man? Think she's telling the truth? I think she's telling the truth. I don't think she beat her husband and tied him up, tortured him with the stabbing, then cut his throat. Nah, it wasn't her."

"You're right," Bauer shrugged. "Look at her – you really think she'd do a dirty job like that? It was probably her boyfriend."

"*Boyfriend?*" I exclaimed. "What boyfriend?!"

"You really are an actress, aren't you?" Crowley chuckled. "*What boyfriend?* That particular ruse would work a lot better if you'd actually bothered to hide all those emails and texts and phone calls."

I pushed out a frustrated sigh. "What the fuck are you talking about?! I don't *have* a boyfriend!"

"Would "No Rest for the Wicked" agree?" Bauer asked. "I mean, the man killed your husband for you – I don't know if he'd appreciate not being claimed."

*... the man killed your husband for you...*

"I... *what?*" I said, suddenly feeling dizzy. "You don't... you don't know what you're talking about. He doesn't even know Kellen. He's not... we're *friends.*"

Crowley leaned across the table, wearing a smirk that made my skin crawl. "Mrs. Stuart... come on now. We saw the video – the things you two were doing weren't very *friendly* at all."

My eyes went wide. "Video? What video?"

"The video we got from your computer, the video you've watched thirty-six times since last year, of you and "Wick" finger-banging yourselves, Mrs. Stuart. Well... *you* used more than just your fingers."

Heat spread over my face as I clenched my fists. "I deleted that months ago!"

"Well, you didn't do a very good job. You've barely been here an hour, and we already have enough from your computer to put you away for good."

"Everything you have is circumstantial at best, Crowley. Cut the bullshit."

I looked up to see that the door had opened again, and a woman was standing there glaring from Crowley to Bauer. The door swung shut behind her, but she kept her stance – one hand propped on her hip, the other clutching an expensive-looking leather commuter bag.

"Demetria Byers... it hasn't been long enough."

Demetria smirked, tucking her hair behind her ear as she approached the table, putting her bag down before she started collecting the pictures of Kellen to put back into the folder.

"Ah, if you only understood how mutual the feeling was." She closed the folder full of pictures and tossed it across the table to him. "This interview is over. You had no business speaking with my client without her lawyer present, and I'll make sure that's mentioned when you try to use anything she's said against her."

Bauer chuckled. "Don't have to use her words from tonight. The evidence speaks for itself. Besides – she hasn't asked for a lawyer."

I opened my mouth to speak, but Demetria put a hand on my shoulder.

"At the restaurant, where your thugs snatched my client away from her friends with a baseless arrest, Chloe McKenna informed the arresting officers that she'd be contacting Mrs. Stuart's attorney. *Me.* She didn't need to ask, because her legal representation was already on the way, and you should have waited. But... you never were one for taking your time, were you?" she asked, in a tone that definitely spoke to

64

history between her and Bauer, but I wasn't worried about *that* right now.

I wanted to know how she was going to get me out of here.

"Now, gentleman, I think we can all agree that you've egregiously overplayed your hand here. The simple fact that my client isn't even in handcuffs right now speaks directly to the fact that you don't believe she did this. Please tell me you don't think this woman brutally murdered her husband, wrote a message implicating herself, and left a bloody knife covered in her fingerprints, all in the condo that *she* pays for, and then went to have dinner with her friends. There's no possible way you don't see that this is a setup," Demetria said, her expression stern as she looked back and forth between the detectives.

"It's not as if your client has been forthcoming with her whereabouts from this morning," Crowley challenged, as if they'd even bothered to ask.

"I was… visiting someone," I piped up. "Almost two hours out of the city, and the same distance back!"

He scoffed. "Can your "someone" corroborate that?"

"I…" I pushed out a sigh. "No."

He shook his head. "You got some proof? Let me guess – no, you don't, because you're lying, and we're *going* to prove it."

"Okay you're done," Demetria interrupted. "I need to talk to my client, and I hope I don't need to remind you that our conversation is privileged."

"Don't worry about us snooping," Crowley said as he stood, and Bauer moved away from the mirror, toward the door. "We're about to go have a conversation with the boy toy. We'll make sure he knows you're lawyered up, Mrs. Stuart."

My lips parted. "What? You know who he is? You have him *here*? How?!"

Bauer laughed. "Oh, did lover boy not tell you he was still in town?"

"Enough! Out!" Demetria demanded, before I could ask any more questions. When she turned back to me, she was wearing the same scowl she'd been giving the detectives. "Why the *hell* would you talk to them?!"

I pulled my head back, surprised at the question. "Why wouldn't I? My husband is dead, and they think I did it!"

"They don't. They just want it to have been you, so they can wrap this case up. You're lucky I got here when I did – they would've had you confessing in another hour."

I frowned. "No, because I didn't do anything. And girl... I don't even *know* you."

"But Chloe does, which is a good thing for you – trust me. I'm going to ask you a few questions that I need you to answer for me as honestly as possible – no bullshit. We're going to fix this, but I need you to be straight with me. Okay?"

"Okay."

"Where were you this morning, between ten and noon?"

"At my father's grave. I stopped for lunch on the way back, but I didn't keep the receipt."

Demetria shook her head. "That's fine. Your Mercedes has GPS. They're going to pull it, and it's going to prove where you were. Next question – the message on Kellen's chest. Beyond the obvious, does it mean anything to you?"

I pushed out a sigh, then swiped a hand over my face. "Um... it's a nail polish name that I came up with. My upcoming holiday collection... Wicked Widow," I explained as my stomach flipped. "All of the names are plays on fidelity, wedding vows... killing a husband. *By Death We Part* is a black matte polish. And um... the card, that came with the roses I got after the break-in. *Partaking all Others.* It's a deep crimson, like the flowers were."

"Partaking, instead of *forsaking*. It's a creative concept, I love it." She gave me a sympathetic smile. "Just... pretty unfortunate timing."

"Who are you telling?" I asked, letting out a dry chuckle. "So... what happens next?"

66

"Well, I'm going to get you out of here, so you can get some rest. I have a feeling they already got back that GPS report, traffic cameras, EZ pass, something, to show that you weren't anywhere near Kellen when he was murdered. Otherwise, they'd already have you booked. They're just trying to get information out of you. Like the "boy toy" they referred to. Who the hell is that? Chloe didn't say anything about you having a side piece."

"That's because I don't! At least... not *really*."

"Monica, no bullshit. Tell what the deal is."

"It's just this guy that I met online, like five years ago. We've never met in person, I don't even know his name, and he doesn't know mine. There's no way he did this."

Demetria nodded. "Okay, so... why do they think he's your "boy toy". Is the relationship sexual in nature?"

"Uh... sort of," I answered, lowering my gaze to my hands. "We've had phone sex. And... webcam sex, I guess you'd call it. One of the very first times we did the webcam thing, I... recorded it, to watch again later. I thought I deleted it a few months back, but apparently not, if it's being considered evidence now."

I appreciated that Demetria's response was just a simple nod. "Okay. I'll do what I can to make sure it's not seen by any more people. But... that still doesn't explain what they insinuated on the way out. "lover boy didn't tell you he was still in town?". He came to visit you?"

"No," I shook my head. "As far as I knew, he didn't even know where I lived, and I didn't know where he lived. But..." I sighed. "After I got hacked, he recommended a computer security firm to me, for me to take all my devices to. It was here in town, which freaked me out."

Demetria's eyebrows crept up. "So... he *does* know where you live then."

"Yeah. I guess so. I haven't talked to him since then."

"And that was two nights ago?"

I nodded, and Demetria let out a hefty sigh as she sat back. "Monica... I understand that you think this man is your friend, but..."

you have to know it's possible that he stalked you, found out where you lived, and killed Kellen to get him out of the way."

"Absolutely not," I insisted. "I talk to Wick all the time – he would already know that Kellen wasn't in the way of *anything*. We lived separately – Kellen with his pregnant girlfriend."

"Okay. So maybe he killed Kellen *for* you. Sees the distress this man is causing, and wants to free you from it."

"No. *No*." I crossed my arms over my chest. "These last few days have been absolutely crazy, but Wick being a murderer – and setting me up to take the fall for it? That's something I patently refuse to believe. It's not as if Kellen was some boy scout. He was fucking half the metro area, he's an asshole, and he was always wrapped up in one scam or another lately. I'm sure there are plenty of people who would love to see him dead."

Demetria gave me a single nod. "Okay. I believe you. But, for the sake of transparency, I think it would be a good idea to call in Renata and Chad. You're being accused of murder, and this alleged affair is what the police are looking at as your motive. It's time we find out who *Wick* really is."

# FIVE

Women never fucking listen.

My instructions couldn't have been clearer – here's an address. Take your computer here to get fixed.

But *no.*

*No.*

She couldn't just roll with it. So instead of taking herself to the colleague I knew and trusted to fix her hacking issue, Sandy had waltzed her fine ass right into the very last place I needed her to go.

My bad – *Monica* had.

I'd been in the shop when she walked in – fine as hell in dark pink slacks that fit her thick thighs and ample ass like they were made just for her, and a navy-blue sweater that plunged low enough in front to show the generous swell of perfect breasts.

"*Damn,*" the customer I was supposed to be helping muttered, confirming my thought that she'd probably pulled the attention of everyone nearby. I didn't know who she was then – she was just a gorgeous woman with a laptop in her hands, obviously needing help.

When she stopped to watch Quentin interacting in the classroom, I thought it was going to be my opportunity to finish with my customer and go to her rescue.

Of course, his ass wanted to talk.

By the time I sent him off to the register to check out, Renata had already gotten to her. And *just* when I was about to take it as a sign of something not meant to be, Renata stepped out of the consultation office to talk to me.

She had a customer who needed my help.

I tried my best not to let my giddiness show as Renata explained that the woman needed a security clean-up for home and office.

I was *great* at security clean-ups for home and office.

*"The way she found out about it all was really bizarre,"* she'd said, gesturing toward the woman sitting at her desk, waiting. *"Some guy she's been talking to online, warned Monica that he thought she was hacked, because whatever virus was trying to use the video chat connection to access **his** computer, and..."*

Renata kept talking, but I wasn't really hearing it. Because, as I looked at the woman in the office, her hand went up to a tiny platinum cross around her neck, twirling it between her fingers, running her perfectly polished navy-blue nails along the outline.

I knew that cross.

I knew that *hand.*

Had seen that cross laying between those flawless breasts, had watched those nails – a different color every time – disappear into the valley between those voluptuous thighs.

It was her.

*Right there.*

She must have felt me looking at her, because her gaze came up to mine. Those big brown eyes didn't show any sign of recognition, but her high cheekbones lifted even more as succulent, pretty lips curved into a dimpled smile, and she... waved.

*Fuck.*

70

I forced nonchalance as I looked away without reacting, as if I hadn't noticed.

"Yeah," Renata said, touching my arm, which brought my attention back to her. "So do you think you can come and talk to her about it?"

"I actually have something else on my plate right now, but um… get her information, we'll run it against the schedule, and see when we can get her fixed up. In the meantime, get her set up—"

"With a new phone and laptop, have her tether the laptop to the phone for internet, and talk to her cell company about a temporary data increase. Duh."

My mouth dropped open. "Damn, Ren, why you gotta "duh" me?"

"Because, you're being weird and she really needs help."

"And we're *going* to help," I assured. "I just… I have something else to take care of first, and then I can get on board."

Renata sucked her teeth. "You'd *better* be."

"And now you're trying to punk me? I thought we were better than that?"

As she stopped to grab a cell phone from one of the supply carts before she headed back to the consultation office, she tossed me a grin. "*Trying*, Chad? Pretty sure I did."

I laughed as she went back into the room with Monica, then took the opportunity to observe while their attention was on each other.

*So this is Sandy…*

Since becoming friends – before the webcam stuff – I'd considered Sandy beautiful, sight unseen. Call it corny or whatever, but I was easily swayed by an intelligent, driven woman, with a great personality. That shit was *beyond* attractive to me.

But *goddamn.*

This woman was flat-out striking.

I knew better than to think it, but my mind took me there anyway – *What the fuck is her husband's problem?* I quickly arrived at an answer though: Stupidity. Not that a woman's looks made it okay to be

71

an asshole, but *shit.* Men with good sense didn't screw over women who looked like *that.*

She had dimples.

On her face *and* on her ass.

The shit just didn't make sense.

All that aside… I had a problem on my hands. I could deduce on my own that recommending a specific computer service company had probably spooked her – I wasn't supposed to know where she was. And in my defense, I *hadn't* known where she was, until the hacking attempt exposed her IP address and location.

The fact that she was right here in the same city had been news to me too.

Hell, the *not* knowing had been part of the appeal of the whole thing – a nice bit of excitement for my everyday life. Still… I'd be lying if I said that seeing her in front of me wasn't incredible. But it didn't mean that I was about to reveal who I was.

It was one thing for our friendship to be housed in phone calls and late-night web chats, with the boundary of anonymity and perception of distance firmly in place. Knowing who she was, knowing that we were right here in the city, possibly knew some of the same people… it felt bizarre.

I didn't know what to do with it, so I did nothing.

Later that night, when I had the urge to shoot her a text, asking if she was okay – normal shit for us, usually – I found something else to do. Same thing the next morning, when I thought about her as soon as I opened my eyes. When Ren asked for my availability for the upcoming week, I gave it to her, knowing it wasn't something I could put off.

I was going to have to face it.

Before that though, I googled the hell out of her.

*Monica Stuart. Thirty-six years old. Graduated Blakewood State University with honors, owner of Vivid Vixen Cosmetics. Married fourteen years to Kellen Stuart, former financial advisor. No children.*

"And fucking fine as *hell,*" I muttered to myself as I browsed the pictures attached to the article I'd found. Apparently, Monica was some

72

sort of beauty icon – a lot of the hits I got on her name were from write-ups raving about everything from her hair to her clothes. There were hundreds on hundreds of pictures of her on red carpets, in photoshoots as the model, candid shots of her directing, shots of her as the client. Knowing these things about her added a whole other layer to the woman I already knew her to be.

What I didn't see were many pictures of her actually *with* her husband.

"Yo!" Quentin called out as he barged into my office with Marcus right behind him. "We gonna have to peel you away from that screen, or what?"

Marcus plopped into the chair across from me. "Come on, bruh. You're not even dressed, and you know the courts fill up quick."

Sitting back, I propped my hands behind my head, looking at them. "Correct me if I'm wrong, but don't you own the gym? It's never occurred to you to just reserve a court?"

"What's the fun in that?" Marcus asked. "Part of the excitement is wondering if you're gonna have space or not. What are you doing anyway? In here pretending to be busy?"

Quentin laughed. "That's what Ren was fussing about yesterday."

"Ren never thinks I'm working," I chuckled. "Nah though, I'm just finishing something up."

"What you working on man?" Quentin asked, and before I could react or respond, he'd turned the screen to face him. I blew out a sigh as a grin spread across his face. "Oh, I see. *That's* what you're working on."

I shook my head. "I can explain."

"Don't have to explain anything," Marcus said, with a low whistle. "*That* explains itself," he added, pointing to a picture that was a side angle of Monica in jeans.

Quentin laughed. "Sure does. Now I'm even more surprised to hear you didn't seem eager to help. Ren said "Monica" was pretty, but lawd. That's a *woman*."

"Kayla know you're in here looking up women?" Marcus teased, and Quentin immediately joined in.

"Whew, I hope not. You know she doesn't play that shit. Gonna roll up here with that Range Rover on two wheels like she did a couple years ago."

"Okay," I said, shaking my head. "So, fuck you, and fuck you." I flipped both of them my middle finger as they laughed, and I couldn't help chuckling too as I shut my computer down and stood up. "Y'all go ahead and grab a court, I'll meet you down there. Who's our fourth?"

"Sam is en route," Quentin answered over his shoulder as they left, and I went to my desk for my keys and cell. As soon as I picked it up, I grinned at the message on the screen.

**"You're going to be there tonight, right? – Kay."**

When I opened up the text thread, I laughed at the video clip she'd included after the message – puppy dog eyes.

*"Where else would I be?"* I responded as I left my office.

**"Working. As usual. – Kay."**

I shook my head. *"I'm not always working, first of all. Second, I wouldn't miss seeing you tonight for the world. I'm hitting the court with the guys, and then I'm not even coming back to the office. Washing up and heading your way. Or I could just head your way, no wash-up. I'll have flowers* 😊*."*

**"Ewww. Hard pass. Shower please. And don't play with me about the flowers! – Kay"**

*"Not playing. Two dozen roses, just for you."*

**"... chocolates too? – Kay."**

I chuckled, then typed out a response. *"Obviously."*

**"Ahhhh! I love you! – Kay."**

*"Yeah, yeah, I love you too."*

74

Kayla was the best thing in my life.

Full stop.

From the time I met her, her presence had brought about a certain sense of fulfillment and peace – feelings that hit me out of left field, just like she had herself. A funny, brilliant, beautiful smart-ass, she was. Her very first words to me, the first time I saw her, nearly eleven years ago, had been *"Oh, your mouth must not work, huh?"* And then, after I assured her that it did, *"Well, use it. Staring is creepy and rude."*

And so it went, from there.

Over the next eleven years, we grew up together – me more than her, because she was already so damned astute. Kay had never been... idealistic. I attributed that to the years before we met – a nomadic lifestyle, surrounded by people who promoted practicality and nonchalance. She didn't want big grand gestures, had no use for anything fancy. Kay yielded herself to exactly one hobby – one singular imaginative thing that she did with near-obsessive enthusiasm.

She danced.

And as antithetical as they were to her insistence on – mostly – frugal living, she *loved* flowers.

So there I was, backstage at the theatre with an armful of roses, waiting to deliver them to her for a job well done. She wasn't the principal dancer in her ballet company – for now, that title belonged to Anais Campbell, a veteran dancer Kay considered the blueprint of a contemporary Black ballerina.

Her *idol*.

Kay had been practically vibrating with happiness when she popped up at *Five Star Tech* to tell me she'd been accepted into the company, and that excitement had been magnified ten-fold once she was promoted from the ballet corps into the position of soloist.

Tonight was the culmination of months and months of hard work for her. The joy on her face when she finally emerged from the dressing room, scrubbed free of makeup and changed into sweats was palpable. As she approached me, stopping to sign autographs from other attendees, the smile on her face grew and grew until she was beaming as she stepped into my free arm for a hug.

"I can't believe you actually made it," she gushed, looping her arms around my waist to squeeze tight. "And these flowers are *amazing*." Her eyes glittered with happiness as she pushed herself up on her toes to kiss me on the cheek before she pulled the flowers from me, practically burying her face in them to inhale. "Thank you."

"You're welcome. You looked really good up there."

Somehow, she smiled even brighter. "You really think so? I lost my footing in that twirl in the second act, and I—"

"Don't even sweat it. It was barely noticeable."

Her smile faded a bit. "But you noticed."

"Kay…"

"I know, I know," she shook her head. "Don't beat myself up, etc. etc. But you know how important this is to me. I'll never be principal with that kind of mistake."

"Fine, so you have a note for improvement for next time. But what you're not about to do is let a tiny mistake ruin your night."

She sucked her teeth. "So what am I about to do instead?"

"Well, don't you have an after-party to go to?"

"*Maybe.*"

I chuckled. "Okay well then *maybe* you should get yourself ready, instead of dwelling on small stuff. Cool?"

"I guess…" She rolled her eyes, but couldn't keep a smile from breaking free as she looked down at the flowers again. "Thank you for coming tonight."

I shrugged. "Told you… nowhere else I'd rather be."

We talked for a few more minutes, and she introduced me to some of her peers in the ballet company I hadn't met. After that, I left her to it, knowing she had a busy night ahead, and made my exit.

The police car out in front of the theatre didn't immediately raise a red flag. Police presence at large events wasn't anything to lift an eyebrow at, so I walked right past it, heading to my car when I heard, "*Chadwick LaForte, stop right there!*"

76

The gasps from the remaining crowd mirrored my own shock as I stopped walking to turn and see what the fuss was. I took a step back, surprised, as I found myself facing the barrel of several guns.

"Man, what the hell is happening?" I shouted at the police officer closest to me, as the others moved to pin my arms behind my back to strap me into handcuffs. It took everything to quell my immediate reflex to get them the fuck off of me, knowing that local law enforcement tended to be trigger happy.

"Chadwick LaForte, you're under arrest for the murder of Kellen Stuart. You have—"

"Who the *fuck* is Kellen Stu—"

Oh.

Oh, *shit.*

"Wait a minute," I insisted. "I don't even know that motherfucker to have—"

"Save it," one of the cops said, as they shoved me into the back of a police cruiser. "Of course you didn't do it. That's what they all say."

I started to say something back, but he'd already slammed the door, which was probably for the best. I had plenty of smart-ass shit to say, but none of it would help my situation. Sitting back, I closed my eyes, focusing on pulling myself together. There was no point in arguing with the cops when the word "murder" had been thrown around. There was only one thing I needed to say to anyone.

"I want to speak to my lawyer."

"What the hell have you gotten yourself into?" Demetria asked as she walked into the interrogation room, already looking more exhausted than I was used to seeing her. Working a few doors down from her at *Five Star Enterprises* made her a pretty regular fixture in my life, and she always looked put-together and ready to destroy someone or something.

She still looked like that now, only… tired.

I shook my head in answer to her question. "Some bullshit. I didn't fucking kill anybody. You *know* that."

Demetria gave me a curious look at she sat down beside me at the table. "I mean… do I? We both know you haven't always been the computer repair guy, so…"

"You're pulling my leg right now, right?"

"Not at all. You were good with a trigger, but knives were your weapon of choice."

I pushed out a harsh breath through my nose as I glared at Demetria. "And I left that life eleven years ago, for Kay. You *know* that."

"What *I* know is that Monica Stuart is a very beautiful woman, and the two of you had a relationship that became sexual in nature. You knew she was married, knew about the drama her husband was putting her through, knew about the latest developments. It's really not a stretch that you might consider getting rid of him for her."

"I didn't even know her damn name until *yesterday*! And I can account for my whereabouts all day today."

Demetria nodded. "Good. *Great,* actually. If both of you have alibis, that's less the police have to try and make their case."

"There is no case," I maintained. "I didn't even know that motherfucker!"

"But you know Monica. Very, *very* well."

"We talked online."

"You did more than *talk*, Chad. Now isn't the time to try to downplay it. They have video. They know you two were more than "friends"."

My nostrils flared at the word *video,* and I sat up a little straighter. "*Video*? How in the hell do they have video, and how the hell do you know about it? What kind of video? From when? Why in the world—"

78

"Okay, one question at a time please!" Demetria interrupted, then took a breath as she pushed her hair back from her face. "They got the video from Monica's computer. She says it's from about a year ago, and it is… an intimate session the two of you shared."

*Goddamnit. She was recording us?*

"You said "she says". That's what she told the police?"

Demetria shook her head. "No. She told *me*. Because I'm representing her as well. Chloe called me when they arrested her, two hours before they arrested you."

"What the *fuck* Dem! You don't think this is a conflict of interests?!"

She frowned. "What? No, not at all. The police are trying to railroad both of you, when *neither* of you is guilty. I can more than handle this."

I scoffed. "How sure are you that she isn't guilty, huh? She recorded us together without my permission. Isn't that a crime?"

"Technically, yes. But it was never intended to be viewed by anyone other than herself, and she'd attempted to delete it. It was recovered from the computer's hard drive. That's the only reason they have it."

"No, they have it because she did it in the first damned place," I argued, not interested in Monica's reasons or semantics. "Our text and email correspondences don't have anything that would make the police arrest me for a fucking murder. The video is what has them thinking things between us are something they aren't!"

"So what are things between you, Chad? Because you seem pretty upset at the idea of being linked to her at all."

"Because I'm being accused of *murdering* this woman's husband! My face is probably on the fucking news right now – what do you think Kayla is thinking, huh? They arrested me right outside the theater, in full view of everybody. Do you know how embarrassing that could be for her, if anybody knew who I was? How embarrassing the shit is for *me*?"

Demetria nodded. "Yes, I understand. But I hope you don't think this is a cake walk for Monica."

"Right now, I don't give a *fuck* what it is for Monica!"

After I made that statement, Demetria's eyes went wide for a second. I could tell she swallowed her first response, but was still getting ready to say something before a knock sounded at the door. Before either of us could actually answer, it swung open, and two detectives walked in.

"Let me save you fellas some time," I started, ignoring Demetria's subtle kick under the table, trying to get me to be quiet. "I did *not* kill anybody, especially over some pussy I've never even had the chance to sniff. You've got the wrong goddamn guy."

The white one chuckled as the other one moved to the back of the room, resting against the wall. "Never smelled it before, huh? That's an interesting way to put it."

"Yeah, well, you get the point."

"Oh yeah," he nodded. "I get it. And so did Kellen Stuart I bet, by the time you introduced him to the dangerous end of your girlfriend's expensive kitchen knife fourteen times before you cut his throat. Is that number significant for you? They were married fourteen years, you stick him fourteen times?"

I shook my head. "I have no answers for you about this shit, because I have nothing to do with it. I didn't fucking stab anybody."

"This time," the black detective chimed in from the back. "We managed to find some interesting information in the parts of your history that aren't redacted, or classified."

"What does my history have to do with this?"

"Let me answer that for him, Bauer," the other detective said.

"Go for it, Crowley."

Crowley grinned. "With pleasure. You see, even if you didn't ever hold the knife yourself, it seems pretty clear that you have the means and connections to have hired somebody for this type of thing. Now, you may not have "smelled it", but you damn sure saw it, and had yourself a good time when you did. We've got your phone records, emails, texts. You talked to Mrs. Stuart multiple times a week on the phone, and share an email or texts pretty much every day. All of that suddenly stopped yesterday. Why?"

"She got hacked."

"Huh," Bauer spoke up. "She got hacked. And *you* are a former CIA hacker, among other, more hands-on things. That's a nice little coinky-dink."

"And that's *all* it is," Demetria chimed in. "That's all any of this is – coincidence, conjecture, and circumstantial evidence. Either you actually *charge* my client with something, or you let go home."

Crowley sighed. "Your alibi checks out anyway, Mr. LaForte. You're free to go. But you stick around town. I'm sure we'll have some more questions for you."

I shrugged. "Anything more you have to say to me, you can do it through my lawyer. You said I was free to go, right?"

Once I got the nod, I stood up, and Demetria followed me out to the hall. "I called Marcus," she said. "He should be waiting up front, to give you a ride back to your car."

"Thanks Dem."

She nodded. "Of course. Five Star Family looks out for each other. I would give you a ride myself, but I need to get back to Monica. They're holding her overnight. Can't get traffic camera history until morning, so…"

"Yeah, well. I'll see you later."

"Really, Chad?" Demetria snapped at me, and I frowned. "What?!"

She rolled her eyes. "She said the two of you have been friends for *five* years. You're seriously not even going to ask me how she is?"

"She hated ol' boy. She's probably celebrating."

"Actually, she's distraught," Demetria corrected, folding her arms. "Regardless of how their relationship had changed, she still lost her husband, in a horrible manner, and now she's being held for his murder."

"None of which has *anything* to do with me." The look on Demetria's face had guilt tugging at my chest, but still… "I can't be involved in shit like this. I don't need my face on the news. How the fuck would I even begin to explain this to Kayla, huh? I wish Monica the absolute best – she's a good woman, and I don't want to see her life destroyed. But I can't have something I don't have anything to do with destroying *my* life either. I have too much to lose."

"Who says you're going to lose, Chad?" she asked, then shook her head. "But… whatever. I get it. And you're not wrong. However, Monica could use all the friends she can get right now. She could use the support. But… I guess we won't be counting you in that number."

I raised my shoulders again. "Nah. You won't."

I left Demetria there in the hall and headed through the police station toward the front, where Marcus was waiting for me. My head was spinning as I moved, trying to make sense of what had seemed like an eternity of waiting, first for Demetria, and then to be released.

It had actually barely been two hours.

Two long ass hours.

Part of me did feel bad about abandoning Monica, if it could be considered that. I cared about her, cared about her wellbeing, but when it came to being accused of murder, I had to put a pause on that. If my friendship, relationship, whatever with her, was threatening my freedom or ran the risk of exposing the people I loved to unwanted or unwarranted attention… for me, the choice was easy.

# SIX

*Vivid Vixen* didn't need me for day to day operations. Even though I typically went in to the office every day, and made myself a part of pretty much everything, there was nothing exclusive to me that couldn't wait.

And at this point… everything had to wait.

Because everything was fucked up.

My friends had been here. Chloe, Nubia, Blake, Kora, among others, had all taken their time out to offer company and comfort, but I wanted neither. In the last four days, I'd had maybe nine hours of sleep. Even my attempts at medically induced slumber had failed, and I had to believe it was a direct result of the series of bombs that had been dropped on my life.

The social media attack on my business.

The cyber-attack on my privacy.

Kellen's attack on my spirit.

The attack against my security at home.

And the *pièce de résistance* – Kellen's murder – which, taken with everything else, felt like an attack on my sanity. It was well-coordinated emotional warfare, the likes of which I'd never experienced, and wouldn't wish on anybody. If this was a battle, I was losing.

*Badly.*

I nearly jumped out of my skin when the alarm on my phone went off, disturbing the quiet of my suite at *Veil*. As hotels went, *Veil* was best of the best – A Drake family property, unmatched in luxury, security, or what mattered most to me at the time: *privacy*.

Those damn photographers had been relentless.

I wasn't a socialite, or some big star. As far as I was concerned, there was no reason for the paparazzi to care about me, and yet when I finally got to leave the police station, in two-day old clothes with uncombed hair, there they were.

*"Monica did you kill your husband?!"*

*"Monica, is it true your company is going bankrupt?!"*

*"Monica, how do you feel about your dead husband's baby with his mistress?!"*

They didn't care how it felt for me. Didn't care that their questions stung, didn't give a damn, in the slightest, that even though my last few years with Kellen hadn't been something to be proud of, I was *still* a woman in mourning.

They just wanted their story.

And I certainly wasn't going to help give them one.

It was too quiet here though.

I didn't want the TV on, for fear I'd see my own face splashed across the screen, being dragged as a woman scorned and a murderer. Social media was a *major* no-no. Chloe didn't even have to forbid me this time – I already knew I needed to stay away.

There were no distractions here – only the opportunity for me to get lost in my thoughts. The only problem was, my thoughts were as riddled with Kellen's slit throat as my sleep was, so neither state held the promise of peace. Darkness seemed to be winning the battle for my state

84

of mind, but while I had the energy, I forced happy thoughts to the forefront of my mind.

Like the first time Kellen and I met. He had a work-study job in the student post office, and I'd lost my mailbox key. He struck up a ridiculous conversation about responsibility, which I quickly learned was a rehearsed, required speaking prompt any time a student misplaced their key. I teased him about it, and he invited me to a party in his dorm, even though we were both freshmen, and freshmen didn't have parties in the dorm.

But *that* freshman had a party in his dorm.

Somewhere, in the depths of an old photo storage account, there were pictures of that night. I grabbed my cell phone, but quickly remembered that it was a new one – I'd never set up anything on it. I went to the website using the mobile internet browser, and simply stared at the login page. I just couldn't remember.

But I *did* have a locked note file with all those old passwords on my phone.

At *Five Star Tech.*

And just like that, my decision was made.

I was going to get my phone.

"Welcome to Five Star Tech! How can I help you?"

I managed to pull a smile to my face for the young woman who approached me as soon as I walked into the store. A brief glance downward at the pin on her shirt told me her name was Taylor.

"Um, yes," I told her. "I had to drop off my phone and laptop a few days ago, but there's a file I need to look at. Is Renata here? She's the one I worked with before."

Taylor gave me sympathetic smile. "I'm sorry, she's not. Baby appointment," she explained. "But, I'm sure someone else in the workshop can help you. Come on, I'll take you back."

This time, when I walked past the classrooms that flanked the hall, both were empty. The store itself was less-populated than last time, something I attributed to the time of day, on a weekday. It was probably a normal thing for them, because when Taylor walked me back to the "workshop", the only consultant on duty was the same guy who *still* hadn't called to schedule that security cleanup.

But then again… Renata knew about the break-in, which was still under investigation, and it wasn't as if I was going home anytime soon anyway.

So I guess it wasn't that big of a deal.

"Chad, perfect! This customer worked with mom a few days ago, and she needs to get access to her phone. You think you could help her?"

Chad gave me the same disinterested look he'd given me a few days ago before he nodded, turning back to the woman he'd been speaking with before we walked in.

"He's our best tech – and that's saying a *lot* with the people who work here. He'll get you taken care of," Taylor told me, and then headed back to the front of the store, leaving me there to be… ignored, apparently.

Chad seemed in no hurry at all to get out of the face of the - admittedly gorgeous - young woman who had his attention. She was intensely focused on whatever he was saying to her, and I couldn't blame her. Now that I was closer than I'd been last time, it was easy to see that Chad was a *lot* of man, tall and broad and seemingly made of pure milk chocolate. He leaned down, planting a kiss on her forehead that made her laugh and give him a playful shove before she walked away. As she passed, she gave me a look that if I didn't know better, I would've read as… hostile.

But I didn't know her, and she didn't know me.

There was no reason for hostility.

"What can I do for you?" Chad asked, pulling my attention back to him. Even though something about his tone sent a strange feeling coursing through my chest, I shook it off, knowing he was the only one who could help me.

86

"I don't know if you remember, but I was here a few days ago, dropping off a laptop and a phone?" When he just gave me a blank stare, I continued. "Well, um… I need something off of that phone. I don't know if you guys have wiped it or anything yet, but I'm hoping you haven't. And my name is Monica Stuart."

Instead of moving to act on my request, he narrowed his eyes, giving me a look reminiscent of the one I'd gotten from his… girlfriend, I guess. His hard stare continued for a few seconds before he nodded.

"Follow me."

So I did.

I was right behind him as he went to Renata's office, using a key ring to get inside. He went to a row of lockers I didn't even notice when I was there before, opening and closing them one by one before he found the one holding my laptop and cell phone.

He was acting so strange that I didn't even bother to meet his eyes when he handed me the phone.

"Thank you," I told him, my gaze remaining on his hands as I took it from him.

And then, I saw the scar.

A familiar, razor-thin line of raised skin, that went from his thumb joint to up past his wrist. I froze as my eyes traveled that line, just as I'd done dozens and dozens of times via webcam. Only this time, as my gaze moved up, there was no abrupt edge of the screen, ending my view.

I could finally see his face.

"I'm guessing Demetria didn't tell you."

Yes.

This was him.

There was no mistaking that voice, and now that I knew this was him, knew this was *Wick*, the man I'd considered a friend, the man who'd… been drawn into a murder case with me… I couldn't understand how I hadn't immediately known it was him.

Because it was *definitely* him.

"No," I said, just above a whisper, as if that was the only appropriate way to speak at such a time. "She told me that they found the person on the other end of the username, but she... she said you wanted your privacy. But I didn't... did you know it was me, when I came in here the other day? Did you get me here on purpose?"

"What?" he frowned. "Hell no. I told your ass a different place to go to, but you walked in *here* instead. No, I didn't know it was you. Why would I do that, when anonymity was our thing?"

I shook my head. "No. No, you're right. I know you're right. Chloe sent me here, because I... I didn't trust the address you gave me."

"You should've."

"You could've been leading me into a trap."

He scoffed. "You've gotta be fucking kidding me. I get arrested for murder fooling with you, but *you* could've been walking into a trap? Hilarious."

"I never meant for that to happen. I had no idea any of this was going to happen. I'm sorry."

"You *should be*," he vented, in a harsh tone that made me take a step back. "Not only do you have me involved with some shit I do *not* need to be involved with, you fucking *recorded us*?"

"I can explain," I insisted, fumbling over my words as I held up my hands to get him to wait. "It wasn't... malicious, I just—"

"You know... I don't really think I care about the excuse. I just want you to get your phone, and get the hell out of here, and don't come back. Your being here just gives the police more shit to talk to me about, and I don't fucking like police, Sandy."

"Monica."

"Whatever the fuck," he shrugged. "I really don't want to hear either one again, to be honest."

I sucked in a breath. "But... I thought we were friends?" I asked, speaking my mind even though I hated how weak and desperate it sounded. "Wick, I am *sorry* that you got wrapped up in this, but you have to understand that this isn't my fault. I didn't kill him!"

"You probably should've," he said, sounding so completely bored of me, of the whole conversation, that it made me physically hurt. "At least this would've all been for something."

"Wick, I—"

"*Listen*—" he interrupted, shaking his head. "I left the drama behind me eleven years ago. I have no tolerance for it, not in my personal life. I wish you the best, but do me a favor – leave me alone."

Those words hit me like a bag of bricks, but I squared my shoulders, held my head high anyway. I'd taken enough emotional beatings throughout the course of my life that I knew how to swallow it for now, instead of letting the feelings bubble over and embarrass me.

Because that's where I was now. In front of the man I'd spilled my deepest heartaches with, willing myself not to cry tears that just a week ago, I would've poured openly.

I should've known better than to think he wouldn't end up disappointing me.

"I didn't come here for you anyway," I told him, keeping as much emotion out of my voice as I could. "So it shouldn't be a problem."

He gave me a curt nod and then left me there with my cell in my hands, feeling like I'd taken a knife to the stomach. Instead of giving in to the weakness in my knees, I steeled myself and powered the phone on, copying down what I needed before I turned it off again, putting it back in the locker he'd taken it from.

I put on tunnel vision as I left Renata's office, making sure to pull the door closed behind me. I didn't even glance in his direction as I made my way out, kept my face expressionless until I made it to my car. And even then… I swallowed my emotions again.

All of them.

*Everything.*

I wasn't even interested in the pictures anymore, at least not for nostalgia's sake. For whatever reason, that little run-in with Wick had reminded me of what Kellen was. My relationship with Wick wouldn't even exist, not in its current iteration, if I hadn't fallen in love with, and married a snake.

This was his fault.

And now, despite the long list of ways my own needs were being neglected, I had to bury his trifling ass. Even in death, Kellen had found a way to taunt me.

"I'm pretty sure I've *never* seen someone need a glass of wine as much as it looks like you do right now," Nubia said, standing over me as I stared absently at the forms spread out over the table.

Who the hell knew death required so much paperwork?

I'd just finished another tense phone call with Kellen's mother, discussing what she wanted for his funeral plans. Despite what her son had turned into, the woman had never been anything but good to me, so I wanted to give her the respect of burying her son with dignity.

I don't think my arrest for his murder had her feeling very warm toward me though.

In any case, when I looked up to find Nubia holding out a big glass of wine, a smile spread across my face.

"Oh God, thank you," I told her, accepting the glass as she laughed.

"You're more than welcome, Mon. Talk to me. How are you feeling?" she asked, rubbing my back for a few seconds as she sat down beside me. "You've been pretty quiet."

I took a large gulp of the wine, swallowing before I answered. "I feel... about like you'd expect. And I have about a billion things left to do before this funeral on Friday."

"Okay, like what? Anything you can hand off to me, or someone else?"

90

"Unfortunately not," I told her, then took another drink. "Thank you for offering, but I'll be okay as long as I follow my to-do list. I've gotta get out of here in the next ten minutes to make my hair appointment though. Thank God that was already set before everything went wrong."

I turned to look at her just in time to see the slight curl in her lip as she surveyed my head. "Yeah, thank God. Cause your weave is looking a little busted right now."

"Oh kiss my ass," I laughed, and she joined in. If nothing else, I knew I could count on Nubia to break up the darkness with light moments of humor.

Just then, a knock sounded at the hotel room door, and Nubia quickly motioned for me to keep my seat.

"It's probably just Blake. I've gotta pick up Trey from the sitter, so she's gonna drive you to that appointment."

I rolled my eyes. "I can drive just fine, dammit."

"Girl, don't nobody care what you're talking about. We're your friends, and we're gonna be there for you all the way through this, whether you like the shit or not. Don't argue," she called over her shoulder as she went to the door. And sure enough, a few seconds later, Blake was walking toward me, with her arms stretched out.

"How are you feeling today sweetie?" she asked, bending to pull me into a hug without me having to rise from my seat. "Wait, don't answer that. I'm sure I already know."

I nodded. "Yeah, probably."

"Well," Blake sighed. "How much you wanna bet that a good scalp massage and a fresh weave will make it all feel a little better."

"That is a bet I will definitely take you up on," I said, rising from my spot on the couch.

I'd managed to drag myself to the bathroom for my personal care that morning, so all I needed to do was grab my keys and purse to head out the door.

"Thank you for sitting with me this morning," I told Nubia, hugging her as we headed out. "Next time you come by, bring the baby with you. I could use a Trey hug and a few of his little toddler kisses."

"Consider it handled, love."

She headed out, with me and Blake right behind her, going separate ways once we made it to the private parking garage. Instead of grilling me about everything that had been happening, or letting the car descend into silence, she treated me to a constant stream of conversation about everything else.

I was grateful for it.

Because, lately, when left to my quiet thoughts, things were getting darker and darker for me. The run-in with Wick two days ago certainly hadn't helped things – now I felt even *more* lost. If that were even possible.

The trip to the salon felt shorter than usual, probably because of Blake's chatter. I glanced around to make sure the parking lot and entrance were free of the journalistic vultures I'd been dealing with more and more since Kellen's death before I opened my door and climbed out.

A day at the salon always felt like a treat to me. My stylist, Tika, always had good stories to tell, the salon supplied wine and champagne, and they'd been a huge supporter of *Vivid Vixen* cosmetics since early on – they had a whole polish display just for my brand. Walking through their door, into that warm, upscale salon energy always made me smile.

Only today... it was different.

A hush fell over the whole salon as soon as Blake and I walked in, and open conversation turned into whispers. Of course, this was something I should have expected after my face had been all over the news, my name dragged through the mud without any evidence. I wanted to leave, but the funeral was in a few days, and Nubia was right – I was looking busted. So instead of shrinking in response to the negative energy, I walked right to the reception desk to give my name.

"Monica Stuart. I have a one o'clock with Tika."

The girl at the desk gave me a strange look, then turned her eyes to her screen, clicking around a little before she tentatively met my gaze.

"I-I'm sorry, Mrs. Stuart. I don't have it on file. It must've been canceled."

I frowned. "What? No, that has to be a mistake. I didn't cancel my appointment."

"It's not a mistake."

I turned toward the source of that statement to find Tika standing a little behind me, arms crossed as she scowled in my direction.

"Excuse me?" I asked, confused, and Tika took another step toward me.

"I *said*, it's not a mistake. I canceled the appointment, because I didn't think I could stand to look at you after what you did."

My frown deepened. "Again – *Excuse me*? What the hell are you talking about, T?"

"*Kellen*. You took him from me!"

My head reared back. "Took him? From *you*?"

"Yes, you jealous *bitch*," she spat, closing that last step between us. "He was going to leave you, and it was going to be me and him—"

"Are you telling me that you were fucking my *husband*, Tika? Are you kidding me?!"

Tika shook her head as a slick little smile curved the corners of her mouth. "No. I wasn't fucking your "husband". I was fucking *my man*, and your chubby ass just couldn't help getting in the way. I hope they throw away the key when they lock your frigid ass up. *Murderer*."

I didn't see red.

I saw black.

And the very next second, one of my hands was tangled in Tika's hair, holding with the tightest grip I could while the other hand curled into a fist to connect with her face.

I heard the screams from the patrons, heard Blake in my ear, begging me to let Tika go while she tried in vain to pull me off of her, but I just... I couldn't.

I was so, *so* tired.

And I had so many questions.

How long had it been going on? How the hell had it started? Did he initiate it? Did she? But I didn't care about any of the answers as much as I cared about shutting her up.

With my fist.

"*Monica!*"

I couldn't say why, but that time, when Blake said my name, it got my attention. I was no longer holding Tika, but my fingers were still clenched tight around a handful of bleached blonde strands.

"Come *on*, before the police get here," Blake hissed, carting me toward the door, and away from where Tika was surrounded by stylists trying to comfort her.

I shook her weave from my hand, intending to follow Blake's instruction, but Mona, one of the older stylists, and owner of the salon stepped in front of us. Immediately, my fists clenched again, but Mona held up her hands.

"I was married thirty-two years," she said in a deep, serious tone. "My husband couldn't keep his dick in his pants either, so I know how it feels, honey. I've done just that," – she pointed to where Tika was being helped to the back, "to more than one hoe myself. Don't you worry about this, alright? We *all* saw her approach you, and rear her hand back to hit you. Didn't we?" Mona asked, glancing at the stylists and clients within earshot. They all knew well enough to nod.

Honestly, I was still a little dazed, still reeling from what had just happened, so I couldn't do much except mirror their nods. "Um… thank you," I told her.

"Mmhmm. Now gone on. I can't have this trouble in my shop."

"Yes ma'am."

I didn't have to be told twice to leave a place, especially when I recognized I'd been done a favor. We climbed back in the car, and Blake drove in silence for several minutes before she spoke up.

"Aiight Holyfield – you wanna tell me what the *fuck* that was?"

I huffed. "I'm not really sure what you want me to say, Blake. I snapped."

94

"Clearly. I didn't know you had hands like that Mon," she laughed. "You didn't break a nail did you?"

"Of course not. They're done with *Vivid Vixen* products. Still perfect."

"Uh huh." Blake nodded. "So what, that was that, a field test? Market research? Is your next slogan going to be, "Whoop that trick, and still have a perfect mani with *Vivid Vixen*?"

"Hell yes. Gotta hire Nubia for the visual. She could sell the hell out of that."

Blake giggled. "I'm just glad it was me with you, and not Nubia. She would've let you kill that girl."

"Because Nubia is a *real* friend."

"Monica, *bye*," Blake shrieked, then turned to me as we pulled to a stop light. "I don't think an attempted murder, not even a week after you're arrested for a *different* murder would be a good look for you. Just sayin'."

I pushed out a sigh as the car started moving again. "No. Probably not." The car was quiet again for several minutes while it all played in my head. I'd known for a long time that Kellen was a whore – he hadn't exactly tried to hide it. I'd watched him flirt with everyone from waitresses to my employees, but I'd really thought that Crystal was it for him. She was the one he loved to rub in my face, the one he'd chosen to carry his child.

She probably thought she was as special as I'd assumed she was.

Turns out, she wasn't.

"I guess he really was just fucking everybody," I mused, shaking my head. "But my hair stylist, though? That's just foul. That's like fucking his barber."

"Yeah," Blake agreed. "It's pretty messed up, Mon. I'm so sorry."

I shrugged. "Nothing for you to be sorry about. I picked him."

"Not like that makes it better. You don't deserve this."

I had no response for that. Because honestly... maybe I *did*. Maybe all of this was the harvest from the seeds I'd sown in my marriage. Not being as supportive as I could have after he lost his job, not caring if he felt emasculated or threatened about my drive and work ethic. The emotional affair with Wick.

I wasn't innocent.

So as angry as I was about the whole thing, there was still an underlying sense of guilt.

A quiet feeling that... *yes.* This was *exactly* what I deserved. And if it wasn't my own karma, maybe it *was* a curse. Maybe I was reaping what my own mother had planted, doomed to repeat her mistakes as my own.

That woman who'd been there at the tech store talking to Wick... that body language certainly didn't say "customer". And yet, before the last week or so, Wick and I had been much, *much* more than friendly with each other.

I was all pissed off at Crystal and Tika for enabling my husband's infidelity, but really? I wasn't much better. When I tallied up my own mistakes... I wasn't sure I had room to judge.

# SEVEN

## MONICA

My damned arms hurt, and I wasn't even finished yet.

I dropped my shoulders and tipped my head back to stare at the ceiling, grateful that I'd – finally – successfully removed the last weft of my sew-in weave, but simultaneously devastated by the knowledge that I still had to unbraid, wash, and blow dry the mass of hair that had been waiting underneath.

*This shit is going to take all night.*

But still, I soldiered on, as I worked on my second bottle of wine. Blake, Kora, Chloe, *and* Nubia all had stylist recommendations for me after my fiasco earlier in the afternoon, but I'd declined all suggestions.

With my luck, the new stylist had probably been fucking my husband too.

The only safe choice was to do it on my own.

I'd convinced my girlfriends to leave me to myself, and found my way into the bathroom with my Bluetooth speaker, some wine, a pair of scissors, some hair clips, and a comb. In the mirror, I'd carefully snipped the thread holding my expensive bundles to the cornrowed hair underneath, until it was all a tangled pile on the floor. Then, I set to work taking down the braids until *my* hair – as in, the stuff that came from my scalp – was all free.

And a mess.

But, I felt lighter.

I washed and deep conditioned, taking the time to give myself a fresh mani/pedi while the products soaked into my hair. Afterward, I picked up my blow dryer, to stretch it out before I plugged up my flat iron. I didn't make it to the straightening step before somebody knocked on the door, which brought a frown to my face.

I wasn't expecting anybody.

Thinking quickly, I managed to tame it into an oversized bun by the time the knock sounded again, and I rushed through my suite to see who it was. I took a step back from the peephole, surprised at who was on the other side. While I was debating whether or not I wanted to answer, he knocked *again,* and I took a deep breath and opened the door.

"Asher," I said, looking up at Kellen's best friend. "What are you doing here?"

His gray eyes widened a little, and he ran a hand over what looked to be a freshly cut fade. "A man can't come check on a friend who's having a tough time?"

"Is that what we are, Ash? Friends?"

He shrugged. "I mean… we used to be. You don't call me anymore, don't write, so maybe not."

"Well, considering the fact that your bestie seemed to always be somewhere he shouldn't, doing something or *someone* he shouldn't… I figured I'd save you the uncomfortable position of having to lie for, or defend him."

Ash drug his full bottom lip between his teeth, chewing at it for a second before he pushed his hands into the pocket of his dark brown leather bomber. "I don't have a rebuttal for that. Other than… thank you."

"Mmhmm."

Neither of us spoke for a moment, but then a slow smile spread across his handsome, lightly freckled face. "So... are you going to let me in, or not?"

I narrowed my eyes a little, considering it before I nodded. "Sure, Ash. Why not?"

I stepped aside for him to enter, not expecting the way I'd be affected by the aroma of his cologne as he passed. It wasn't exactly the same as Kellen's, but it was similar enough that it made my eyes water with tears I had *no* intentions to shed.

"This is a nice ass hotel," he said, looking around as I closed the door. "Pat said you were holed up in some "ten-star" hotel, but now I actually believe her."

*So that's how he knew where to find me.*

Pat was Kellen's mother, and I'd given her my contact info at the hotel in case she needed to reach me before the funeral. Not that there was much conversation necessary between us now that Kellen was gone, but still. She was my husband's mother.

"So you've talked to her? To his family?"

Ash nodded. "Yeah. They uh... wanted me to talk to the police."

I frowned. "Talk to the police? For *what*?"

"To... help gauge their conduct on this trip for the funeral, from what I gathered. They wanted to know... if you were guilty. If you killed him."

"That is ridiculous, and you know it. I did *not* kill Kellen."

He lifted his hands, motioning for me to calm down. "That's what I told them, and what I told the police too. They reached out to me, for questions. I told them everything I knew, because I want them to catch whoever did this – but I know it wasn't you. You loved him... even when he didn't deserve it."

"Told them everything?" I asked. "What is *everything*?"

"I don't know," he shrugged. "Just... possible motives and shit I guess. Women, shady business deals, debts."

"Debts? What *debts*? I paid for everything, why the fuck would he have *debts*?"

"Business debts."

"What business? Kellen didn't *have* any business besides screwing anything he could fit his dick in. He didn't *work*. What business, Ash?!"

"Monica, *damn*," Ash said, approaching me to grab my shoulders, holding me still. "Look, I don't know everything my friend was into, and that's not a conversation I'm about to have with his widow. I just want you to know, that the police know there are angles other than "mad wife" to explore. Angles that make more sense."

I pushed out a breath through my nose and shook my head. "Sorry. It's just that this is a lot."

Ash nodded. "I know," he said, stepping in closer, and moving his hands from my shoulders to my face. "*I'm* sorry. For everything you're going through right now. Anything I can do to help?"

Again, I shook my head. "No. Not that I know of, anyway."

"Come on," he grinned. "There has to be something."

I chuckled. "Ummm… do you have a spare time machine lying around? Cause if I just go back and change a few things around…"

"*Really* now," he said, walking away to take a seat at the counter, and motioning for me to follow. "That's a line of conversation I'll bite. What would you change?"

I scoffed. "Man, too many things to name. So many mistakes."

"Ah, don't wimp out on me Monica. At least one thing. Come on."

Wrinkling my nose at him, I fought – and lost – the urge to smile. "Well, I definitely wouldn't have gone to that frat party Junior year."

"Which party?"

"Boy you *know* which party," I laughed. "Me, you, Kellen, Amanda, drunk as fucking *skunks* walking home in the snow, no coats, stopping every five minutes because somebody had to puke?"

Ash's eyes went wide. "*Yooo*. Yes. Yeah. Yep, all that. Definitely take that one back. That was *not* a good look for any of us."

100

"Not at all. Whatever happened between you and Amanda? I never really understood why you two broke up?"

He sighed. "Just… grew apart I guess. Shit happens. What looks good in college looks a little different once you're grown."

"I sure do know all about that," I said, then closed my eyes. "Anyway… what about you? What would you take back?"

"Ah, shit," he said, crossing his arms as he sat back in his high-backed bar chair. "Uh…. Shit. Okay, so… I had this little work-study job freshman year, right? So, one day I stayed up all night studying, took the test the next day, and then I was so exhausted that I just couldn't keep my eyes open. So I called in, and they called somebody else to take my place. Well *that* dude ended up getting an opportunity that should have been mine. I regret that shit to this day."

"What was the opportunity?" I asked, and Ash shook his head.

"See, now you're all up in my business."

I laughed. "Oh, is that it?"

"Yes, it is. You don't see me telling you how to run your little press-on nail company."

"Oh my God, *nooo* you didn't!" I shrieked. "My "little" company, that's what you're doing right now?"

He shrugged. "I mean, I call it like I see it. Not like you've been on magazine covers, lists of entrepreneurs to watch, signing exclusive deals with major cosmetic stores, anything like that."

I tucked my top lip between my teeth, trying my hardest not to grin like a fool. "So you've been keeping up with me, huh?"

"Hell yeah I have. Gotta keep up with your investments, make sure they're growing, right?" he said, nudging my shoulder.

"Ah, but I bought you out two years ago, Ash," I reminded him, and he nodded.

"Yeah, and I let you off cheap. Should have charged a "knew you way back when" fee on top of the value of my stake in the company."

"But because we're *friends*, you didn't do me like that."

"*Only* because we're friends. If you were anybody else, I'd still have my ten percent."

Now *that* was a memory to hold on to.

Four years ago, not too long after Kellen lost his job, Ash had taken a chance on me. *Vivid Vixen* was a fledgling company back then, still considered indie in the nail world. I had the drive, and I had the ambition – what I *didn't* have was the money.

But I knew people who did.

Some were friends, and some weren't, but everyone I approached, I approached with the same energy. "*I can do this. It will be big. If you invest in me, I promise you will get your money back, if I have to mow lawns and wash dishes to do it.*"

I don't know if it was friendship, genuine belief in me, or simply a desire to get me out of their face, but I ended up with the money I needed, for the building I was in now. My *own* production facilities, my *own* research lab, my own *everything*.

Two years later, I bought back every single percentage of my business I'd sold to make it happen. Ash had been one of those investors.

"I'd think you'd congratulate me on being a shrewd enough businesswoman to know you were a softy, and take full advantage."

He laughed. "Uh, that's… a way to look at it."

"The only way to look at it."

"Well, in that case, I'll drink to that… if I had a drink."

I rolled my eyes. "Wow. Very subtle way to tell me you'd like a drink."

His shoulders hiked up. "I mean, I'm not gonna pretend I don't see that very nice mini bar over there, that I just imagine is full of top shelf liquor."

"Oh I'm sure," I told him, standing up from my seat. It wasn't until I was halfway there that I got a little self-conscious, remembering that I hadn't bothered with underwear underneath my yoga pants and tank, since I wasn't expecting company. Suddenly, I felt like I was jiggling all over the place, but when I glanced back, Ash's attention was out the window, admiring the view of the city.

"You still drink that frilly shit from college?" he asked, once we made it to the bar. "Lemon Drops, Appletinis and shit?"

I fake-gasped. "I'll have you know that my tastes have matured. I drink sweet red wine now, the cheaper the better," I laughed. "You still a *Mauve* and coke man like your friend?"

"Til' I can't lift the glass by myself anymore."

He was quiet as I fixed the drink for him, and then slid it to him. He looked at it, confused.

"You're not going to have one?"

I shook my head. "No sir, I was halfway through my second bottle of wine when you knocked on the door, so I probably shouldn't."

"Just a sip, Monica. Come on. Enough to drink to Kellen's memory… the good years."

My eyebrows went up when he first mentioned drinking to Kellen, but honestly, the good years we'd had together definitely deserved a toast. I splashed enough *Mauve* into a glass of my own for just a sip, laughing when Ash grabbed my hand while I was still holding the bottle, to tip in a little more.

"Okay, now that's more like it," he said, raising his glass, and I followed suit, even though I really was feeling a bit tipsy from my drinking earlier. "To a friend, a husband, to… a deeply flawed man, who was loved in spite of, and taken before his time. Cheers."

"Cheers," I said, clumsily tapping his glass with mine before I swallowed the liquor inside. "Oh, shit," I chuckled, putting a hand to my throat as the *Mauve* burned its way down.

"Goddamn lightweight," Ash scoffed, shaking his head as he chugged his drink back.

"Whatever. I'll be right back," I told him, leaving him at the bar to duck into my room. If he noticed that I'd put on the matching jacket to my yoga pants when I came back, he didn't react, or say anything. But, it was more for *my* comfort anyway.

Having my titties out around my dead husband's best friend wasn't a good look.

I took a seat on the opposite end of the couch from him, and didn't think twice about it when he moved closer to the middle as he started talking. That was just *Ash*, always wanting to be right in your face as he talked, and talked, and *talked*, but honestly, I didn't mind. As adamant as I'd been about wanting to be alone, the company was nice, and being around Ash really did make me remember the good times I'd had with Kellen, which were honestly plentiful.

Four years of friendship, friends with benefits, dating, being exclusive, breaking up, fucking, hating each other, and then cycling through it all again. That had been college. After that, those first ten years of marriage, building our careers, trying and failing to start a family, learning each other and growing together. Ash had been a pretty consistent presence around our home – he and my friend Amanda, who'd dropped off the face of the earth apparently, after she and Ash broke up.

But it had been beautiful, even with the dark moments. Really, *really* beautiful.

Until it wasn't.

"Hey, I'm gonna grab another drink," Ash said as he stood. "You want one?"

I shook my head. "No thanks."

While he was off taking advantage of the – probably expensive – mini bar, I took a peek at my phone, my heart racing when I saw that I had a text from my lawyer, Demetria.

**"Great news – I think you're in the clear. I got Sam Turner to look into the investigation. Police are heavily pursuing other angles, possible suspects. They may have more questions for you later, but hopefully this helps you rest a little easier. – Demetria Byers (Olivia Pope)"**

*"Yes, that IS great news. Any developments with the break-in at my house, or the hacking?"*

104

"Not yet, but I'll stay on Sam about it, and keep you posted. – Demetria Byers (Olivia Pope)"

"Oh, and Monica, SERIOUSLY, try to get some rest. – Demetria Byers (Olivia Pope)"

*"I'll try. Thank you."*

"Do you remember that night before you and Kel got married, how he kept calling, and calling, and calling you?" Asher asked as he returned to his seat beside me, drink in hand.

I nodded. "Vividly. I could hear all the loud ass partying and debauchery in the background, and y'all told me it was just butt dials."

"It was *not* butt dials," Ash laughed. "Kel was *wasted* beyond belief, and the strippers wouldn't leave him alone."

"Um, it was his bachelor party! Why would they?"

"Because he wanted them to." He shrugged. "He was cool with the lap dances and stuff, but then, it all started getting more and more raunchy, and it was messing with his head. He spazzed a little bit. He didn't want anything to do with all that – all he wanted was you. He was terrified that something might happen that night that would… I don't know, disappoint, or disrespect you, and he didn't want that. I guess when he called though… he couldn't find the words."

"Wow."

I blinked, hard.

The truth behind that story was… unexpected, to say the least. Kellen had never been the kind of guy who *wasn't* up for a good time. As a matter of fact, I would imagine that a stripper in his lap, a drink in his hand, and titties in his face was how Kellen would *define* a "good time". Back then, it never would have occurred to me that he would take it beyond that, but being distraught enough about whatever was happening at his Vegas bachelor party to feel bad about it?

"It *had* to have been the liquor," I said, shaking my head. "That's the only way that makes any sense to me."

Ash hiked one shoulder, then dropped it. "Maybe, but I think it was more. He loved you just that much, that he didn't want to mess it up."

105

"Yeah," I scoffed. "That sentiment certainly faded."

"Life changes all of us," Ash agreed, then took a long sip from a drink that looked to be more *Mauve* than coke. "He lost his job and never recovered."

"Well, when you're a black man, insider trading allegations will do that to you."

"They fucked him over. Left him bleeding out."

I swallowed, then dropped my gaze to my hands. "Yeah… and I didn't do anything to try to stop it."

"Monica, don't do that shit," Ash warned, putting his hand on my knee and squeezing. "You *did* do something. You worked, while he was down."

I sucked my teeth. "Oh please. All that did was make him resent me."

"Not at first though."

"Right. He cared about not disrespecting me, at first. He *loved* me, at first. He wouldn't cheat on me, *at first.* Whoop-de-fucking-doo. You keep wanting to talk about what he did at first, but like Janet said – what the *fuck* had he done for me lately?"

"Whoa, *shit,* Monica," he chuckled. "I wasn't… I wasn't trying to upset you. I'm sorry, I just miss my friend, and I'm trying to focus on the positive memories, instead of… the other shit."

"Yeah, well, I don't quite have the same luxury. In case you forgot, your *friend* was murdered in the condo he lived in with his pregnant mistress, and paid for with money I earned. Since we're strolling memory lane, did you talk to your boy about how *fucked up* that was?"

"As a matter of fact, I *did*," he insisted, any humor from before completely removed from his tone. "Don't think that just because I considered the man a friend, I supported that shit. He was wrong, and I told him so."

"But he didn't give a damn, did he?" I snapped. "I know you loved him as a friend, and I loved him as a husband, but don't you sit in my face and try to martyr him in death as if he was perfect in either role."

"Hey…" His tone was soft as he reached for my hand. "That's not what I'm trying to do. I'm not trying to upset you. I'm sorry."

I closed my eyes as his thumb moved back and forth across my palm, then shook my head, trying in vain to hold back tears. "*I'm* sorry. My emotions are all over the place today. One second, I'm reminiscing my damn self, and the next I'm wondering why the hell I chose him in the first place."

Ash's grip on my hand tightened, and I looked up to find him staring, with clear sympathy in his eyes. "Well, first of all, for the record, he and I *both* thought you were too good for him," he told me, sitting his drink down on the glass coffee table, freeing his hand to swipe away the tears that had started spilling down my cheeks. When I laughed at that, he grinned. "There we go, there's that beautiful smile again."

"Whatever, Asher."

"I'm not lying on you," he teased. "And second… I'm pretty sure that what you're feeling… the up and down, the regrets, the wondering… it's all a normal part of the grieving process. I don't want you beating yourself up over it."

"Yeah. Maybe you're right," I told him, then squeezed his hand. "Thanks Ash."

"Thank me for *what*? For doing the shit a friend is supposed to do?"

I shrugged. "Well… yeah, actually. I mean, you and I were friends back then, sure, but Kellen was your *homie*. You could easily have pretended I didn't even exist, which is what I expected. You're the only one of Kellen's friends to reach out to me at all."

"Definitely don't take *that* personal. Over the last year or so, Kellen pushed everybody away really. I was the only one who gave him any pushback, so there's no telling where their heads are with all of this."

"*Wow.*" I frowned. "I didn't know that. But I guess there was no reason I would've, since it's not like I was around him either. Once I moved into the house by myself… that was it. I tried to pretend he didn't even exist."

"Which meant pretending *I* didn't exist," Ash reminded me, making me shake my head.

"Not intentionally, but… you're right. And that's my bad. We used to kick it *so hard.* Me, Kellen, you, Amanda… I wonder if she even knows about Kellen. Have you talked to her at all lately?"

"Nah," he sighed. "Haven't heard her voice in years."

I nodded. "I might try to call her tomorrow. I used to try all the time, but she never answered, so I just stopped."

"Recently?"

"No, this was years ago. Around when she up and left after y'all broke up. I never did hear her side of that story by the way."

Ash shrugged. "I told you, we just grew apart. She wanted to move back out west, and I wasn't interested. Neither of us wanted to do long distance, so the choice was made. She thought keeping up with each other would just keep us from being able to move on, so I respected her wishes and let it go."

"Ugh. She was probably right, but still. That was my homegirl, and she just disappeared. I bet she stopped taking my calls because talking to me would remind her of *you.*"

"Sure, blame me for everything."

"I'm not *blaming* you, just saying," I laughed. "I miss those times."

"So do I. And now, it's down to just us two."

*Damn.*

It sounded so gloomy when he phrased it that way, but… he was right. Through college, and after, the four of us had been super tight. Double dates, Sunday breakfasts, trips. I'd honestly thought we'd be friends forever, until Amanda up and disappeared. Once she was gone, and it was me, Ash, and Kellen, I started feeling like a third wheel in their bromance, so I left them to their manly shit, and ended up tight with other friends – Blake, Kora, Nubia, and Chloe. And now, like he said… both of our partners were gone.

From the foursome of friends we'd started with, it really was down to just us two.

When I looked up at Asher again, I noticed how much lower his eyelids had gotten, no doubt from the *Mauve* he'd drained from his now-empty glass. But there was something else... a gloss of sadness in his eyes that made me feel so bad for him. My relationship with Kel had severely deteriorated over the last years, but his hadn't. Ash was mourning the loss of a dear friend.

"We're gonna be okay," I told him, covering his hand with both of mine before I moved to get close enough to pull him into a hug. "I know you miss him. And I'm sorry for *your* loss," I said, wrapping my arms around his shoulders.

"Thank you, Mon." His voice was thick with emotion as he rested his head in the curve of my neck and shoulder, returning the hug and squeezing me a little. "That means a lot."

I pulled back to see his face. "Like you said... this is what friends do for each other, right?"

"Yeah... right."

For several seconds, Ash stared at me with those half-closed eyes, and then suddenly his face was coming closer – *too* close – to mine. It only took a moment for me to register his intent, but by that time, his lips were already on mine.

"Asher, what the *hell*?!" I asked, jumping up from my seat as soon as I pushed him away.

For a moment, he looked dazed, and then his eyes went wide and he stood too, holding up his hands. "Monica... *shit*. I... I'm sorry, I didn't mean to... *shit!*" he exclaimed, swiping a hand over his head. "I didn't... I wasn't... I'm so sorry, you have to believe—"

"Ash, *chill*," I told him, attempting a soothing tone, even though my heart was racing with the shock of what had just happened. "It's... it's not a big deal, okay? You've been drinking, and we're both emotionally raw right now, and... I know you didn't mean anything by it."

"Monica, I am *sorry*."

I nodded. "I know, okay? You didn't drive, did you?"

"No. Not tonight. I uh… I used a car service."

"Perfect. So, call your service, so you can get back to… where are you staying?"

"I'm at the Drake. A regular five-star property – everybody can't afford this big-money shit like you," he teased as he pulled his phone from his pocket – something I was glad for, because it broke the heavy, awkward tension in the room.

"I'm only here because the privacy was necessary," I assured him. "Otherwise, my behind would be somewhere else too."

"Yeah, yeah. I uh… I got the car ordered, so, I'm gonna go ahead and bid you goodnight before I go wait down in the lobby."

I sucked my teeth. "Boy if you don't stop. Waiting down in the lobby for what? Like you can't keep your hands off me or something? *Please.*"

"I just think it's probably for the best, after that," he said. "And you weren't expecting company anyway, so I should probably let you have your room to yourself again."

"If you say so, Ash. I just feel like ten years from now, this story is going to turn into, "do you remember that time you kicked me out of your hotel room", and I'm telling you now, me and you are gonna box."

He laughed. "You aren't gonna fight anybody Monica, you're too pretty for all that."

Immediately, my thoughts went to earlier in the day, when I'd tried to snatch Tika bald, and I shook my head. "You know, you're right."

"Conceited ass," he chuckled. "I'll see you at the funeral, right?"

"Since it's probably poor form to plan it all and then not show up… yes. You will."

"Good. Good night Monica."

"Good night, Ash," I called after him, rolling my eyes at the fact that he threw up his hand to wave, instead of giving me a hug. Once he was gone, I let out a heavy sigh, trying to push out all the conflicting feelings about Kellen that his visit had stirred up.

110

In two days, we'd be committing his body to the ground. With any luck, I'd bury these feelings with him.

# EIGHT

*"What the fuck is your problem?"*

I pulled out my earbuds and looked up to find a very angry-looking Renata standing over my desk, obviously ready and willing to get much louder than she'd been when my music was still blasting in my ears.

"Ren... can I help you?" I asked, confused about what I'd done to draw such rage, so early in the morning.

Her nostrils flared. "Yes, you sure as hell can, by telling me why in the world you took it upon yourself to tell one of our clients to "never come back". Who do you think you are?"

"The man who owns a third of this business," I answered, completely calm. "And I'm guessing you're talking about Monica Stuart?"

"You're goddamn right," she snapped. "As much as that woman has been through in the last week, you cannot tell me she deserves you being an asshole to her."

I dropped the earbuds onto my desk, and pushed away the hard drive I'd been working on. "What she's been through? Look, there's more to this than you know, so—"

"Oh please. You're talking about *you* being "NoRestForTheWicked"? I figured that out in two minutes alone with her laptop, did you forget who I am?"

I raised my eyebrows. "Are you taking this personal?"

"Yeah, actually, I kinda am. I told this woman that we would get her back on the path to normalcy, and now that's out the window. She came to me – to *us* – for help, and you send her away? Why, so nobody would know your little secret?"

"Because I got arrested for fucking *murder* behind my association with her. And Ren... you *know* that I can't be wrapped up in any bullshit."

Renata let out a sigh. "Yes, I know. I understand perfectly, Chad. You were fucking CIA, I understand that you need to keep a low profile. But I've never known you to be... a *fuckboy*."

"*Whoa*," I said, raising my hands. "A fuckboy? Seriously?"

She nodded. "Yeah, seriously. I saw how long you and Monica have been friends. Only a *fuckboy* would be selfish enough to abandon a woman he's been as intimate with as you and she have. Yeah, you got arrested. I recognize how fucked up that is, but you are not a pussy – far from it. So get over it, and *help me help her*."

My jaw tightened as I leaned back in my chair, spotting the obvious passion in Renata's demeanor. But what I didn't get was, "Help her with what, Ren? It's a murder investigation. It's not like there's shit we can do about it."

"Not the murder investigation." She shook her head. "But the hacking? The break-in?"

I frowned. "Wait a minute... break in?"

"Yes, a break in, at her home. Panties scattered all over the place, art and books destroyed, roses smashed on her front doorstep."

"Was she home when it happened?" I asked.

"For the break-in, no. But the roses were left at the door while she was inside, after discovering it. She called me, and I called Marcus, who called Sam."

"Marcus didn't say shit to me about that."

"That's something you'll have to take up with him. But it's irrelevant. With everything going on, I can't help thinking it has to be connected."

"Sounds like the former FBI agent in you coming out," I said, which drew a smile from her.

"Yeah. And I'm trying to pull the *Agent* Calloway back out of you. I've seen your files, remember? You used to rock with Inez and Savannah back in the day, and *those* bitches are the toughest women I

114

know besides Mimi. And Quentin is your blood. If *they* respect you, I know you're a bad motherfucker, and between us and the rest of the team, we can figure this out."

I sat back in my seat, shaking my head. "Ren... I left all of that behind me for a reason. For a *damned* good reason."

"Which I understand, but—"

"I'm *not* gonna be dragged back into it. Especially when I have Kay to consider."

Before Renata could respond, the door to my office swung open again, and I looked up to see Quentin.

"Hey..." he said, looking suspiciously between the two of us. "Y'all good in here? Steven said he saw Renata storm in here upset about something... I don't need to referee, do I?"

Ren sucked her teeth. "Of course not. Chad loves me."

"And you love to take that for granted," I said, grinning as she flipped me off.

"Whatever. Q, your timing is actually perfect. I was just about to remind Chad of the story of how you reacted to finding out I was the mystery girl you'd been chatting online with for all those years."

Quentin's face blanked. "Oh, shit. You know what? I think I hear somebody call—"

"Uh-uh," Ren laughed, pulling him into the doorway. "You bring your butt in here and tell him how much you regretted being mean to me."

"I wasn't *mean*, it was more like—"

"Quentin."

He pushed out a sigh. "Aiight, cherie. I wasn't necessarily Prince Charming at first, but you have to understand *why* I was angry."

"I do," she assured him, planting her hands against her chest. "And, I understand why Chad is so upset with the Monica situation. But it's just that – the situation. Yes, the video was a mistake, but the police would've wanted to question you anyway. You're blaming her, but this isn't her fault. None of it is."

"I get that, but it doesn't change the fact that I don't want anything to do with the drama of that whole situation."

"What about once it's over?" Quentin asked, apparently surprising both of us, from the way Ren's lips parted. But then she turned to me too, waiting for me to answer the question.

I shrugged. "What do you mean?"

"I mean... once the drama has passed. Because, it *will* pass. And then what do you do, when you miss your friend, and the shit that seemed so big in the moment... you realize it wasn't even worth a damn – let alone worth the loss of that friend."

"Listen," I started, shaking my head. "I get what y'all are saying... I *do*. But it's really not that simple. Honestly, I'm not even pissed anymore – I just can't be a part of this."

For several seconds, neither of them said anything. When Renata did start to speak, Quentin hushed her, kissing her on the forehead.

"Babe... let me talk to Chad alone real quick, aiight?"

"Yeah," she nodded, then slipped out of the room as Quentin dropped into the chair across from me at the desk.

"Aiight man... not to be on any sappy shit, but... you want to tell me what's *really* going on? Because you say you're not pissed anymore – cool. You say you're not trying to have unwanted attention or scrutiny on you – understandable. But we *both* know that you could help Renata help Monica without your name even being involved if you wanted it that way. What I think is that you... don't want to be involved with Monica at all, and it has nothing to do with this murder shit. So... what's up?" he asked, propping his hands behind his head.

I shook my head. "There's nothing up. You pegged it – I just don't want to be involved."

"But you were *very* involved before all this shit went down. I wasn't trying to be all in your business, but Ren gave a little background. What's different now vs a week ago?"

"Proximity," I answered. "A week ago, I thought she was halfway across the country. Now she... hell, she may as well be next door."

116

"So?"

My eyes widened. "*So*? You say that like everything can just flip back to normal."

"No, I'm saying it like... why does it matter? You care about this woman, right? So, why wouldn't it be a good thing to learn that instead of being hundreds of miles away, she's right here where you can see her, touch her, in real life? I don't get how that's not a *better* situation."

I let out a dry chuckle. "Because you're thinking like a man who's been married for five years. Like a man who doesn't have certain countries he can't step foot in. A settled man. One who doesn't need to be able to get up and go at the drop of a dime."

"You don't live that life anymore though, bruh. You keep saying how you don't want to get dragged back into it, but it sounds to me like you're keeping yourself there. It's okay to settle in and make a life for yourself. I mean... who, besides all the former law enforcement and government agents that you work with at Five Star, do you even talk to?"

"Kayla."

He laughed. "Come *on*, man. She don't count."

"Fine. Monica. Well, *Sandy*."

"Okay then! So you're gonna throw away your one – relatively – normal human interaction... for what? Actually... while we're here, I need you to explain how the *fuck* your former-CIA ass ended up in a damn anonymous whatever-the-fuck-y'all-call-it in the first place?"

"For exactly the reason you said – normal human interaction. I didn't know who she was, she didn't know who I was. I only gave the details I wanted to give, she did the same. We could communicate from anywhere, because she... lived in my computer, as far as I knew, you know? And talking to someone who was just... completely removed from everything... it was refreshing."

"I don't get you man," Quentin laughed. "If you were happy to talk to her then, but now that you know the two of you are in the same place... it's game over?"

"Yes."

"But that doesn't make any sense, unless you're… afraid of what might develop. That's it, isn't it?"

I shook my head. "Man… I'm really not trying to talk about this shit. *Really.*"

"And that's cool," Quentin said, putting up his hands. "But… let me ask you this – and you don't even have to respond – a year, five years, ten years from now… are you going to be able to live with the fact that someone you cared about needed your help, and you chose not to do it, based on a part of your life you swore you wanted to put behind you?"

True to his word, Quentin stood up and left, not even looking back to see if I would respond. Probably because we both knew I wouldn't. Still though, the damage was done.

He'd effectively watered the seed of doubt his wife had planted, and the goddamn thing was already blooming.

*Maybe I really was thinking about this the wrong way.*

When I said I wasn't pissed at Monica anymore, that was the truth. The whole situation was aggravating, but I understood that she wasn't the villain. It was just all-around fucked up.

With that said, the last thing I needed was continued interaction with her, bolstering the theory that I'd killed her husband for her, or that we'd cooked up some scheme together. I didn't need to be hauled into the police station again, didn't need some local gossip columnist posting my picture online for the whole damned world to see.

I wasn't trying to accept an invitation for trouble at my front door.

Quentin was right though. I could help with the other stuff right here from the comfort of my office, or at home, and never have my name officially connected to anything. The problem in that was, even if the authorities didn't know I was helping, Monica would. And she would be grateful, and want to talk, to thank me or something, and that meant being in her face, or hearing her voice, or smelling her scent on the paper if she simply sent a card.

I didn't need that.

118

But I wanted it, bad.

Which was *exactly* why I needed to let the shit go.

Things were perfect when she was outside of my reach. When all I could do was imagine her face, or pretend smelling her perfume was like having her *actual* aroma in my nose. Before she was close enough to touch… or taste.

Yes, we were friends, but it served no one's interests to pretend that there wasn't more to the story – a story I knew better than to start in the first place. Monica was… an attachment.

I'd spent half my adult life in a career that considered *attachments* grounds for dismissal. *Don't develop personal relationships* was damn near part of the job description.

It wasn't an easy thing to let go of.

Family were the first ones I relaxed that rule for, once I hung up that particular hat for good. Their number was limited enough that it was easy, eventually, to justify friends – a few from my days at Blakewood State, but mostly fellow government agents or law enforcement – people I met during my stint as a Tech Analyst with the FBI, before I stepped away completely.

Women… were a whole other animal.

Of course I had flings – I was a man with certain needs, so that had been a constant. And it wasn't as if I didn't see the value of women beyond sex. Being a friend was the type of thing I could handle – I was actually pretty damned good at it, I thought. But once other shit got involved – other shit being romantic feelings – that was where it tended to fall apart. And with Kay having been such a large part of my life, for years…I couldn't say that I felt a particular inclination to change that.

I didn't feel incomplete. There was no deep, underlying sense that something was missing, no craving for long walks or cuddling in front of the fire. Between Kay, my *Five Star* family, friends, and work, my life was full.

*Not if you leave Monica hanging though.*

"*Fuck*," I said out loud, scrubbing a hand over my face. Whether or not I wanted to admit it, Monica, as Sandy, had developed a certain importance in my life. When she told me vague details about a great deal she'd closed for her business, I was genuinely happy for her. When she hit me up randomly to ask about my day or see if I'd managed restful sleep, it made me feel cared for. And when the clown ass motherfucker she'd married hurt her... I wanted to do *exactly* what the police had accused me of.

So, to answer Quentin's question... no.

I *wouldn't* be able to live with myself knowing that she'd needed something I could provide, and I'd done nothing to help.

Closing my eyes, I heaved out yet another one of those hard sighs, then opened my desk drawer to pull out my cell phone. Before I could overthink it, I dialed a number, chuckling when the woman on the other end answered with a long, drawn out, "*Helllloooo?*"

"Ren..."

"Yes, Chad. How can I help you?"

I drummed my fingertips on the cool surface of my desk, glancing at the forgotten hard drive I'd been working on as I contemplated my answer.

"Monica Stuart. I need her laptop, and have her bring in her home desktop too. If I'm going to figure this out for her... I need all of it."

"*You're not as smart as you think you are, motherfucker,*" I muttered as my fingers flew over the keys, easily bypassing the attempt that had been made to keep me from seeing the exact method that had been used to breach Monica's computers. I wouldn't call it amateur work by any means, but the hacker – probably someone hired from more obscure, less than legal reaches of the internet – definitely wasn't elite.

That made *my* job a little easier.

I'd taken Monica's things to my home office with me and gotten comfortable, knowing that there was little chance of me getting any sleep – my default setting these days. Instead of setting myself up for frustration, I'd made my way straight here after my workout and shower, and settled in. The room was dark, my music was cranked up loud in my ears, and I was making progress.

Whoever hacked her was *all* the way up and through Monica's business.

The corrupted files were hidden in innocuous places, and all had innocuous names, so the chances that a typical user, or even the typical computer repair guy, would have found them, were slim. What they lacked in sophistication, they made up for by not being messy. I still had no idea who inserted the flash drive that did all the heavy lifting, but I *did* have my doubts that the hacking was personal.

As I navigated through everything in front of me, I realized that even her company's cloud server had been infected, and I had a suspicion that it had been the target in the first place. Production schedules had been downloaded, and in some cases, *changed*, so that they'd been over- or under – producing certain products, leading to shortages or surpluses, both of which could affect company goodwill and bottom line. And from what I could tell, more than one formula from her skin care products had been changed – by the system, not by one of her scientists – which meant that some products weren't even being produced as intended.

*"But quality control should be catching that,"* I mumbled to myself. That thought was barely out of my mind before I found the bundle of quality reports that had been suppressed from view by anyone other than the System Administrator. Someone, somewhere, had been giving those products the go-ahead to be sent to select clientele – online beauty influencers, celebrity spokespeople, and a few specific salons.

*No wonder Vivid Vixen* was getting trashed on social media. Monica thought the beauty vloggers or whoever were being paid to lie about the products, and say bad things. But... they weren't lying. The problem was in the production chain itself.

I backed out of that without touching anything, to avoid tipping anyone off. Eventually, I would take over the system and add better security measures, but for now, gathering information was key.

I navigated back to the laptop itself, and into the last folder I hadn't checked – labeled *Recipes*. A love of cooking was something Sandy… no, *Monica*… had mentioned to me on many occasions, but having such a folder on her work laptop rang an alarm bell for me. And sure enough, once I had clicked a few levels deep into the folder, I found something that made me frown, and lean a little closer to my screen.

A gateway for surveillance feeds.

The first one didn't surprise me very much – it was Monica's house. The front and back doors, her kitchen, her living room, and office – two angles of all points that could be used for entry. She'd probably turned them back on after the break-in.

Next was the *Vivid Vixen* building, which was full of security cameras. The building was dark now, and quiet, but I could easily imagine those screens filled with action. It wouldn't be any trouble at all for someone to watch every single detail of a day at *Vivid Vixen*, from the comfort of their computer screen.

The last one though… I didn't understand it. It was a single camera, aimed at an empty, unfamiliar living room. From the angle, it had to be up in a corner or something, and the view was partially obstructed. But everything that *was* visible was crystal clear. As I watched though, brow furrowed in confusion, it slowly became clear that I wasn't looking into someone's home… I was looking into a hotel suite.

A chill crawled up my spine as Monica came into view, illuminated by the glow of the TV. Her nose was red, and her glossy eyes were rimmed in a similar hue – obvious signs that she'd been crying, which pained me. Hearing it had always made me want to punch a hole in something, but *seeing* her pretty face so clearly distraught made my chest feel tight. She dropped brusquely onto the couch, an action that pulled her barely-tied robe open even more, almost revealing her

122

obvious nudity underneath. My eyes narrowed as I thought about someone else – someone sinister – watching her in this state.

*I can't just ignore this.*

As I wracked my brain trying to remember what hotel Renata had said Monica was in, the subject of the surveillance lifted a wine bottle from the coffee table to her mouth, tipping it back. Once she'd gulped down whatever she determined was enough, she practically tossed the bottle down, then dropped her face into her open hands.

There was no audio, but it was obvious that she was sobbing.

*Fuck.*

I got up from my desk, searching for the client card Renata had given me, with all of Monica's contact information. I frowned when I saw, in neatly printed letters, that Monica was staying at *Veil*.

They were *supposed* to be known for going the extra mile in discretion.

Back at the desk, I used my own laptop to open a private chat window to send a message. I wanted to protect Monica's privacy, but in her current state, alarming her didn't seem like a good idea. I didn't have the firepower here at home to do anything about a camera in a hotel room across town. But, I knew someone who might.

[open secured chat with user_ grimreapher]

[norestforthewicked: yo. u around?

grimreapher: only if your big sexy chocolate ass has something good for me.]

I chuckled, shaking my head as I typed back a response.

[norestforthewicked: stop playing. heard you're laid up with a hotel magnate now.

grimreapher: nah. that nigga is laid up with *me*.

norestforthewicked: well wake him up. unauthorized eyes on my client under the shroud.

grimreapher: not possible. no cameras in the rooms.

norestforthewicked: C33.]

A few minutes passed without a response, and I could imagine Willow – who'd appropriately dubbed herself the "Grim ReapHer" in the hacking world – cursing to herself as she realized I was right.

[grimreaper: nigga. is this monica stuart?

norestforthewicked: focus.

grimreaper: which means yes, it is. how the fuck is she this fine while she's a weepy drunk? impressive. goddamn she's fine.

norestforthewicked: agreed. but, focus please.

grimreaper: fine. i'll suppress the signal for now, and then get someone in there to get the actual camera while she's not in her room. who did she piss off? veil is impossible to break into – somebody wanted eyes on her *bad* to pull this off.

norestforthewicked: yeah. that's what concerns me. thanks will.

grimreaper: anything for the man that caught me but didn't keep me. 😊 you hitting that?

norestforthewicked: goodbye.

grimreaper: which means yes, you are. good for you. i'll have the camera delivered to the store so you can check it out, but keep me in the loop. the twins will want blood over this.

norestforthewicked: I would expect nothing less.]

[/secure chat closed]

Just as she said, I watched the feed from inside Monica's hotel room go black, and pushed out a sigh of relief. My agitation with getting arrested and shit aside, the fact that she was being consistently violated in one way or another was pissing me off.

Fuck it.

I wasn't waiting anymore.

It was probably going to take me the rest of the night to complete, but I cared very, very little about that as I started the process of sanitizing everything. I inlaid new security protocols as I went, so there was no chance of her network getting infected again. When I finished everything, I would put together a report she could use to at least repair the damage done to her business while we found the culprit.

124

Between me, the Drake family, and the police... whoever did this had a problem on their hands.

I couldn't *wait* to figure this out.

# NINE

A good wife would have cried.

After all the tears I'd shed in the week before Kellen's funeral, I'd certainly had plenty of practice. But somehow, once we made it there, and I was sitting beside his sobbing mother on the front pew of the church she claimed to have raised him in, I made a… controversial decision.

I wouldn't cry over him again.

Not one single, solitary, miniscule tear.

His pregnant whore cried enough for both of us.

And so, I just sat there and endured it. The fact that I had to share space with the woman who'd shamelessly, blatantly inserted herself in the – admittedly wide open – space that Kellen and I had carved in our marriage was the last humiliation I had to tolerate. Well… I didn't have to, but I did. There were too many eyes on me not to, besides the fact that his mother deserved for this day to go by with minimal drama. Kellen was only in his thirties, and had been killed in a manner I couldn't describe as anything other than horrible.

It was fucked up, honestly.

She'd never been anything except kind to me, both before and during my marriage. Now though, she'd made her choice, and I wasn't bothered. She and Crystal clutched fingers and sobbed together the whole time – the perfect picture of grieving mother and her sham of a daughter-in-law. My hands remained empty for the entirety of the funeral, save for the program and a woefully dry handkerchief.

On the other side of me, Asher couldn't seem to help making me regret the microscopic hint of cleavage that showed with the dress I'd

127

chosen. I'd called myself being modest, but his roving eyes had me feeling like I was on display – and had me questioning just how "accidental" that kiss was.

Until I smelled the liquor on his breath.

*You'd probably need a few drinks to get through your best friend's funeral too, Mon.*

Just when I thought my contempt for this day couldn't grow *any* deeper, Kellen's mother had invited Crystal to the mic, for a final kind word before we moved to the graveyard to commit his body to the ground. I could feel the whole room staring at me – a mix of pity, disgust, and simple-minded delight at what they perceived to be a slight against me. Like it was some sort of *gotcha*.

But… as Crystal stood up there crying about the loss of the love of her life, I stifled a smile, wondering what kind of accidental karma had come my way. My cheating husband was finally out of my life, and I didn't have to give up half of my business or money to make it happen.

Hell… I had nothing to cry about.

But that was yesterday.

By the time Kellen's lawyer was showing me and Demetria into a small conference room for the reading of his will, the day after the funeral, I was back to feeling nostalgic, or whatever the hell the feeling was. The feeling that it made no sense, at all, that at thirty-six years old, I was widowed.

He stepped out, and while I had a quiet moment, I allowed myself a few tears. Beside me, Demetria offered me a few tissues from a packet in her purse, and I accepted. I'd been surprised – no, shocked, actually – that my presence was even required at such a meeting. Having his affairs in order was something I expected of Kellen, even if I wasn't quite sure what "affairs" he had… other than the ones that involved him screwing half the east coast. What took me off guard was the idea that my name was listed on anything he had.

I quickly dried my face as the door swung open again, and Patricia – Kellen's mother – and Crystal appeared, along with the

128

flustered-looking lawyer - Eric. I gave Pat the courtesy of a nod, and Crystal the courtesy of not whooping her ass.

"Mrs. Stuart – uh – Monica," Eric stammered, closing the door behind him as he stepped in, clutching a file folder. "These two have insisted on sitting in on this meeting, but they have no legal right to—"

I raised a hand to stop him. "Can we please just get this over with?" I asked, not caring to hear about… whatever. "It makes your job easier anyway right, to just talk to all three of us at once?"

"Well, Monica…"

"Eric. Please. Just read the will, or whatever you called me here for."

He pushed out a sigh, and sat down. "Okay. Well, Kellen didn't have a formal will, but he did have assets and policies that I personally managed for him. Because he didn't have a will, anything that doesn't have a specifically named beneficiary, of course goes to you, Monica. He had various investment accounts, plus retirement accounts, with a combined value of…" he flipped his folder open, thumbing through a couple of pages before he continued, "A little over four-hundred thousand."

Across the table, Crystal huffed, and my eyes left Eric long enough to look her dead in her face, daring her to make another sound. She pinned her hot-pink lips together, crossing her arms as she dropped her gaze.

"He only had the one life insurance policy, with a benefit value of two million. The listed beneficiary of that policy is… Monica Stuart."

"What?" all four of us asked at the same time, only Crystal's pitch was somewhere near a scream.

Eric shook his head. "Crystal… I've already explained to you – if Kellen had other wishes for his assets, or that insurance policy, he never expressed it to me. I asked him on several occasions about drafting a will, but he always ended up canceling the meetings. I'm sorry."

"You're *sorry*?!" she shrieked, pushing herself up from her seat. "What the *fuck* is that supposed to mean to me?" Her hand drifted to her barely swollen belly, and I had to look away. "You honestly expect me to believe he didn't bother to make sure me and his child were taken care of? He *loved* me!"

I couldn't help the ugly peal of laughter that broke from my lips as I turned my gaze back to hers. "Girl, I can't believe you expected better from an unemployed, married man living off his wife."

"Kellen was a good man! It wasn't his fault he was stuck with you!"

My eyes went wide. "A good man? Little girl, you'd better wise up *quickly* if Kellen Stuart fit the criteria to be given such a title in your mind. Lazy? Yes. Trifling? Sure. Vindictive? Oh baby, you'd better believe it. But *good*? Girl, grow the fuck up."

Crystal's nostrils flared, distorting her pretty peanut-butter toned face as she fought back tears. "I see he was right about you. You're about to walk out of here with almost two-and-a-half million dollars because of him, but you're still sitting here slandering his name. This is why he loved me. Why he wanted *me*. Because I loved and supported him like you never could."

"Huh," I said, as a smirk spread across my lips. "Answer a question for me, baby girl... where exactly did that get you? Because it looks to me like *you* are about to walk out of here without your wife-financed sugar daddy, with nothing but a baby that's going to destroy that tight little body to show for it. I know the dick was good, it really was, but Crystal...was it *really* worth it?"

"*Monica!*" Pat scolded, and I did my best not to roll my eyes.

"You know what?" I asked as I stood. "Let me just save everybody some drama – I don't want a goddamn thing from Kellen." I turned to Demetria, looking back and forth between her and Eric. "I don't ever want to see this money. Give it to his kid. In a trust or something. Can we do that?"

Demetria nodded. "Yes. If you're sure that's what you want."

"It is. A trust, that *she-*" – I tossed a hand in Crystal's direction – "can't touch. Just like... I don't know, a stipend or something, so she can have prenatal care, and so the kid can play soccer and get braces. I

130

don't care. Demetria… you and Eric work out something fair. Do not ever speak to me about it again."

Both lawyers nodded. "Understood."

I grabbed my purse, intending to leave, but hesitated for a second when I heard a quiet, "thank you," from across the table. I looked back to see Crystal looking much less self-assured than she had before. Instead, she looked exactly like what she was – a twenty-three-year-old girl in glamorous makeup and hair to make herself look grown, in a fucked-up situation because she wanted to play games that were much more mature than she was.

She looked… too familiar.

"Do *not* thank me," I told her in a voice that must have communicated exactly the danger she was in, because she took a step back. "Please understand that I am *not* doing a goddamn thing for *you*. You and Kellen were too busy being trash to make sure the life you created was taken care of. *Somebody* has to do what your silly asses didn't bother to. He or she deserves a fucking chance, and when your kid is all grown up, and you watch them take it… make sure you remember the bitter bitch that gave it to them. And weep over the fact that it wasn't you."

I didn't give anybody a chance to say shit to me – I left. More than anything, I was pissed that I'd pulled myself away from a fresh bottle of wine to come to a meeting, when this could've been handled over the phone.

"Monica!"

I started to keep walking, but the familiarity of the voice just wouldn't let me do it. I pushed out a sigh, and then turned to see what Pat wanted.

"Yes?" I asked, trying to keep the edge of irritation out of my voice as she approached me, with tears in her eyes. "What can I do for you, Patricia?"

She gave me a sad smile. "I know I hadn't seen you in a few years, but… no more "Mama Pat"?"

"I…"

"Please," she said, waving me off. "I'm just... talking. You don't need to explain yourself, when I walked in here with... her."

I nodded. "Yeah."

"I'm sorry. For... for thinking that you could've been the one to do... *that* ... to my baby. You were always the sweetest young lady, and you've grown into a woman that I've been proud to call my daughter. But I'm..." she sniffed loudly, obviously trying to hold back tears. "I'm getting to be an old woman, Monica. An old woman who just lost her child. Wrong as he was, he was *mine*. You understand?"

"I do."

"He told me that you... that you couldn't... that you two had tried, and tried, but... that girl in there..." Patricia pushed out a sigh through her broken attempts to articulate herself, but then a smile broke through on her face. "She's carrying my *future*, Monica. All I have left of my baby, after I thought I'd never get that. Because he said you guys couldn't. But now—"

"Patricia, please," I interrupted, swallowing the lump building in my throat. "I don't need any further reminders of my... deficiency... in that department. Just be happy that you're finally getting that grandbaby you wanted. I understand. And I'm happy for you."

Right in front of me, Patricia's face crumpled. "Monica, I'm—"

"Goodbye, Pat. You be blessed, okay?"

She opened her mouth like she wanted to say something else, but then she nodded. "Okay sweetheart. And you as well."

I returned her nod and then turned around, getting down the hall as quickly as I could while trying not to look like I was rushing. Once I made it to the elevator, I pressed the button and prayed for an empty one, breathing a sigh of relief when that particular wish was granted.

Inside the elevator, I pressed the button to get to the parking garage, then closed my eyes as the doors shut. I bit the inside of my lip, trying my best to keep it together.

As if everything else happening wasn't enough... I hadn't expected to get slapped in the face today with two ugly truths.

132

I really, *really* was glad for Patricia. I remembered the bleak, tear-filled conversation where Kellen and I had explained that we'd never be able to give her the biological grandbabies she so desired in too-vivid detail.

It was my fault.

It was *me*.

I was the problem.

But back then, Kellen loved me too much to *ever* phrase it in such a way. We put my body through the ringer to try every possible method, traditional and otherwise. It wasn't happening.

But ultimately, we were still happy... I thought.

Apparently, a child with his DNA *was* more important to him than I was, because he'd certainly had no issue rubbing its existence in my face. Which only made it more surprising that he hadn't taken the time to make sure his new family was taken care of if something happened to him. It wasn't as if he was trying to hide them from me – he'd *flaunted it.*

But... one thing I'd learned very early in life was that a man who was reckless enough to conceive a child outside of his marriage couldn't be counted on to do what was right. Whether it was a celebrity with a "break baby", my own husband, or my own father.

And... *fuck.*

I'd tried so hard not to end up with a man like my father.

All that trying... for *nothing.*

As the elevator hummed down to the parking garage, I soothed myself with the conclusion that this unpleasant ordeal was my chance to pay my own undeserved favor forward. Once upon a time, a woman who should have held nothing except contempt for my very existence had been generous to me. Not selflessly, but that was fine. She did something for me that unquestionably set the stage for... just about every good experience of my adult life. Her gift to me had a price, as did my gift to Kellen and Crystal's child.

The price I paid?

*Never come back here again.*

The price Crystal would pay?

Knowing that I, the wife she'd despised, had done more for her child with a single check than she ever would.

*Huh.*

*I guess that gives Crystal some commonality with my mother.*

The elevator chimed to let me know it had arrived at my floor, and I sucked in a breath as I stepped out, quickly making my way through the elevator bank and out to the parking garage. My phone started ringing as I slipped between a row of cars, and I dug into my bag for it as I kept moving toward where I was parked.

My fingers closed around the phone at the same time I spotted my Mercedes – not exactly the place of refuge I needed, but it would work for now. I glanced to make sure nothing was coming before I stepped out to cross the driveway, then looked down at my phone as I moved, frowning at the unknown number.

Suddenly, the bright glare of headlights enveloped me in the dim garage, blinding me for a moment before common sense kicked in, and I bolted out of the way of the fast-approaching car.

*"Watch for pedestrians asshole!"* I screamed at the back of the car, even though it had already whipped around the curve and disappeared. Flustered, I took the last few steps to my car and quickly located my keys, locking myself inside once I'd gotten in.

I couldn't decide if getting hit by a car would have been a good or bad way to end this day.

"Boss lady… you *sure* you don't want to call it a night?"

Instead of looking up from my computer, I pushed a sigh out through my nose before I responded. With my eyes still focused on the screen, I told Kim, "I'm not going anywhere. But, I've already kept you here past eight. If you want to leave, you can."

No response came, but I could still feel her lingering in the open doorway to my office. When I looked up, she was watching me, with palpable uncertainty in her eyes.

She was smart to be worried.

Three days after Kellen's funeral, I'd sat down with Renata from *Five Star Tech* to hear what she referred to as a status report. Listening to her explain just how methodically some unknown person had run roughshod over my security had sent me through a wild range of emotions. Rage, humiliation, disgust. And when I found out that formulas had been altered, quality reports falsified, inventory logs misrepresented, all without my knowledge… all I wanted to do was vomit.

It was a fucking *mess.*

A mess that, as far as I was concerned, should *never* have happened. The day after that meeting, I had my ass back in my office, grieving period be damned. The processes we had in place shouldn't have even allowed for it, and as my executive assistant, Kim should've been able to tell me this had gone wrong before someone else had to. Was it *all* her fault? Of course not. But she knew what her role was in this company – making sure I had what I needed to fulfill *my* role.

CEO and President.

And if *I* was out of the loop on vital information that affected the day to day operations of *Vivid Vixen*, what the fuck were we doing here? What the fuck did we have? If shit like *this* was going to get by me without a second look while Kim sat and collected her salary for nothing… why were we here at all? And where the hell had she been while somebody was planting a bug or whatever the hell I was supposed to be calling it, on my computer in the *first* place?

But she'd been with me a long time.

So.

She hadn't gotten cursed out.

As far as I was concerned though, my job was the only executive level position that was secure. And to be honest… even that was a little shaky. *Five Star* had already done the work of reconfiguring my tech security, but everything else was up to me. Scheduling product recalls, putting a hold on product innovation to revisit and possibly revamp every single one of our current formulas, recounting product inventory, working with Chloe to manage the complete, total, massive PR nightmare… it was enough to make the second buyout offer I'd gotten from *Canvas Cosmetics* two weeks ago look really, *really* sweet.

If it was even still on the table.

Not that I *wanted* it to be on the table.

*Canvas* was a giant in the beauty industry, sure, and it would be cool to see where they could take the *Vivid Vixen* name with all the resources they had at their disposal. But it would be just that – the name. None of the heart and soul and *hustle* I'd put into building into the successful business it had become. I hadn't reached a point yet that I was ready to give it away.

So… it had to be fixed.

"What can I do for you?" I asked Kim, who was still standing in my doorway looking lost. "Didn't you say your mystery boyfriend was in town this week? I *know* you'd rather be in his face than mine. Go ahead and go home."

She sighed, then stepped out of the doorway… *into* my office, instead of out. "Um… may I speak freely?" she asked, pushing a handful of long twists over her shoulder.

"Please do. What's on your mind?"

"You are. Forgive me if I'm speaking out of turn, but… should you really be back already? You just buried your husband after a horrific crime, not to mention all the other *crazy* stressful things that were happening. And all of this with Vixen is just more stress piled on top of it. I just don't want to see you make yourself sick."

I propped my elbows on the desk, resting my chin on my hands before I pushed out a deep breath. "Kim… I appreciate your concern for my wellbeing, but as we've recently discovered to be woefully true – this business isn't going to run itself. I'll be fine."

"But, don't you think—"

"But *nothing*, Kim." My tone was stern enough that Kim's eyes went wide for a second before she disciplined her expression back into nonchalance. "I'll see you tomorrow."

"Not if you come have a drink with me?" she suggested, her voice edged with an almost-desperate quality that was the only thing keeping me tethered to my resolve of not cursing her out.

Still, I let every ounce of my annoyance show on my face. "Okay, what is the issue here?" I asked, *really* giving her my full attention. "You've lamented multiple times over the years about not getting to see your long-distance boo as often as you'd like. You come in this morning bubbling with happiness because he's here. Leave for lunch, stay gone two hours, come back with your hair all over your head and a smile you can't keep off your face. I keep you here until eight tonight, running you through the ringer trying to get this company back on the tracks. It's finally time to go, and yet... I can't get you out of here. You have a man to warm your bed and presumably good sex waiting for you, but... you want me to come out for a drink? Make this make sense to me."

Kim shrugged. "Well... that's just it. I... have someone to go home to. And you..."

"Don't," I finished for her, struggling to suppress the veil of rage that had just fallen across my shoulders. I could take it if she was just trying to cozy up to me to save her job, but *this*?

This... *pity*?

"Kim... do yourself a favor," I said, in a low voice as I turned my gaze back to my computer screen. "Leave. *Now*. And let's pretend we never had this conversation."

"Yes ma'am!" she replied immediately.

But... long seconds went by, and I could still feel her in my office.

"For some reason, you are still here."

That seemed to spur her to action, and a moment later, I was alone.

Little did Kim know, that was exactly how I *wanted* to be.

Her leaving meant that this area of the building was empty, and I could set my mood exactly the way I liked it. Lights off, with only the glow of my computer illuminating the room, and my music cranked up loud in my earbuds. It was like being on my own little dark bubble – visual disturbances eliminated while I grooved to whatever was in my ears. It put me in a good space – a space I desperately needed to be. A place where I could work, work, work, without the pesky distractions of loneliness or grief.

I stayed there for hours.

It was only once I reached the point where I could no longer ignore the hunger clawing at my belly that I broke away, cursing myself – and Kim – for the fact that my usual desk stash of protein bars was depleted.

I picked up my disregarded cell phone, clearing the usual pile of text notifications from my friends off the screen. According to the bright white numbers, it was nearing midnight.

I needed to at least *try* to get some sleep.

My insomnia had already been getting worse, but the events of the last week had taken me to a whole new level of sleep deprivation. I sighed as I closed the screen of my laptop, thinking about the wine and narcotic cocktail I'd used the night before just to piece together a measly three hours of restless sleep. That had only exacerbated my already fucked up mood to the point that I'd woken up already sick of the current day.

But there had to be some light at the end of a tunnel *somewhere* for me.

I hoped.

I pulled myself out of my daydream to realize that without the glow of my screen, the office was darker than I expected. My mind quickly deduced that I was missing the ambient light from the sconces in the reception area – a switch Kim must have flipped on her way out.

Since my cell phone was still in my hand, I turned on my flashlight feature, using it to gather my things, and put the files I'd pulled from the safe in my office back in their secure place.

138

Incorporation documents, investment records, patent files, and documentation on all of *Vivid Vixens* original formulas – what I'd been looking at today, for comparison purposes – were all kept here. Many things were kept in digital storage, but there were certain things that I – correctly, it seemed – considered too risky to keep in such a way.

Files on a server could be hacked. But the chances that anyone would get into my safe, with its dual lock system – dial and digital – were very, *very* low.

It just felt... safer.

Once I had that done, I hooked my purse onto my shoulder and made my way out of the office, realizing for the first time how... eerie it felt without lights. Unlike my house, where I'd memorized my way through it in the dark, every shadow or shapeless mass seemed like something – or someone – lurking in obscurity, waiting to pounce.

The low *thump* I heard just as I stepped into the reception area didn't help.

I couldn't tell if it had come from in front or behind, but as just as quickly as my brain registered fear, I told myself to calm down. It wasn't as if the building was empty – my product scientists stayed late often, and the warehouse had late hours too. That was why we kept overnight security – more people to add to the list of reasons to be hearing things.

Shaking my head, I laughed at my own ridiculousness.

Now, I was just being paranoid – probably side effects of a murdered husband and a severe lack of sleep. With everything I'd done today, there wasn't much else I could do besides the thing I hated most – waiting. So instead of rushing to the office in the morning, maybe I'd gift myself that spa day Chloe had mentioned... not even two weeks ago.

*Wow.*

So much had happened in such a short time that the conversation in Chloe's kitchen felt like something from months past. Then, hearing that my computer was being hacked had felt like my world was crashing down. I had no idea that *much* worse problems were headed my way.

And I had no idea that the man who'd warned me about the hacking would no longer be my friend – a blow I hadn't even had the capacity to process quite yet. For now, all I knew was that I missed him.

Did I understand his anger?

*Of course.*

He was a Black man, unfairly accused of murder and hauled in for questioning in a climate where a seemingly simple interaction, even for the innocent, could end with the police taking your life. I couldn't even imagine how stressful it was, especially when I considered that Wick had never even seen my face, let alone Kellen's before all this happened. Him getting pulled into that was fucked up, honestly. And if I were Wick, I wouldn't want to see me either.

But… that feeling wouldn't last forever, would it?

*Could* it?

Eventually, once this all passed, he would come around. He would see that as unfair as that whole situation was for him, the experience was doubled, maybe even tenfold for me. I wouldn't reach out to him, because I'd never begged my damn *husband,* so I certainly wasn't about to beg another man for anything, and because he'd asked me not to, so I planned to respect that.

*Wick* would do the reaching.

And I would get my damned friend back.

Eventually.

And maybe then, I'd get some damned sleep.

I smiled to myself again – this time over the sluttiness of thinking about another man giving me a sleep-inducing orgasm when my husband hadn't even been in the ground a whole week. I was so busy with my internal giggling that I barely caught it when I heard that same *thump* again – only this time, much closer, and now that I was really listening, followed by a sound that made my heart slam against the front of my chest.

*Breathing.*

"Who's there?!" I asked, fumbling with my phone to bring up my flashlight again. As soon as I pressed the button, something –

140

someone – knocked the device from my hands. Before I could react, scream, do anything, I felt something connect with the side of my head, and pain bloomed immediately behind my eyes. A gloved hand clamped over my mouth and nose, cutting off my ability to breathe as I struggled against the body pressed behind me.

Using my perfectly manicured nails like claws, I dug into the hand and arms that were holding me, causing enough damage to make my assailant drop his hold. As soon as my mouth was uncovered, I took the opportunity to scream, and run.

"*Help!*" I belted, as loud as I could as I moved toward the door that would get me out of the reception area, hoping that I would be lucky enough that security was walking the halls at this time. "*Somebody, ple—*"

Pain ripped through my head again as my attacker grabbed me by the hair, yanking me backward at an angle that sent me tumbling to the ground, dazed. The next thing I knew, I was being flipped over on my back, and hands were around my neck.

Somewhere in the room, my cell phone was on the floor, sending my flashlight beam directly at the ceiling. The ambient glow was enough for me to see the dark outline of my attacker as his hands closed tighter around my neck, squeezing so hard that my vision went hazy.

Vaguely, I registered that my cell phone had started ringing, but my assailant didn't care. My weak attempts to claw at his hands didn't matter either.

I was fading… fading… *fading.*

And then… nothing.

# TEN

This was why we weren't supposed to get attached.

The barely-restrained anger, the shallowly-buried fear, the willingness to disregard your training, your rules, maybe even your mission, all because of a short phone call, and a handful of words.

*"Come to the hospital. There's been an incident."*

An incident.

An *incident.*

An "incident" didn't say shit, but set off dozens of horrific possibilities in my head. So many that, as soon as I hung up from that call from Marcus, I got up from my desk to get dressed. Kay was sleeping, and I let her stay that way, giving her a kiss on the forehead before I pulled the covers up over her and left, making sure to set the alarm on my way out.

As I headed to the car, different scenarios played out in my head – none of them ended well. But there was little use in giving in to those thoughts when I had no details – that was another part of protocol, never giving more information than absolutely necessary over the phone. And apparently, Marcus only deemed it necessary that I know Monica was at the hospital, and I should come.

The rest, I would find out when I got there.

I didn't like how the shit felt. Was there distance between us now? Yes. But that didn't mean I wasn't going to be concerned about her. Was she sick? Had she passed out from stress? Had she done something to herself? Had someone done something to her? All that shit was swimming around in my head, to the point that by the time I made it to the hospital I was agitated as hell, and ready to fuck something up.

As soon as someone told me what the hell was going on.

Following the instructions Marcus gave, I found my way to the restricted area of the hospital where Monica was being kept – a string I knew someone in *Five Star Security* had pulled. I recognized the guard at the door, and he immediately moved aside to let me through.

"They're in P5," he told me, pointing out one of the doors that lined the hallway. Through each door, there was a private waiting area, and beyond that, the actual hospital room. Marcus and Chloe were the only ones waiting in Monica's.

"Aiight, I'm here now," I said, addressing Marcus after I'd greeted Chloe. "Can somebody tell me what the fuck is going on?"

Marcus nodded. "Chloe knows better than I do, so I'll let her tell the story."

My eyes immediately went back to Chloe, who gave me a wry smile. "I suppose that's true, but even I don't know very much."

"Anything you can give me. Y'all called me in the middle of the night for a reason."

She tipped her head. "Well, yes. Of course. So… today was Monica's first day back at the office – she told no one that she was going ahead of time, as far as I know. I thought the distraction was probably good for her, so I didn't press it, but I'd been checking in with her every few hours to make sure she was okay. Around eleven tonight, she didn't respond. I knew she'd decided to stay at the office late, so I didn't think much of it, but about an hour and a half later, she still hadn't replied, so I called. When I didn't get an answer, I tried to call her direct line in her office, but I kept getting a busy signal, which was odd for her business line at that time of night. That's when I called the building security. *They* insisted that she was just fine, sitting at her desk working according to the cameras. But I insisted that someone go and physically check. Put eyes on her, not just watching through a screen. And… that's when they found her."

My eyes went wide. "Found her? What does that mean?"

Chloe let out a breath, and when she spoke again, her voice was shaking. "She'd been attacked."

"Attacked *how*," I managed to grunt, my gaze stuck on the closed door to the hospital room. "What are her injuries?"

"Concussion. And um…" – her voice broke again – "Pretty bad bruising, uh… around her neck."

"She was choked."

Chloe nodded, and then cleared her throat. "Yes. Until she passed out. And… um, she was hit in the head, with something. Doctor says she'll likely have a headache for a few days, but other than that, she'll be okay."

"Yeah. Physically maybe. Should I even ask if a culprit has been found?"

"Ha. *No*," Chloe scoffed, shaking her head. "The useless security at her building didn't even discover anything amiss until I called. Whoever did this had recorded part of the security feed earlier in the night, and had the cameras from her office, reception area, and hall playing on a loop. They called the police of course, but the culprit was already long gone. I called Marcus to meet me at the hospital, just in case whoever this was wanted to finish the job once it was realized that she'd survived. She needs protection."

"Which is why I called you," Marcus cut in. "Our client roster is completely full right now – *I* shouldn't even be here. I have Mimi acting as attendant for me right now, but that's a temporary solution. I know you've told me over and over that you aren't interested in playing protector, but—"

"I'll do it," I said, interrupting whatever long-ass spiel he was about to go on. "Why exactly didn't we already have her under protection already?" I asked, hoping to hear something that would make me feel a little less guilty about not having insisted on it before now. But before now, there hadn't been a physical threat to her, there was no reason to think someone wanted to do her bodily harm.

Now we knew different.

"She didn't want that," Chloe answered, after Marcus gave me nothing but a shrug. "I asked her about that after her place was broken into, but she was adamant. Said she wasn't a celebrity, didn't need a bodyguard."

I let out a dry laugh. "So, was that before or after somebody turned her husband into a human pin cushion?"

"Before. But now…"

"She doesn't have a choice," I said, finishing that sentence for her. "Marcus. Safehouse?"

He shook his head. "Everything we have is either occupied or on reserve. We're already in process of setting up a few others, but you know it takes time."

"Yeah. It's fine. She'll stay with me then." Marcus nodded, but Chloe made an odd sound in her throat that made the two of us turn in her direction. "Problem, Chlo?"

She cleared her throat. "Well, it's just… don't you think we should wait to speak to Monica before these decisions are made?"

"No. For what?"

Her eyes went wide. "Well, we could start with the fact that I was under the strong impression that you wanted nothing to do with Monica, and insisted that she stay away from you, which will likely be difficult if she's taking temporary lodging in your home. Wouldn't you agree?"

"And, that's my cue to leave," Marcus chuckled, giving Chloe a quick hug before he turned to me. "Listen… Sam says that Monica's office was trashed, and it looked like whoever did this was after access to the safe. Monica just happened to be there."

I nodded. "So she wasn't the actual target?"

"Maybe not. But, we don't want to count on that, and then…"

"Right. I've got her."

Marcus grinned. "I know you do. I've been begging your ass to leave *Tech* and come to *Security* since we started this shit, and you always told me no. I didn't realize all you needed was the right damsel in distress to get your act together," he teased, and I waved him off.

"Man, fuck that noise. I'll get up with you later."

"Uh huh. Bye Chloe," he called, as he headed out the door.

146

"Goodbye Mr. Calloway. Always a pleasure." Once Marcus was gone, Chloe's attention came right back to me. "Please don't think you're going to get out of explaining exactly what the energy will be between you and Monica *if* we come to an agreement here. She has no family worth mentioning, so her girlfriends... we're *it* for her. So you get to talk to Mama-Bear Chloe tonight."

I shrugged. "Well, Mama-Bear, there's nothing to come to an agreement about. Until Monica is released from the hospital, I'll be here. Keeping her secure. When she's released, her temporary place of residence will be my – very comfortable – guest room, where I will continue to keep her secure. Until we know who is behind all of this, and the threat is eliminated, I will—"

"Keep her secure," Chloe finished. "Yes, you said that, but you have to understand... it is very curious to me that you've gone from *"Don't come around anymore"*, to fucking... Liam Neeson, or something. Explain yourself."

"Shit changes."

She huffed. "Oh, is that what's happened?"

"Yes," I nodded. "It is. Now that I have the full picture, and more and more shit keeps piling up, I'm approaching it differently. I was pissed, and now there's no room for that. I feel bad that all of this is happening to her."

"She doesn't need your pity," Chloe snapped, stepping closer. "She needs someone to give a damn!"

"I *do* give a damn," I shot right back, suddenly incensed at the suggestion that I didn't. "Even before all of this, I gave a damn, back when she was crying and hurt because her "girlfriends" were too busy wrapped up in their men to really be there for her when that bitch-ass husband of hers really showed his ass last year. Remember that?"

Chloe's tight jaw and lack of response let me know that I was right on the mark.

"I may have needed a few days to sulk and lick my wounds," I told her, taking advantage of her silence, "but don't you get this shit twisted – it didn't take all of this for me to give a damn about Monica – I already did, before I saw a face or knew a name. I'm not about to go back and forth. I told you what the fuck I was doing, and I don't particularly give a damn if you like it. I don't particularly give a damn if *Monica* likes it. I said I would protect her, and that's how it's going to go. Are we clear?"

Chloe's eyes narrowed at me – not in a scowl, but more like... scrutiny. She looked at me like that for several moments, until I raised an eyebrow at her. Then, she nodded. "Yes."

"If she doesn't have family, I guess you're next of kin."

"I'm her emergency contact."

"Cool. Then, if you have questions or concerns, I'll hear them."

For some reason, that made her smile, which she quickly tried to hide by tucking in her lips. "Uh... no, no questions, Chadwick. I'm very clear now on where you stand, and I am very confident that Monica will be... uh... *safe*... in your hands."

"This feels like a setup," I said, and Chloe laughed.

"No, no setup. I just... saw what I needed to see from you."

I furrowed my brow, confused. "Which was...?"

"Feeling. But, enough about that. Let's discuss our plan of action."

*"Where is she? I want to see her!"*

I looked up from the computer in my lap to glance at the door, wondering who the hell was being loud outside Monica's hospital room. Whatever meds she'd been given upon arriving at the hospital last night had kept her asleep thus far, and I preferred to keep it that way. Based on what I knew about Monica, I doubted she'd been getting much sleep lately. She needed whatever rest she could get.

148

I hadn't laid eyes on her yet. I was on the other side of the curtained partition, still digging for a culprit for all of this while her girlfriends took turns at her bedside. Chloe had left a few hours ago, and Kora Oliver – an award-winning stage actress and singer who Kay idolized – had taken her place. Now though, Kora peeked from around the curtain, a question in her eyes as I met her gaze, and nodded.

"Yeah. I hear it too."

I put the laptop down beside me and stood, pulling out the concealed weapon I wasn't technically supposed to be carrying. But getting caught with it was an issue I'd tackle only if it became an issue.

For now, I wanted whoever the fuck was on the other side of that door to be quiet.

I opened it just enough to see out of, and found myself face to face with one of the security guards that worked the floor. His hand was lifted like he was about to knock, but he dropped it when he saw me.

"Hey, man… sorry to bother you. But you have someone—"

"Asher Ross. Tell her it's Asher Ross. I need to see her," I heard, then looked past the guard to see some light-skinned dude with gray eyes looking pitiful.

"I don't know who that is," I told the guard, even though I'd just finished compiling a guest list from Kellen's funeral, and identifying their relationship to the deceased. From my preliminary search, it appeared that "Asher Ross" was *Kellen's* friend.

What the fuck did he want with Monica?

For all I knew, *he* was the person who'd attacked her last night.

"Did he say Asher?" Kora asked.

I looked behind me to see the curtain partially open, and behind her, Monica was awake – it was her hand using the remote control to raise the top part of the bed, but I couldn't see her face.

"Yes," I answered Kora's question. "But I'm not sure if visitors are a good idea yet. Has the doctor even talked to her while she was awake?"

Kora frowned. "You might be right. But let me ask her if she wants to see him. I know he's a college friend."

149

My hopes that she would say "no" to a new visitor were quickly dashed when Kora came back with a smile. "She agreed to see him. You can let him through," she said, looking at me expectantly.

I gave her a nod, and then went back to the door. "You patted him down?" I asked the guard, who nodded.

"He wouldn't be down here with me if I hadn't." The guard glanced over his shoulder and then looked back to me, lowering his voice. "Look man, I'm sorry for even bringing his ass down here. He was insisting, and looked like he was about to cry, and—"

"You're good," I told him, then pulled the door open to let Asher come in, even though I didn't want to. With everything happening, her homegirls were the only people in Monica's life I trusted, and that was mostly because Chloe vouched for them. For now though, with nothing except my own suspicions about this dude and his begging-to-get-punched face, I couldn't deny her seeing him if she wanted to.

But it wasn't going to keep me from keeping an eye on that motherfucker.

For whatever reason, Kora seemed to have the same idea, because instead of leaving, she simply stepped back from the bed. She didn't even close the curtain back before she came to stand next to me, crossing her arms in a stance like mine as we watched Asher bend to greet Monica.

A short prickle of anger rushed through me before it settled as a throbbing in my temple as I watched him kiss her forehead, then keep his hand cupped on her face. I had friendships with women, sure, but they never involved the type of lingering touches he was giving. I frowned a little, wishing I could see her face, see *her* reaction to him, but at this angle, he was blocking my view of her.

I was getting ready to move to a new position when my phone started buzzing in my pocket. A quick glance told me it was Kay, who'd probably just realized she'd woken up to an empty house. I made a mental note to call her back later, then returned the phone to my pocket. I felt eyes on me, and I when I looked up, Kora was staring right at me.

150

"So… who is Kay?" she asked, keeping her voice low so we wouldn't draw Asher and Monica's attention. "Wife? Homegirl? Girlfriend?"

"An off-limits topic," I answered, chuckling at her attempt to pry. "And none of your business. I don't know you."

She sucked her teeth. "Boy stop, you know you wanted to ask for my autograph. I'm guessing "Kay" dragged you to one of my shows?"

"Multiples, actually," I grinned. "How did you know?"

"Because you didn't ask, when we were introduced. Most people I meet, they recognize my face as familiar, even if they can't exactly place it, so they ask. You didn't. So I assumed… correctly."

A satisfied smirk spread across her lips, and I laughed.

"And here I was thinking you were just cocky," I teased.

"Oh, I'm that too. I'm very good friends with four other beautiful women. We *have* to be cocky, or we'd eat each other alive. Confidence is a prerequisite around here."

I nodded. "I see. So… why don't you go ahead and spill the beans on why you sparked up this conversation with me now?"

Kora's eyebrows lifted. "Am I that obvious?"

"No. I just assumed…correctly."

"Ahh. Well-played."

"I know. Now…. You wanna answer my question?"

She pushed out a little sigh while her gaze moved to Asher and Monica. It settled there for a few seconds before she looked at me again, stepping a little closer, speaking a little lower. "I don't trust him."

"You think he did this to her?"

"No," she said quickly. "Not this. His concern feels genuine, but it's like he's… too concerned. I don't know if he did anything or not, but something isn't right. I feel it."

"What do you know about him?"

She shook her head. "Not a lot. I know he invested money in *Vivid Vixen* four or five years ago, before it really exploded. He was good friends with Kellen. They all went to college together. He was dating Monica's friend."

"You know the friend's name?"

Kora frowned. "Um… Ashley? Amy? Amber? Something with an *A.*"

"You met her before?"

"Yeah," Kora nodded. "A long time ago, maybe six or seven years. She was… odd."

"How so?"

Kora shrugged. "I'm not sure how to describe it. Just, the way she looked at and interacted with Monica. A little too eager, a little too interested. A little too… enamored. Like she wanted to peel Monica and wear her. Kinda how Asher is looking at her now," Kora mused.

I followed her gaze to where Asher had taken a seat beside the bed, his profile still blocking my view of Monica's face. I couldn't see what Kora could, but the reverence had trickled even into his body language.

A solid knock at the door pulled me from my observation of Asher. I fought the urge to groan when I went to answer and saw who was on the other side, but still stepped aside to let the officers in.

"Well, look who we have here," Detective Crowley said, loud as fuck for no good reason. "Loverboy. We thought you would've skipped town once you were cleared."

"Loverboy?"

I stopped fighting that groan at the sound of Asher's voice, and a few seconds later, he was right in front of Detective Crowley.

"What the hell are you talking about?" he asked the detective, and then turned to me. "What the hell is he talking about? I thought you were security?"

"I am. And you can see yourself out, so that Monica can talk to the detectives."

"Not until someone explains what the hell is going on," he said, crossing his arms as he looked me right in the face.

*Here we fucking go.*

"Listen, man," I started, stepping right into Asher's face. I had him by a good 3-4 inches and at least fifty pounds, something he seemed

152

to only realize now that we were closer. "Don't make this something it doesn't have to be. You can see *yourself* out, or *I* can put you out. I think we both know which one you'd prefer."

He stared for a few more seconds, then narrowed his eyes. "I'll wait outside."

"You'll go home. After she talks to them, she needs her rest," I said, firmly enough to leave no room for debate. The only person coming back in here after she talked to the police was Kora, who didn't give me closeted psycho vibes like "Asher" did.

"Come on, Asher," Kora intervened, grabbing his arm to pull him toward the door. "He's right. Monica needs to rest after everything she'd been through. You can walk out with me."

Asher didn't give Kora any resistance – they were gone a few seconds after that. But Crowley and Bauer both turned to me, as if they were waiting for something that must have gone over my head.

"Are you going to talk to her or not?" I asked, and Crowley chuckled.

"Uh, yeah. Just waiting for you to step out."

I shook my head. "Don't think so. You two have tried to railroad her once, and it's not happening again. I know her rights, and mine, and you aren't talking to her alone. I'm not going anywhere."

"Her rights?" Bauer scoffed. "What, are you her legal counsel or something?"

I shrugged. "Well, I do have a law degree, so sure. Call it whatever the hell you want. I'll be right here while you're talking to her."

To stress my point, I finally stepped to the other side of that curtain, where Monica was, to stand beside the bed, bringing us face to face for the first time since that day in the store. I knew she was in bad enough shape that the doctor had insisted on keeping her overnight, but I didn't expect her to look so… fragile.

I swallowed hard as I took in the troubled apprehension in her eyes, the shadows underneath, and the lurid purple bruising around her neck. I knew from experience *just* how hard someone had to compress to make markings like that – evident hand prints, if you knew what you were looking at – and the shit made it a little hard for *me* to breathe.

"Fellas," I said, turning to the detectives. "Look, can this wait? She's not in—"

"It's okay," Monica spoke up, catching me off guard with the roughness of her voice – a quality I *would never* have used before to describe how she sounded. "I just want to get it over with, so... what do you need from me?"

"Just a few questions, Mrs. Stuart," Crowley said, stepping up to the foot of the bed. "Would you like your boyfriend to step out, give you some privacy while we talk?"

Monica narrowed her eyes. "He's my *security*, and I would feel much more comfortable if he stayed."

"That's fine." Per usual, Bauer parked himself near the window, away from the action, leaving Crowley the work of being the asshole.

"So... you claim you were attacked last night, at your place of business?" Crowley said, flipping open a pad to take notes.

"It's not a claim. It's a fact."

He shrugged. "Fine. Tell me what happened."

"I got attacked in my office."

Crowley looked up, glaring at Monica. "Can you start from the beginning, with details?"

"Yes. I was... I was working late. My assistant had already gone home, but I stayed back, trying to finish up."

"Why were you there without your assistant? If you were working, wouldn't you need assistance?"

Monica puckered her eyebrows. "What? No, not necessarily. These were all things I needed to do myself. Emails directly to certain people, things like that."

Crowley wrote that down. "Okay, so you worked late. Until when?"

"Midnight, I think."

"You think?"

"Yes," Monica snapped. "I *think*. I have a concussion, so it's a little fuzzy."

Crowley's face turned just enough red to notice. "I... uh... yes, of course. Please continue."

"Thank you. So, I shut down my computer and packed up, and I left. Wait... no, I stopped to put some files back in my safe."

"What kind of files?"

"Important ones. Why?"

"Just trying to get a clear picture ma'am."

"Fine. Financial documents. Proprietary formulas. Things like that."

"Okay. So you put the files back in your safe, and then you left the office? I thought you said you were attacked in your office?"

Monica shook her head like she was confused. "No. I... left my office and went into the reception area. It was really dark – darker than it should've been. Someone had turned the ambient lights off."

*On purpose.*

"Someone like who? Who had access?"

"Any of the housekeeping staff, security, and my assistant Kim, I guess. And she has an assistant, who comes in a few times a week."

"Your assistant... has an assistant?"

"Kim's job is very demanding," Monica told him. "If I have to pay someone to assist her, I'm more than happy to do it. I just need the work done."

Crowley nodded. "Fair enough. So what happened in the reception area?"

"I heard a sound, like someone was there. I ignored it at first, but then I heard it again. And I... I heard someone breathing I think. So I called out... I asked who was there. And then... something hit me in the head. I remember screaming. He had his hand over my mouth, and I used my nails to dig in, so he let me go. I tried to run, but...my hair. He grabbed me by the hair, and dragged me to the floor, where it was cold. Really cold. And then... his hands were around my neck. And that's the last thing I remember."

From the window, Bauer asked, "You're sure it was a man?"

"No," Monica answered. "But they were strong... much stronger than me. I couldn't fight him off. And it felt like a man. Smelled like a man."

"Huh. That makes this even more interesting."

"Why?"

"Because," Crowley said, pulling a picture from the pocket of the notebook he was using, "This message was written in nail polish on top of your desk. This mean anything to you?"

*Was the polish dry when they arrived? How much time would that have taken?*

When he handed her the picture, I leaned in too, frowning at the *"WHAT'S YOURS IS MINE"* painted across the glossy surface of Monica's desk.

*It's not the same person*, I thought, but didn't speak aloud. The detectives could surely use their own investigative skills to compare the shapes of these letters to the ones from messages left at the scene of Kellen's murder and the break-in at Monica's house.

"It's another one of my polish names, from the Wicked Widow collection," Monica said, pushing the image away from her. In it, her office had been ransacked, and it was probably disturbing for her to see it that way. "That color is gold, just like the polish."

"They used the exact polish that matches the name?"

Monica shook her head. "No. They aren't out yet. It was supposed to launch next week, but I had to recall every last bottle from the stores. They have to be quality checked again."

"So, you're saying that no one had access to this nail polish, to know the names or their corresponding shades?

"Of course not – what kind of marketing would that be? Lots of people have had access, because I want people using it, and telling their followers, friends, and family about it. It's been all over social media, just not available to the general public."

"Got it," Crowley said, scribbling away. "Anybody besides you have access to the safe in your office?"

"Not currently, no. I changed the combination yesterday."

*That must have pissed someone off...*

"What made you do that?"

"I don't know... intuition maybe?"

Crowley lifted a brow. "You don't trust your employees?"

"I wouldn't put it that way. It was just that, with so much going on, I wanted a little extra assurance. Just being careful."

*Nah. She doesn't trust Kim. Good.*

"Right." Crowley studied Monica for several long seconds before he spoke again. "You know anything about Tommy Woods?"

*Tommy Woods, local mob affiliated loan shark?*

Monica frowned, thinking for a moment before she answered. "No... it doesn't ring a bell. Should I know something about him?"

"Not unless you make a habit of breaking the law," Crowley answered, with a chuckle. "In the crime world, the man is a king... and your husband was one of his loyal subjects. Died owing the man close to two hundred grand. Based on what we know about Woods, we think he's a viable suspect. He may be trying to intimidate you in an attempt to collect what he's owed."

Monica shrugged. "He can have his damned money, I don't care. Kellen had that covered in death benefits – take it from there and leave me the hell alone."

"Ma'am, Woods is a criminal. We're not in the business of giving them what they want after they've committed crimes."

"I don't really care what business you're in – I care about my life. If paying him money I don't even want is what it takes to leave me the hell alone, it's exactly what I'm doing."

"We don't even know for sure that it's him."

"Then why the hell are we talking about it?" Monica snapped.

"We're updating you on the case, ma'am. Do you know anyone else who might be interested in harassing you? Anyone who'd want to hurt you?"

"Like *this*?" Monica said, then pushed out a sigh. "No. Not like this. Is that all? I'm tired, and would like to rest, please."

"Well, actually—"

"Yes," I said, stepping forward. "I think that's enough. You heard her."

"We have more questions."

"And they can wait until she's feeling better."

Crowley and Bauer exchanged a look, then nodded, briefly making me wonder if I was going to have to physically *put* them out, but then Crowley inclined his head in my direction.

"Fair enough. Mrs. Stuart, we'll speak with you again soon."

"Yeah, make sure you arrange that with her lawyer," I said, subtly guiding them toward the door. I didn't see Kora, or anyone, in the waiting room, so I went back to the bed to find Monica curled up on her side, eyes closed, face half-buried in her pillow.

I dropped into the chair beside the bed to get eye level with her before I reached out to gently touch her arm. "Hey... you good?" I asked, when she opened her eyes to look at me, revealing the impending glossiness of tears.

"No. Not at all. Thank you for getting them out of here."

"You don't have to thank me for that. You've been through a lot. You need time to process, and grieve, and... heal."

She scoffed, and then rolled onto her back, staring up at the ceiling. "I didn't think you cared about all of that. Right? Mr. *Leave Me Alone.*"

I grinned. "Okay. I deserve that. I was harsh with you because I was pissed, and scared, and... pissed. I took a fucked-up situation out on you, and for what it's worth, I'm sorry for hurting your feelings."

It took a few seconds for her to give me any indication she'd even heard what I said, but then she turned in my direction just enough to look me in the face. "It's worth a lot. Apology accepted."

My eyebrows shot up. "Damn, that quick? You're not gonna make me grovel, beg, none of that?"

"Nah," she laughed. "I understood why you were pissed. If this situation were the other way around, *whew*. You'd be every derivative of "fuckboy" under the sun, and that status would be *permanent*."

158

"Well, shit. It would really be like that?"

"Hell yes. But besides that… With everything getting turned all upside down, I need all the trustworthy friends I can get right now. Do I *look* like I'm in a state to be pushing people away when they're trying to help?"

Immediately, my eyes went to the bruises on her neck. Self-consciously, she lifted her own hand, covering them.

"It looks bad, doesn't it?" she asked. "You're looking at me like I'm pitiful, just like Asher did."

"I don't think you're pitiful," I answered quickly, shaking my head. "Not at all. Yes, the bruises look bad, I'm not going to lie to you. But… you survived it."

She scoffed. "Yeah. This time."

"Nobody is going to touch you. Because to do that, they have to get through me, and nobody is getting through me. You understand?"

Monica smiled. "I thought you were a computer geek. Now I'm supposed to buy you as *Billy Badass*?"

I shot her a grin as I leaned in closer to the bed. "How exactly did you know my codename?"

"Oh please," she laughed, just as the door swung open. I was on my feet quickly, weapon drawn, getting in between her and whoever had come in without knocking or announcing themselves.

"Whoa, *shit*!" the doctor exclaimed, putting her hands up. "What the hell is happening?!"

I lowered the gun. "My bad, Doc. I have to be on high alert."

"Well, it's just us," Kora said, from beside the doctor. "You can put that away."

She was right. So I did. And then I stepped away from the bed, back to the other side of the curtain to let her have some privacy while the doctor checked on her. I went back to my chair, back to my laptop, back to my search for the truth.

# ELEVEN

"I really just feel like I should walk over there and beat her ass, that's all I'm saying."

I tried – and failed – not to laugh at Nubia's antics as we wrapped up the "mandatory" self-defense class at *Five Star Fitness*. I'd only been released from the hospital the day before, so I was supposed to be doing more observing than anything else.

That wasn't what *I* wanted though.

What *I* wanted was to be prepared, to know what to do if and when somebody put their hands on me again. *I* wanted to be able to kick ass. So as soon as my babysitter – Wick – stepped out of the room, leaving me with Kora, Nubia, Blake, and the instructor, Mimi, I was right in the mix with the others. At first, I'd worried I'd have to talk Mimi into letting me work with everyone else, but as soon as I told her I didn't want to just watch, mischief sparked in her eyes, and she grinned.

*"Well get your ass up here and let's work then."*

And work, I had. I still had a little bit of a headache, and my neck was bruised and sore, but physically, I was okay. I was halfway afraid to close my eyes or be alone, but that wasn't about to keep me from learning how to protect myself.

After the class, we left the room to refill our water bottles at the machine, and that's when I noticed the woman I'd seen Wick kiss at *Five Star Tech* was there, and had stopped Mimi to talk. She really was gorgeous – tall, smooth pecan-toned skin, and a body that was pretty much made for the leotard she was wearing underneath a simple ballet skirt.

I could definitely see her appeal – a fact that I mentioned to my friends. *"So that's the "Kay" he basically told me to mind my business about?"* Kora had asked, and of course, the conversation went left from there, which was how we arrived at Nubia's proposition of "whooping ass".

"Nubia, come on," Blake laughed. "You can't just fight somebody because she's dating your friend's... online fuck buddy slash bodyguard."

Nubia sucked her teeth. "Speak for yourself. I carried a whole ass pregnancy through a round of chemo, and maintained bad bitch status the entire time – I can do whatever I put my mind to."

Blake countered, "Don't you have the reputation of the new TV network to worry about?!"

"Oooh, you're right, I do... Okay, so pull out your phone and record it. Monica, Kora, make sure nobody else records it. This beatdown is going to be on WAWG, exclusively. I'm gonna make so much damn money. This is great."

"Stop it," Kora scolded. "We don't even *know* that he's dating her. Monica, you said he kissed her on the cheek, or forehead or something right? She could just be that man's friend."

"Of course she could," Nubia said, her tone soothing as she sidled up to Kora. "But... we know how *you* like to do with *your* "friends". Don't we?"

"You just *love* bringing that up, don't you?"

Nubia shrugged. "Yes, I do. You know I do. But my *point* stands. Sure, she could be his "friend", but let's not pretend it means she's not climbing those big broad chocolate shoulders on the regular."

"I'm gonna have to agree with Nubia here," I chimed in. "I mean, he and I are "friends", and... look what *we* were doing."

Blake nodded. "And besides that...am I the only one a little annoyed that there's no way she's older than like, twenty-five? *If* that? What is with these men going after babies?

162

*I* could answer that. "Perky tits and naivety, usually," I said, thinking about Crystal's immaturity and lack of planning. A smarter woman would've at least made Kellen put some type of plan in place for her, *especially* if she was having unprotected sex, and not trying to prevent pregnancy. Really though, that may have been simple stupidity, and nothing to do with her age.

But, to answer Blake's *other* question… no. She *wasn't* the only one annoyed that Wick, or Chad, or whatever, was at least forty, cavorting with what I considered to be a young ass girl. It reminded me of my husband, which was a major turnoff – a turnoff I probably needed, since after we left the gym, I would be spending my first day in *his* home.

We probably needed to reaffirm those boundaries as "friends"

As if we'd thought him up, the man himself appeared, soaked with sweat and dressed to work out. My crew and I were tucked out of the way in the corner next to the water machine, so I simply watched as he went straight to where Mimi and Kay were standing, kissing Kay's forehead before he said something to Mimi.

Suddenly, three sets of eyes were on me as Mimi pointed in our direction. Wick said something else – probably "thank you" – to her, and then grabbed Kay's hand and started moving in our direction.

*"I know this motherfucker isn't bringing her over here for introductions,"* Nubia hissed in my ear, and I immediately shushed her, turning back just in time for Wick to plant his little girlfriend right in front of us with a big smile.

"How are you ladies this morning?" he asked, earning a pleasant "good" from Kora and Blake, an extra dry "fine" from Nubia, and a raised eyebrow from me. "You still feeling okay Monica?"

"Mmmhmm," I nodded. "How are you?" I asked Kay, whose eyes went wide in apparent surprise that I'd spoken to her.

"Oh, um… I'm good," she answered, tucking her hands behind her back.

Wick shook his head. "Kayla is playing shy, but she's only here this early to meet you. All of you," he amended, before dodging a swat Kay aimed in his direction.

"That's *not* true!"

He scoffed. "Yes it is. Your ass isn't even usually out of bed this early, since you don't have classes until this afternoon."

His words brought a sheepish smile to her face, that said he said telling the truth. "You didn't have to say that in front of them."

"Ah, don't be embarrassed. Get excited. You want me to show them how loud you squealed when I mentioned them to you?"

"Could you *stop*," Kay whined, which only made Wick chuckle harder.

"She loves you – all of you, really – but especially you, Kora. She's heavy in ballet now, but she wants to get more into modern dance, and stage acting."

"Oh how *sweet*," Nubia said, and me, Kora, and Blake all turned to give her a death stare about her tone. "Your boyfriend is introducing you to your idol, huh?"

"*Boyfriend*?!" Kay blurted, sounding – and looking – absolutely disgusted as she stepped away from Wick like he was contagious. "*Gross!* He's my dad!"

"Dad?!" Nubia, Blake, Kora and I asked in unison, mouths open.

Wick's eyes narrowed in confusion. "Yeah… dad. Can somebody explain…?"

"Oh honey, we thought she was your sugar baby," Nubia shrugged, stepping forward. "Our bad."

Kora laughed. "No, *we* didn't think that. In any case, it's nice to meet you, Kayla," she said, extending a hand, which Kay eagerly accepted. "Would you like to talk? I can probably give you some resources to get you started, if you really would like to move into stage work."

"Or TV," Nubia interjected. "I was hating before I knew ol' boy was your daddy, but you're beautiful, and I need fresh faces on my network."

164

Blake shook her head. "No, that face belongs in *magazines*, and on the web, and I can get you there baby girl. Let's chat."

While my friends argued over their newfound project, I was left facing Wick, who still looked confused.

"*Sugar baby?*" he asked me, and I shook my head.

"Well, it's—"

"No, I *know* what it is. I just… don't understand why you thought—"

"I didn't!" I corrected immediately, embarrassed. "I mean… not exactly. I did think she was your girlfriend after I saw the two of you at *Tech* that day. I mean… you kissed her."

"On the *forehead*."

"I didn't know!"

"I told you I wasn't with anybody though. You really think we would've been doing what we were doing before all this if…?"

I shook my head. "I am the absolute *wrong* person to ask a question like that. Remember?"

My question seemed to have the desired intent – reminding him that before my whole life fell apart, the shit was never together to begin with. I was married to someone who didn't let a silly thing like vows keep him from doing whatever the hell he wanted. And there was little use in pretending as if I were innocent myself – I certainly wasn't thinking about Kellen's ass when I was spraying Wick's cologne in the room to set the mood.

It wasn't as if I had room – at all – to judge.

Wick scrubbed a hand over his head, looking away instead of answering my question. When he brought his attention back to me, he asked, "You ready to head out? I left you with Mimi while I got my own workout in, but I'm sure you probably want to check out your new digs."

"Temporary digs," I corrected – more to make sure he didn't think I planned to intrude any longer than I absolutely *had* to, than anything else. "And I intended to ask you about that – I thought you were supposed to be protecting me. What if someone had burst into the classroom and grabbed me?"

Wick laughed. "Well, first of all, they would've had to make it through Naomi, and they would've been biting off more than they could chew with that one. Second, my workout was only about thirty minutes. The rest of the time, I was watching you."

I frowned. "We were in the classroom by ourselves. Are there cameras in there or something?"

"Yes, there are cameras, but I was just on the other side of the glass. From your side, it was a mirror. From my side, it was a window."

"So you were watching me through two-way glass? And that doesn't seem creepy to you?"

He chuckled. "I'm supposed to be protecting you, remember? Isn't that what you just said? Besides... you handled your business in there. I'm proud of you."

I bit down on my lip as heat rushed to my cheeks. "Seriously?"

"Yeah," he nodded. "I see you worked up a little sweat, with your headband, and your ponytail," he laughed, reaching behind me to flip my hair, which only made me blush harder. "You looked cute."

My eyes went wide. "Cute?"

"I didn't stutter," he said, crossing his arms over his broad chest, putting those powerful biceps of his on full display. "You showering here, or at ho—at my place?"

"Um... I think I'll wait until we make it to your place. Maybe I can actually settle in afterward, and get some work done. I have to, before my whole business falls to pieces."

Wick frowned. "It's not that bad, is it?"

I scoffed. "Yeah, it only seems that way because Chloe is on the case. She's managed to keep the attack out of the press, which is helping a lot, but I had to admit fault on sending out a bad batch of product to our core group of influencers, which is just... bad business. Luckily, I'd listened to Chloe and hadn't issued any nasty responses when the accusations first happened. At the very least, we were able to put out a gracious statement."

166

"So you're good then, right? If Chloe is handling the PR, what is there that's more important than you taking a few days to get some peace?" he asked, and I shook my head.

"Everything else it takes to keep my business running smoothly, since apparently I can't count on the people I *hired* for that purpose." I took a deep breath after I answered that question, knowing that getting myself worked up didn't help anything. But I was annoyed – *supremely* annoyed – about the problems that had been going on right underneath my nose.

Problems that were exacerbated by Kim's sudden, unexplained absence.

It was too much of a "coincidence" for me to believe that the inability for anyone to get in touch with her was completely unrelated to my attack and the attempted break-in at my office, but I wasn't as quick as everyone else seemed to be to jump on the *"she had something to do with this"* bandwagon. In fact, I was more than a little bit worried about her.

Kim had been with me for years and years – since before the cash infusion that had really taken *Vivid Vixen* over the top. While the details of that – among other things – had been kept private, Kim knew more about my company than anyone else, and had *done* more, money aside, than anyone else. Yes, I was pissed about the oversight that got us to this place, but I wasn't ready to throw her away. Not without *proof.*

Something that was sorely lacking in way too many categories of my life.

"We'll figure out what's going on," Wick assured, putting a hand on my shoulder just long enough to squeeze before he let it go. I had to immediately cross my arms to hide my beaded nipples – a reaction that had happened instantly when he made contact with those big ass hands.

But… I wasn't supposed to be thinking about him like that.

Self-imposed when I thought he had a girlfriend or not, I planned to keep the vow I'd made myself about keeping my lust to a minimum. Although I understood where he was coming from, and forgave him without reservation, Wick's attitude with me that day in *Tech* was a red flag I had no plans to ignore. The very last thing I needed or wanted was for a man to have me out here looking stupid.

*Never* again.

"You want to let your girls know we're heading out?" he asked, oblivious to what was going on in my head. But now that my mind had gone there, I couldn't let it go. Even after I'd said my goodbyes to my friends and climbed in the passenger seat of the sleek Tesla Model X that Wick pulled to the private exit of the gym, I was still turning it over.

"So you're really just… good now?" I asked, interrupting his boring dialog about the security protocol he needed me to start following.

He pulled to a stop at the next light, and raised an eyebrow at me. "Meaning?"

"Meaning…you were *really* pissed at me about the police arresting you, and now you're just… letting me stay at your house. What changed?"

"The situation," he said simply, as we started moving again. "For what… two days? I was pissed at *everything* related to that whole ordeal. Once I talked to Renata, found out the other things that were happening, it made me step back and look at it differently. So I agreed to help you – before you were attacked, and we talked in the hospital – because everything else aside, I still saw you as a friend in need. I'm sure you've been mad at a friend longer, over less."

I smiled out the window. "Yeah, I definitely have. And I was meaner than you too, but that doesn't make it sting any less. You hurt my feelings."

"And I'm sorry for that, truly. I have a question though – have you considered how *I* felt?"

"Of course I have," I said, turning back to him. "I would've been pissed about getting arrested too."

He shook his head. "Nah, I'm talking about *before* that. I'm talking about how you dropped me like a New Year's resolution after I warned you that you were getting hacked. Now, I understood not hearing from you that particular night, because I know you had to be freaked out.

168

But it wasn't until I realized it was *you* sitting in Renata's office, playing with that cross necklace, that it dawned on me – you thought *I* had something to do with that shit. How else would you have ended up in my tech store, after I gave you a *great* recommendation to someone else?"

"In *my* city," I defended. "We were supposed to be anonymous – why the hell wouldn't I find it suspicious that you knew where I lived?"

"Because I'd *just* told you that whatever virus was on your computer was trying to use the connection to get access to me. I could see where the attempt originated from."

I sucked my teeth. "But I didn't know all that!"

"But you knew *me*. Well… kind of," he conceded with a nod. "Look, I'm not going to sit here and pretend I don't understand that it was scary for you. I know it was, and I understand why you asked Chloe to put you in touch with someone who could help – someone who just so happened to be me. But think about that – we'd been friends online for more than five years, and *incredibly* close for almost two. I tell you something thinking that I'm helping you, and you decided to just… not talk to me. For two days, even though we usually talked multiple times a day, every day. I only knew you were okay because I *happened* to recognize you. Then next thing I know… I'm getting arrested. Talk about some shit that stings…"

Oh.

I *hadn't* considered that.

But it didn't mean I was ready to take the responsibility I knew was mine.

"You could have reached out."

"You're right. I could've. But with you already being suspicious of me, what would your response to that have been?"

I sighed. "Probably not great."

"Exactly."

"But that doesn't change the fact that you were mean as hell, while I was going through a really rough time. I *needed* you."

"And I get *all* of that, but I need you to understand this little rift or whatever didn't *start* with me "being mean" to you. It started with you deciding to cut off communication, and me finding out that you recorded us without my knowledge, leading to who knows *how* many people seeing what was supposed to be a private act."

"I told you I was sorry about that!" I insisted. "It was only ever supposed to be for *my* eyes."

He shook his head. "Sandy... I don't want or need an apology from you. The shit happened, we can't do anything about it now. This isn't about laying blame on anybody – I'm just trying to put it all out there and make it clear that my anger didn't happen in a vacuum. I know you're going through hell right now, and it feels like everything is falling apart, but you aren't the only person with things at stake. Did you know that I used to be in the CIA?"

My eyebrows went up. "No. And to be honest, I'm really not here for a conversation that definitely feels like you're blaming *me* for *you* being an asshole. But, I'll let you finish. Tell, me, what does you fooling around with computers for the CIA have to with this?"

He chuckled, deflecting my attempted jab. "*Everything*. I didn't *fool around with a computer* for the CIA – I dropped international bodies for them. Disrupted foreign governments. Brokered arms deals. And okay, yeah, maybe I hacked a few things. I've had assignments so classified that I, literally, would have to kill you if I told you. You don't come away from that without making the kind of enemies that probably don't know your real name, but if they happened to see your face on the news by some twist of fate – say, getting arrested in connection with the murder of a beauty mogul's husband – it could be a problem for you and everybody you love. If it was just me... okay, fine, maybe that's no big deal. But I have a *child*. Yes, she's technically a grown woman, but when *I* look at her, I still see the face of the ten-year-old who got dropped on my doorstep after she lost her mother. So let's go back to the sting of knowing you didn't trust me, add finding out you'd betrayed my privacy, and top it all with a little "*I'm the only parent Kayla has left, and I'll be goddamned if she loses me too.*" and you tell me you don't understand why I told you I didn't want to see your face."

I swallowed, hard. "Well, when you put it like that..."

170

"Look, Sandy—"

"Monica."

"Sorry. *Monica*," he said, reaching over to put a hand on my knee. "I swear to you – this is *not* about me trying to make something your fault. I'm not holding *shit* against you, not looking for an apology, none of that. From my interactions with your friends, I can tell there was some "*Girl, fuck him*" type talk, and I *get* it. Reasons aside, I *was* an asshole to you. I *did* make a decision without all the facts. I *wasn't* there when you needed me, and I'm sorry, full stop. I just want you to see where I'm coming from, and what factored into my words, so you don't think that's all I am."

I turned in his direction, frowning as I put my hand over his. "Wick, I—"

"Chad."

"Sorry. *Chad.*"

"I'm just fucking around. From *your* lips, I prefer Wick."

"If you don't stop playing…"

"I'm gonna get in trouble?"

"*Wick!*"

"Hm?"

I couldn't help smiling, shaking my head at the way he wiggled his eyebrows at me before he put his eyes back on the road. Being up close and personal with the funny, goofy moments we'd shared so many times on the phone felt… good.

Better than it needed to.

"What I was *trying* to say was that we've known each other for a long time. My opinion of you is very, very high. I knew there was more to you than that. And so do my friends, if you're concerned about that."

He shook his head. "I don't know. They didn't seem too fond when y'all were accusing me of being a sugar daddy."

"Oh God. Please don't remind me about that," I said, covering my face with my hands.

"Don't remind you? I'm *never* going to let you forget," he laughed, earning the glare that I shot him after that.

"It's not my fault you never told me you had a kid!"

"But why would you even think that?!"

"Uh, because she's tall and gorgeous and I saw you kiss her?"

"On the forehead, like the *baby* she is," he argued, and I shook my head.

"Forehead kisses aren't just for babies."

He shrugged. "But she is, indeed, a baby. She's *barely* 21. I'm 43, Monica."

"That certainly didn't stop my husband."

"I'm not your husband. Not remotely the same kind of man."

I opened my mouth, intending to argue that he didn't even know Kellen, and therefore had no idea what kind of man he was, but… that wasn't true. He knew *plenty* about Kellen. It was just that he only recently knew his name.

"Hey," I started, ready to shift the subject away from Kellen and the painful memories that line of conversation would undoubtedly bring. "You realize I've learned more about you today than in all our years of knowing each other?"

"Not true," Wick countered, as he turned into the neatly manicured driveway of a gated community. "You know already knew plenty about *me*. Now you're just in my business."

"No I'm *not*!" I laughed. "You're the one being all chatty," I told him as he keyed in a code that opened the gate, then drove through. "Actually, now that I think about it… I'm pretty sure I dominated our phone conversations. I've done so much unloading on you, but I'm not sure you've ever done that with me."

"Maybe our needs were just different? You needed to talk, and… I don't know. Maybe I needed to listen? I'm not sure what it was, but I do know I greatly enjoyed our conversations. I like listening to you."

I scoffed. "I'm pretty sure it's *very* lonely on the island of men who *like* listening to women go on and on about their emotions and other trifles."

"I'm okay with that. I don't like being grouped with the rest of these motherfuckers anyway," he said, then turned the car off after he'd pulled into the driveway of a gray-bricked craftsman style home. "Let's get you inside."

I looked at the house, then back at him. "Wait... *this* is your house?"

"Yes," he said simply, then climbed out of the SUV, coming around to my side to open the door. "Why do you sound so surprised?"

I stepped out, looking around at the neatly polished neighborhood, with houses of all different styles that somehow still blended to create picture-perfect harmony. "I don't know, I just expected something more... rugged."

Wick laughed as he easily hefted my heavy suitcases out of the cargo hold, sitting them down in the driveway so that he could close the door. "Couldn't raise a kid in a bachelor pad, you know?"

"Right," I nodded. "I guess I have to get used to seeing you as a dad now."

He smirked as he grabbed the suitcases, carting them past me toward the door. "As long as you remember that I'm *Kayla's* father. Not yours."

I bit my lip to keep my expression from telling on me as I tried to discern the meaning behind that statement. Was he telling me not to expect to be taken care of, or reminding me that, even in his current role of protector, he was *still* a man. A man who, now that he knew my face, had seen pretty much every inch of me. Maybe reminding me that things between us weren't exactly platonic.

Not that I was in any danger of forgetting.

Inside Wick's home, I learned that my assumptions about his living space were way, *way* off base, especially after seeing the outside of the house. I'd imagined him in a sleek loft apartment in the city, with an expensive view, but this was nothing like that. The spacious, modern kitchen was swoon-worthy, and based on the well-worn pots and pans hanging over the island, actually got used. The pool, patio, and barbecue pit made me think of Saturday dinners filled with friends and laughter. The living room was full of comfortable seating that made it obvious that the space was functional.

There was nothing rugged, or specifically masculine about it. It was just... a *home*.

Well... almost.

I took mental notes as he explained different security functions of the house – bullet-proof glass windows, triple-bolted outer doors, panic buttons and hidden weapons caches, in addition to the state-of-the-art security system that had a tiered hierarchy of contacts that made my head swim.

"And," Wick added, "I have my neighbors keeping an eye out for anything out of place. This neighborhood has quite a few retired agents, but next door in particular, the house with the teal door – those are friends. Harrison and Savannah. If for *any* reason something happens here, and you need to get out of the house, you go straight there. But, that's pretty unlikely. The safest bet is the panic room on your end of the house."

My eyes went wide. "Panic room?"

"Yeah. What, you thought I was playing about my past, and the need for precautions?"

"No," I said. "I just... it's intense."

"But you'll be *safe*," he reminded me. "Come on, let me show you the upstairs."

I followed him up the stairs, staying behind him as we moved along the hall. "This is Kay's room up here," he told me, pointing to another short set of stairs in the middle of the hall. "It was the attic, but I converted it into a whole suite up there for her. She's in and out though – she stays with friends closer to school some nights, or the boyfriend she thinks I don't know about. I'm down here at this end. Bedroom, office. If you're ever looking for me, I'm probably in the office. And then, down here," he said, leading me to the other end of the hall, "Is the panic room I told you about – I'll show you the other one too, and give you the codes for both – and then... your room."

I grinned as soon as he opened the door to it – it was obvious that at least *one* of my friends had been through, from the way the dresser had been set up like a vanity to the specific bedding in the room.

174

"Chloe was here," he said, as if he'd read my mind. "She wanted to make sure it was comfortable for you, so we made a few adjustments to the guest room. That's why you stayed with her last night, instead of here. It looks okay for you?"

I nodded. "It's perfectly fine. Much more than I expected. Thank you."

"Thank Chloe," he shrugged. "She also insisted on booking a massage for you, later this afternoon. They'll set up in here."

"Oh! Nice. Okay. Um… I guess I'll get settled in then. Maybe take that shower."

"Cool. I'll grab your suitcases from down—" he stopped as his phone started ringing, frowning at the screen once he'd pulled it from his pocket. "Give me a second," he said, then stepped out of the room to answer it.

While he was off doing that, I took the opportunity to look out of the window, taking in the lush green lawn, and trees that bordered his backyard. There was a seat there, so I dropped into it, closing my eyes.

Even with the medically-induced sleep I'd gotten in the hospital, I was still *so* tired. Mentally, physically, emotionally, I was completely exhausted, and my already sketchy sleep habits had just been worse with everything happening over the last few weeks. If I were lucky, the change of pace would be exactly what I needed to be able to relax enough to get the restful sleep I desperately needed.

"Monica?"

It took more effort than I expected to pull my eyes open and find Wick standing over me.

*Did I fall asleep that quick?*

Damn.

Maybe that class had taken more out of me than I thought.

I gave Wick a sheepish smile, embarrassed that he'd had to wake me up. I knew something was wrong when he didn't smile back.

"What happened?" I asked, pushing myself up from the window seat as he pushed out a sigh.

"That was Marcus. We found Kim."

# TWELVE

No steps forward, five steps back.

That's the kind of pace it felt like we were working at, just adding more and more questions, without getting any answers, and I was tired of it.

*Monica* was tired of it.

She hadn't said much on the way to the hospital where Kim had been taken, after her landlord found her passed out in her apartment, so badly beaten that her doctor had insisted on keeping her sedated.

She hadn't said much on the way back, either.

Now, we were back at home, where Monica had retreated to the guest room. I made my way to the office, completely content to just sit and *think* for hours, until I figured *something* out.

Kim was lucky that we'd been looking for her. After three days of unanswered attempts to contact her, no activity on her bank account, and no outgoing messages or calls, Marcus had finally taken it upon himself to go to her building. A few bills in the landlord's palm had convinced him to take Marcus upstairs, and that's when they found her –

with a rope around her neck, and "*Untying the Knot*" written in money green nail polish on the floor beside her.

I wasn't sure which detail bothered Monica the most.

The hospital got in touch with Kim's family, who'd been trying to get in touch with her too. I managed to sneak in a conversation with her mother, where yet another question was introduced – who was this mystery long-distance boyfriend that Kim was telling people about, but couldn't convince to be introduced?

None of her friends or family, Monica included, had met this guy, but apparently Kim was crazy about him. It took a little prodding, but eventually her mother had remembered a name – Dave, or David – that automatically set my suspicion sensors off.

*David Asher Ross.*

Monica had brushed that off immediately, insisting that there was no way Asher and Kim were dating. But when I pressed her about her reasoning, she couldn't give me anything more than an assumption that they wouldn't do it without telling her, knowing the connection she had to both of them.

Personally, I wasn't so sure.

I was willing to admit that on paper, Asher looked like a model citizen, but my gut told me he wasn't to be trusted – something that rarely, if ever, led me astray when I listened. Just because I couldn't find anything on him didn't mean he wasn't a snake. And that thing with the names? Way too much of a coincidence for me to let it go. So I wasn't about to.

My moral objections to hacking Kim's Facebook account lasted about two seconds before I was in her inbox, scouring for that name.

"*Jackpot*," I muttered to myself when I came across messages from a "Dave R", but when I tried to go into the conversation, I frowned. I didn't have the ability to click on his name like I should've, and the profile picture was blank. Kim's side of the conversation was still there – and it was obvious that this was the right Dave, from the tone of the messages – but there were never any responses.

"*He deleted them... but how?*"

178

Searching "Dave R." on Facebook gave me more results than it made sense to try to sift through, so I didn't even try. Instead, I left Kim's account and hacked my way into Asher's, searching for any signs of her.

Asher's inbox was completely clean, as if he either didn't use it, or made a habit of deleting messages. Since that was useless, I shifted my attention to his pictures, scrolling all the way to the beginning of them.

That's where I found Monica.

She was a common fixture in his pictures, mostly in a group, but by herself often enough that the casual observer might think she was his girlfriend. Initially, because everybody looked so young, I thought maybe these were pictures from college, but Monica was thirty-six. Facebook wasn't even invented until after her college years. But, these were definitely the years right after.

From wedding pictures to BBQs to fireworks at a lake, it was obvious that their little group was tight. Kellen and Monica were glued at the hip, looking just like the happy couple that the rings on their fingers implied. Asher, and the woman I could tell from the captions and tags was *"Amanda"*, just looked... like they were there.

Many of the pictures were just three of the group, while the other person took the picture. Even with that dynamic, even though this was *Asher's* Facebook page, the clear subject of most of the pictures was Monica, with Kellen as an afterthought. She was always sandwiched between Kellen and either Asher or Amanda, both as attached as her husband seemed to be. I guess I shouldn't have been so surprised – Monica was magnetic, and beautiful – but now I understood the comment Kora had made.

These pictures showed a vibe of borderline obsession.

As I scrolled, and time went on, there was a clear shift. Monica's presence in the pictures dwindled as they got older, or... maybe there were just fewer pictures. Snapshots of friends turned into snapshots with the cigar club, colleagues, proof that he'd met and shook hands with the president. I expected to still see Amanda's face, since I was under the impression they'd dated a while, but her appearances were few and far between, until they just... stopped.

Following a hunch, I clicked over to her profile, which was still active, but apparently defunct. Her pictures showed the same adoration for Monica that Asher's had, from group pictures to kissy-face selfies, and then... nothing. Her last few posts coincided with her complete disappearance from Asher's page, and since then, there hadn't been a shred of activity.

*This shit is strange.*

I made a mental note to ask Monica about Amanda again, and see if I could get any more details from her on that. Something about that whole situation was off. In the meantime, I left Facebook and let myself into Kim's email accounts to see what, if anything I could find there that was out of place.

I still had the records from when I shut down the hack at *Vivid Vixen*, so I cross-referenced the timestamps on when that sabotage had started against all of Kim's email accounts. There didn't seem to be any clear pattern, but there *was* a particular name that stood out.

*Glen Pearson.*

I backtracked through the emails until I found what I was looking for – Glen Pearson, owner and CEO of *Canvas Cosmetics.*

Why would Kim be talking to *him*?

Using his name as a keyword, I searched through the emails again. A quick perusal showed that Kim hadn't actually been communicating with him, she'd been going back and forth with his executive assistant. Both assistants had been intermediaries in a surprisingly informal offer for *Canvas* to purchase *Vivid Vixen*, and take over the business operations. As far as I could tell, there wasn't a number on the table – the conversation was more about establishing the interest of both sides.

It was, however, one-sided. Monica wasn't remotely interested, and she made that clear.

About a week later, shit started going wrong – yet another thing I wasn't willing to accept as pure coincidence. I made another mental note – look further into Glen Pearson.

For now though, I was still on Kim.

After finding out that another of those cryptic nail polish messages had been left at the scene, Monica had sat at Kim's bedside and cried guilty tears, feeling like the attack was her fault. Personally, I wasn't moved. Sure, it was messed up that someone had kicked her ass, but I wasn't prepared yet to say, "she didn't deserve it".

And once I pulled up her financials – not to see if they'd been used, which had been the focus when we couldn't locate her at first – to look for any suspicious patterns, I was even *less* convinced. Ten different ten-thousand-dollar payments, over the course of six months, made her look a *lot* less than innocent.

*What the hell is your sneaky ass doing, Kim?*

I played that question in my head as I followed the thread of those payments, trying to figure out who they were from. It wasn't very smart to accept bribes or whatever it was in her main bank account like this – it was sloppy. But whoever was on the other end of those payments had covered their tracks well, sending me digging for even the flimsiest thread that I might be able to tug, to lead me in the right direction.

When I found that thread, it simply confirmed what I already thought.

There *was* a connection here to *Canvas Cosmetics*.

Those payments were from the well-hidden account of a company *Canvas* had purchased more than thirty years ago – *Blissful Beauty*. When they made the purchase, they'd immediately shut down *Blissful's* operations. It was clear that they just wanted them out of business, eliminated as competition.

So… why was *Blissful* paying Kim, who worked for *Vivid Vixen?* There were no products being made, nothing. But as I dug further, I found that *Blissful's* former owner, Miranda Cline, now sat on the *Canvas Cosmetics* board of directors.

Those motherfuckers were up to something – the question was *what*.

Was the goal to scare Monica into selling her company? And if so, why did they want it so bad? And why do things that could ruin the company's reputation, if that was the case?

Once again, I was working with more questions than answers. And, even if I could tie the sabotage and hacking to *Canvas Cosmetics*, there were things that still didn't make sense. Like Kellen. Corporate sabotage was one thing – murder was a whole different ballgame.

Murder was… *personal*.

That was what felt off about all of this, at least from where I sat. If Monica had enemies on a personal level – the kind who would kill, steal, and maim – wouldn't she *know*?

Actually, hell… maybe she did, and just didn't realize it.

I pulled myself up from my chair just as the doorbell rang, interrupting my intention to talk to Monica. I picked up my tablet, tapping the screen a few times to get to my cameras, frowning when I saw some buff motherfucker on my doorstep, holding a massage table.

Ignoring the doorbell, I went back to the email from Chloe, which had included the details for the massage she'd booked for Monica. Sure enough, homeboy at the door was the one whose picture and other identifying information was there in the email – the guy that *Five Star Security* had vetted and approved.

Did I *really* feel like opening the door and letting this dude touch Monica?

*Hell no.*

Did I want to have to answer for it to Chloe and Monica if I sent him away?

*Hell no.*

So… I went to open the door.

"You can wait *right* here," I told him, after letting him into the foyer. There were cameras covering every room downstairs, so I wasn't too worried about leaving him while I went to check on Monica, and make sure she was ready.

After I knocked, she came to the door in a silky robe that I hoped she wasn't naked underneath. I knew that was standard protocol for a massage, but it didn't mean I wanted to know that motherfucker downstairs was going to get a front-row view of this particular glory.

"Was that the masseuse at the door?" she asked, leaning into the doorframe.

I nodded. "Yeah. You good? You still want to do it?"

"Do I still want to do it?" She let out a dry laugh. "I'm not even sure it's an option at this point. I need *something* to work out some tension, and I think this massage may be just the answer. Will you be sitting in?"

*Hmmm.*

I hadn't even considered that, but now that she mentioned it...

"No. I want you to be able to relax, without distraction. I'll be right outside the door though, and the masseuse has been vetted. You're safe."

She smiled. "In that case... I guess you can go ahead and send him up."

"Cool. I'll get him."

Back downstairs, I found the masseuse exactly where I'd left him. "Good," I called out, and he looked up as I descended the stairs. "So you know how to follow directions. I have a few more for you, so I need you to listen hard. I don't want us to have any misunderstandings."

"Of course not," he nodded. "I'm listening."

"I will kill you," I stated simply, casually, as my number one point. "That's not a threat, or a tease, or just something I'm saying to keep you in line. I *really will* fucking kill you, and that's the main thing that needs to be understood. Okay?"

He swallowed hard. "Uh... yes sir."

"Good. If you make her uncomfortable, I will kill you. If you upset her, I will kill you. If you touch her inappropriately, I will kill you. If you purposely see something you aren't supposed to see, I will kill you. If you *accidentally* see something you aren't supposed to see... I will kill you. Don't do it. Don't chance it. Don't think you'll get away with it, because you won't. You will not make it out of this house alive. You understand?"

"Yes sir."

I clapped a hand on his shoulder. "Good. Come on. I'll show you where you can set up."

True to my word, I showed him up to Monica's room, regaling him with an explanation of the myriad different ways I really could kill his ass if he put even a *toe* out of line. I watched him like a hawk as he introduced himself to Monica, frowning when she blushed over something he said. What? I had no idea, because I was too busy thinking about killing him to listen.

What the fuck was wrong with me?

He set up his little table and equipment or whatever the fuck, then stepped out of the room with me while Monica got situated on the table, under the sheets he'd laid out.

"Hey," I said, standing shoulder to shoulder with him as we waited for Monica to be ready. "You remember what I told you?"

He raised an eyebrow. "That you'll kill me?"

"My man," I told him, clapping him on the shoulder again. "Glad to hear you got the message."

I grinned at him as he nervously inched away. After a few moments, he knocked on the door, and must've heard Monica call out that she was ready, because he practically bolted through the door, closing it behind him.

I went straight to my office, grabbing my laptop and a chair to drag back down the hall, sitting my ass right by the door. I distracted myself by doing what I was supposed to be doing anyway – searching for answers to what was happening with Monica. The sooner this was over, the sooner I could…

What?

The sooner I could *what*?

What exactly was it that I wanted out of this situation anyway?

I still vividly remembered that conversation with Quentin, which seemed so long ago, instead of just a few weeks. I'd gone on and on

184

about how things were different now that Monica and I were in arms reach of each other, and yet here I was, jealous as if I had a right to be.

*Did I* have a right to be?

After all, it wasn't as if she and I were strangers. The all-night conversations, intimate acts, all the laughs we'd shared, all the tears I'd soothed... the shit had to count for something, right? Even if she was legally bound to another man at the time, there was no denying the *emotional* bond that we'd shared.

But what the fuck did *that* matter?

Hadn't I told myself that being in the same city killed the appeal of it all? Hadn't I been *so* goddamn sure my interest would wane? Hadn't I been convinced that the *mystery* was what kept me so enthralled, the suspense of what was behind the curtain, and that once the secret was revealed, the fun would be over?

Yeah.

I had.

But...

I was wrong.

Really, *really* fucking wrong.

I liked seeing her laugh, and smile. I liked having confirmation of what I'd always known – that she was beautiful, in and out. I liked knowing that she really *was* a boss, she didn't just play one on the internet. I liked... *her*.

But again, that wasn't news.

Just confirmation of something I had no idea what to do with.

The buzzing of my cell phone pulled me from my thoughts. As soon as I saw Chloe's name on the screen, I answered, stepping away from the door so that my voice wouldn't travel through.

"Open the door for me please," was the first thing she said, a request that made me frown.

"Huh?"

"I'm at your front door," she explained. "I didn't ring the bell in case Monica is still with the masseuse."

Oh.

I made my way down the stairs to collect her, wondering what she wanted. Once she explained that she just wanted to check in on Monica, I led her up the stairs to the room, where the door was still closed.

"Oh wow," Chloe commented, glancing at her watch. "They've been at it a while, haven't they? I assumed she'd probably end up wanting a little extra time, but I only booked him for an hour."

My eyebrows went up. "An hour? He's been in there with her for nearly *two*."

Nope.

Before Chloe could stop me, I'd turned the doorknob, only intending to peek in and make sure everything was good, but then I saw – "Motherfucker where are your goddamn clothes?" I growled, wondering why the *fuck* ol' boy was giving a massage in nothing but his boxers – *not* the uniform he'd been wearing when he came to my door.

"Chadwick, *please*," Chloe pleaded, grabbing onto my arm as I shoved the door open all the way and started toward the table, intending to take apart the "masseuse" limb by limb. She thought she would stop me, but I just dragged her along.

Monica had sat up on the table, looking sleepy and confused as she tucked the sheet around herself. Ol' boy looked rightfully terrified as he backed up, hands raised in deference.

"Whoa, man, I'm just doing my job!"

"Like hell you are!" I bellowed, scowling at Chloe when she managed to put herself between us.

"Chadwick, *stop*. It's part of the massage! Just a gimmick, and you are *ruining* Monica's rest and relaxation. Collect yourself!"

My eyes bugged out. "Collect myself? *Collect* myself?! This motherfucker is in his boxers in *my* house, and you want me to collect *myself*? You're about to be collecting pieces of—"

"Wick!"

Monica's voice cut through my anger, and I turned to where she was perched on the massage table, wrapped in nothing but that sheet.

186

"He's not going to be giving me a happy ending, if that's what you're all fired up about," she said, her tone half-annoyed, half-amused. "It's *just* a massage."

"Just so we're clear though," Chloe interjected, still standing between me and the masseuse. "Happy endings *are* included in the package I booked for you, so if you want him to do that, he can dear, just tell him you want to add it."

"*Chloe!*" Monica scolded, barely stifling a laugh while I was standing here seeing red. "Will you stop teasing him, and get him out of here?"

"Of course dear," Chloe said, smirking in my face as she tried – and failed – to push me backward. "*Move*," she insisted. "Let's let her finish up."

I let out a frustrated grunt, but followed what Chloe was saying and reluctantly left the room. As soon as the door was closed behind us, Chloe turned to me, clear mischief in her eyes.

"Well, he's *quite* handsome, isn't he?" she asked, and I shook my head as my hands clenched into fists.

"Chloe, what the *fuck* is this?" I hissed, trying to keep my voice down. "You didn't say shit about naked massages and happy-endings and shit. You made it seem like… I don't know. *Not* this!"

She folded her arms. "I made it seem like exactly what my friend needed, and it was. Did you see the bliss on her face before you barged in there like a Neanderthal?"

"All I saw was the fact that the motherfucker was touching her, and neither of them have clothes on."

Chloe shrugged. "Monica is a grown woman, it's no business of yours. She needs to relax, and she needs to sleep, and I certainly don't see you stepping up to do what needs to be done."

"Excuse me?"

"You most certainly are."

"*What the fuck is happening right now?*" I muttered to myself, and Chloe laughed.

"You're jealous, is what's happening right now. And it's rather delicious."

I shook my head. "So that's your role now? Antagonizing me about your friend?"

"For as long as it's amusing, yes," she quipped, before a grin spread across her face.

"That's not very nice."

"And neither were you. Monica may be over it, but I don't have to be."

I sighed. "I thought, at the hospital, that I was back on your good side?"

"Oh, Chadwick. You *are*," she said, reaching up to cup my face in her hands. "But that doesn't mean that I won't still torture you." She dropped her hands to prop them on her hips, shifting to business mode. "Now, tell me – are we any closer to knowing who is behind all of this?"

Scratching my head, I dropped back down into the chair. "Maybe? I know that Kim has been paid a hundred thousand dollars in the last six months, by a subsidiary of *Canvas Cosmetics*. It still needs to be investigated further, but I'm pretty confident in assuming that she was being paid to help sabotage the company. I'd put good money on a bet that she was the one who put the virus on Monica's computer, and made sure that it stayed covered up long enough to put their plan into action."

"*Canvas Cosmetics*? *Really*? That seems… I don't know. This is all a bit of overkill for a corporate takeover, is it not?" Chloe asked, and I nodded.

"That's the same thing I thought. Which is why I say we need to keep investigating. Somehow, all of these crimes are connected, and it has to be deeper than somebody wanting to buy *Vivid Vixen*. And I have every intention of figuring it out."

Chloe smiled. "I have full confidence in you, Chadwick. If anyone can find an answer, I know it's you. Are you going to tell Monica?"

188

I let out a heavy sigh. "I'd planned to, but... I don't know. I feel like she's gotten enough bad news today. I don't want to add to it, but I also don't want her feeling guilty about Kim when I'm pretty sure she has something to do with all of this."

"Right. Monica said that she'd changed the combination on the safe in her office without mentioning it to anyone. She *also* said that Kim was pretty adamantly trying to get her out of the office that night. What if Monica getting attacked was simply a case of her being there at the wrong time? The detectives seemed certain that the safe was the target, but the contents were intact because only Monica knew the combination. If getting access to that safe was part of Kim's job..."

"Maybe the beating was retaliation for the failure with the safe. I mean, a job like that... you really only get one shot. You fail, and your target adds another layer of security, moves what you're looking for to another place, and so on."

Chloe nodded. "Exactly. I just don't understand why Kim would turn on Monica that way though. Certainly Monica expects a lot of her, but I know for a fact that she's extremely well-compensated for her time."

I shrugged. "Beats me. But whenever she wakes up... she has some questions to answer."

Chloe and I both glanced behind us as the door to the guest room opened and the masseuse stepped out, back in his clothes, with his bag and table in tow.

"Oh, are you finished?" Chloe asked brightly, and the young man nodded, nervously creeping toward the staircase.

"Yes ma'am."

"Wonderful. I'll show you out," she offered, stepping between us again and guiding him down the stairs. While Chloe handled that, I went straight for Monica's room, looking in at exactly the right moment to catch a – glorious – glimpse of her ass cheeks peeking underneath boy short panties as she pulled her Blakewood hoodie over her head.

"*Shit*, my bad," I called out, backing away and closing the door. "I was just making sure you were okay. Probably should've knocked."

Not even five seconds passed before she pulled the door back open, creamy caramel thighs on full display as she stood there pantless, in just that hoodie. "Yes, you should've. But it's not like you haven't seen *all* of me anyway."

"Still. I'm sorry."

She nodded. "Yes, still. And, apology accepted. And to answer your question, I'm fine."

"Enjoyed your massage?"

She smirked. "Yes, as a matter of fact. I did. And now, I am going to take advantage of my relaxed state, and try to sleep. Unless you'd like to barge in and interrupt *that* too."

I scrubbed a hand over my face. "Yeah. I'm... as the young folks say, tripping, huh?"

"Yeah, a little bit. Who knew you'd be so wildly jealous and possessive of a woman you said you never wanted to see again?"

"Never gonna let me forget that, huh?"

"You forget I thought Kayla was your girlfriend, and we can call it even. Deal?"

"Deal. And for what it's worth... the jealousy is blowing me too."

Monica grinned. "Good to know."

"Rest well. Okay?"

"I am certainly going to try," she sighed, glancing around the room behind her. "A glass of wine would probably help. You have one of those lying around?"

I cringed. "Actually, no, I don't. I try not to keep it around the house."

Monica's eyebrows lifted. "Oh, right, you told me that. Your precarious relationship with alcohol. You mentioned it, but you never explained what happened."

There was silence between us for a few seconds before her eyebrows went up a little further.

"Oh, shit," I said. "That was a hint, wasn't it?"

She hiked one shoulder. "Yeah, a little bit."

190

"Right. Uh…" I cleared my throat, then pushed my hands into the pockets of the sweats I'd changed into after my shower earlier, before we'd gone to the hospital to see Kim. "So… eleven or so years ago… my life got turned upside down. I was minding my business, between ops, and I get a knock on my door. Surprise, you have a child. She's ten. Her mother – a fellow government agent, living abroad – was killed in the line of duty. So this beautiful little girl – looks *exactly* like her mother – doesn't have anyone except you now. I was still young. Still a little wild. No plans of settling down anytime soon, let alone having children, but… she was here. So I had to adjust. *Drastically.* Resigned from the CIA, landed a desk job with the FBI. Bought a house suitable for a family. And I… do my best, you know? But I'm trying to raise a pre-teen girl who is grieving the loss of her mother, dealing with my own feelings about learning that Lisa had died – grief, confusion, *anger* that she'd never told me our fling had resulted in a child."

"Wait," Monica interrupted, holding up her hands. "You had this fling, and then never saw her again?"

I nodded. "Yeah. She was stationed in Prague. I was… hell, twenty-one, twenty-two? Kids, honestly. I was still an agent-in-training. We had fun while I was there, and I actually *wanted* to keep in touch. Not gonna lie, she was seven years older than me, and had my young ass sprung. But she didn't want that. For her it was like… holla if you're ever back in Prague."

"And you were never back in Prague."

"No. I wasn't. I never saw her alive again, but here was this little girl, with her face. Just dropped into my lap, turning my whole world upside down. I didn't know what the fuck I was doing. I was confused, and angry, and… *scared*. I was really fucking scared. A drink at night to help me sleep turned into three. Turned into working from home so I could drink during the day, while Kay was at school, and have time to be sober for her. That's how you *know* your ass is a drunk, when that's your rationale, as if your responsibility to your child is only during their off hours from school." I stopped, letting out a dry chuckle. "But…

anyway… social services stopped by one day. Surprise visit, to see the state of the home, talk to me while she was at school."

Monica put a hand to her mouth. "Wick… *no.*"

"Oh yes. The quick version? They took Kay from me, because they felt I couldn't provide a suitable home. This little girl who'd already lost the only parent she knew, but was finally, *maybe* starting to feel a little bit of normalcy, kinda *maybe* starting to trust me… ripped away, again."

"But you got her back, right?" Monica asked, her eyes glossy and wide. "They didn't put her in the system, did they?"

"Only because I fought. Tooth and nail, I *fought*. Whatever classes they told me to take, I was there. AA, I was there. Random breathalyzer, whatever the hell they wanted, I did it, because I wasn't going to let my daughter down," I told her, clearing my throat after I finished. "And that, is the Saturday morning special story of my, as you stated, "precarious relationship" with alcohol."

Monica stepped forward, wrapping her soft hands around my wrists. "Stop it. Don't downplay that, as if it's…"

"Corny? But it is."

"So what if it is? It's also what makes you so much more of a man than… others."

"Am I interrupting something?" Chloe asked from the stairs, and I stepped back from Monica's doorway.

"Nah," I told her, shaking my head. "I was just about to go back down to the office. She's all yours, Chlo."

Before they could protest, I'd already scooped up my laptop and chair and headed back down the hall, to the safety of my office. The further I was from Monica and her questions… the better.

192

# THIRTEEN

*"I thought I told you what to do?"*

I looked up from my computer to see Amanda standing in the doorway to my darkened office. Only a bit of moonlight streaming through the open window made it evident that it was her – a face I hadn't seen in two or three years.

"Amanda!" I jumped up from my seat, excitement coursing through me at the sight of my friend. I started to round the desk, intending to get to her and pull her into a hug, but then *she* moved.

Something about it wasn't right.

As she made her way towards my desk, her movements were sluggish, but jerky at the same, like she was half asleep, or like… like she wasn't in control. My own movements stalled, leaving me frozen to the spot as my brain struggled to make sense of what I was seeing. And then, she shifted her head, and I saw it – a jagged hole, right through her forehead, framed perfectly by her hair.

A scream built, then stuck in my throat, refusing to break free, even as Amanda reached the front of my desk. She put her hands down, leaning over the desk to speak as a trickle of blood spilled from the open wound in her head.

*"You were given instructions. You disobeyed. So now you pay."*

That scream finally came.

I closed my eyes, trying to shut out the horror of what was in front of me, screaming my throat raw in hopes that someone would hear me. And *save* me.

*"Monica! Monica!"*

Hands wrapped around my arms, gripping me tight, and I immediately went into defense mode, swinging my fists at whatever I could connect to.

*"Monica!"*

The hands gripped harder, moving to my wrists to keep me still. I tried to move my legs, to kick, run, anything, but something had them confined. So I did the only thing I *could* do – I channeled Naomi Prescott, remembering what she'd told me to do in class.

I tucked my chin, and then thrust the top of my head toward *whatever* the hell the thing was that had me hostage. I didn't have the leverage to put a ton of power behind it, but it was enough that the hold on my hands went away.

*"Did you just headbutt me?! Open your goddamn eyes, Monica!"*

Huh?

When I opened my eyes, I was no longer in my office, in the clutches of undead-Amanda. I was... in bed, tucked under the warm confines of the covers. Wick was sitting at the side of the bed, scowling at me as he put a hand to his nose to check for blood.

"What the *fuck* was that about?" he asked, and I cringed.

"Sorry," I said, untangling my legs from the sheets to crawl to where he was sitting so I could see where I'd hit him. "Are you okay?"

He scoffed. "I'm fine. Are *you* okay? You were screaming your head off. I thought somebody had gotten into the house or something."

I sat back on my knees, embarrassed. "Oh. Uh... no, not exactly. I had a nightmare, I guess. It was super vivid. Felt real."

194

"Okay, so *that's* why you tried to smash my face in with your head," he chuckled. "Just so you know, you need a little more power behind it if you want to stun, or do real damage."

"I gave it all I could in the moment. That thing had my hands."

"You mean *I* had your hands," he corrected. "You got me with a pretty nice left hook before that though. You may have been having a dream, but you were kicking real-life ass."

I cringed. "Sorry."

"No need to be. Are *you* okay?"

"Yeah," I nodded. "I'm fine."

"You want to talk about it?"

"*No*," was my immediate answer. "Not at all. I want to forget it as soon as I possibly can."

"Understandable."

He gave me a nod, and then stood, picking up a gun he had to have brought in with him from the bedside table. It was then that I realized he wasn't wearing anything but his boxer briefs. I had to bite down on my bottom lip to keep my mouth from dropping open.

*Lawd.*

I'd seen that body at least a hundred times, but always from a screen. A screen that, apparently, had never done him justice, because my eyes were glued to him like it was brand new to me. In his clothes, Wick was handsome. Without them, he was other-worldly – meticulously chiseled, coated in polished mahogany skin. From a side view, the boxer-briefs left nothing to the imagination – a tight, perfect ass, ample bulge in the front, powerful thighs.

It took *everything* in me not to audibly groan before I turned away, burying myself underneath the covers again to hide how hard my nipples had gotten through the thin fabric of my nightgown.

"I'm gonna let you get back to it, if you're good then. Try to get some sleep... if you can, after that."

I nodded. "Yeah. I'll try."

"Lights off or on?" he asked, from beside the light switch at the door, even though he'd shown me controls beside the bed earlier.

"On. Please."

There was clear sympathy in his eyes before he bowed his head to acknowledge my request, and dropped his free hand away from the switch. "Good night."

"Good night," I called after him, even though *come back* was what I really wanted to say.

Even before the nightmare, I'd been iffy about being in the dark. What had formerly served as solace now held unseen danger – intruders lurking in places just out of my reach, waiting to attack me. I didn't want to be alone in the dark – or hell, the light either. But I felt childish enough wanting the lights on. It would be the definition of "doing too much" to ask him to stay.

I re-situated the pillows and then laid back to close my eyes. As soon as I did, the first thing I saw on the backs of my eyelids was that bleeding wound in Amanda's head.

My eyes popped open and I sat up, shaking my head before I decided to just get my laptop, and get some work done. It didn't look like sleep was in the cards for me tonight.

*Hmph.*

*Sleep is overrated anyway.*

I couldn't seem to let it go.

After being up most of the night with it in my head, and then spending most of the morning with it, I couldn't shake that horrible image of Amanda from my head. I rarely, if ever, had nightmares, and when I did, it was never anything like *this*.

What the hell did it mean?

As I sat at the desk in the guest room, my failed attempts at focusing on work kept leading me back to that image. It had to mean something, right?

196

Frustrated, I snapped my laptop closed and picked up my cell phone. I didn't even blink when I found myself in the contact list, navigating to Amanda's number, and hitting the call button.

*It's not going to ring.*

I braced myself, waiting to finally hear the little message telling me that the number was no longer in service. But, like always, it rang. It rang, and rang, with no answer, until the voice mail message picked up – Amanda's chipper voice asking the caller not to leave a message she wasn't going to listen to, and to text her instead.

"Why the fuck won't you answer?" I asked the phone, after disconnecting the call. It didn't make sense for it to always just ring. Did she have my number blocked?

No.

Why would she have my number blocked?

Shaking my head, I unlocked the phone again, navigating to a different contact – this time, Amanda's aunt. She was the one who'd raised Amanda, the one who came to help her move into the dorm room we shared, the one who yelled for her at graduation. Parentage had always been a touchy subject for Amanda – something I could relate to, though we had different reasons. I always thought she had it good though – at least she had *somebody* in that role, to love and support her.

I couldn't say the same.

In any case, as the phone rang, I wondered how Sheila would react to hearing from me. She'd always treated me kindly, but we hadn't spoken in a long time – even before Amanda's disappearance. After, I never felt quite comfortable calling her out of the blue – what if I *had* inadvertently done something to Amanda that pissed her off so bad she just didn't want to speak to me? How awkward would that conversation be?

So I let it go.

But now, after that dream… I couldn't. As close as Sheila and Amanda had been, surely she would be able to at least assure me that Amanda's brain was intact, and that she was *not*, in fact, rocking a bullet-sized hole in her head.

Or at least, that's what I hoped.

In reality, Sheila broke down crying as soon as I explained who I was.

"I haven't seen her in years," she explained in broken words, her voice laden with emotion. "The last time I talked to her, she called me so excited. She was going to move in with Asher – they were looking for homes together. And then she was just... gone."

I frowned. "Wait a minute... moving in with Asher? She never told me that, and neither did he. It was never mentioned."

"She definitely told me that. After not hearing from her for a week, which was unusual, I went to her place, and used my key to get in. The place was completely empty. All her furniture, everything, gone. I managed to get in touch with her landlord, and she told me that Amanda had sent in a legal document relinquishing her lease, with a check big enough to pay it out. She even sent me a copy, but that signature... it wasn't Amanda. But that woman didn't care, as long as she had her money."

My frown deepened as I sat back in my chair, processing Sheila's words. "Why would Amanda do that, though? It doesn't make sense. I know she moved to Denver to be with Asher before... do you know where they were thinking of buying?"

"Further east. Up there with you, and Kellen. And... oh, Monica. I'm so sorry to hear about what happened to him. You two always looked so happy together, and that's so—"

"I'm fine, Ms. Sheila," I interrupted, not wanting to go down that road. "I mean... thank you, but... I'll be okay. I'm just a little concerned about this thing with Amanda. It's not like her to just... disappear like this. Do you know anyone else who might know?"

Instead of the "no" I was expecting, there was a long silence on the other end of the line, before Sheila pushed out a sigh.

"I called her mother. And that... *woman* ... had the nerve to ask me why I was calling her about it. As if Amanda isn't her flesh and blood. *The best decision I've ever made was handing that thing to you*

198

*the moment it was born.* Can you believe she actually said that to me? About her own child?"

Yes.

Yes, I could.

Amanda had drank a little too much more than once, getting loose enough at the lips to tell me things she wouldn't dare when she was sober. Horrible things her mother said whenever she was around, the deep insecurities Amanda felt about the woman's obvious abhorrence of her.

Those were the moments that kept me grounded, instead of envious, of the relationship Amanda had with her aunt, who doted on her. Flawed as my mother may have been, she'd never hated me, at least not in that way. Amanda may have had a bomb auntie in her life, a role I could've used myself, but at least I didn't have a mother who loathed my very existence.

"That's really sad," I agreed with Sheila. "And I'm going to take it to mean she hadn't heard from her either."

"If she had, she didn't tell me."

I pushed out a sigh. "Okay. This whole thing is nuts. How does somebody just disappear, and no one who knows her has any idea what happened?"

"Oh I *have* an idea of what happened. That boy happened, and he did something to her!"

I frowned. "What boy? Are you talking about Asher?!"

"I sure as hell am. I always knew something wasn't right about him, but I couldn't pinpoint it, and Amanda didn't want to see it. I believe he did something to her. He killed her!"

My heart dropped. "Ms. Sheila, *no*. I've known Asher about as long as I've known Amanda, and I know he would *never* hurt her. He *loved* her."

"Sure, as long as she was playing the little role he wanted, and following his orders!"

"Wait a minute – *what*?" I asked, sitting forward. "What does that even mean?"

"Nothing. *Nothing*," she said. "Never mind. I have to go."

"Wait, Ms. Shei—"

"Don't call here again pretending like you were really Amanda's friend."

"Pretending?!" I gasped. "Excuse me?"

"You heard me," Sheila hissed. "You think I don't read on the blogs that you and your husband were having problems? And every time you start having problems with Kellen, Amanda started having a problem with Asher, sneaking off on long trips, for days at a time."

"What the *hell* are you implying?"

"I just find it funny that your husband drops you for a younger version and my Amanda disappears at the same time. Like someone needed her out of the way, like they thought you and your husband were splitting."

As offended as I was by the absolute *bullshit* she was insinuating, I couldn't help noticing the increasing drag on her words, as if she couldn't open her mouth completely. My heart sank a little as I remembered, just before she was gone, Amanda telling me about Sheila's increasing dependence on painkillers, after an accident at work.

*Maybe that's why she's talking crazy.*

"Ms. Sheila, I have no idea where this is coming from, but I assure you – there has never been anything except friendship between me and Asher *or* Amanda. I had nothing to do with any problems they were having, and I don't know anything about whatever it is you're trying to say."

Sheila chuckled, but it came through as muffled, like she was laying with the phone against her face. "You might now. But they knew. I knew. Your little secret. I know."

"What secret?"

"I… know it. You can't hide it forever. Folks… always trying to hide babies. Giving babies away. Paying people off and…. Sending them away."

Those words made me swallow hard. "What? What are you talking about?"

200

No answer ever came.

Whatever pills she had taken consumed her, and all I could hear on the other end of the line was her faint snores. I pushed out a sigh, then hung up the phone.

Part of me regretted calling. Questions without answers were becoming a running theme that only served to add to my perpetual frustration. Amanda was missing, Kim was in the hospital, Kellen was dead, and I was in someone else's home, recovering there from being attacked in my office because I couldn't go to my own.

I was tired.

That exhaustion was what led me out of my seat and down the hall to Wick's office. I peeked in when I didn't get a response to my knock on the door, but he wasn't there.

I found him down in the kitchen, sitting at the counter with a plate of food. He'd asked me earlier if I was hungry, and at the time I'd turned him down. Now though, the smell of Thai basil and the sight of those noodles had my stomach growling – which reminded me I'd turned down breakfast too.

"Hey," he said, looking up when I stepped in. "You changed your mind about lunch? Grab a plate, there's plenty."

I gave him a sheepish smile. "Well, that's not exactly why I came looking for you, but um… are those drunken noodles?"

"*Our* favorite," he replied with a grin. "Yes, they are."

Following his urging, I sat down across from his place at the counter while he stood, grabbing a plate and fork for me. A few minutes later, I was digging into the spicy sweet goodness, unconcerned with how it might look.

I was hungry.

"So why were you looking for me?" he asked, once he'd handed me a glass of water and returned to his own plate. "Everything okay?"

I nodded, swallowing a mouthful of food before I spoke. "Yes, everything is fine. I just… I called Amanda's aunt, hoping that maybe she'd heard from her, but I ended up with more questions than answers.

It was such an odd conversation… about halfway through, she completely switched up on me."

Wick stopped eating to look at me. "What kind of questions?"

I thought about it for a few moments first, as I twirled a forkful of noodles on my plate. "Questions like… why didn't she tell me that she and Asher were planning to move here, before she disappeared? Especially since according to Asher, they were broken up. Or, why does her aunt think that *I* had something to do with problems between Amanda and Asher?"

He scoffed. "Well, you already know my answer to that."

"Yeah, I do," I told him, rolling my eyes over his insistence that Asher was secretly in love with me. "And you already know *my* thoughts about *that*." I was quiet for a few seconds before I continued. "She thinks Asher… did something to Amanda. Something to get rid of her, I guess so he could be with me. But there was never anything romantic between us. We went to college together, he was my husband's best friend. And, he's *my* friend. Even if I could buy that Asher secretly had a thing for me… murder? *Really?*"

Wick shrugged. "Well… maybe it's not as much of a stretch as you think?"

"You're only saying that because you didn't like him coming to see me at the hospital."

"No, I'm saying that because I didn't like him coming to see you at the hospital, and because Kim's "boyfriend" has the same initials as him, and the shit is suspicious."

"You think everything is suspicious."

"Because it is. Including that Kim."

I huffed. "Right, you thought *she* was guilty of something too."

"She *is* though," he countered, putting his fork completely down. "I know you don't want to believe that she would betray you, but I have proof – somebody from *Canvas* has been paying Kim a lot of money. Kim has full access to your office… to your computer… you see where I'm going with this?"

202

I shook my head. "Hell no, I don't. Not only are you accusing Kim, you're accusing a company that helped pioneer the black beauty industry of what... trying to take me down? In *this* manner? *Why?!*"

"I don't know *why*, Monica, but I do know *what*. I know you want to believe *Canvas* is above reproach – you probably grew up using their brands, and maybe you still do. Maybe you admire the way they built and grew their business. Maybe you want to think they're just flat out better than this. But numbers don't lie."

"But they can damn sure misrepresent the facts! About a year ago, Kim tried a new lipstick from them. A test product. It broke her face out really badly, and she wanted to put them on blast, but I talked her into just emailing someone at the company, to see what recourse she had. She followed my advice, and now I see that she got paid for her discretion. Good for her."

Wick sat back from his plate, smirking at me. "So... she used a sample product from a popular company, and had a breakout, huh?"

"Yes, she did."

"Just like all those influencers who used those test products for *your* company, and had those breakouts? Quite the coincidence, isn't it?"

I frowned, confused. "Wait a minute... what are you saying?"

"I'm saying that she *played* you, and has been working this shit for a while, if this was a year ago. She was testing you – gauging your reaction. I bet you she didn't suggest that *you* should just pay those women off to "be discreet" about it when your shit was breaking people out."

"I never *got* any emails. They just went straight to bashing me online!"

He shook his head. "Oh, but you *did*. See, Kim intercepts *all* of your *Vivid Vixen* emails – she deleted them before you ever saw them, and said nothing. Luckily for you, the web service you use keeps backups, and they were kind enough to send them to me. Monica, *Vivid Vixen* started as an indie brand – some of those influencers had been fans of yours from day one. You *really* think they wouldn't try to contact you first to find out what was going on?"

I blinked, hard. "Wait...no. Kim said that... no, this can't be true."

"I'm sorry. But it is. I don't know what they have on her, how much she's supposed to be getting, if they're threatening her to make her do it, or... I don't know what. But I *do* know that Kim is not on your team. Did you ever actually see this supposed breakout?"

I had to swallow the lump in my throat before I could answer. "I... no. She... she worked remotely for the whole week. Said she was too embarrassed to leave the house."

Wick nodded. "Yeah. Probably more like... she couldn't look you in the face knowing what she was doing."

Yeah.

Probably that.

Absently, I shook my head as I pushed away my plate, suddenly disinterested in the noodles.

"Hey," Wick said, reaching across the counter to grab my hand. "I know it's hard, but... try not to let it consume you. We're going to figure this out."

I scoffed. "Will we? Because... here I am again. More and more questions, not *nearly* enough answers."

"Yes, we will. Kim is going to wake up, sooner or later, and she's going to tell us what she knows."

"What if she knows *nothing*? What if she can't even remember? What then?"

"Then we follow a different lead."

"Like what?"

He shrugged. "At this point... *anything.* It doesn't have to be today, but at some point, we're going to have to sit down and have a real conversation about your enemies."

"I don't *have* enemies," I insisted, throwing up my hands. "I don't fuck with anybody, specifically to prevent anybody from fucking with me! I run my business and I *mind* my business."

"That may be true, but somewhere along the day, some feathers got ruffled, and—"

"You'd better not say a damn thing about chickens coming home to roost."

Wick grinned. "I mean, I wasn't planning on it, but… it's accurate."

"It's cliché."

"Doesn't make it any less valid."

I sighed. "Yeah, I guess. Hey… can you hack into something for me?"

"One of the few things in this life I can guarantee, gorgeous. What is it?"

"It's Amanda… Amanda Gordon. Can you find out who pays her phone bill?"

He raised an eyebrow at me. "Uh… yeah. Give me a second," he said, then pulled his laptop in front of him. I chewed at the inside of my lip as his fingers flew over the keys, and several minutes later, he stopped to read something on the screen. The corners of his mouth curved into a triumphant smile that he suppressed as soon as our eyes met.

That was all the answer I needed, really.

But I asked anyway.

"Who?"

"Asher."

Hearing the answer out loud still made me cringe, even though I'd expected it. Instead of responding verbally, I nodded, then climbed down from my stool.

"Monica…"

"I'm fine," I lied, keeping my face averted toward the stairs. "I'm just… tired, from last night. I'm going to lay down."

I was relieved when he said nothing – giving me a pass to continue on my way. As quickly as he'd given me that, I had no doubt that, with time, he *would* figure this out, and give me all the answers I needed.

I just hoped my view of the people I cared about wouldn't get destroyed in the process.

As usual, sleep eluded me.

But what did I expect really, with the lights on full blast because my grown ass had found a sudden fear of the dark?

I tried to reason with myself that it made sense, that I shouldn't feel bad about what had to be just a temporary aversion, but I kept coming back to the same conclusion – that trying to sleep with the lights on was just silly.

So I turned them off.

And then laid there in the dark, terrified, and painfully awake.

I'd drank the chamomile tea, squeezed drops of lavender oil into my long, relaxing bath. Lavender candles, lavender-vanilla body butter, lavender pillow spray.

That lavender shit didn't work.

So I took the pill – the "guaranteed sleep" that had always been hit or miss for me, and tonight only served as another miss. So not only was I wide awake, and afraid, I was also *pissed.* I had no grand ambitions to cure cancer or end world hunger. I just wanted to *sleep.*

Why was that so goddamned *hard*?

I turned onto my stomach and buried my face in my pillow, wondering if suffocating myself *just enough* to pass out was a possibility. Turning my face to the side, so I could breathe, I laughed out loud at my own ridiculousness. Tentatively, I closed my eyes, hoping that simple darkness was all I would see.

*Thank goodness.*

I pushed out a sigh of relief.

Instead of thinking about how bad I wanted to sleep, and my frustrations that I couldn't, I focused instead on clearing my mind of everything. My breathing slowed as I sank further into the mattress,

206

cocooning myself in those luxurious sheets. After a few minutes, my eyelids grew heavy on their own, staying closed with no effort on my behalf.

And then they popped open, in unison with a booming knock of bass.

The music only lasted a few seconds, not even long enough for me to recognize the song. It was, however, long enough to snatch sleep from my grasp as I sat up.

Once again, I was wide awake.

I turned my legs out of the bed, but hesitated for a moment once my bare feet sank into the lush fibers of the carpet. It probably wasn't a good idea to go poking around Wick's house at night, but he'd told me to make myself at home. Since sleep was obviously not on my agenda, those noodles from earlier could certainly take its place.

As soon as I stepped out of the guest room, I was bathed in darkness. Briefly, I wondered if it was some sort of security measure for the house to be *so* black, but then I realized the real problem – my eyes hadn't yet adjusted to the light.

More specifically, hadn't adjusted to the pale blue light streaming under the door to Wick's office, which made the rest of the house seem even blacker in contrast.

*What is he doing up?*

As soon as that question crossed my mind, my destination changed, and I was padding down to his office on bare feet. I wavered at the door, but then swallowed that little bit of uncertainty before I grabbed the knob and turned, pushing the door open.

*Knock, Monica. You should have knocked first!*

But, the door was already open now, and there he was, laptop open on the desk, leaning back in his chair with his forearm draped across his face. I didn't even have to see his eyes to read the exhaustion that laid heavily across his shoulders, reminding me of the shared ailment – chronic insomnia – that was the reason our paths had crossed in the first place.

I started to just back out. He hadn't moved, or looked up, so obviously he didn't even realize I was there. But then my eyes fell on the desk again, and I couldn't help the gasp I let out – a sound that got his attention immediately. He sat up, dropping his arm from his face to reach for his weapon. Before he pointed it, he recognized me, and opened his mouth to speak – probably to ask why I was there.

But my question was going to come first.

"Why is there a liquor bottle on the desk?" I asked, stepping forward. "Did you—"

"No. It's not open," he explained, looking me right in the eyes.

"Okay, but why is it here at all? I mean, this is your house, and you don't owe me any explanations, not really, but… after that whole "precarious relationship with alcohol" thing, I didn't think…"

I let my words trail off, not really sure how to finish the statement. And from the look on his face, Wick seemed as lost for words as I was.

"It's… hard to explain," he said, reaching forward to pluck the bottle from the desktop to cradle in his hands.

I crossed the room quickly, coming around to his side of the desk where I took the bottle from him, and then perched myself on top of the desk. The bottle went on the other side of me, out of sight, and out of reach.

"Try anyway."

He chuckled, leaning back in his chair again to scrutinize me. His eyes landed on my breasts just long enough for me to realize I'd neglected to pull on a robe over my thin nightgown, then came respectfully back to my face.

"What, are you a counselor or something now? Always trying to get me to talk about my feelings."

I shrugged. "It's not like you didn't play that role for me long enough. I should return the favor, right?"

"What if it doesn't feel like a favor?"

"What if it *is*, even though it may not feel like it right now?"

208

He grunted, then propped his hands behind his head. "Am I talking to Monica, or Sandy?"

"Same girl. Stop stalling. What's with the liquor bottle? What is it that's driving you to want to drink?"

"It's not that simple," he said, shaking his head. "I don't... *want* to drink. I mean... I do. It relaxes me, mellows me out, sometimes helps me sleep, sometimes helps me *think*. And I just enjoy a good glass of *Mauve*. Sue me. I *want* to have a drink. Just one. But I don't want the consequences. And so... I just look at it."

I frowned, confused, as I tried to absorb what he was saying. "But... *why*?"

"I..." he sighed. "I can't give you the neat explanation you're probably looking for. What I told you is what I have."

"No," I shook my head. "I get that part, I'm saying... why now? What's going on?"

His eyes went wide. "Are you seriously asking me that? I've got you in my house for protection because somebody has decided to wreak havoc in your life. And I... I'm *missing* something. I can't figure out how to fix this for you, and it's fucking with me."

"So you want to drink because of *me*?"

"No! *No*. That is *not* what I'm saying, not blaming anything on you. You asked what was going on – that's what's going on. But it just... is what it is."

I scoffed. "What it *is*, is that *my* mess is spilling over onto you – exactly what you were concerned about."

"No," he corrected me, with an extra layer of bass to his tone that sent a little shiver up my spine. "What it *is*, is that I am a man with a certain weakness that has absolutely *nothing* to do with you. So don't put it on your shoulders."

"I'm not—"

"Yes, you are. Just like you used to wear your husband's infidelity like it was your burden to bear. It wasn't. It was his. This is mine. *Not* yours."

"But you *just* said—"

"No, I didn't," he said, then smirked at the frustrated growl I let out. "Stop trying to make this about you, when it isn't. And I'm managing, by the way. This bottle is about five years old. Purchased right around the time Kay turned 16, and wanted to start dating. I pulled it out again when that little motherfucker broke her heart, because I need a distraction to keep me from killing him. And I just looked at it. Pulled it out *again* when she stayed out past curfew the night of her prom, and was brought home by the police, drunk as a sailor. And I needed a distraction from killing *her*. And then again when she spent her first two years of college at a school across the country, that had an amazing dance program that she just *had* to attend. Then, I needed a distraction to keep the worry from killing *me*. I always just looked at it. I'm never gonna open that bottle, Monica. It's... symbolic."

I stared at him for a long moment, trying to figure out... something. *Anything* about this man. "Symbolic of what? What does it represent?"

He grinned. "When I can properly articulate a direct answer to that, you will be the first to know."

"I'll take the indirect answer for now."

"God, you are persistent, aren't you?"

I shrugged. "You gonna tell me, or not?"

"Yeah, I guess," he chuckled. "I guess it's like... looking at this liquor, I know the possible consequences, right? Maybe I have that drink, and it's fine. But maybe it's not. Maybe I have that one, and it's like trying to eat just one chip. Not possible. I don't want to take that chance, don't want to spiral. And so, for these few minutes, or few hours, I can look at it. Maybe even hold it. But I can't indulge. I have to put it away. You following me?"

"Yes."

"Okay. So... my anger at this kid that broke my baby's heart, right? Spreading rumors about her at school, harassing her and shit. I'm *pissed. Livid.* But I know the possible consequences. Maybe I just go talk to him, and he listens respectfully, and it's fine. Or maybe, he pops off at the mouth, and I pop off with my fist, but he's a kid, and you can't

210

hit kids, so now my ass is in jail for something I should have handled differently in the first place. I don't want to take that chance. I can think about it. Maybe even *dream* about it. But I can't indulge that anger. Gotta put it away. Can't indulge the fear. Gotta put it away. Can't indulge the worry. Gotta put it away. And it's not even about… suppressing your emotions, never facing it, not like that. Just about facing the possibility of what might happen if you indulge that weak ass humanity, and give in to doing things that only bring negative consequences. The bottle is… a reminder. And a distraction. Distract myself from doing something like finding Asher and snatching him up and kicking his ass until he tells me everything I want to know. Because I remember that he's *definitely* the type of motherfucker that would press charges, and it would be stupid to bring that on myself."

"Wow."

He tipped his head to the side. "Wow?"

"Yes, wow. That is… quite a way to think… but I get it. I think."

"I think you do, and you just want to give me a hard time. What are you doing up, snooping around anyway?"

I rolled my eyes. "Well, *somebody* decided to crank their music up loud as hell, right when I was finally about to drift off to sleep."

"Oh, damn, you heard that? My bad. My headphones disconnected for a second, and I tried to shut it off. I hoped it didn't disturb you."

"No such luck," I said. "So, I got up to go looking for those noodles from earlier, saw your light on. Decided to…"

"Be nosy?"

I grinned. "If you want to call it that. What are you doing up anyway?"

"The same thing as you. Can't sleep. Nothing helping. The usual."

Our eyes met, and I raised an eyebrow at him. "You know… it's been a while, but… if you think back, you might remember that there used to be something that helped both of us with our… shared problem."

"Oh yeah? What's that?" he asked, keeping his gaze locked on mine.

For about five seconds, I just stared at him, reconsidering what I'd started. But then, I pushed his laptop aside so that I could position myself right in front of him on the desk, propping my feet up on the arms of his chair.

He stayed where he was, reclined with his arms behind his head as he watched me. I leaned back, using one arm for leverage as I hiked up the hem of my gown and opened my legs.

I wasn't nervous.

I'd shown myself to him already, time after time. The only difference now was that he was close enough to touch… only he didn't.

I did.

Without pulling my panties aside, I ran my fingers over the sensitive bud of my clit. With his eyes on me, all it took was a barely-there touch to make myself tremble, and for a little gasp to escape my lips.

"Is this ringing a bell?" I asked, switching gears to push my hand inside my panties to touch myself with no barrier between. I was already soaking wet, aching for *him* to be the one touching me, but I still didn't push my underwear aside to let him see.

"Not yet," he told me, in the deeper, lust-filled tone I recognized from all those late-night video calls. "Keep playing."

I did what I was told.

I played.

I teased and stroked and rubbed until my thighs were shaking so hard I could barely keep my feet planted on the arms of the chair. So, Wick did it for me, grabbing my ankles to keep me steady as he stood up, stepping between my legs.

"Don't stop," he told me before he hooked my legs around his waist to free his hands. Before I could respond, his hands were buried in my hair as he lowered his mouth to mine.

I didn't stop.

Even as he kissed my breath away, my fingers kept working. Even as his tongue sunk into my mouth, stroking deep, my fingers kept working. Even as his teeth nipped at my bottom lip, my fingers kept working. As his fingers grazed my scalp, lighting even *those* nerves on fire, as he groaned into my mouth, as I got wetter and wetter, as that firmly twisted spring of pleasure wound tighter, and tighter, and *tighter*... my fingers kept working.

Until they couldn't.

Until *I* couldn't move, paralyzed by the sudden, overwhelming impact of the orgasm I'd been waiting on far too long. I wanted to scream – *tried* – to scream, but Wick swallowed it in the kind of kiss I didn't know I craved until it was happening to me – long, slow licks and sharp nibbles and soothing suckles that I felt all the way down between my legs.

But it wasn't enough.

I *needed* more of him.

My hands went to the waistband of his sweats, intending to tug it down, but he immediately caught my wrists.

"What are you doing?" he asked, a question that made me frown, because I thought it was obvious. My face must've given him a sufficient answer, because he smirked, then stepped in closer. Close enough that now I could feel the gift I'd been trying to unwrap right between my legs, hot and heavy and making me throb, even with the layers of close between us.

His one-handed grip on my hair tightened, just enough to tug my head back a little, so that I was looking up at him in the pale blue illumination from his computer. "Monica... I have... fantasized about having you. Smelling *you*. Not your perfume. *You*. Not just seeing this skin. Touching it. Tasting it. Tasting *you*," he said, bringing the hand I'd used to play up to his mouth. "If you think," – he stopped to lick my index finger – "I'm going to let you," – then ring finger – "rush me..." – then middle – "You couldn't be more incorrect." He closed his mouth over all three fingers, licking away any traces of... *me* ... that remained.

After that, he brought his mouth back to mine, to murmur, "I have every intention of taking my fucking time," against my lips.

And then he kissed me again.

Harder this time, in an urgently, brutally passionate way that contradicted what he'd just said, but had me squirming on the desktop, ready for more. His hands drifted to my shoulders, down my back, to my waist, then hips before he tucked them underneath me, grabbing my ass to lift me up in a fluid motion that he made seem effortless. He never broke the kiss as he moved us from his office to his room. It wasn't until he'd lowered me to the bed that he separated his lips from mine.

Both my mind and heart were racing as he flipped on the lamp beside the bed, then pulled me right to the edge, in front of him. He reached underneath my flimsy nightgown to hook his fingers in the sides of my panties, and then slowly dragged them down my legs before he dropped them to the floor.

And then he just… stared. Raked his eyes over me, in a slow, meticulous perusal from my toes to the top of my head.

"*What?*" I asked finally, suddenly feeling self-conscious about everything from my hair, which *had* to be all over my head, to the softness of my body, to the simple cotton nightie and panties that were a far cry from the extravagant *Scantalilly* I'd fantasized about seducing him in.

The way he grinned at my question caught me off guard – it wasn't a sexy smirk, it was outright… giddy. He laughed a little, then ran his tongue over his lips before he leaned down, planting his hands on either side of me on the bed as he brought himself to eye level with me.

"Told you so."

My eyes narrowed. "Uh… what?"

"I said, *told you so.* All those times on the phone, I called you beautiful, and your response was always, *boy stop, how you know?*" he teased, mocking my voice.

"Whatever, I don't sound like that."

He grinned again. "Maybe not. But still. I was right. This whole time… I was *right as hell.* You are *so* goddamned beautiful."

214

I… *shit.*

That caught me so off guard that my eyes watered with emotion before I could even catch myself, but Wick was too busy kissing me again to notice. And I was too busy kissing him back to dwell on self-deprecating thoughts about how silly it was to get emotional over something as simple as being called beautiful, but it was… it was *more than that.*

More, that I would have to pinpoint and interrogate at a different time, because it was hard to be introspective when large, hot hands were gripping your ass, lifting you up to move you backward across a big, California-King sized bed. Even harder when the owner of those hands stopped kissing your lips to kiss and suck your neck, then tug the top of your nightgown down to lavish your nipples with the kind of attention they'd been sorely lacking for years. Completely impractical when he stopped to just yank the gown over your head, and trail kisses from your breasts to your belly-button, unfazed by the rolls or dimples or stretchmarks and kissing those too, until he made his way down to where you've only been touched by yourself and your gyno for *years.*

And when he spread your legs, leaned in and inhaled, let out a deep, satisfied groan, then looked up at you with the smirk of a man who'd just hit the lottery before he dove face first, tongue out… well… it was just fucking impossible to focus on anything else.

In next to no time, my hands were tangled in his sheets, gripping for something, *anything* as my back arched away from the bed. I tried to push back, but he caught me, arms locked around my thighs as he buried his face between my legs, licking and biting and sucking and *"ohmygodwhatthefuckpleasedon'tstop! Please! Please!"* I screamed, damn near biting a hole in my lip as he did some type of… *something* with his tongue that made me feel like I was about to turn inside out.

He had his whole mouth on my clit when the dam burst, and I climaxed, *hard.* He kept me locked exactly where I was, bucking against his mouth as my orgasm hit me in waves that seemed to keep going on, and on, and on, with every rasp of his tongue.

215

When that storm finally calmed, and he released me to the bed, I felt thoroughly wrung out. I kept my eyes closed, with every intention of riding that wave of bliss straight into sleep, but the distinctive sound of a condom wrapper opening let me know Wick's intentions were different.

As they *should* be.

My eyes fluttered open when I felt his hands on me again, and as soon as he lowered his body over mine, I was wide awake, and ready. I raised my hands, cupping his head to bring his mouth down to mine for a long, sex-laced kiss that I wouldn't have minded indulging for much longer than he did. For some reason, he pulled back, and met my gaze with an expression I couldn't read.

"What?" I asked, and he blinked, then shook his head.

"Nothing, gorgeous," he replied, even though there was definitely, *definitely* something. But then, he sank into me, slowly, deftly, gliding through my wetness in one long, deep stroke that we *both* moaned loudly at the end of. He stayed there for a moment, dipping his head to kiss me again as my body opened and adjusted for him, and then… it was on.

My mouth dropped open and stayed that way as he pulled back and then plunged again, and then again, and then again, coming after me with deep, languid strokes that made it hard to catch a breath. He hooked my legs around his waist, pressing into me with his body flush against mine in a way that created a delicious friction against both my clit *and* my nipples.

It was… magnificent.

"*Wick*," I breathed into his ear as I locked my arms around his neck, burying my face in the space between. "I…*shit* you feel so *good*," I whined, digging my nails into his back. That little compliment seemed to spur him on, because he adjusted a little bit, and then he was somehow blissfully deeper, stretching me, grinding against a spot that made me dig in harder.

"Nah," he grunted at me, pulling my head back so that we were face to face. "That's *all* you."

216

He kissed me again – an unhurried, skillful perusal of my mouth with his tongue that I quickly realized he was using as a distraction. The next thing I knew, my legs were hooked over his shoulders and he was so far in me I felt it in the depths of my stomach. Those long, deep plunges started getting deeper, and faster, and harder, until my little whimpers and moans of pleasure became a steady refrain of *"ah, ah, ah, ah, yes, ah, ah, yes, ah, yes!"* and then devolved into an incoherent, open-mouthed hum.

When he finally pulled back from that, settling into a slower rhythm, I somehow found enough breath to tease, "I thought you said you were taking your time?"

He grinned, pushing my knees into my chest as he lowered himself down so our lips could meet. "That was before I'd been inside you, gorgeous."

I tried to smile back, but ended up biting my lip as he started moving again, so deep now that every stroke brought his hips flush with mine. I closed my eyes, letting pleasure take over as he drove into me, kissing me at the same time, in a delicious sort of harmony that sent me rocketing into the middle of yet another orgasm.

And *then*, I really was done for.

I could barely feel my legs as Wick plunged into me one last time, with an animalistic grunt that sent a pleasurable thrill up my spine, adding to the euphoria I was already feeling. We didn't even untangle from each other – I just closed my eyes, enjoying the pleasant weight of his body covering me.

Sometime later, I felt him move away, and then move *me.* I started to protest, thinking for some reason that he was taking me back to the guest room, but then I felt the warmth of the sheets covering me before he climbed in behind me, closing me up in his arms.

And then, I gave in to one last thing my body had been craving, for the longest time.

*Sleep.*

# FOURTEEN

This was way too comfortable.

Way, *way* too damn comfortable.

But still, I didn't move, for fear of disrupting Monica's state of deep sleep. Well... that, plus the fact that having her in my bed felt good.

She'd showed up at the door to my office around one in the morning. Woken up ready to go at it again around five, and gone back to sleep immediately after. Now, it was damn near ten in the morning, and I'd just opened my eyes, feeling better rested than I had in months.

No matter how contented I was at the moment, nature was calling. I carefully lifted the arm Monica had draped across my stomach, then detangled my legs from hers so that I could climb out of bed to relieve myself.

While I was washing my hands, my stomach started rumbling, protesting the fact that I hadn't eaten since that lunch the day before. I left the bathroom, doing a mental inventory of my pantry while I threw on boxers and sweats. I wondered if I had the ingredients to make waffles.

Monica liked waffles.

A glance at the bed told me she was still fast asleep, curled in a ball now under the covers. Before I could stop myself, a wide grin had crossed my face. Countless times, I'd imagined this moment, but always with the knowledge that it was outside of my reach.

Only... it wasn't.

It was right here in my face.

And as much shit as I'd talked – internally and externally – about how having her within arm's reach would lower my interest… my *actual* feelings were the total opposite.

I was *very* fucking interested.

Instead of standing in the doorway staring at her like a creep, I made my way downstairs. Halfway down the staircase, the scent of bacon hit my nose, and I frowned.

"Kay, you down there?" I called, and I relaxed as soon as I heard her distinctive giggle.

"No, it's a breakfast-making burglar," was her sarcastic ass response, and I shook my head as I followed the aroma down to the kitchen, where I found Kayla standing in front of the waffle maker, pulling one out to add to a stack that she'd already made.

"To what do I owe the honor of being graced with your presence – and waffles – your majesty?" I asked, stepping beside her to plant a kiss against the side of her head.

She shrugged. "I don't know. I mean, I really just came to grab some clothes, since you're playing bodyguard, but then I peeked in your office, looking for you, and I saw…"

*Holy shit, what did she see?*

My thoughts were moving a hundred miles per second, wondering when she'd arrived home, and what it was that she'd seen. Monica on my desk? Me carrying her out? *Fuck. Where did I take her panties off? Did I leave them on the office floor?*

"This," Kay finished her statement, reaching under the cabinet for the bottle of *Mauve* I'd left on the desk last night. I'd been a little too distracted by the woman in my bed to even think about going back for it.

Kay put the bottle down on the counter, then turned to me with her hands propped on her hips.

"What?" I asked, even though I knew damned well *what*.

She shrugged. "Well… you only pull that bottle out when I've done something, or somebody has done something to me. And since

220

nobody is on *my* bad side, I figure I'm on yours. So... you want to talk about it, or...?"

I narrowed my eyes. "So... bacon and waffles are what... a peace offering?"

"Uh... something like that."

"Okay, out with it. What did you do that you think I've found out about?"

Her eyebrows perked up. "Wait, so... you don't kno—I mean... so you're not mad at me?"

"Should I be?"

"Huh?! *No,* daddy!" she insisted, suddenly *way* too damned cheerful. "It's just that I thought that *you* thought that I did something, but I really didn't, so if you're cool, I'm cool. We're cool. Everybody's cool. I even made a waffle for Monica too."

*That* was it.

Right there.

The over-sell.

"You're *not* a good liar, Kay. I thought we went over this before?" I asked, chuckling as I sat down to eat my bribe waffles before she really told me what the fuck was going on. She'd either wrecked the Range Rover she *begged* for as a birthday gift, was back to trying to hustle me into paying for her to have her own apartment, needed money, or... something that was too awful for me to even name, but I was expecting to hear any day now.

"Why do you think I'm lying?" she asked, in her definitely-withholding-the-truth voice. "You've always been fair with me, and consistent. I have no reason to—"

"You're laying it on too thick baby girl," I interrupted, holding up a hand. "Just tell me how much you need."

She sucked her teeth. "Why do you always think I want money."

"Because you *always* want money, Kay. You think I'm playing, but I'm gonna make your ass get a job. You see where Taylor always is between classes. *Working.*"

"But Taylor doesn't have an important part in a real show, with long, hard, exhausting rehearsals, *or* a boy—a... *boy-ottomless*... list of responsibilities... like *I* do."

I gave her a blank stare as I chewed my mouthful of waffles, then swallowed. "Boy-ottomless. *Boy-ottomless*, Kay? With a straight face, you just tried to make that work. Okay, K-Pain."

"K-Pain?" she asked, confused.

I grinned. "Yeah. Like, T-Pain. Rhymed "mansion" to "Wisconsin". Wis-*can*-sin? Remember?"

"No."

"Yes you *do*," I insisted. "That song, "I Can't Believe It". You remember that!"

She held up a finger. "Hold please." I watched, amused as she picked up her hot pink, tutu-ed phone case, fingers flying over the screen as she looked it up. "Yeah, I was like twelve when that song came out, so..."

"You're just a hater," I said, brushing her off. "Hating on *my* joke. K-Pain is funny."

She cringed, shaking her head. "But it's... not though."

"Maybe you're right," I grinned. "But your painfully unsuccessful attempts to conceal the fact that you have a boyfriend are *hilarious*."

Her oversized afro puff shook as she stepped back in overdone faux-shock. "Why would I be pretending not to have a boyfriend?"

I shrugged. "Ol' Khalil probably wonders the same damn thing," I told her, almost making her choke on the sip of orange juice she'd just taken. "If he asked *me*, I'd say it was probably because you knew I would look into him, like I always look into them, and you probably didn't want me to know he had a record, cause you're in *loooove* with him. Am I right?"

"Daddy, you didn't!"

I laughed. "Oh, but I did. Months ago. I looked all up and through his shit, because I wanted to know who he was if he was going to be dating *my* baby girl."

Her eyes went big and glossy, like they always did when she was getting ready to go into full-on daddy's-girl mode. "But that's not *fair*. It's a violation of his privacy, and you don't even know the full story to judge him based on him having a record, and—"

"Kay, *damn*," I said, motioning for her to kill the noise. "I haven't said anything to you about him. If I had a problem, he would've disappeared by now. You don't have to explain yourself like this to me – you're grown, even though you like to pretend otherwise when you think you're in trouble. I just want to keep you safe. I saw the letter from the judge in his file, all that shit."

*And I put a Lo-Jack on his piece of shit car.*

"And you approve?" she asked, getting right in my face. "You're okay with him? You like him?"

I sucked my teeth. "Ain't nobody said all that. I just don't think the little motherfucker is going to get you into anything you can't handle, which is as far as I care to reach. You're old enough to buy alcohol, which makes you old enough for me to mind my business. Just don't fuck it up."

"Ohhh, you should *meet* him," she gushed. "He paints the most *amazing* murals, and he's teaching me how to eat vegan, which is *great* for me as a dancer—"

"Hold up," I said, with a piece of bacon halfway up to my mouth. "Is pork vegan?"

She grinned, and shook her head. "You *know* it's not. Just don't tell."

"Who would I tell?"

"Khalil."

"Why the *fuck* would I be talking to Khalil?"

She stepped back, giving me another sheepish grin. "Well, because… I… maybemovinginwithhimnextmonthifthat'sokay???"

"Man, *hell* nah, it's not okay!"

"You *just* said I was grown though!"

I threw up my hands. "Then why the hell are you asking me?!"

"Because I care what you think, and I want your blessing, duh." She said those words with a pout, and a strain to her tone that instantly softened the scowl on my face.

"I'm glad to hear that you still care what I think, baby girl. And what I think is that you're way too young, and its way too soon for you to be moving in with *anybody*. I'm not giving you my blessing for this, but I know you'll do whatever it is *you* feel is best. I just hope you consider it long and hard. And consider that I really will make that motherfucker disappear if he's not doing right by you. So I mean, if you *really* want that on your hands..."

"Daddy, stop it," she whined, then pushed out a sigh. "It was really just a thought. Not even something we're seriously considering. Not yet. I just wanted to know what you thought."

"I think Khalil needs a real job, or you're going to need one. Cause I'm not paying rent for you to lay up under him."

She sucked her teeth. "Do you *really* think I would expect you to?"

"I mean, you *expected* that Range Rover, so..."

"Enough about me," she said, brushing that line of conversation off. Kay was spoiled – unabashedly so, and I knew it – but she *mostly* had a good enough head on her shoulders that I didn't feel about it. I was making up for the years I hadn't known her, and I didn't give a fuck what anybody had to say about it.

I grinned at her attempt to deflect. "Oh, you're ready to change the subject now, huh?"

"Yes, because I want to know *why* you brought the liquor bottle out if you've known about Khalil for months?"

"Why don't you mind your business, and I'll mind mine?"

She raised an eyebrow. "Oh. So it's about *her*," she said, not even bothering to hide her eye-roll.

"Ten minutes ago, you were making a waffle for *Monica*, and now she's just... "her"? Damn, cold world."

Kay shrugged. "Sorry. I'm still salty about that whole wrongful arrest thing, and now I find out she has you pulling the *Mauve* out."

"I didn't say it was her, you *don't* know the full details about the arrest, and we're past that anyway."

"I bet you are," she said, smirking. "I peeked in your room looking for you too. Imagine *my* surprise to find—"

"*Noooo!*" My hand went to my chest as I immediately filled that sentence with the worst possible scenario, but Kay lifted her hands, shaking her head.

"*No!* You think I'd be in here cooking waffles if I'd walked in on that?! I'd be… at therapy, or something. Ew. No, you two were just… sleeping. Looking all… peaceful and adorable or whatever. But my point was… of course you're past the arrest, if she's posted up in your bed looking cute like a Woman Crush Wednesday or something."

I grunted. "Not that it's your business, unless you want to talk about where *you* woke up this morning, but, we got past our friction before… that happened. Because we talked. Like grown-ups."

"*Not the only thing y'all were doing like grown-ups*," she muttered, around a mouthful of bacon, making me scowl.

"Aiight… let's talk. Go ahead and spill. What's with the attitude?"

"I don't have an attitude," she insisted. "It's just… weird. You haven't brought a woman to the house since Dirty Diana."

I coughed, trying not to choke on my juice. "Shit, I forgot about that," I laughed.

Kay gave me a look that said she was unamused. "*I* haven't. She hated me, for no reason!"

"You were seventeen, Kay. She definitely had a reason."

"Whatever. I'm just glad you dropped her before she moved in… with her box of toenail clippings.

I shuddered, remembering the horror I felt when I'd stayed overnight at her house, and accidentally knocked over the box she kept on her dresser.

I'd dealt with some *interesting* women in my lifetime.

"Please don't remind me of that shit," I told Kay, shaking my head. "Just be glad I recognized the crazy before the feelings got too deep."

"Oh, I am," she nodded. "But, I thought that dealing with her had scared you off bringing anybody home. Apparently not though."

"In my defense, Monica was already here. But... I'm not really sure why you care baby girl."

"I mean, it's not that I care about you... doing whatever, it's just... it's different, is all. Just makes me wonder."

I frowned. "Makes you wonder what?"

"If... if she's like mom." As soon as those words left her lips, she shook her head. "Wait, I mean... I don't know how to express it, not really, but... you'd told me about her already, you know? Back when she was "Sandy", your friend from online. And, I'm not stupid, I know you dated the whole time I was growing up, all of that. But you never talked to me about them. Not even Diana, not really. But just... in conversation, you would tell me a funny story you'd heard from *Sandy*, tell me *Sandy* had recommended a movie, or a show, or... whatever. And your face would kinda light up, and all of that. Like you liked her."

My mouth opened a little, struck by what was honestly a revelation to me. I'd never mentioned Kayla to Monica, because I was purposely keeping the details minimal. But I didn't realize that talking to Kay about Monica, even innocuously, had been such a natural, normal thing.

"Anyway," Kay went on, "When I was younger, I made up this whole narrative in my head, that you hadn't gotten married, or settled down with anybody, because you were pining away after my mother. And I know that's not true, but still. It's what I wanted to believe. Relationships were inconsequential to you, because that's how you were trained... except for me and... Sandy. So... my narrative shifted. And Sandy, to me, was like a stepmom that I'd never meet, or see, but... you had *someone* in your life that made you happy. So I never felt bad about you not having a girlfriend or anything, because you had Sandy. And I filled in details for her. Details... from my mother. So then now, here we

226

are, and Sandy is actually Monica, and at first you were mad, but then you weren't, and then you left in the middle of the night because she was hurt, and I saw how you looked at her at the gym that day when you were talking, and now... she's in your bed. And I know it's childish, and silly, but... if she's taking that place as a woman in your life *for real* now, I just... I want to know if those details I filled in are right. I want to know if she's like my mother."

*Ah shit.*

I swallowed the sudden lump in my throat and pushed my plate away, reaching forward to grab Kay's hands. "Baby girl... you don't know how much I wish I could tell you yes, Monica is like Lisa. But... she's not. I've tried to be age-appropriately transparent with you about the relationship between your mother and me, but since we haven't really talked about it since you became an adult, let me put it this way... your mother used me for my body, Kayla."

"Oh my *God*, Dad!" she whined, sounding disgusted as I laughed.

"I'm sorry, sweetheart, but that's just the real deal. She was an older woman with a certain sex drive, and I was a young man that could handle it. Your mother was, as you kids would call it today, *a savage.*"

Kay giggled at that. "Goals," she laughed, a little too hard.

"I don't know about all that, young lady," I scolded, trying to keep a straight face, but I couldn't. "But nah, seriously... your mother was an amazing woman. It's unfair that she was taken away from you so soon, but you consider yourself lucky for the years you got to spend with her."

She nodded. "I do. I just... I wish I could've had them with both of you."

"Yeah, I do too. But... that's not the way it went, and... all we can do is make the best of it now, right?"

"Right," she said, and smiled. "So... I'm guessing that means Monica is *not* a "savage"."

I chuckled. "Nah, I don't think so. With business, maybe, but on a personal level... no. I think you'd like her a lot though. She's smart, she's sweet, she's funny, she—"

"Always has a bomb mani-pedi," Kay mused.

"How do you know?"

She wrinkled her nose, looking at me like I was crazy. "Duh, because I follow her on Instagram. Her nails, hair, clothes, skin, life, are all goals. Well... maybe not her life right now."

"Ah, damn. Come on, Kay..."

"What?! I'm just saying, her life isn't exactly enviable right *now*. Maybe it will be, like... later though."

"How about, instead of talking about *her* life, you tell me about yours. Come on. What's up with you, besides ol' boy?"

"Daddy, we talk every day. Not much has changed since yesterday. Oh! Wait, actually – I might be getting moved up on the stage! Anais has a crazy stalker ex, so the director is considering pulling her from the show to keep her safe. But... I don't know. As much as I'd love to have that spot, I don't want it to be because Ana is being threatened, you know?"

I nodded. "Yeah, I get that. Has she talked to the police?"

"Yeah, but they won't do anything since he hasn't touched her, even though she's terrified. It's like they don't even care."

"Sounds about right," I grunted. "I think you should put her in touch with Marcus. She shouldn't be having to deal with this shit."

"I think you're right. I'll talk to her tonight. For now though, I have to get going if I want to make it to campus for my 11:30."

"Aiight K-Pain," I told her, standing to pull her into a hug before I kissed her forehead. She pulled back, just to scowl at me.

"K-Pain is *not* happening, stop it."

"Don't be a hater all your life," I called after her as she headed toward the front of the house to leave.

Surprisingly, she'd left the kitchen mostly clean. She *really* must've been feeling convicted about that boyfriend of hers. But honestly, even with his felony record – busted hanging with the wrong

228

crowd when he was just out of high school, a fate that could've *easily* been my own – Khalil seemed like a good kid. I'd used the resources at *Five Star Security* to run a few test scenarios past him, when he and Kay first started dating. Fast, easy money, but the kid never did bite.

I was impressed.

It was too soon, to me, for her to feel like we needed to get introduced. I'd run off enough knuckleheads to recognize that the ones she brought to me after a month or two were the ones she knew weren't shit, she just wanted me to give her confirmation.

Khalil had been around for nine.

With this one, I could tell, she really liked him, and he was good to her. She didn't want me to run him off before she was ready for him to be gone... or she was waiting until her feelings were strong enough that she didn't care what I thought about him. Either way, I was cool. Actually, I thought he was good for her. He was a little bit older than her – he was just twenty-five, but still – and more mature. Grounded. Humble. Made enough money as a painter to actually support himself, between commissioned work and his fairly popular business. I *liked* him for her.

I couldn't tell *her* that though. Not yet. She'd run the other way.

With Kay headed off to school, I went upstairs to look in on Monica, expecting to find her still asleep. What I found instead was an empty bed, which caught me a little off guard. It hadn't occurred to me that she would leave.

I stepped out of my room and went down to hers, knocking on the door first instead of just walking in. I had to knock twice to get her to answer, and when she did, her whole vibe was just... *off*.

I narrowed my eyes, confused about why the hell she was standing in the doorway, cracked just enough for her to stick her head out instead of opening it to let me in.

"Uhh... what's going on with you?" I asked.

"What? Nothing," she said, shaking her head. "I just um... I came to take a shower, and put some clothes on. Get my day started. You know, the usual."

"Oh." I pushed my hands into the pockets of my sweats. "You know, uh… you could've used mine, right?"

"I didn't want to be in your way, you know. Figured I'd get myself back to my own space, give you yours."

I tipped my head to the side. "Did I give you the impression that there was a problem with you being in my space?"

"Um… no. No, you didn't."

"So then why…" I paused, meeting her eyes in search of some kind of explanation, only to have her stare right back, offering none. Which was an answer in itself. "*Ohh*," I said, as understanding clicked into place. "This… isn't about *me* at all, is it?"

"No, it's not," she said, sounding relieved. "I… woke up feeling a little confused, and so—"

"*You* need some space. Got it."

She raised an eyebrow. "Really? Just like that?"

I shrugged. "Yeah. I didn't survive Kay's teenage years not being able to take a hint about when a woman wants to be left alone. When you're ready to talk, you just let me know."

She tried to hide it, but a little smile crept to the corners of her mouth as she nodded. "I will. And um… I heard you talking to her. Just a little, because I wasn't trying to be nosy, I just went looking for you, and I heard you two downstairs. Didn't want to interrupt."

"You could've. She made you a waffle."

"*Really?*" she asked, genuinely surprised.

"Yeah. I put it on the warmer for you."

"Okay. Thanks. But, no, I couldn't have walked into that kitchen looking quite as… freshly fucked as I did. I figured it was best to come and get cleaned up while you two had your time together. You should know… she's going to appreciate you *so much* when she gets older. I mean, I'm sure she does now too, but… I think about what a difference having a father like you would've made when I was her age, and…"

When she didn't finish that statement, I knew there was more heartache behind her words than what her voice gave away.

"When did he pass away?" I asked, and she shook her head.

230

"He's still alive, as far as I know, I just never knew him. I had a stepfather, for a while. The closest thing to a real parent I ever had, and *he* died when I was fifteen. I only knew him a few years, but he was good to me, so I always go put flowers on his grave on his birthday. Good thing for me, because this year, that was the day Kellen died. My commitment to taking him those flowers was my alibi."

My eyebrows went up. "Shit. That's some kinda luck."

"Or... none at all. Depends on how you look at it."

She dropped her gaze to the floor, looking so forlorn that it made my chest hurt. "Hey," I said, getting her to look up again. "We could find your biological father. I'm usually pretty damn good at tracking people down."

"No," she said immediately, with a sardonic little laugh. "I misspoke. I *know* who he is, we just never had a relationship... because of the way that I came about. I don't even know if he knows about me, but... I know about him. There's no need to track him down."

"Oh. Shit, I'm sorry."

"Don't be," she shook her head. "I'm okay."

The look in her eyes told a different story, but again – I knew when to stop pushing.

"I'm going to let you get back to your morning," I told her. "But, in a couple of hours, I want you to come down to the basement."

She frowned. "You didn't show me a basement. What's down there?"

"It's the door right behind the stairs. You can't miss it. And to answer your question... you'll find out when you get down there."

"You're really not going to tell me though?" she asked, surprised.

"What, and ruin the surprise?"

I winked at her before I turned away, heading to my office first to set a few queries in motion before I went to clean up – myself, and my bedroom.

I didn't know what Monica was being weird about this morning, after what I'd thought was an incredible time last night, but I chose not to focus on it when I had a lot of other things to do. It was only a matter of time before Monica went stir-crazy, being confined to a house that wasn't home to her. We needed to get this shit figured out, so that she could be back to her own space, like I knew she wanted.

As soon as I sat down at my computer, I went to the list I'd compiled of things to look into further.

*Kim's finances – what made her agree to work with Canvas, and does she have other accomplices?*

*Canvas – motive? Has to be deeper than just wanting Monica's company.*

*Asher – psycho motherfucker. I can just feel it. What the fuck is he up to? Besides Monica, what did he have against Kellen?*

*Kellen – who killed him, and why? He had beef with Monica, so why not use him instead of getting rid of him?*

*Amanda – where did Asher bury the body?*

What stood out to me most were the questions about Kellen, so I decided to focus my energy there. It only took a few minutes to get knee deep into the hole of personal debt he'd built around himself with bad investments in tech and crypto-cash ventures that never took off. Up until three years ago, when he... magically, I guess, paid it all off.

Only it wasn't so magical.

A few minutes after I found *that*, I realized he'd been able to pay off that debt with a loan from a "banker", Tommy Briggs who was well-known to be connected the criminal fringes of society. Looking through his financial records, I could see where he'd been cashing out investments and other assets to stay on top of bi-weekly payments toward the loan. He was still wrong as hell, but seeing this put the fact that he'd been living off of Monica in a different light. In addition to being trifling, the man was desperate, which had the potential to lead to an ugly situation.

In this case, more than just potential.

From the looks of things, Kellen had dug himself into a hole he couldn't get out of, and the only ladder he had available was robbing Peter to pay Paul. And sure enough, earlier this year, around the same time those big payments had started for Kim, they'd started from Kellen too, originating from the same source.

*Canvas* had been using him too.

"But why kill him?" I mused out loud, frowning at the screen. If I was working from the assumption that *Canvas* was behind the hacking, Kim's attack, Monica's attack, and the break-in and Monica's house, I had to assume that Kellen's murder was part of it too. Everything except the hacking had one of those messages with it – the names of the nail polish colors.

It *had* to all be connected.

What was the motive though? Exactly *what* was the catalyst?

"Why use the nail polish names? There has to be a reason. *Has* to be a reason."

After thinking about it for another few minutes, I navigated to my internet browser and typed a simple string of keywords as a query into Google.

*Monica Stuart Vivid Vixen Interview Wicked Widow*

Immediately, a dozen or so articles popped up, many of them just referring back to one main article – an interview she'd given with *Sugar and Spice* magazine.

*"I got the idea from Twitter, actually,"* she'd told the interviewer. *"There was this picture going around of this woman in this really gorgeous, lavish sheer gown, with feathers, and the caption on it was something like, "what I'm wearing to my much older husband's funeral after he "mysteriously" dies. And I mean, I'm not gonna lie, I chuckled at it, you know. There's like this fantasy or something, of being the tender young thing for some dinosaur of a man, and he leaves you everything. I guess it sparked something in my imagination, because before I knew it, I was jotting down these names for colors that this woman might wear. "Gold-digger Goals" as this lush, intense gold tone, and "Poison Potato Pie" which is gorgeous fall orange, and "Champagne at the Funeral" – a beautiful pearlescent nude. That's just a few of them. I've gotten some pushback about it, which is to be expected, but I really just wanted to do something different and sexy and*

*fun. Of course I'm not advocating murder – I think nail polish is considered contraband in prison! I just wanted to flex my creative muscle and tell a story – a fictional story."*

Okay, so, that was innocuous enough that I didn't see how the creation of the collection could factor into motive. Maybe the names were just convenient ways to torture Monica – which, at this point, was exactly what I considered all of this to be.

And I was *pissed* about it.

A knock at the open door to my office made me look up, to see Monica standing there, looking good enough to eat – again – in jeans and a BSU tee-shirt, with her hair pulled up in a ponytail.

"Hey… you said two hours, right? I thought we were meeting downstairs?"

My eyes went immediately to the time in the bottom corner of my screen. "Oh, shit. My bad. Yeah, let's get to it," I told her, pushing back from the desk to stand. "I just need to throw some shoes on."

"Is what I'm wearing fine?" she asked, looking down at the blue Sperry's on her feet.

"Absolutely. You are very, *very* fine," I said, winking at her as I eased past her in the doorway to get to my room. She rolled her eyes about it, but couldn't help the smile that came to her face, which had been my goal anyway.

A few minutes later, I was opening the door for the stairs that led to the basement. I flipped the light on, then motioned for her to lead the way, which she did without any complaint.

Even with the light for the stairs, the basement was pretty dark until we passed a certain point. Then, step by step, everything lit up, activated by our movements until Monica let out a gasp as we reached the bottom.

"*Wow,*" she whispered, stopping where she stood to put her hands on her hips as she stared in awe. "That is… a lot of goddamn guns."

It *was* a lot of goddamn guns.

But, I wasn't without my reasons.

234

If the white boys with no military or law enforcement training could build up their arsenals with guns bought off the internet, my ass was building up an arsenal too. Anybody that came here looking for a problem would definitely get it. I'd first taught Kay to use a simple handgun when she was sixteen, and I'd had her down here at least once a month since. She knew how to use everything in this room, from the lightweight pistol, to the hunting rifle, to the AR-15 I hoped I never had a reason to use.

As long as Monica was here, I was going to make sure *she* knew how to use one too.

"Point out what you think you'd be most comfortable with," I told her, leading her to the handgun case. I have all different types, different ammo caliber, different grips, different weights. We can find something that works for you."

She sucked in a breath. "Oh, um... probably something like what I already have. I took a class a few years ago. Once it was clear that Kellen wasn't interested in being a protector anymore."

"That's good. So you know how to protect *yourself*. How to keep your gun clean, loading and unloading, all of that?"

She nodded. "Yeah, they taught me all of that."

"Perfect. So we should just be able to run through a refresher then. What do you have right now?"

A semi-blank look crossed her face. "Um... a Glock? 9mm I think?"

"Okay. How many rounds does it hold?"

"Excuse me?"

"Bullets," I laughed. "How many bullets?"

"Oh! Six."

"Okay. Any idea what model it is?"

That blank stare came back, and she shook her head. "No. But, it's upstairs with my things."

"Not necessary. If you're already comfortable with that one, we'll introduce you to something. Glock is a great brand, and I have a few down here myself, but the CIA raised me with a Sig, so that's my brand of choice." I keyed in the code that would let me open the case, then picked up a pistol I thought she'd be able to work with. But when I handed it to her, I couldn't do anything but frown at the way she was holding it – her grip was off-kilter, her trigger finger placement was awkward, and if she fired the way she was holding it, her thumb was likely to get broken by the hammer when it slid back.

"Okay, *wow*, that is really wrong," I told her, stepping behind her and reaching around. "You want to make sure your thumbs are under *here*," I said, making the adjustment. "And keep your hands here, so your finger is free to pull the trigger. Always have it at eye level, okay? You aren't shooting anybody's feet. If you have it out, you need to be ready to kill. Show me. Pull the trigger."

"What?!" she exclaimed, stepping away. "I'm not about to fire this gun in here, with all these other guns!"

I raised an eyebrow. "Didn't say anything about firing it. I said pull the trigger. It's not loaded, Monica."

"Oh. Shit, tell me *all* the details please," she laughed. "What good is pulling the trigger if there aren't any bullets?"

"I just want to know that you'll actually do it."

"Oh. Sure, here," she said, pointing it right at me, and pulling the trigger. I heard the little click confirming that she'd actually done it, and crossed my arms, shaking my head.

"Really? You pointed *at* me to do that? What if I'd forgotten to unload it? What if I got it mixed up with a different one?"

Monica frowned. "Uh, sorry *Mr. Chadwick*," she said, rolling her eyes. "You told me to pull the trigger."

"Yeah, because I assumed you would be mindful of gun safety, Ms. *I Took a Class*. You just forgot all of that shit, huh?"

She sucked her teeth. "You don't have to be *mean*."

"Nobody is being mean to your ass, you could've shot me, woman! On *accident*. If I'm going to take a bullet, I want it to mean something, please."

With the gun still in her hands, loosely now, she crossed her arms, potentially dangerous weapon just floating every-which-way.

236

"You're *trying* to give me a heart attack, right?" I asked, pointing at how she was holding the gun.

"Oh! Sorry," she said, correcting herself – somewhat – by pointing the gun at the floor, standing like she was posing for a 90s gangster rap poster.

*What the hell did I get myself into?*

"Okay… how about we start all the way at the beginning? Is that cool?"

"Whatever you say," she muttered, in a tone that made it clear I had gotten on her nerves. For what, I didn't know, since I hadn't pointed a gun and pulled the trigger at her, but whatever. We were gonna make the shit work.

It turned out that she really did *know* the basics, they'd just gotten a little shoddy in her memory from lack of practice. Once we spent some time going over it all again – basic gun safety rules, loading and unloading, breaking it down to clean it, etc., I was confident that she was ready for the next thing.

"Got something else to show you, gorgeous. Come on. And bring your gun."

The expression she took on was one of suspicion, but still enough curiosity that she did what I asked, following me around a corner, where she let out another gasp.

"Oh my God! Is this a *shooting range*?! In your *house*?!"

I chuckled. "Yes, it is. Fully insulated and reinforced so no bullets get out. *Majorly* ventilated so that all the gasses and poison and shit don't stay in. You ready to practice?"

"*Hell yes*," she said, wearing a goofy ass grin as she turned to me. "Where are the bullets? Let's do it. I'm ready to gear up!"

"Oh so *now* I've got you excited, huh?" I asked, pulling her over to outfit her with goggles and ear protection. "You don't have an attitude anymore?"

"I didn't have an attitude," she argued. "You just… hurt my feelings, is all. You were acting like I didn't know what I was doing."

"Hey," I said, grabbing her chin to point her face up towards mine, and looking her right in the eyes. "You... *didn't* know what you were doing though," I teased, laughing when she snatched away from me to head towards the ammo.

"You're gonna get enough of teasing me while I have a gun in my hands," she called over her shoulder while I put on my own ear protection and goggles.

"You ain't gonna do shit," I shot back, yelling so that she could hear me through the ear cuffs. "Worry about hitting these targets."

"I'll just pretend they're you."

"Oh you're not going to hit anything if you do that. May want to pretend it's Kellen."

I regretted that shit as *soon* as it was out of my mouth. Hell, before. But, I said it as soon as I thought it, before my brain could send the *that's a mistake, motherfucker* signal to my lips.

I hadn't even been looking at her when I said it – I had turned to pull my ammo of choice from the shelf. When I looked at her, her eyes were on her weapon, but her hands had stilled in the middle of loading her gun. She was frozen.

Yeah.

Big fucking mistake.

"Monica... shit, I am *so* sorry."

That seemed to snap her out of her trance, and she shook her head. "No. Don't be. You're right."

"But that wasn't... I didn't mean that like a joke about him being dead, I just meant that—"

"That he was a piece of shit?" she supplied for me. "That he constantly disrespected me, had zero regard for our marriage vows, and doesn't deserve even half of the consideration I've given him, since his death? You are absolutely right," she said, with a heavy sigh. "He treated me like garbage... and that's just based on the things I *know* about. There's probably a whole lot of heartbreaking things I'm – blissfully – not even aware of." She blinked hard, several times, a move I recognized as an attempt to fight back tears.

238

I *hated* how right she was.

"Still," I said, unable to dispute any of the words she'd spoken about her husband. "I shouldn't have said that. And I'm sorry. I wasn't thinking."

She shrugged. "Don't be sorry. Like I said... you're right. He may be dead, but that's no tragedy for me. And he doesn't deserve for me to act like it is."

The next twenty or so minutes were... tense. We got her loaded, and set up in one of the two firing bays I had, and then I let her loose with a target page, which she completely murdered with haphazard shots. Then, she carefully reloaded her weapon, and killed it again.

And then again.

And then again.

The tension left her shoulders after that.

Once she seemed a little less angry – and I hoped to God it wasn't *actually* my face she saw as she was doing all that firing – I joined her on the other side of the bulletproof glass that separated the firing bays.

"Hey... you good?" I asked, approaching her cautiously while she was reloading.

She looked up at me with a smile, and nodded. "Yeah. Sorry about that getting all intense on you like that. I'd had something on my mind, and then your comment about thinking about Kellen as my target kind of... pushed me over the edge."

"Again, I am *so* sorry. It wasn't funny, and—"

"The hell it wasn't," she giggled. "Listen... seriously, you don't have to be sorry about that. It's not our fault he got himself murdered and I can't even joke about killing him anymore. He's even getting on my nerves in death, and it's pretty annoying."

I chuckled. "Tell me how you really feel then, damn."

She took a deep breath. "Yeah... I don't even know how I feel about anything these days. Everything is all upside down, and I'm just... a little lost. But I'm okay. I'm here, I'm focused. I need to be able to do this, and now that I've... wasted all these bullets," she said, motioning at the shell casings all around her feet, "I should probably get you to help me actually hit something."

"You've been hitting... the page. Which is something," I said, trying to give her a little encouragement, but it only made her shake her head.

"Uhh, nah. I need to be able to hit a target. With consistency. *Help*."

I grinned. "Yeah. I've got you."

And I did.

The next hour that we were down there was much more fun, with Monica being an eager student. She took direction well, easily applying the running stream of tips I gave her, until I had her emptying a whole magazine straight into a target.

"*Oh my God!*" she squealed, as soon as she'd pumped the last bullet right into the center of the target. She followed her proper steps first – turning on the safety, and then putting the gun down before she snatched her ear protection, turning to me with an excited shimmy. "Do you *see that*?!" she asked, and I nodded, taking off my own ear protection before I opened my arms to pull her into a hug.

"Yeah, I did. That was *really* good! Listen, you keep practicing like *that*? Nobody can fuck with you, gorgeous."

She tipped her head up at me, beaming as I looked down into her pretty face. "And it felt *ah-may-ziiiing*," she gushed, doing another one of those shimmies. Only this time, she was still in my arms, body pressed too close to mine for me to let too many more shimmies go unaddressed. "I feel *really* bad ass right now."

"You *looked* really bad ass too. I should've grabbed my phone, so you could see a video of your technique, which helps you adjust and improve. We'll remember that for next time."

She grinned even harder. "There's gonna be a next time?"

"There has to be. Shooting properly is something you use or lose. You *have* to stay in practice."

"Okay," she nodded eagerly. "When? Tomorrow?"

240

"Nah," I laughed. "Your arms will probably be sore. But maybe the day after that, okay?"

"Yeah. Um… can I do one more round?"

"Of course. Load up."

I let her out of my arms so that she could load up. Just as she was lifting and aiming, I touched her shoulder, in a gentle reminder that she didn't have her ear protection on.

"Thank you," she shouted, when I picked them up and put them on her head, adjusting to make sure her ears were covered. I stayed behind her, adjusting her grip, critiquing her stance until she was perfect, and ready to fire.

But I still stayed behind her.

"What are you doing?" she asked, half-turning to face me as I wrapped my arms around her waist, putting my body flush against hers.

"Being a distraction. You don't think it's always peace and quiet at a moment when you might have to pull a gun, do you?"

"I don't think I'd have you all over my neck either though," she giggled, shying away as I trailed my lips over the back of her neck.

"*Fine*," I said, stepping away to give her room. "No distractions then. Go ahead and make it happen."

I grinned at her as she carefully fixed her stance and grip, then pointed and aimed again. She squeezed the trigger six times, pausing between shots to adjust her aim, just like I'd shown her, and at the end, she had another really good page of targets.

"Know what would be hot?" she asked, turning to me as soon as she'd followed her safety protocol with the Sig.

"I'm looking at something now, but go ahead," I told her, making her blush as she pulled off her goggles.

"I was thinking, if I get really good, I can do like, a collection of polishes in badass colors. But they would have to be a really good, high durability gel polish, so your mani doesn't get chipped while you're loading and unloading, all of that. *Ooh!* The "Bulletproof" collection. And I'll find a black police officer, and a female soldier, and a woman who goes hunting, and then just like, everyday women, you know?"

"It sounds like a great idea. A campaign like that might even get more women into learning to shoot for self-defense too. And these days…"

Monica nodded. "Right. Necessary. *Ahh*, I'm already excited about it," she mused, then gave me another big grin. "Thank you," she said. "I needed this today."

"Thank you, for being a willing student."

She raised an eyebrow, then stepped toward me. "Thank *you,* for being a patient teacher. And… protector."

I was the one to take a step this time, closing the gap between us. And then, I kept going, backing her up against the wall. "No need to thank me. This isn't a favor, Monica. I have you here because I want you here. *Safe.*"

She ran her tongue over her those soft lips, looking up at me with her eyes wide. "Why?"

"Is that a real question?"

"Yes," she shot back. "And I want a real answer."

"You think I'm scared to give you a real answer or something, and you've gotta demand it out of me?"

She shrugged. "Yeah. Probably."

"You're right," I countered, and her serious expression broke as she laughed. "No, seriously though… when I say that I consider you a friend, that I care about you… I mean that."

For several seconds, she just stared, and then… "Is a *friend* all that you consider me?"

"Is that really a conversation you're trying to have right now?"

"No."

I chuckled. "Good. Me either."

After that, she gave me another of those long stares, and I couldn't tell if she understood how sexy that shit was, especially with her hands gripping the sides of my tee shirt. I leaned in, bringing my mouth down to hers to press a soft kiss to her lips.

"Let's go back upstairs," I suggested, moving my hands from her waist down to her hips.

242

She held my gaze, eyes full of lust, nipples hard enough that I could feel them pressing into my chest through her shirt, and… shook her head.

"Not for what *you* want to go back upstairs for," she told me, with a disappointed little sigh after. "I'm guessing you didn't notice I was barely walking straight after last night… and this morning. *She* needs a little TLC first – and *not* from your dick… Wick."

"But I can treat her with *all* the tender loving care she needs, in all kinds of other ways, without even taking my boxers off."

She smirked. "And I believe you. The problem is, if we do that, I'm definitely going to want you to take your boxers off. I happened to already have a high appreciation for what you keep in there, but after last night's first-hand experience with it…"

"Mmm," I grunted. "You sure do know how to stroke a man's ego. Sure would like you to stroke something else though."

"I know. And… as much as I would like to indulge that… rest isn't all I need."

I raised an eyebrow. "Tell me what you need."

"Clarity, Wick. And unfortunately… the kind I need… you can't give."

I closed my eyes to take a deep breath as I caught her meaning. "Not about me?"

She nodded. "Not about you. Remember that whole… woke up feeling confused thing?"

"I do. Still confused?"

"Very."

Reluctantly, I eased myself back, giving her some space, because I knew, without her explicitly stating it, that it was what I needed to do. "Do me a favor?" I asked, and her eyes immediately perked up.

"Of course. What?"

"Don't hesitate to tell me when you're… no longer confused."

Rolling her eyes, she laughed, then turned to pick up her weapon, goggles, and ear protection, to return to their proper places.

"Don't worry," she said, with a smile that seemed… promising. "You'll be the *first* to know."

# FIFTEEN

*A nice lunch with my friend will help me be a lot less confused…*

That shameless use of sex as a bargaining chip was what got me out of my sequestered status at Wick's house, and at *Sucre Noir* sitting across from Blake. The man himself was sitting a few tables down, occupying a booth alone in the half-empty restaurant. That had been another condition – coming at an odd hour. The fewer people Wick had to keep an eye on, the better. And it was a condition I was totally fine with, as long as it meant being somewhere other than the house, and getting to see my friend.

Even if she was looking at me like I was crazy.

"You know," I started, taking a sip from the blueberry lemon drop the server had placed in front of me before moving on. "I wanted to have this conversation with you, because out of everyone, I thought you'd be uniquely qualified to understand the awkward position I'm in."

Blake lifted a carefully arched eyebrow, then sipped from her own cocktail. "Okay. You're not wrong about that," she admitted, once she'd placed the glass back on the table. "We're in the "held on to a cheater" club together, sure. But… our situations are completely different, Monica. You have to understand that?"

"But I don't," I responded. "Or… wait. I *do*, but…" I closed my eyes, pushing out a little sigh. "Kellen had his faults. But he was still my husband, and *I* made the decision not to leave."

"With damn good reason."

I scoffed. "Was it though? I mean… think about how different my life could be right now, if I hadn't just pretended Kellen and his mistress didn't exist for damn near two years. If I'd just taken the time to find a lawyer and gotten this over with? All this time and energy wasted, simply because I… chose to just ignore it, and focus on my business. Which is how my marriage got where it was in the first place."

"What have I told you about taking *all* the responsibility for that?" Blake asked, frowning. "I'm not going to sit here and blow smoke up your ass, tell you that your actions were perfect, or pretend that you couldn't have been better at meeting your husband's needs. You already know the deal with that. But you know what? Kellen had options, just like you did. He could've talked to you. He could have divorced you. He could have talked to a therapist, sought counseling. But *he* chose to step outside of your marriage. *He* broke your vows. So it doesn't make sense to act like it was all you."

I sighed again. "I know that part, Blake. But… Okay… I know I don't talk about this a lot, but you remember me telling you about finally getting my mother to talk to me about my father?"

"Of course," she nodded. "For lack of a better term… your mother was the side chick."

I laughed a little. "Right. Not supposed to get pregnant, and *definitely* not supposed to have the child. But she did, and… that was the end for them. But not for me. She gave me his name, and I dug and dug until I got what I needed. An address. And I mean… I went."

"You wanted to see him, Mon. That's human nature. He was your father."

"That is *not* how his wife saw it. As soon as she saw me, she knew. Told me I looked just like my *whore* mother. And I… how could I

246

even be mad, you know? There I was, the clear evidence that her husband had a weakness." I pressed my lips closed for a second, just remembering. "He didn't know about me. I found that out, that day. He'd paid my mother to have an abortion, and instead of doing that, she just decided to stop seeing him."

"Oh, damn."

"Pretty much," I said, with another humorless laugh. "But… the reason I bring this up, is because… after she wrote a check big enough to make me agree to stay away, she said something to me. Something that I've carried, without even realizing. I hadn't even remembered that conversation, but she told me to choose wisely, or I would end up writing a check like that someday. She warned me. And you know… I was a kid, barely eighteen. I used the money for college, and I brushed her words off, because I thought I was *so* fucking smart. I would prove her wrong. Marry a man who would never put me in that position. That *would* never be me. Until it was. And it was something that I… I couldn't face it."

Blake reached across the table to grab my hand. "I *get* that Mon, I swear I do. You stay, because you don't want to fail. You don't want your relationship to just be another one that didn't work out, and you don't want people talking, and because you *love* his stupid, trifling ass. And because you want to believe that he can be better, and that you can be better, and that you can figure it out. You want to believe that it was just a mistake, or a whole bunch of them, but that you have something together that's *bigger* than that. You want to believe he can go back to being the man you loved, or if he's not, that he's going to be a new and improved version that you can fall in love with again."

I nodded. "Yes. *All* of that. *Yes.*"

"*No.*" Blake sat back, shaking her head. "No, Monica. Because it's not enough for *you* to believe it, and want it, and *crave* it. He has to be right there with you. Do you know how many stupid bitches I got called, because I didn't leave Mykel? And you were there, Monica, you know – that motherfucker *took me through it.* Embarrassed me all in public, hoes in my house, in my bed. And hell, maybe I *was* a stupid bitch, but I loved his dumb ass, and I wasn't ready to go anywhere. Not until I hurt him first."

I smirked a little. "Oh, I remember. The popular thing is "screw his friend, screw his uncle". But *you*, my friend…"

An evil little grin spread across her face. "Ah, yes. That infamous trip with his biggest rival in NBA. And I didn't even have to fuck Scott. I just posted pictures of me and him together in Miami, and Mykel cleaned his shit up *quick*. And I still made his ass chase me for two years before I took him back. But you know why that worked out for me?"

"Why?"

"Because *Mykel* wanted it to work. He wanted me. He wanted *us*. It wasn't enough for just one of us to be there – we *both* had to be on the same page. I don't mean this in an insensitive way, but… that wasn't what Kellen wanted. And if someone has decided to check out of a relationship, all the *wanting* in the world isn't going to make things magically be okay."

"I know. I *know*. Trust me, I keep reminding myself that Kellen wasn't… he wasn't the same anymore. That layoff ruined him, in more ways than one, and it was just downhill from there. I *know* it's not all my fault, and I *know* that by the time of his death, he was… lower than trash, to me. But as much as I *hated* him… there was…"

"Some part of you that still hurt, when he died? Some part of you that still *loved* him?" Blake shrugged. "Honestly, I would think there was something wrong with you, if you *didn't* feel this way. Emotions are… complex. Maybe you hated "*unemployed with a pregnant mistress*" Kellen, but "*handing out your polishes on the way to work*" Kellen could still get in your panties. You still loved him because you still remembered who he *used* to be. The person he'd become hadn't quite purged you of those memories yet. But… he hadn't been that man for a *long* time, Monica. Emotionally, physically, he'd moved on, even if a court of law wouldn't say the same. You'd been single in every way except on paper for damn near two years. His death doesn't reset that clock. You get to move on. It's *time* to move on."

248

I shook my head. "His body isn't even settled in the ground."

"And what, pray tell, does that have to do with *you*?"

"I've been a widow for... hell, not even a month. And I'm already letting someone else touch me."

Blake frowned. "Bitch, that man has been exploring your guts via webcam for at least a year, why are you acting like it's brand new?"

"Because that was a *fantasy*," I hissed back. "*This... he* is *real*. A real live man with *real* equipment. Not *my* fingers, *his*. Not a dildo, a *hot*, hard dick. I... Blake... nobody else has touched me. I lost my virginity to him, when I was a sophomore. Never did anything with anyone else. When we graduated, I married him. So for another fourteen years, no one but him. And now..."

"So, what... it was awkward or something?"

"*No.*" I pushed out a heavy breath, and closed my eyes. "It was... *God* it was amazing. And I don't even think it was because it had been a while, I think *he* was just amazing. And I didn't even think twice about it, Blake. I wanted him. I initiated it. And I loved *every single second*. And then we did it again, and I loved it more. But then... I woke up the next morning, feeling... alien. Like it was someone else in my body, someone else who'd let another man touch, and please them in such a way. It *couldn't* be me because *I just buried my husband.*"

"Girl, let it *go*," Blake groaned, sounding exasperated. "Wait – I do not mean to sound so blunt, or like I don't see where you're coming from, but *honestly*. Let it go. I don't know that Chad is your "one true love", or whatever the fuck. What I *do* know is that after he got arrested for fooling with you, claiming he wanted nothing to do with you, and so on... that man over there is... right over there. You feel me? Shifted his workload to make *your* shit his main priority. Rushed his ass to that hospital to see about you. Put you in *his* house to keep you safe. Keeps looking his sexy chocolate ass over here at you like he thinks you're gonna disappear into thin air. *This* is behavior that you reward."

I rolled my eyes. "Reward? I should grant him access to my pussy because he's being nice?"

"Uhh, cut the shit. He's being quite a bit more than "nice", and you know it. Stop playing. And, no, I'm *not* saying that you should use pussy as a reward, because pussy is plentiful – he can get that anywhere. I'm saying that, from where I'm sitting, it seems like a dead asshole – sorry – is being given more consideration than the live one with the big dick. And that doesn't make a ton of sense to me."

"Hold up," I said, raising a hand. "I never promised you sense and logic, I said *lunch,* bitch. You get what you get."

"I can tell," she said, laughing as she picked up her drink for another sip. "Seriously though… Monica, we have watched you… shrink, over the last two years. It's like when you walked in on him with that girl, part of you perished, and you shifted your focus solely to *Vivid Vixen.* Just, work, work, work, and if you weren't working, you were half doped up trying to sleep, and if you weren't wrapped up in that, you were… playing with your pussy on the webcam, or whatever you and Chad were doing."

"Blake…"

She shrugged. "I mean… am I lying on you?"

Instead of answering, I just gave her a blank stare, which she responded to by smirking. "See? Exactly. *Anyway*," she kept on, before I could interject, "My point is, I've seen you more since all of this than I had in like the whole year before that! And I didn't even know you could fight, but you *literally* snatched that bitch in the beauty shop by her wig."

"Wow," I laughed. "That seems like a lifetime ago. *So* much has happened since then."

Blake nodded. "It really has. Hate it took a murder and getting choked to see your ass, but here we are."

"Blake!"

"What?"

"You've been spending too much time around Nubia. *Entirely.*"

"I… am not even going to deny that. The woman is a bad influence, but we love her," Blake laughed. "But really, Monica. If you can… try to think of all of this as… a rebirth. I know you're having to make some changes to the company, hiring new people, all of that. I think you should apply that to your personal life too." She stopped talking to smile. "I still remember when the internet just *exploded* with news about Mykel and where he was putting his dick. While everybody else was *allll* over my back about leaving him, and not being stupid, blah, blah... you called and asked me what you could do for me. And then you came all the way to San Diego, and you got me out of bed, and did my nails, and my hair... you remember that?"

I nodded. "I do. I remember the headlines from those pictures when I took you out to lunch looking like new money too. *"Blake Hollis Unbothered in La Jolla"*."

"*Girl*, Mykel was hot about it too!" she giggled. "But I bring that up as just... an example of what I mean when I say you are *amazing*. I know Kellen's favorite thing to call you was *bitter*. *Miserable*. And... when it came to him, maybe you were. So fucking what? That's over. It's the past. You deserve to be happy. You deserve to smile. You deserve *good dick*. Okay?"

I laughed. "I... Okay. Okay."

"Okay," Blake repeated, with a triumphant smile. "Now if you'll excuse me, I need to catch Mykel before he leaves to get on this plane. I'm ovulating, and he has to shoot up the club while it's still poppin'."

"Ah, still working on that baby, huh?"

"Yes. Fingers crossed that this is our month."

"Your lips to God's ears," I told her, standing with her for a hug and a kiss on the cheek. "Bye honey. Milk him dry."

She laughed. "I certainly plan on it."

Once she was gone, Wick didn't waste any time abandoning his table to join mine.

"I know, I know," I told him. "You're tired of wasting away in this stuffy restaurant. I just have to get the check, and then we can go."

He shook his head. "Actually, I love this place. I came over because we *need* to go. I want to take you by *Fitness* for another self-defense session before we go back to the house. And I'd like to get there before dark."

"The gym?"

"The *house*. Part of protecting a client is being aware of my surroundings. It's easier to be aware when it's not dark."

I chewed on my bottom lip for a second. "Okay, Mr. Professional. I don't have gym clothes. What do you say about *that*?"

"I say that I definitely asked you to put workout gear in the bag I had you to pack."

"The bag you had me pack for the car, in case we had to go on the run?"

He smirked. "The bag I asked you to pack because I knew I wanted to take you to the gym after lunch."

"Oh."

"But, for what it's worth, you should *definitely* keep a bag with a few passports, at least two handguns, a hundred rounds of ammo, and a sturdy knife handy... in case you have to go on the run."

I sucked my teeth. "You're playing with me."

"Am I?" he asked, wearing an expression that made it hard to tell if he was serious or not. "Anyway – the check is already taken care of, so we're good to go."

"What do you mean, it's already taken care of? As in you paid it?"

"Yes, as in I paid it."

"No one was expecting you to do that. I just wanted you to bring me, not to cover it."

He shrugged. "I knew that. And if you're about to go all *independent woman* on me, save it. You can definitely pay me back if you want to, cause you and your friend went a little loose with those twenty-dollar cocktails, and the shit wasn't cheap."

"Uh-uh, Big Money," I teased, grabbing my purse. "You got it. Thank you."

"You're welcome," he said from behind me as I led the way to the front of the restaurant.

Once we reached the front doors, he amended our positions, keeping me just behind him, with a firm grip on my arm until we made it

252

to his Tesla. Inside, the heated seats had the car comfortably warm versus the bitter cold outside, making it easy to settle in for the ride across town to the gym. There was quiet between us for most of the ride. I couldn't say what was on his mind, but I was deep in thought, turning Blake's words over and over in my head.

She was right.

Kellen's death *didn't* – or at least *shouldn't* – reset the proverbial clock on whether or not it was okay for me to move on from our relationship. The *fact* was that our relationship had been over for at least two years, that I knew of. Who knew what was really going on in Kellen's head when we were going through the motions of counseling? When he was playing along with the purchase of a home he never had any real intentions of being the man of, or letting me believe that maybe we really could work things out?

He was already checked out.

It made no sense for me to be worried about if anything was "too soon".

Hell, it probably wasn't soon enough.

Maybe I was making too much of it. Timing aside, I was a single woman, and could do whatever the hell I wanted – including my temporary bodyguard. And that brought me to another thing I felt was being lost in all of the chaos – Wick had earned a place in my life before the nonsense even started.

It was funny that Blake brought up that trip to see her when she lived in San Diego – it was on *that* trip that my online identity had been forged, and when I first found out *NoRestForTheWicked* even existed. A simple response to a post on a message board – about where to get the best drunken noodles in the city – had ended up spinning off into a friendship that had helped keep me sane over the next five years, and something I'd treasured pretty deeply for the last two. He'd listened without judgment, soothed my tears, made me laugh… helped me sleep. All while the man I'd taken vows with was laid up with another woman.

And this was no one-sided thing.

As Blake had so easily noted, despite Wick's cold treatment and harsh words when he was still fuming about his arrest, he hadn't been able to stay away. Before he and I even spoke again, he'd dug in his heels and started the work of helping me, like the friend he'd already proven himself to be. Hadn't been afraid to apologize, or express his *own* hurt to me. And when all of this confusion came to a point of me needing to be protected, he'd been the first to step up – had *insisted* on it.

When it came to choices for "moving on", I could do much, *much* worse than Wick. And after four years of personal stagnation, while I allowed the dregs of my marriage to emotionally drain me, it was important – no... *crucial* – that I actively work to surround myself with people that made my life better.

Wick was qualified to be in that number.

"Aiight gorgeous, let's get to it," he said cheerfully, oblivious to the dissection that was happening in my head. "I think we'll have plenty of time."

Inside the gym, he showed me to a private area I hadn't seen before – a series of rooms with padded floors, with heavy bags of varying size hanging from the ceiling. Looking around, I quickly noted that we were alone, with no sign of Naomi to be found.

"Um... are we early?" I asked, accepting my bag when he handed it to me. "And why is the class back here today, instead of that room up front?"

He sauntered over to a wall lined with boxing gloves and other gear, selecting a protective headpiece before he answered. "I didn't say you were coming to class. I said we were having a session. There's a partition back there where you can get changed."

After he said that, he held up the headpiece, comparing it to the size of my head before he nodded, putting it down on the table against the wall as he scoured for one for himself.

"Uh, excuse me... so... *you're* going to be my instructor today?"

Wick turned to me, eyebrow raised. "That gonna be a problem, Stuart?"

254

He looked me right in the face, daring me to challenge him – a dare I had no interest taking him up on.

"Not at all," I told him, then turned with my bag on my shoulder to go to the area he'd pointed out in the small room – a tiny corner, cordoned off by a wall. All that was on the other side was a chair and a few hooks, so there was little distraction as I traded my blazer and boots and jeans for sneakers and workout gear. Still, by the time I came around the wall to get back to Wick, he'd already changed and picked out protective gear for both of us.

"Okay," he said, giving me an approving nod. "Let's get to work."

The first thing he did was run through the basics with me again – the stuff I'd learned with Naomi three days ago. Using the heel of my hand to strike an attacker under the nose, a quick neck chop, or eye-gouging, all intended to cause enough pain or disorientation that I was able to get away, and try to run. Those were all easy to remember, as well as fairly easy to execute, so we moved quickly from those, into what to do to break out of certain holds.

I focused hard on what he was telling me, especially when he started explaining what to do if I was being choked. Going through the motions of it brought back ugly memories, but by the time we'd gone through his whole list, I felt convinced that even if I was overpowered, I wasn't going down without a fight. If someone tried to mess with me again, I would at *least* be leaving a mark.

"So... how do you feel?" he asked, as if he'd been reading my mind. "Confident, I hope. You've been doing well, between here and the gun range."

I nodded. "Yeah. I feel pretty good. In theory, at least. In practice, I may end up just screaming in the attacker's face, or fainting or something."

"Nah," Wick laughed, shaking his head as he approached me. "You hit me with a decent headbutt the other night – I would've been fucked up if you'd actually had the leverage to put some force behind it."

"That's how I got loose from the guy who attacked me at my office too, only he was behind me. And... still caught me... and choked me... so... I'm not that sure any of this stuff works, but at least I *feel* like I can do something."

"It definitely works... under the right circumstances, with the right conditions. But you said something key – you *feel* like you can do something, and that's half the battle. Anything you do with confidence is always going to get a better result than the shit you do while going about it like you're scared. You have power. Don't be afraid to use it."

I smirked. "Yeah, I hear you with all the motivational stuff, but um... I was expecting to get to punch something. I'm supposed to be using my power, right?"

Wick smiled. "So what, you want to do a little bit of sparring or something?"

"As in, hitting each other?" I cackled. "Have you seen your arms, man? No thanks."

"No, as in, you trying to hit me. I'll be doing something else."

My head dropped, eyes narrowed as I looked at him. "Something like *what*?"

A different, mischievous sort of grin spread across his face as he walked away from me. "Oh, you'll see."

I watched, curious – and a little concerned – as he went back to the wall containing all the boxing gear, and lifted the tabletop, which apparently housed a storage compartment. I frowned when he turned to me holding two bright blue sections of pool noodle.

"Okay, you ready?" he asked me, and I immediately shook my head.

"What? No, I don't even know what's happening."

"I told you already." He switched the pool noodles to one hand, then grabbed a pair of boxing gloves before he approached me. The pool noodles dropped to the ground while he helped me into the gloves, and after he bent to retrieve them, he stepped back. "Try to hit me."

"What?"

256

"Come on, Monica. Imagine I'm… I don't know, a chipped manicure. Take your best shot."

Feeling completely awkward about it, I planted my feet how I was supposed to, and tried to jab him – an action that was immediately met with a swipe from the pool noodle. The lightweight foam didn't hurt at all, but the fact that he'd blocked me with it was strangely… infuriating.

So I jabbed again.

And got blocked again.

*Fuck!*

This time, I aimed low, only to get blocked again, and to add to my annoyance, Wick bopped me right upside the head with the other noodle, and then grinned.

Oh, it was *on* now.

I launched myself at him, pouring all my energy into one jab after another, trying my best to land even a single blow, but I couldn't. By the time I stopped, bent at the waist with my gloved hands against my knees, trying to catch my breath, I was soaked with sweat and had gotten bopped on the head, neck, shoulders, even my ass, a good fifty times.

Wick wasn't even panting a little.

*Sonofabitch.*

"What's wrong, gorgeous? I thought you said you wanted to punch something," he said, still wearing that stupid ass grin.

"Shut up."

He chuckled. "Why I gotta shut up? I'm just saying I expected more out of you, but you're in here playing games, wasting time. You gonna get up and do this or what?"

*Okay.*

Without warning, I straightened up and launched myself at him again, *determined* this time to at least get *one* hit.

"Oh, *shit*," he laughed. "Here we fucking *go!*"

"*Ugh!*" I growled, his laughing only making me more frustrated, only making me go after him harder. I could literally feel the energy draining from my body with every blow, and knew I couldn't keep it up much longer. Something flashed in my mind – something he'd just told me, not even an hour ago.

*It's either you or them – you use whatever move you have, but you take their ass down.*

Okay.

Wick's eyes went wide as I took a step back from him, and then reared back, putting my weight on just one leg as I aimed a kick in his direction.

"Oh, okay Ronda Rousey," he laughed, *again*, easily deflecting that too. "That's right, give me everything, give me all you got! You've had a fucked up last few weeks, I know you're pissed. Let it out. Come on! *Come on!*"

"Ahhhh!" I screamed, right in his face, throwing punches, jabs, kicks, *everything* I had left, and he deflected it all, over, and over, and... over. There was no triumph for me, no moment of victory where I finally landed a blow, and I wasn't sure if I was pleased or pissed that he wouldn't let me win.

Finally, I stepped back and didn't step forward again, completely spent after digging into my last reserves of energy.

"Ah, man. That's it?" he asked, dropping the sticks to amble up to me. I was bent over again, wheezing as he leaned to put himself at eye level, looking me right in the face. "That's all you got? Damn."

I didn't even think about it.

It was something like a reflex that had me pulling my arm back, then aiming my glove straight at his face. I didn't even feel the impact of my fist, I felt in my elbow, in my wrist, reverberating all the way up to my shoulder.

And then I realized I hadn't hit him at all.

He'd caught me by the wrist, with my glove barely an inch from his face. Once I processed that, I swung with my other hand while he was still holding me, only to have him easily snatch the power out of *that* jab too.

258

His next move happened so quickly that I didn't even realize he'd done anything until I was hitting the padded floor, falling flat on my back. And then he was on top of me, wrists pinned up by my head, legs caught between his, and his head far enough back that my "signature" headbutt was out of range.

There wasn't shit I could do.

"You know, I'd be pretty pissed at your attempt at a cheap shot... if I wasn't so fucking proud," he said, but made no moves to let me up. "I told you to do whatever it took. Good job."

I let out a huff. "You're up there, I'm down here. How is that a good job?"

He grinned. "Monica... I have *no* problem letting you be on top. Just say the word."

"Let me on top."

"Cool."

"Ahhh!" I squealed, closing my eyes as he easily flipped us over so that he was the one on his back, leaving me to fall naturally into a position where I was straddling him.

"Yeah. This is much, much better," he teased, hooking his hands behind his head as he grinned up at me. "Do your worst. I can take it."

*Ugh!*

I couldn't keep a smile from forming on my face, so I shook my head. "Whatever. The moment has passed."

"Ah, don't tell me you're mad at me now. What did I do?"

"What did you do?" I sucked my teeth, then twisted to awkwardly pick up one of the pool noodles between my gloves, pressing tight to hold it firm enough to wack him upside the head a few times, like he'd done to me. "Not fun, is it?"

"That? No. But the way you're rocking your hips to hit me...*goddamn*," he grunted. "*That*, you're going to have to stop."

I narrowed my eyes and then pushed backward, landing so that I was right on top of his dick. And rocked again. "What? *That*? What are you going to do if I don't stop?"

"*Why*," he asked, easily sitting up, with me still planted in his lap, "Are you messing with me, knowing you're... confused?"

"Am I?"

"Aren't you?" he countered, meeting my gaze with a stare so intense I had to look away.

"Can you take these off for me?" I held up my gloved hands with my eyes still averted, and he undid them without a word, tossing them onto the mat beside us. "What?" I asked, finally giving him my attention again, when I could still feel him looking at me. "You have something you need to say?"

"*Need* to say? No. *Want* to say?... maybe."

"That's not a *maybe* kind of question," I told him, trying my best to remain unaffected by the feeling of him between my legs. That was the problem with teasing a man, you ran the risk of getting yourself hot and bothered. Even with the layers of our clothes, it was prominent – thick, and hard, and bringing back memories that made me involuntarily clench.

The grin he gave me made it clear that he'd felt it.

"How is that for you to decide?"

I scoffed. "Maybe because *I* asked the question."

His eyebrows went up. "Oh. I guess that makes sense."

"What was it that you wanted to say?" I asked, trying to bring him back to what he was clearly attempting to deflect.

The glitter of amusement left his eyes, replaced by... something else, as he shrugged. "I was just... wondering where you were, mentally, with all of this. With everything. Trying to get a gauge on how you're feeling. You haven't said much."

"Excuse me? I feel like talking is all I've been doing."

"Not about... *you*. We've talked about the shit that's been happening, talked about me, talked about Kay, talked about our friendship, and so on, but... there hasn't been much about *you*. Are *you* okay?"

Maybe I was just still a little sensitive from my conversation with Blake earlier, and then getting hit with that goddamn noodle a million times. Or maybe my emotions weren't buried as deeply as I thought.

Whatever it was, that question brought hot, immediate tears to the backs of my eyes, and I blinked hard, trying to clear them away.

"Um...why do you ask? Do I seem like I'm not okay?"

"Do I seem like I give a fuck what you *seem* like? Cause I don't. I asked if you *are* okay, not if you *seem* to be."

I let out a huff. "Well. Um..." I shrugged. "Honestly, not really. I have someone trying to destroy my company, and maybe kill me, and I don't know who I can trust, and my husband is dead, and I can't sleep in my own bed, and... I mean... I'm managing. But I... no. I don't think I'm okay."

Those last words came out in a rush, each one tumbling over the next as I tried to hold back inevitable tears. Embarrassing tears, that I tried to hide by removing myself from Wick's lap, to get away, but I was barely off of him before he pulled me back, closing me up in his arms.

It felt just as I'd imagined.

All those nights he'd talked me through my tears about my husband, I'd dreamt about this. That should have been when I knew I was in trouble, that I was taking it too seriously, that I was too invested. Fantasizing about sex was one thing – fantasizing about being held, being comforted... that was a whole other.

Instead of holding back, I let loose, sobbing into his shoulder to release all the tears I'd stored up in the time that had passed since I swore I wouldn't cry about any of this again. It had been completely random, a promise I'd made myself in an attempt to be strong.

Being "strong" hadn't helped.

At all.

For these few moments at least, accepting my own vulnerability was... *relieving.*

Wick didn't say a word. He just held me, letting me bury my face in his neck as my tears soaked his shoulder. When they subsided, he eased me backward, so he could see my face. He used his thumbs to clear the residual moisture from my cheeks, and I didn't even bother trying not to smile when he leaned in, kissing me on one cheek, then the other, before he brought his lips to mine.

I closed my eyes, letting myself get lost in the soft pressure, feeling like it was exactly what I needed. An instinctive moan left my throat as he left a gentle nip at one corner of my mouth, and then the other.

"I know you're tired," he said, in his rich, soothing tone. "Let's get you home."

I wanted to protest, but he was right – I was exhausted. I climbed off his lap and then let him help me to my feet before following him to that table to spray and wipe down all the gear we'd used, and put it all away.

When we were done, I hesitated. And he must have caught whatever vibe I was putting off, because he stopped too, looking down like he was waiting for me to speak. But… I didn't have anything to say. Not with words, at least. I reached up, grabbing two handfuls from the front of his shirt to bring his mouth down to mine.

We were definitely on the same page. Because no sooner than our lips had touched, he was grabbing me by the hips to ease me backward, then picking me up to seat me on that table. He stepped between my legs, bringing his hands to my face to keep me where he wanted me as he dipped his tongue into my mouth, tasting and exploring.

"*Mmm.* Pull your pants down," I moaned, closing my eyes and letting my head fall back to give him better access as he trailed kisses down my neck.

I shivered at the sensation of his laughter against my skin as he came back up to my ear. "No protection on me, gorgeous."

"I couldn't have your babies if I was trying, handsome. And no one but you has touched me in two years, and I'm pretty sure you've done full background checks on any booty calls. We don't need it," I told him, with my fingers still wrapped in his shirt. "*Pull your pants down.*"

262

His hands went to his waistband, and my hands went to mine. In just a few seconds, we were both partially disrobed, just enough to make the connection we needed to make.

Yes.

*Needed.*

I bit down on my lip, relishing the slow, delicious friction as he sank into me, then grabbed me by the thighs, hiking my legs around his waist. He leaned in, capturing my mouth with his as he planted his hands on either side of me and pressed in.

"*Goddamn*," he grunted, then sucked in a breath before he locked eyes with me. My mouth fell open, but I didn't drop my gaze – I was spellbound by the intensity in his eyes as he deliberately, meticulously stroked me, burrowing so deep that it held an edge of gratifying pain.

So, *so* good.

Good enough to forget everything *except* how good he felt, with his tongue in my mouth and his hand up my shirt, cupping my breast and squeezing my nipple, and his dick buried to the brink. I dropped my hands to his ass, pressing my nails into his firm glutes, encouraging him to go deeper, if possible, and *goddamn*, it was.

I didn't give a shit who heard – I let out a gasp that was exactly as loud as my body wanted it to be, followed shortly by a steadily streaming chorus of his name.

"Ah, *fuck*," he growled into my mouth, and then kissed me harder, cutting off my ability to make a sound, or hell – do *anything* – with the notable exception of taking everything he was giving me.

And he was giving me *plenty*.

Soon, the training room was filled with the distinctive sounds of our connection – our shared moans, the creaking legs of the table, and the loud, sensual *smack, smack, smack* of skin on skin as he stroked me faster.

Deeper.

Harder.

Until I couldn't take it anymore, and he couldn't either, slamming into me with one last growl as he emptied himself into me, and I clenched around him.

We stayed connected for several moments, panting together until our hearts slowed back to a normal pace, and we could breathe. I glanced down, really noticing for the first time that I hadn't even gotten my yoga pants and panties all the way off – they were still halfway on one leg, twisted and dangling around my foot.

Wick followed my gaze, and chuckled, though he had no room for a laugh at my expense, not with his sweats and boxers still caught around his knees.

I closed my eyes as he kissed me again, suddenly. He pressed his forehead to mine, then carefully slid out of me.

"I'm guessing you made it past that confusion, huh?" he asked, bending to pull his pants back up around his waist. I started to reach for my own, but he stopped me, grabbing the unoccupied pant leg to untwist them for me, and then pull both sides up over my feet.

"Thanks," I said, as he helped me down from the table, so I could pull my pants up all the way. "And… Somewhat."

"Anything I can do to turn that "somewhat" into a "completely"?" he asked, and I smiled as I looked up at him, right into his handsome face.

"Don't worry," I told him. "You're already doing it."

# SIXTEEN

"Is this okay?"

*Why is that even a question?*

My eyelids were clenched shut, face screwed up, goddamn toes curled – okay, maybe that was why she'd asked. But, yes, it was okay. It was so, so, *so* much more than okay. She had me in her mouth, slurping and sucking and gagging, and I could not be *any* fucking better.

To answer her question though, I grunted a *fuck yes* that made her stop running her tongue around the head, teasing me, just long enough to grin before she swallowed me again.

She'd caught me coming out of the shower and insisted on this. Insisted that her "confusion" was being rapidly replaced with "clarity", and I didn't catch any emotional undercurrents that made me argue with that. If she was down, then so was I, *hell yes.*

But then... she'd apologized before she started.

*"I haven't done this in a pretty long time,"* she warned, right before she had me moaning, groaning, ready and willing to scream like a little bitch, because her mouth felt *just that damn good.* And if her personality, intellect, business acumen, humor, beauty, body, and the

glory of her pussy hadn't been enough to persuade me that Kellen was King Dumb-ass for letting her go...

*This* had me far – *far* – past convinced.

I wasn't *trying* to choke her, but shit... I lost the battle to *not* bury my hands in her hair, keeping her in place as I drove up into her mouth, into her throat. And she... *goddamn*... she took it in stride, moaning and swallowing me deeper and just... continuing to be perfect.

It was just about time to warn her of an impending eruption when she pulled completely away, wiping her mouth with the back of her hand before her eyes landed on me in a sexy, mischievous grin. She held her audience – me – completely captive as she slinked across the bed, climbing over me, straddling me, then holding my dick exactly where she wanted it before she sank down.

*Heaven.*

That was what this had to be, having Monica on top of me, hips moving in slow circles that didn't skip a beat as she raised her hands to remove the band from the ponytail I'd ruined. Her golden-streaked hair fell around her shoulders like a mane, making her look even wilder, even sexier than she already did.

I hadn't even known that shit was possible.

I remembered, some time ago, having to coax her into showing me her body. Not because she didn't *want* to, or didn't like it, but because she was afraid *I* wouldn't like it – a lie from the pits of hell, based on bullshit put in her head by her husband.

And now here she was, completely nude, the room completely lit, grinding on top of me like she was having the time of her life.

I really, *really* hoped she was, because that would make two of us. If that first night had been good enough to have me ready to sniff behind her like a greedy puppy, then *this* – feeling her, again, with *nothing* between us – I... might be in trouble. I tried to keep telling myself that it was just sex – damn good sex, at that – because she hadn't given me any indication that it was more than that.

The *problem* was, I'd had good sex – damn good sex, at that – with my fair share of other women over my forty-something years, and I

266

couldn't say that it had ever been like *this*. Hell, even when Kay's mother, Lisa, had my young ass sprung, I couldn't ever remember thinking long-term. Like… *long*, long term.

But with Monica, I'd found myself, more than once, wondering exactly what I needed to do in order to not mess this up, how to make sure she remained in my life, in this capacity, and more, for a long ass time.

The shit felt so right that it *had* to be wrong… right?

I blinked away those pesky thoughts, shifting my focus back to the present – Monica had reached behind her, between my legs, cupping and massaging my balls, which didn't give me much choice.

*"Trying to kill me,"* I muttered, making her laugh – a sound that hit me right in the chest before I turned it into a moan with my hand between *her* legs, teasing her clit. She whimpered, rhythm broken as I pressed harder with my thumb, then moved to pinch her swollen, sensitive bud between my thumb and forefinger.

*"Ahhh,"* she moaned, as I moved my fingers back and forth, using her distracted state to sit up.

With one hand still between her legs, I fisted the other in her hair again, pulling her lips to mine. I wasted no time dipping my tongue into the sweetness of her mouth, savoring her as she started moving again. I left her clit to give my attention to her soft, full breasts, filling both hands, to cup and squeeze before I brought my fingers to her hardened nipples.

I pulled back, just enough to cover her lips, chin, neck, and collarbone with soft kisses as I made my way down to her breasts. Her breath started coming in soft gasps and whimpers as I nipped along the outline of her light brown areolas, following each nibble with a soothing lap from my tongue. Her knees clenched against me, fingers went to my shoulders, digging in for leverage as she kept riding me, struggling not to get overwhelmed with pleasure.

A flash of annoyance washed over me as my doorbell rang, and Monica's hips stopped moving.

"*Mnn-Mnn*," I grunted, around a mouthful of her nipple. "Don't stop."

Whoever it was, they could wait. I didn't do drop-in guests, and I *damn* sure hadn't invited anyone to come over. After the way our trip to the gym had ended earlier, I'd hoped that once we made it back to the house, my night would go *exactly* like this. I had no plans of letting someone interrupt it.

I sucked her nipple, hard, and Monica's head fell back as she moaned. The other nipple, I pinched, and she moaned even louder. From there, I fell into a rhythm, spurred on by my name starting to spill from her lips. A second doorbell ring went unanswered, and I *honestly* didn't give a single fuck.

We were having a moment.

I felt the tension building in her body, especially once I returned my free hand between her legs, destroying any semblance of control she had over her movements. The ringing doorbell changed to a pounding knock, and I still didn't care, because Monica was getting loud, and her thighs were shaking, and she was just *dripping* wet, and those three things were infinitely more important than whoever was at the door.

A familiar tingle started in my groin as Monica gave up on moving up and down, opting instead to sink as far down as she could, and keeping me there as she ground in blissful, torturous circles, and I matched those circles with my thumb on her clit. Suddenly, she went rigid, and her body constricted around me, milking me until the eruption she'd started with her mouth finally came.

After that, we *both* collapsed, and then laughed at the insistent, alternating ring of the doorbell and knocking at the door.

"*Goddamn*, I can't afterglow in peace?" I asked out loud.

Monica laughed as she pulled herself up. "I'm going to get in the shower while you handle that," she said. "And then… can we talk about dinner? Between the sparring and the sex, I've worked up an appetite."

"My dinner is already here," I told her, reaching to grab her as she stood, holding her long enough to bite her on the ass cheek before she wiggled away, squealing.

268

"Get the door," she said, her tone firm but her eyes sparkling with happiness as she gestured toward the front of the house. Without saying anything aloud, I mentally filed the way she looked right now – completely content and well fucked – into my favorite things.

I was about to have a bad ass attitude with whoever was at the door for making me have to look away.

I didn't even bother trying to suppress my annoyance as I threw on a tee shirt and sweats, and I took my damn time getting to the door. I was already there by the time I thought about the camera feed connected to my phone – I could've just glanced at it to see who my insistent uninvited visitor was, but, again... I was there now.

The lights around the front door were connected to a motion detector, so I could clearly see Harrison and Savannah, my neighbors, on my front porch. My eyes narrowed.

*What the hell do* they *want?*

A little concerned now – not about *them* doing anything. I knew Savannah from my CIA days, knew she was solid – about what would bring them to my door so late, I went ahead and pulled it open, and was met immediately by Harrison's scowl.

"It's about goddamn time. You know how long we've been waiting out here?"

"You know what you almost interrupted?" I shot right back – a response that he immediately caught on to, and his expression changed from annoyance to understanding. "What is so important?" I asked, and Harrison's scowl came back as he bent to snatch a wriggling, human-sized bundle I hadn't noticed from the ground beside him.

"Found this motherfucker creeping around the woods behind the houses. He set off our motion alarms, but he says he's looking for your special guest."

My eyes narrowed as Savi reached up, pulling off the hood they'd put on the intruder's head.

*Asher.*

His eyes went wide at the – admittedly – sadistic smile that spread across my face. "Well. I can't say I'm surprised to see you at all.

Bring him in," I told Harrison, stepping back to let them through. Savi followed shortly behind, and I closed and locked the door as they took them into the kitchen, forcing his bound form into a chair. As I watched, they made quick work of switching his bindings so that he was immobile, trussed to the legs and back of the chair.

Without removing the gag they'd secured around his mouth, I bent to look him directly in the eyes. "Mr. Ross. Where have you been, bruh?" I asked, then pulled a chair in front of him to sit down. "You've been a hard man to find, which is interesting to me. You see… I think you're a fucking creep, at best. Murderer at worst. But I'm a fair man. I don't have anything that's not circumstantial, so I'm going to give you an opportunity to explain yourself. We're going to take your gag off, and me and you are going to have a conversation. Okay?"

There was already a nasty purple bruise spreading around his eye – courtesy of Savi, more than likely – making him look completely pitiful as he nodded. I motioned for her to remove the restraint from his mouth, and as soon as it was gone, he started flexing his lips and jaw, undoubtedly trying to restore feeling to both.

"Let's get started. Where is Amanda Gordon?"

"I don't know."

"That's a lie. *Don't fucking lie*," I warned, getting right in his face and grabbing the back of his head. "*Do. Not. Fucking. Lie.* Okay?"

"I'm not lying!"

I narrowed my eyes. "Okay. I see you want to play games." I got up from my chair, going to the knife block on the counter to grab the kitchen shears from the middle. I held them up in his face. "Every lie is gonna cost you a finger, and motherfucker, *I don't bluff.*" I went around behind him, opening the shears and pulling one of his pinkies between them. "Okay… let's try again, from a different direction. What the fuck are you doing here? How did you find this house?"

"Blake Hollis," he answered immediately, visibly shaking now that I'd introduced the possibility of real, lasting bodily harm. "I… she had lunch today, with Monica. I've been… taking turns following her friends. I knew one of them would see her eventually. And then I followed the two of you to the gym, and then back to this neighborhood. I couldn't get in though. Didn't know which house."

I let go of my grip on his fingers and straightened my stance, staring down at him. "Okay. Keep that up, with all the detail. Why are you trying to get to Monica?"

"Because I care about her! I just wanted to make sure she was okay. That she was safe. I heard about what happened to her assistant, and wanted to know if she was being taken care of."

I frowned. "She's being taken care of *just* fine."

Asher looked up, and something in his expression changed. I watched the facial tics spread, from fearful anxiety to rage. "You... you *smell* like her. *Why do you smell like her?!*" he screamed at me, fighting against his bindings. "Did you *touch* her?! You *touched her* didn't you?! I'll kill you if you touched her!"

I stepped back, exchanging looks between Savi and Harrison, who smirked at right around the same time I did. "Untie this motherfucker," I said. "I want to see him back this shit up."

"Chad... come on," Savi said, pushing out a heavy sigh. "You know he doesn't know what he's getting into."

I shook my head. "Nah, he came sneaking around here "looking for Monica", let's see what he planned to do. He wants to be bold, let his ass be bold."

"So you *did* touch her?" Asher asked, obviously stuck on that, and sounding damn near on the verge of tears.

Savi glared at me, communicating the obvious that maybe ol' boy was unstable, but that didn't keep me from wanting to kick his ass.

"Not your business," I growled at him, moving to stand in front again. "You said you "*heard*" what happened to Monica's assistant. Are you claiming you weren't behind that shit? Cause I find it mighty coincidental that her boyfriend, who we can't seem to find, has your middle name, and your same initials."

"I don't know her," he claimed. "Don't know what you're talking about. *Where is Monica?!*"

"You think I'm bluffing," I said, grabbing the scissors again, and rounding the back of his chair to snatch his finger. "Not gonna warn you again – *why did you beat Kim up?*"

"I didn't!"

I closed the shears, and Asher screamed so loud that he *almost* drowned out the sound of a new voice in the kitchen.

"*What the hell is going on?!*"

Luckily for Asher, I'd lost some of the ruthlessness from my days in the CIA – instead of snapping the shears closed, which could've taken his finger off at the bone, he had a fairly superficial cut. Nothing to be crying about like a fucking wimp, but here we were.

"Asher?!" Monica cried, when no one said anything. "What are you doing here? Why is he tied up?" she asked, directing that question at me. "Did you *cut* him?!"

I frowned. "I mean… a *little*. Not that bad. He'll need like ten stitches tops. Maybe twelve."

"A little?!" she scowled at me, then turned her attention to Asher. "Are you okay?"

He pulled away when she tried to touch him. "You screwed this motherfucker, didn't you? We just buried my best friend, and you're already screwing someone else?"

Monica took a step back, turning her scornful look onto him. "I fail to see how that has *anything* to do with you, Ash. Especially when you tried to kiss me!"

*Wait a fucking minute!*

"I apologized! And I told myself I would give you time to grieve, only to find out that you're already—"

"You can stop right there, because you don't know anything about what I'm *already* doing," Monica snapped, and *then* looked to me for confirmation. I shook my head, acknowledging that I hadn't even been the one to bring up that line of conversation. "How about you tell me what you're doing here!"

"I'm *bleeding*," he whined, and me, Harrison and Savi all rolled our eyes.

272

"I've had worse paper cuts," Savi muttered. "You're getting soft, Wick. Fifteen years ago, he'd be down to one finger by now."

"Fatherhood. Got a heart now, I can't help it," I complained, which only made Monica scowl at me harder.

"We'll get bandages for you," she told Asher, being nicer than he deserved, when all I was thinking about was making him clean up his own damned blood from my travertine floor. "And untie you. *Why* is he tied up, and being tortured?!"

"If I was going to torture him, for real, we'd be in the basement, where it's soundproof. This is… this is just a little interrogation."

She propped her hands on her hips, looking mad as hell and sexy as hell, even in yoga pants and the BSU hoodie she must've thrown on after her shower. "What gives you the right to hold and interrogate someone?!"

"The fact that he was sneaking around on our private property, trespassing, just adding to the list of reasons I don't trust this creepy motherfucker," I answered. I knew I hadn't just been imaging things after lunch – I knew something felt off, like we were being watched, but I hadn't seen anything that confirmed my suspicion. Now I knew – this motherfucker had been lurking around. "And I'm not untying him until we get some damn answers."

"I don't know anything about what you're talking about," Ash whimpered, sounding faint, like he was about to die of that little wound that was already starting to clot.

His speaking up made Monica turn her attention back to him. "But you do know *something*, Ash. I feel like you know more than you're telling about Amanda, and I've been trying to get in contact with you about it. You haven't been responding to my texts or calls. Why?"

"Just busy, I swear. I swear, Monica."

"Too busy to return a text or call, but you can find time to stalk me to find out where I am?! That doesn't make sense, Asher! Nor does it make sense that you never mentioned you and Amanda wanting to move here. And why the *hell* are you still paying her phone bill? To throw me off? To make me think she's still alive?!"

"To hear her voice!" Asher blubbered, breaking down into tears. "She left the phone, when she left. I'd always paid the bill for her, since college. Even though we broke up. I… I call to hear her voicemail message sometimes."

*Creepy motherfucker.*

"Where is she, Ash?" Monica said, her tone much softer than before, letting me know she was actually falling for this bullshit. "Is Amanda alive?"

"I don't know. I don't *know*," he insisted, and Monica lifted her eyes to mine.

"What about Kim?" I asked him, still holding those shears, and ready to finish the job with his pinky. "How are you involved with her?"

"I'm not, I swear." He shook his head. "I don't know her."

Immediately, Monica raised her hands, motioning for me not to touch him. "Asher, you know that's a lie. You met her when you toured the company before I was even in the building I'm in now. And over the years, you've seen her, talked to her, at least a half-dozen times. Please… don't lie to me."

"Okay, we've met, but I don't… I don't know her like that. I haven't seen her, I swear. Please, I need to go to a hospital."

"I don't believe a word out of this motherfucker's mouth," I said, grabbing his hand and positioning my scissors again, ready to finish the job. "He's going to tell us what he knows, one way or another."

"*I don't know anything! I don't know anything!*" Asher started screaming, fighting against his restraints so hard that the chair bucked, at the same time that Monica came at me, trying to get me to stop, and next thing I knew… homeboy's pinky finger was on the floor.

"Hey… this shit *isn't* my fault," I said, as the whole room went silent – Monica and Asher in shock, Harrison and Savannah in thinly veiled amusement, turning away, trying not laugh.

"What the *fuck?!*" Monica screamed at me, at the same time Asher started yelling his head off again.

274

"It was an accident! I was just trying to scare him, but you tried to grab me, and his dumb ass moved the chair, and… snip snip. My bad!"

"*Your bad*?!" Asher and Monica asked, in unison, just before Asher's head tipped to the side, passed out from either fear, pain, or blood loss.

Always cool under pressure, Savannah shook her as she stepped past me, going for the fully stocked first aid kit she knew I kept under the kitchen sink. "I got it. Somebody pick his finger up, and put it on ice. Harrison, go next door and get my bag. You cut through the joint, right? Not the bone?" she asked, and I shook my head.

"Not the bone, I would've had to snap."

She nodded. "Good. Get your lady out of here and talk to her before she passes out too."

Knowing Savannah was right, I turned around to do just that after dropping the shears down on the counter, but Monica immediately shied away, staring in disgust at my hands.

They were covered in blood.

I turned to the sink to wash them, but when I looked back, Monica was gone, and there was only Asher left in the kitchen, with Savi bent behind him, carefully cleaning his wound. I didn't have the medical training that she did, so I left her to it to figure out where Monica had gone.

"What the *fuck* was that?!" her voice sounded, as soon as I turned into the foyer, where she was walking back and forth. "Tell me what is going on!"

I grabbed her by the shoulders to stop her pacing, turning her to face me. "I know that probably looked like a really bad—"

"Probably?! *Probably*?! You just *cut his finger off!* With fucking… kitchen shears, like you were deboning a chicken! *Oh my God!*"

"It's really *not* that big of—"

"Oh don't you *dare!*" she hissed. "Not a big deal?!" She shook her head, then took a deep breath in what seemed like an attempt to calm her nerves. "I... so... you weren't exaggerating, about what you did for the CIA... were you?"

I lifted an eyebrow. "Monica... even if I'd cut his finger off on purpose – which I *didn't* – it would honestly be pretty low-level, on the list of things I've done."

She swallowed hard. "Right. I guess the CIA doesn't exactly hand out hangnails."

"No. They don't. So... what... you're scared of me now or something?"

Her eyes came up to mine, and I gave her the respect of not shifting my gaze, even though the way she was staring had me uncomfortable as hell until she finally answered. "No. I'm not. But... you have to understand if I don't really feel like I can trust my gut right now. I never thought Asher was capable of being involved in this, and yet... here we are."

"So you do think he was involved now?"

She shrugged. "I think it's fishy that he's been out of touch since I left the hospital, and then pops up here. And I think he's lying."

"About Amanda?"

"About Kim," she said, wrapping her arms around herself like she was cold, as Harrison came back through with Savannah's medical bag. "He's talked to Kim. Flirted with her. I tried to set them up on a date, but the timing didn't work out, and then it would've been long distance too."

"Like a long-distance boyfriend?" I asked, and Monica immediately picked up on my allusion to Asher being Kim's mystery boyfriend.

She shook her head. "Honestly? I don't know anymore. Not at this point. I wanted to think that one of them would have told me there was something going on, but he and Amanda were keeping secrets too."

"Asher is the common denominator. Who knows what he was telling Kim? *He* could be the reason she turned on you. Hell, who knows what lies he was feeding Amanda? Maybe she *is* alive, and is just avoiding you because of something he said?"

276

Something flashed across Monica's face, but she cleared her expression so fast I got the impression she didn't intend to tell me. But at this point, it was time out for secrets.

"Monica, come on," I urged. "You know something, don't you? Tell me."

She huffed. "It's not... It's not like *that*, it's just... when I talked to Amanda's aunt, I got the impression that Amanda thought there might be something going on between me and Asher. But I have *no* idea why she would think that."

"Because you have no idea what he was really telling her."

"You're right," Monica said, looking defeated. "And Amanda was always sort of troubled... her aunt was the only real family she had, so she really clung to me, and to Asher. She hasn't talked to me, hasn't talked to her aunt, so that leaves Asher. And... I feel like he has to know more than he's saying."

"Okay then so let's make his ass say it." I motioned for her to follow me back to the kitchen, where we found Savannah wearing some type of magnifying glasses while she reattached Asher's pinky finger on a makeshift surgical table, while he was still bound. "He awake?" I asked, and Harrison was the one to answer, as Savi kept working.

"Yeah, but loopy. She gave him a sedative, and a local anesthetic.

I nodded. "Cool. That means he can still answer questions. Monica... come on."

Her eyes went wide at my mention of her. "Me? I don't—"

"He's most likely to respond to you, and I think you know the right questions to ask. You know details, history, that I don't. I know this is something you can do."

She didn't appear to be thrilled about it, but she stepped forward anyway, taking the hand I offered to lead her into a chair in front of Asher. As soon as she was seated, he opened his eyes, blinking until he focused on her.

"Monica..." he groaned, and she cringed a little before she responded.

"I'm here, Asher. But I... I have some questions, okay? You have to answer them before these people will be willing to let you go. Okay? Ash... I need you to tell me what was going on with you and Amanda, before she left? I'm not blaming you, okay? I just want to know what happened to my friend."

He let out what sounded like a cough, but quickly devolved into a weak laugh. "She... she wasn't your friend," he said, his words slurring as a result of the sedative. "She h-*hated* you. Thought you were everything wrong with her life. No-not... not your friend."

"Hated *me*?" Monica asked, incredulous. "Ash, that's absurd. What would you think that?"

"You were—... weren't supposed to be there. Be here. She hated you because she hated you. Why don't you unna-un-understand?"

"Because you're not making sense!" Monica snapped, clearly getting annoyed. "First Sheila, and now you. Stop talking in riddles!"

Asher's head rolled back. "You talked to Sh... Sheila? She knows. She knows everything. Everything. She kept Amanda."

"This is..." Monica sighed. "This is ridiculous. Can you... could you give him something to make him more lucid?" she asked Savannah, you shook her head, not taking her eyes off her work.

"No. I need him to be still."

Frustrated, Monica looked at me, shaking her head. "This is useless."

"Ask him about Kim."

"But he's—"

"Just *ask*."

She scoffed, but turned back to Asher, looking him in the face. "Tell me about Kim. How are you involved with her? Are the two of you dating."

Asher's eyes closed, and it seemed like pulling them open again was a struggle. "No.... No. It was her fault that.... Her fault they hurt you."

"Her fault that *who* hurt me?"

278

"The…. The break-in. She betrayed you. I…. I never would've done that. But you… and her… and her…. You're all the same. Ungrateful… *bitch*," he spat, with more energy and vigor than any other words he'd said, and the only thing that kept me from lunging at him was the hand that Monica held up, wordlessly urging me to chill.

"Ungrateful bitch," she repeated. "Me? You're talking about me, Ash?"

His face crumpled, but no tears came this time. "I *loved* you… you don't understand. I was…. Always the one keeping you safe… taking care of you. I exposed Kellen and you… didn't even care. You stayed, but it was never supposed to be him."

"Explain, Ash. You say I don't understand, so explain."

"It was *never* supposed to be him. Never. From the start. He wasn't even supposed to be at work that day. Should've been me."

Monica frowned. "Wait… *wasn't supposed to be at work…* Asher, are you talking about the day Kellen and I met? You're the one whose shift he took over?"

"He… just wanted to fuck you. That was it. And you let him."

"Kellen and I were dating for nearly a year before I had sex with him. I was a virgin, you creepy bastard," Monica hissed, which only made Asher laugh.

"He wasn't. No. He wasn't. He was screwing half the campus behind your back. And… screwing Amanda."

"What?" Monica's eyes went wide. "*What*? What the fuck did you just say?!" she asked, snatching him by the collar when he didn't respond, and wouldn't open his eyes.

"*Hey!*" Savannah shouted. "This is delicate work, I can't have you snatching him around!"

"He needs to answer me! Wake up!" Monica screamed, right in his face, just before she smacked him with so much force that it sent his head lolling uselessly on his neck.

"He can't wake up if you knock him out," I told her, grabbing her around the waist to pull her away, only to have her employ – well, attempt at least – one of the defenses I'd taught her, to get out of this very situation. Luckily for me – and probably Asher – I was quick enough to readjust, which only made her angrier.

But I couldn't let her at him.

Enough had happened already that would be hard as hell to explain, but at least Harrison, Savi and I had the connections to possibly explain it away. Monica didn't have those kinds of resources, and I wasn't about to allow her to be further implicated, even if I empathized with her pain.

I didn't let her go until we were back upstairs, and I was between her and the door. As soon as she was loose, she went right back to pacing like she had in the hall.

"Tell me I didn't hear that right," she said, in a desperate tone that made my chest hurt. "Tell me that he didn't say that Kellen was… no. There's *no* fucking way. They didn't even live here!"

"Maybe he meant before… like back when you guys were in school, or lived closer?" I supplied, about two seconds before it occurred to me that it wasn't helpful. But Monica had already deflated, hanging her head as she scrubbed her hands over her face.

"Yeah," she nodded. "You're probably right. Hell, maybe that's why she hated me? Maybe she wanted Kellen all along. And Asher wanted me. So… those two were just a match made in hell from the start. I feel… so fucking *stupid* right now."

"It's not your fau—"

"How can it not be?!" she asked, before I could even finish. "I have been *surrounded* by snakes, for damn near eighteen years! And it just… it doesn't make sense."

"Monica… liars are very good at what they do – especially when it comes to someone like you, who… just wants to see the best in people she cares about. It's not your fault that they chose to take advantage of you."

She shook her head. "You keep trying to make that point, but what it all boils down to is me being stupid. That's it. Bottom line. I devoted so much time and energy into dreaming up and building my company that I didn't even see the shit developing right underneath my nose. And it turns out, with all the attention I was giving it, it wasn't enough for me to see that my right hand was sabotaging me. So... please stop saying this isn't my fault. Because this time... that doesn't hold up to scrutiny. I know you're just trying to make me feel better, but... please."

"Fine. I'll stop saying that, and instead I'll just ask... what *will* make this better? Tell me how to fix, and I will."

"I just want to know why this is happening to me. What did I do, and who did I do it to, that my karma for it is *this* kind of pain."

I gave her a single nod. "Understood."

She stared at me for a moment, and I wondered if she was thinking the same thing as me – that solving this shit had been the goal from the beginning, and nothing seemed to bring us any closer. It was easy for me to pledge and promise answers, but actually *getting* those answers was proving to be problematic beyond belief. But... somebody knew something they weren't telling. I had to believe it would come out eventually, and bring us to where we needed to be.

"I think I'm going to take a bath," she said, and I nodded again.

"You can use mine, if you'd like. It's bigger. Got all the cool jets and stuff."

That *almost* brought a smile to her face, and she stepped in, closing the distance between us. When she anchored herself with her hands on my biceps, pushing up on her toes, I met her halfway for a soft, lingering kiss.

"I *would* like that," she told me. "Thank you."

"You're welcome."

After that, I left her to it, going back downstairs to find Savi cleaning the kitchen up. Asher and Harrison were gone.

"You got him finished up?" I asked her, and she nodded as she looked up from the pile of bloody paper towels on the floor.

"Yep," she told me through her surgical mask. "And gave him a little something that will make the details of tonight pretty fuzzy, *if* he decides to go to the police. I know you probably wanted to question him more, but we both know..."

I nodded. "Yeah. He's told us all he will without more… extreme measures. And I wasn't kidding about not having the stomach for it now."

"I know," Savi said, and I didn't have to see her mouth to know she was smiling. "That's why Harrison and I stayed to help."

I sucked my teeth. "Come on, don't play me like that. You're a mother now!"

"Who held my bloody, messy babies right after birth, and dealt with literal shit of all colors and textures, and more kinds of vomit than you want to hear about. I'm not squeamish. You didn't get Kay until she was older."

"I… you raise a fair point, Sav."

"Oh, I know. Harrison is taking tonight's guest back to his car, and wiping everything down. We already cloned the cell phone we found on him. I'll get you those files."

"Thank you, Savi."

"Mmhmm. Just know you owe me one. You're lucky my babies are with their grandparents right now, but as soon as they get back, my husband and I are doing date night. Guess who's babysitting?"

I cringed – Savannah's kids were adorable little energetic bundles of *terror*. "Uncle Chad from next door?"

"Damn right. How is Monica?"

"Eh… as you'd expect."

Savi nodded. "Right. Do you need help? Between Inez and I…"

"Not yet," I answered quickly, shaking my head. Between her and Inez, heads might roll, and I wasn't ready for that yet. "I have a few avenues that I hadn't taken before… things I was hesitant to do, but now… might be time to go blackhat, and get this figured out."

"Just don't get caught."

I plucked a surgical mask from Savi's open bag, then joined her on the floor to get Asher's blood out of my tile.

"I never do."

# SEVENTEEN

"Your boyfriend?" Bhavna leaned in, taking a break from snatching my eyebrow hairs from my face just long enough to subtly cast a glance in Wick's direction before she continued.

"No," I told her. "Just... um... a special friend."

She lifted a perfectly groomed brow at me, and smiled. "My dear, I have never seen a woman's "special friend" come and sit in the room while she got her *yoni* waxed. Only lovers."

"Okay but can you mind your business, Mrs. Patel?" I asked, even though I laughed before I had to go still again for her to finish. This was yet another trip out of the house I'd had to negotiate for, but it was necessary. My monthly grooming kept me feeling human, and now that I had someone actually looking at me again, it was even more important.

"Do not get angry with me, Monica, I am just asking questions. You are so much more radiant now than the last time I see you, I have to ask. I want to know the secret, even though I already know *your* secret?" she teased.

"And what's that Bhavna? What do you think you know?"

"I know that tall, handsome man is the reason you are glowing. Specifically, his *lingham*."

"Could you not?!" I asked, in a whisper-yell-laugh that made the subject of our conversation look up from whatever he was occupied with on his tablet.

"I have to tell the truth, Monica. You are done now."

Still giggling at our exchange, I sat up straight, looking in the mirror at my flawlessly shaped brows. "There is magic in that thread of yours Bhavna," I told her, then reached into my purse for enough crisp bills to pay for my services and a hefty tip. "As always, thank you my love."

"You are welcome. I see you again for brows in *three* weeks – not four. *Three.*"

"Is that shade, B? You trying to say I'm too much work when I wait the extra week?"

She grinned. "I have to tell the truth, Monica."

"Mmmhmm. I'll see you next time!"

With Wick in tow, I left the salon, feeling refreshed, and relaxed, and... way too cute for Wick to be blocking like he was. He was all over me, obviously feeling extra-protective since that thing with Asher two days ago, because his eyes wouldn't stop moving.

"This is a disaster waiting to happen," he muttered, repeating his ill feelings about coming to the luxury mall for what had to be the tenth time since we'd ventured out.

I stopped walking to face him. "Well, lucky for you, I'm done. I just need to pee before we get back in the car for that long ass drive back to your house. I'll be right back."

"Whoa, *hold up*," he insisted. He stepped in way before I could reach for the door of the bathroom we'd stopped in front of. "A public bathroom? You can't be serious."

"Well, my bladder sure is," I told him. "I'll just a be a second. And I don't want to hear about you coming in the *ladies'* room. There's no assassin waiting to get me while I pee."

"You don't know that."

284

Sucking my teeth, I stepped around him to open the door. "I guess I'll just have to take that chance."

He must've agreed about the lack of danger, because after a harsh sigh, he let me into the bathroom unimpeded. At first glance, the bathroom seemed empty – which wasn't uncommon at such a random time of the day, on a weekday. But I'd just reached for the door to one of the stalls when I heard a familiar voice, from a different one.

"Girl, I *knowwwwah!* I cannot wait to drop this fucking baby. Since his damn granny wants him so bad, she can have him."

*Crystal.*

I quickly surmised that she must be on the phone, since I couldn't hear the other side of the conversation. But what I *could* hear was enough to confirm what I already knew – the girl was trash.

"Bitch, you think I'm playing, and I'm not. I only got pregnant because I thought the nigga had money. But I guess I'm the one looking like boo boo the fool, getting pregnant by a mark."

*A mark...?*

"*Hellllll no!* Nigga didn't have shit but a debit card linked to his wife's account. She was the one with money. Hell, I should've let *her* get me pregnant. She deserved better than his corny ass. Can't believe I faked it as long as I did, but at least I got paid."

*Paid?*

"Byeeee," Crystal cackled. "I told you from the beginning I was getting paid to fuck him. The baby was supposed to be an *extra* come up, cause I thought I was dealing with Obama-level niggas. Now I'm out here fucking up my body for the same type of nigga I was dealing with on the streets. Can't stay off the damn toilet either."

Crystal laughed at whatever was said on the other end of the line. "No such thing as TMI hoe. But seriously – soon as I have this baby, the turn-up has to be... on some next level shit. Soon as my six weeks is up. Granny can have her replacement son, and I can move on. I don't even give a fuck about the money from the will anymore. I got paid for what I did, and I've got my eyes on bigger and better. Wifey bitch can do whatever she wants."

*Wifey bitch? Seriously?!*

"No, she's actually cute. Like... bad bitch status to be honest. And all he ever did was complain about her weight, like he don't realize big girls ain't with the bullshit anymore. Homegirl is a baddie. And his ass could barely get it up half the time. I wouldn't have been surprised if she really *was* fucking his old boss like he thought she was. He was *so* obsessed with what she was doing, and I swear it didn't seem like she was bothered. Until that day she threatened to kill his ass, and baby I don't blame her. I wouldn't let a nigga who could barely get his dick hard play me out either."

The toilet flushed, muffling her next words, shortly followed by the running water of the sink.

"Uh, no bitch!" I heard her laugh, as she tore off paper towels to dry her hands. "I always said if I was going to wreck homes, it was going to come with a price, and I was well-paid, okay? And now, I'm about to get his mama to pay me for this baby, then I'm moving somewhere sunny, bih."

The bathroom door clattered closed, and I stood there, reeling about what I'd just overheard. With all the other drama happening, it – strangely – had never even occurred to me that Crystal may have been paid to disrupt my relationship with Kellen.

But it made perfect sense.

And... it made me wickedly happy.

Kellen had been *so* convinced that she worshipped the ground he walked on, so to find out that her loyalty to him had been tied to a paycheck was delicious. And her long-term con, of getting Kellen's mother to pay her off to keep the grandson she wanted so damned bad she was willing to drop me?

*Ha!*

My opinion of Crystal was suddenly so much higher.

I hurriedly finished my business in the bathroom, damn near breaking my neck from trying not to fall into the toilet while I hovered over it. I was excited, finally feeling like maybe this was a useful lead, and I transferred that excitement to Wick when I left the bathroom. My

286

mouth was running at a hundred miles per minute all the way to his Tesla, and he pulled his tablet back out as soon as we climbed inside.

"Okay. Tell me what I'm looking for," he said, fingers poised over the screen, ready to type.

I blinked. "Um... Crystal's bank accounts. We need to know *who* paid her to go after Kellen. And maybe once we know that, some of these things will start connecting. Amanda's disappearance, Kellen stepping out... what was the catalyst?"

"Okay, let me start with the first thing – Crystal's bank account. Whoa... she has one-hundred eighty-thousand dollars and some change. And it looks like she has expensive ass tastes, too, because she started a lot higher... fifteen thousand dollars a month, dating back for the past two years. No payment since Kellen died."

"That's a lot of damn money just to screw Kellen."

Wick nodded. "Yeah, but it was more than just screwing him, right? You said yourself, it was like he was in love with this girl. Got her pregnant, was building a life. Whoever set this up, they wanted this to be insurmountable."

"Right," I said, processing his words, and trying to make them stick. "Can you see who that was?"

"Gimme a second," Wick muttered, fingers flying over the screen for several moments before he came to a stop. "Asher. Again."

That hit me like a blow to the chest. Even after all the drama of the other night, I'd been holding out hope that Asher would prove us wrong, that he really hadn't been a part of anything crazy, but at this point... those odds were nonexistent.

"At the house, the other night... he said he'd exposed Kellen, but you stayed. Maybe this is what he was talking about," Wick said, which made sense. He'd initially hired Crystal, probably planning to orchestrate me catching Kellen in the act with her. Only, I'd done that by accident anyway, and wound up deciding to stay.

It hadn't worked.

"Okay, so we answered that. We know Asher paid Crystal to play that role. But she mentioned something else... she mentioned

Kellen thinking that I was sleeping with his former boss, but that news is mind-blowing, to me. I've been around Brad Barker *maybe* seven or eight times in the years that Kellen was at *Barker Financial,* and never, *ever* alone."

"That may be true, but someone convinced Kellen that wasn't the case," Wick said, shrugging. "And you have to admit it makes sense. You told me on multiple occasions, that you felt like he hated you. I know you think you committed some horrible slight against him by not babying his grown ass after he lost his job, but that never quite felt right to me. But this... this does. I mean, think about it – Brad Barker is a major player in finance – hell, even *I* know his name. Now, if I'm Kellen, and I believe that you're sleeping with this guy, it's setting off all kinds of questions in my head. Including, "is this the reason no one will hire me?". Not only are you stepping out, you're playing with my money, and *those* are reasons to start hating somebody."

I pushed out a breath. "I guess it does make sense, but also... it doesn't. What would make Kellen even believe something like that? And if he did, why wouldn't he confront, or expose me?"

"That's... a great question. One I don't have an answer for really. Unless... maybe he was just biding his time. Kellen seems like he was a pretty calculating man, and he was being paid by someone at *Canvas* too. If he confronted you about Brad, that's it – the fun's over. But if he's working with *Canvas*, planning your demise, I could see that making him patient enough to kinda slowly whittle you down, and hit you with that last blow at the worst possible time."

"Right...," I murmured. "Someone else just got to him first. But I still wonder why he would even believe such a thing about me."

"This might have something to do with it," Wick spoke, bringing my attention to him. He leaned over the main console, pointing to something on the tablet screen. "You see this? When I looked at Kellen's email history before, I didn't go far enough back. But these right here? These are emails between Kellen and an encrypted account. Those attachments you see there? Screenshots, supposedly of texts between you and Brad."

"I have *never* exchanged texts with that man," I declared. But for all Wick – and apparently Kellen – knew, that was a lie, because those screenshots looked convincing. They looked *damning*, actually, since that was indeed my phone number.

"You don't even text like this," Wick said, leaning in more so that he could see the screen too. "The cadence is off. And this sexting is horrible," he laughed.

I cringed. "Yeah, it is. But Kellen and I didn't really text – we *lived* together at this time. So it's not like we went back and forth enough for him to pick up on that, like you did. Is there a way you figure out who sent these?"

"Not from my tablet. I need my wired connection. But even with that, there's honestly no telling. Finding the banking information is actually easier, believe it or not."

"Oh, wow. Well—"

My words were interrupted by the chime of a ringing phone, reverberating through the car. The console screen lit up, displaying that Wick was receiving an incoming call from "Calloway", which I knew by now meant Marcus was calling.

"Talk to me," Wick said, his way of answering the call.

"Kim woke up. They finally got the swelling to go down, from around her brain. She's still fuzzy... had a hard time recognizing her mother and siblings. But she's awake."

Wick made a triumphant motion with his fist. "Okay. Okay, good. Awake is good. Lucid and eager to spill the beans would be better, but we'll take awake. Can we get in to talk to her?"

"That's a negative. Doctor is refusing any kind of interrogation."

"As expected." Wick glanced at me, and then looked again, this time fixing me with a long look. "Okay, so... no interrogation. Fine. What about a visit from her concerned employer, just checking in?"

Marcus chuckled over the speaker. "You know... I don't see how anybody could have a problem with that."

"Bet," Wick nodded, reaching to pull on his seatbelt and motioning for me to do the same. "We're on our way."

I didn't really like hospitals.

There was no deep, overwhelming trauma there, but after watching my mother and the only father I'd ever known waste away due to diseases that had rendered them regular fixtures at places like this, and then my own bout with infertility, and most recently, having to spend a few days here myself, I was just... not a fan.

I did *not* want to be there.

Especially when I had to feign support for Kim, with the things I knew now. But I wanted answers more than I wanted my anger, at least for now.

So I smiled in her mother's face, played nice with her family, got them nice and comfortable and offered to pay for their lunch, so they could have a little break while I sat with her, alone.

And then I sank down into a chair beside the bed, unmoved by the heavy bandaging around her head, or the deep bruising around the eye that wasn't covered by gauze, and asked her the question that had been burning me up since I first discovered the double-cross.

"*Why*, Kim?"

Instead of answering my question, she looked away, and a few seconds later, a fat tear rolled from her eye.

"*No.*" I shook my head. "*No.* you don't get to sit here and be a victim after what you've done. You're going to tell me *something*. Were you sleeping with Asher Ross?"

"N-no," was her feeble answer, and it sounded as if she'd had to force it out. When we arrived, the doctor had been clear that her "talking" was limited, and they feared she'd suffered some sort of stroke, from the head trauma. I hadn't expected it to be quite this bad though.

"Was this about money? You betraying me?"

"Y...yes."

"Not because you hate me? No personal vendetta?"

"No."

*Small wonder.*

"So… is somebody sick or something?"

That got another yes, but it only made me more frustrated.

"Okay so why not just come to me for help, instead of going about it like this? You had to have known I would do all I could for you, as long as you've been with me."

Very subtly, Kim shook her head. "N-not… not e-nough."

"Not enough… as in, you didn't think I could give you enough?"

"Y…yes."

*Shit. Must be bad…*

"Who, Kim? Who is sick?"

She closed her eyes again, leaning back into her pillows like she was tired. "Mama," she whispered, and I nodded. I *had* noticed that the woman had lost a lot of weight since I'd last seen her, and was looking a bit fatigued. But speaking of fatigued – Kim seemed to be suffering from the same. As much as I wanted to ask more questions in this vein, to understand why she'd betrayed me, she had more pressing answers to give.

"Kim. *Kim*," I said, getting her to open her eyes. "Do you know who did this to you? Who beat you up?"

Barely, she nodded. "Yes."

"Who? I need a name, Kim. Who did this?"

She turned her head away from me. "N…no."

"*Yes*," I insisted, turning her face back toward mine and holding it there, not caring if it hurt. "*Answer* me. Who did this?!"

"I… *can't.*"

"Yes you *can. Tell me!*"

Kim squeezed her eyes shut as a few more tears rolled down her cheek. "I—"

"Don't you fucking tell me you can't. It's the least you could do! *Give me a name.*"

"I'm… *sorry.*"

"Keep it. I don't want it. What I *want* is a name, Kim. *Who*?!"

"A…ash. Ash...let… I…"

I stepped back, feeling like I'd been punched in the chest. Truthfully, that was the answer I'd already been expecting, but it didn't make it any less painful to hear.

"Asher. Asher did this to you," I whispered, more to myself than to her. I'd so wanted to believe that even if he were obsessed with me, even if he was a closet creep, that harming a woman was a line he wouldn't cross. If he'd done this to Kim… what had he done to Amanda?

"N…no. No. *N-no. no!*"

In front of me on the hospital bed, Kim had gotten upset, and a pang of guilt flashed through me. Her eyes were closed as she shifted back and forth, flinching like she was being hit, and I wondered if my questions had brought up a repressed memory of the attack.

"Kim… hey, Kim," I said, laying hands on her in an attempt to calm her. "I'm right here. Nobody is going to hurt you. He isn't going to hurt you anymore. We'll tell the police, and they'll make sure, okay? Asher will never touch you again."

"No," Kim whimpered, shaking her head. "Ash… le… *no.* No, *Ash—*"

"Hey, you are *okay*," I told her again. "Do you… do you know why? Did he say why he did this."

Kim went still, and then opened that one good eye to stare up at me. "Y-you. The… the office."

"This was retaliation for the office?" I asked, trying to clarify, and she nodded.

"Okay. Okay."

I took a deep breath, trying to swallow the revulsion I felt, knowing that whatever delusion Asher had about our relationship, he'd done this because of me. Instead of subjecting her to further questions – questions that could wait – I left the room, finding Wick waiting for me in the small waiting area in the hall.

"I was just about to come and check on you," he said, standing as soon as he saw me. Something about his tone sparked a little thread of suspicion, and I stepped back.

"What is it?" I asked. "What happened?"

He pushed out a sigh, propping his hands on top of his head. "Uh… Amanda's aunt. Sheila. I had the idea to try to look further into the family, see if there might be someone else who knew something, and…"

"Just say it. Please."

"She… she's dead, Monica. That was the first thing I found when I started searching. She was found yesterday. Overdosed on prescription pain meds. The police don't think there was foul play."

"That's *bullshit*," I shot back, crossing my arms. "It's bullshit. Completely. I just talked to her, days ago Wick. And now she's just gone? You think that's a coincidence?"

He glanced around, making sure we were alone before he answered. "No. I don't. Especially not when Asher was on a flight there early yesterday morning, and a flight back a few hours later. I didn't think much of it, because he attended a meeting that had already been on his itinerary for weeks – I know because I hacked his schedule. But finding this now…"

"It's too convenient. When Asher was there in your kitchen… you remember how he reacted when I said I'd talked to Sheila? He said she knew "everything". What is *everything*? And why didn't he want me to find out?"

"It's still circumstantial. It's something we can take to the police like we have a case."

"But we do," I insisted. "Maybe not for that, but Kim told me – it was Asher who attacked her. In retaliation, for me getting attacked at my office. I… Wick, I *barely* want to believe that he could hurt a woman like this, but I cannot keep being naïve. We need to tell the police. He needs to be brought in."

Wick nodded. "You're sure she said it was Asher?"

"Yes. *Yes.* I mean… she's a little out of it, and it was hard for her to speak, but… yes. I'm sure."

"Okay." He reached out, grabbing my elbow to give me a comforting squeeze. "I'll call Sam right now."

He pulled out his phone, stepping away to do just that. I turned, trying to give a bit of privacy and happened to look up in time to see a nurse stepping out of Kim's room, and rushing off down the hall. Just seeing it gave me an eerie feeling, like something wasn't right.

Had I freaked Kim out with my questions?

*Shit. I hope I didn't upset her too badly.*

But even if I did… I had to come to grips that it really wasn't my problem. This particular bed was one that Kim had made for herself.

Instead of pacing the floor, I took a seat, burying my face in my hands. I was still processing the possibility that Asher, the guy I'd known and loved as a friend for nearly half my life, could be a killer. It was a hard, bitter pill to swallow.

If I was acknowledging that he'd attacked Kim, and left the message on her floor, I had to believe that he was responsible for everything else as well.

Kellen's murder, the break-in at my home, at the office. The business sabotage. Amanda's disappearance.

All of it.

And for what?

Get rid of Kellen, and then make me so miserable that I fell into his arms, looking for comfort? It seemed like a long shot – like flat-out craziness, actually – but so did the entire last few weeks of my life. And when everything had been going bonkers, it stood to reason that the motive behind it all would be bonkers too.

But… did that *really* explain this?

If Ash was behind everything, where did *Canvas Cosmetics* fit into this, if they fit at all? Asher had done very, *very* well in the finance sector – he had money to blow. What if *Canvas* didn't have anything to do with any of this – which I strongly suspected anyway, because what would *their* motive be? – and Asher had simply figured out a way to cover his tracks by implicating someone else?

*God, this is all so… chaotic.*

Hopefully, I'd be able to get some answers to the chaos soon enough.

"Okay, I talked to Sam," Wick said, interrupting my thoughts as he approached where I was sitting. "He's sending officers to pick Asher up. I already told him there might be a few… complications with the paperwork, after Asher's unexpected drop-in the other night. But, he felt like what I gave him was at least worth talking to him again. So, we'll see where it goes from here."

I nodded. "Sounds good."

"Are you okay?" he asked, dropping to a squat position in front of me. "I never trusted his ass, but… I know you did. Something like this can't be easy for you."

"It isn't," I said, chewing on my lip for a second before I shook my head. "But, I can't keep ignoring what's right in front of me. If Asher did this, he needs to pay for it. And if he didn't… well… I just hope he gets a really good lawyer."

Those words had barely left my lips when an alarm started blaring from somewhere. It only took a few seconds to ascertain that it was coming from Kim's room. The next thing I knew, doctors and nurses were rushing in.

Immediately, my eyes went to Wick's and the nod he gave me told me he was thinking the same thing I was – here was yet another incident that was too-well timed to be coincidental.

"I was *just* in there with her," I whispered, standing up as Wick straightened from his squatted stance. "She was in bad shape, but stable. Suddenly now she isn't? Kellen, Sheila, - two people who could've given me answers, dead. What do you want to bet that Kim is next?"

"You think that Asher is what… finishing the job? You don't think if he wanted her dead, she would've already been?"

I shrugged. "Honestly, I don't know what to think anymore. But... I just have this feeling, and I know you do too. This is *not* happenstance."

"I agree with you, but Asher isn't here, and hasn't *been* here. At least not since we have."

"Okay, so he got someone else to do it. Someone like... the nurse. The *nurse*. When you were on the phone with Sam, a nurse came out of the room and practically ran to get out of here. Two minutes later, that alarm went off, and I did *not* see her in that rush to get back in there."

Wick's eyes narrowed, and then he walked away, pulling his laptop from his bag. He waited a few seconds for it to power on, and then his fingers were flying over the keyboard as he stared at the screen – a state I knew not to bother him in.

"Come here," he told me, a few moments later, motioning at the chair beside him. When I sat down, my eyes went wide – he'd hacked into the security camera feeds for the hospital. "This is our hall, right here," he said, pointing. "Now if I rewind back, instead of watching live... is this her? Right there?"

"Yes," I nodded. "But... we can't see her face."

Wick sighed. "Yeah. Purposely angled away. She knew the camera was there. Probably where all the cameras are, and how to avoid them. Shit."

"Right. *Shit.*"

My disappointment only magnified when I looked up to see Kim's family coming down the hall, looking full and content from my suggested lunch. They had no idea what they were about to walk into. And just as I was working up the courage to stop them before they opened that door, the doctor stepped out, hands on his hips as he looked around.

I knew that look.

He was looking for the family.

And apparently, Kim's mother knew it too. Before the doctor even opened his mouth, she crumpled right there in the hall, sobbing as her other children tried to pull her back to her feet. Tears welled in my eyes too – despite what Kim had done, she'd been with me so long that she was like a younger cousin to me. It was completely unfair – completely fucked up – that her mother was going to have to bury her.

Especially since a desire to take care of her mother was what had gotten her wrapped up in all of this in the first place.

It was sad, for sure, but… mostly, I found myself feeling guilty. Had I flirted with Asher? Stared a little too long, accidentally brushed against him at a party, *something* to make it make sense that he thought we would be together. Had I inadvertently been leading him on? For it to come to this… there had to be *something*.

Right?

Wick and I slipped out, to save me the heartache of dealing with her family… for now, at least. I knew that at some point soon, I would have to talk with them, addressing the fact that I no longer considered Kim an employee, after finding out how she'd double-crossed me. For now, my head was spinning with everything I'd learned today.

All I wanted to do was lay down.

In the car, I closed my eyes for the long drive home, not opening them again until Wick's phone rang. Curiosity drew my gaze to the console, where "Turner" was displayed as the incoming caller. Wick glanced at me first, seeming to hesitate, but I stared right back, and nodded. I didn't have a good feeling about it, but I wanted him to answer.

"Talk to me," he said, and Sam answered right back.

"We got him. Heading down to the station now."

Wick grinned. "Good. He have anything to say for himself?"

"Not really. Wanted to call his lawyer. And… he wants to speak to Monica Stuart. I wouldn't advise it though. This motherfucker is a wack job, through and through."

"Why do you say that?" Wick asked. "You found something in his apartment? Proof?"

Sam was quiet for a second. "Not of what he's accused of, not yet. But… Ms. Stuart would definitely have grounds for a stalking charge."

"Wait, what? Sam, explain."

"I'm just gonna send you some pictures I snapped. Shit is self-explanatory."

With that, Sam ended the call, but a few moments later, I heard the phone buzz again. I looked at Wick, even though he was driving, waiting for him to give me what he knew I wanted.

"*Fine*," he sighed, after a few minutes. "You can pull them up on the console screen."

I did exactly that, opening up the text thread with Sam after Wick keyed in the numbers that unlocked his phone. For a second, I just stared, not fully processing what I was seeing, but then a blunt wave of nausea hit me as the image focused.

Pictures.

Hundreds, maybe thousands, of pictures of me, lining the walls of Asher's apartment. I could tell just based on my hairstyles that some of the pictures were older, but others were very, *very* recent. Not promotional shots, or images taken from my social media. Clandestine shots of me at the grocery store, at the gym, from a gap in my curtains. Racy pictures I'd sent to Kellen back when we were still on good terms. Shots where I'd flashed the camera, shots where I'd… pulled my panties aside. Pictures that were only ever meant for my husband's eyes, and now…

"I'm going to be sick," I said aloud, and Wick immediately pulled over, even though we were nearly back at the house. I barely had the door open before the contents of my stomach relieved themselves from my body. With my head still hanging, I stepped away from the car, trying to take in gulps of fresh air.

After a few moments, I felt Wick's hand on my back, but I was so mortified that I stepped away, shaking my head.

"Monica… I am *so* sorry. But Sam is lead on this now – he took over the whole thing. He took those shots to send me, so that we would know the full scope of this, but if I know him – and I do – he's making sure no one else sees *these* pictures."

I scoffed. "What, he's gonna destroy evidence? Is that what you're saying to me?"

"I'm saying that he'll make sure you aren't further violated, yes. Cops make shit disappear all the time. Nobody will blink about this. I know that doesn't make it okay, but… I hope it at least… I don't know. Tell me what to do."

Just the fact that he wanted to make it better almost brought a smile to my face, but I was still so disgusted that it wouldn't surface. Just knowing that Asher had intentionally surrounded himself with those images – my personal, *private* images – every single day…

"Let's get you to the house, okay?" Wick asked, wrapping his arms around my shoulders to lead me back to the car. There, he pulled a bottle of water from a compartment in the armrest, and I used it to rinse out my mouth before accepting the gum he'd offered.

I appreciated that he didn't say anything for the rest of the short drive home. His mind was racing – I could just tell – but whatever he was thinking, he kept it to himself.

There was a Range Rover – Kay's – in the driveway when we pulled up, but Wick didn't immediately seek her out. He took me to his room first, running a bath and settling me into it before he left me to myself, to soak, and to… think.

But I didn't *want* to think.

What I wanted was to not think about any of this, for *all* of it to go away and *stay* away. Earlier, I'd considered all of this to be overwhelming, but that was nothing when compared with… *this*. Those pictures… that had been the thing that launched me over the edge, whereas before, I'd just been toeing the line.

*Where did he even get them?*

That was the question plaguing me now. And the other shots… had he been following me? *Stalking* me, like Sam had suggested? Whatever the case, it occurred to me now the danger I'd been in without

299

knowing. I'd been alone with Asher countless times, and the only time he'd indulged his apparent desire had been that night in the hotel.

But he'd seemed so apologetic, so ashamed of himself afterward.

Had that just been a test?

Was he simply gauging my reaction?

I pushed out a deep sigh, and closed my eyes. I was feeling sick to my stomach again, and I'd already brushed my teeth twice before Wick put me in the bath.

There was no sense in making myself queasy over someone else's actions, when I had enough other things to be stressed about. Instead of running it over in my mind any further, I kept my eyes closed, and focused on pushing away every thought.

When I opened my eyes again, the water was cold.

As I woke up, my body reacted to the frigid water with violent shivers, so strong that I barely pulled myself out. I silently thanked Wick for the heated floors in his bathroom, and the towel warmer he'd draped my robe over.

I let out a long sigh as I wrapped myself in the heated terry cloth, then looked around, realizing that there was no longer any daylight streaming in from outside.

*Was I really in the tub that long?*

My heavily pruned fingers and toes said yes, but I was still skeptical as I pulled open the door to the bedroom. Surely Wick would've checked on me before now, not letting me stay in a cold bathtub for hours. But… the clock beside his empty bed told the same story as the darkened sky.

Something had to be wrong.

When I opened the door to his room, the hallway, and most of the house, was dark. There was a light on behind the door that led to Kay's room, and behind the door to Wick's office. I chose the office.

Without knocking, I opened the door to find him seated at his desk with his head down, resting in his hands. Immediately, my eyes shifted, searching for the bottle of liquor that he'd had before, but the desk was empty, save for his laptop and other knick-knacks.

300

"Wick," I said, and he looked up with red-rimmed, wrathful eyes, that quickly softened when he realized I was at the door.

"Monica... shit... are you okay?" he asked. "I... completely fucking forgot you were here. I... *fuck!*" he exclaimed, loud enough to make me flinch. Still, I stepped inside, closing the door behind me.

"Hey..." I made sure my tone was soothing, but didn't move any closer. "Tell me where your head is at?"

He pushed out a sigh, then shook his head. "Kayla. Somebody tried to grab her as she was leaving rehearsal earlier."

"Oh my God! Is she okay?!"

"Yeah. Khalil was with her, and Kay... can fight, for lack of a better way to put it. So, she's fine. She's safe now. I'm just pissed that it happened. Some officers came by and took her statement."

I put a hand to my chest, pressing it into the steady thump of my racing heart. "Good. I'm glad she's safe."

"Yeah. Me too," he said, and then sat back again, quiet.

*Too* quiet.

"Um... you said you were pissed. At... me?" I asked, leaning back against the door.

Wick's eyes came back to me, narrowed. "Monica... what do you think?"

I swallowed the lump in my throat. "I... I think yes. I think that this is the reason you didn't want to be involved with me in the first place. Why you never wanted to see my face again, because of how it might involve, or hurt Kay. I wouldn't blame you, for being pissed at me. I would be pissed at me. You don't have to pretend to *not* be pissed at me. I'm a big girl. I can take it."

His eyes narrowed even further as he sat forward. Even with his mouth closed, I could tell he was running his tongue over his teeth, thinking.

"Monica... why do I get the feeling there's something you aren't telling me?"

His gaze was so intense that it already felt like he was seeing right through me. Yet again, I was reminded that this man was nobody's regular "computer geek". He'd been trained to spot lies – and expertly tell them too. But I had the feeling that between us, there was only one potential liar in the room.

Potential I couldn't force myself to live up to.

Not now that his daughter was involved.

"Because there is," I whispered.

Across the room, Wick stood, then came around to the front of his desk. He leaned back into it, taking a seat on the edge before he motioned for me to step forward.

I didn't *want* to, but it was like I was being pulled by some invisible thread. As soon as I was in front of him, he gently grabbed me by the wrists, with his thumbs at my pulse points.

"Tell me, Monica. *Now.*"

"Glen Pearson is my father."

The words tumbled out immediately, with barely any pressure from him. As soon as I said it, I felt like a weight had been lifted – I'd never spoken those words out loud to anyone still living, not even Kellen. But that relief was short-lived, as Wick realized the gravity of what I'd just told him.

"Glen... Pearson," he repeated, with a tightness in his jaw that hadn't been there before. "As in... owner and CEO of *Canvas Cosmetics*, Glen Pearson?"

With my lips pressed tight together, I nodded, and he pushed out a rough sigh that made me flinch.

"Monica... what the fu—*why* are you just now telling me this?!"

"I didn't think it mattered!" I exclaimed – well, tried. "It's not common knowledge. *No one* knows. Not even him!"

Wick frowned. "How the *fuck* would he not know he had a kid?!"

"Are *you* really asking me that question?!" I shot back. "You didn't know about Kay until she was damn near a pre-teen, Wick!"

"I..." whatever he was going to say, he swallowed it, knowing I was right, even though the situations were completely different.

"My mother… was never supposed to get pregnant. And when she did, she was supposed to have an abortion. He *paid* for an abortion. She used the money to pack up and leave instead."

Wick pulled his head back. "Wow. *Wow.*"

"Yeah. Wow. She moved away, had me, raised me by herself. Never contacted him again, never asked for anything. She only finally told me who he was because I threatened to stop speaking to her if she didn't."

"Wouldn't he recognize your last name as the same as hers? See you, and connect those dots? He had to have looked you up when he tried to buy your company."

I shook my head. "I took my stepfather's name, when he and my mother got married. And then, I married Kellen, so I was Monica Stuart. And as far as seeing my mother in my face… I'm thirty-six years old, and it's not like the two of them were in love. She was his mistress, Wick. Probably one of many. So… I doubt he was pining away every night, trying to remember her face. It was more likely that he was trying to forget."

"Okay. Okay," he repeated with a heavy sigh, still holding my wrists. "So… your father owns *Canvas.* The same company whose account signed all these crooked ass checks. You're telling me now, *why?*"

"In case it matters. Even though… I never thought it did. My reasoning was that, he has to still be in the dark about it, because if not… why come after me with this kind of tactic? I've never dropped a hint, never said a peep, to anyone. He has no reason to think I'm a threat, no reason for all of this. So I just keep thinking… there's no way it's him."

Wick dropped his head back, looking up at the ceiling for a bit before his gaze came back to me. "I… don't disagree. It makes no sense for him to come at you like this. The Asher angle is a better fit, but that puzzle is still missing a lot of pieces. I just… I really would've liked to know this before now. For the sake of transparency."

I nodded. "I know. I *know*. I swear, if I'd thought that it mattered…"

"I understand. You've really never told anyone else?"

"No," I said, giving him a wry smile. "The only people who ever knew my mother was pregnant were him and my mother. And… his wife, when I showed up as a teenager, looking for him. She wrote me a check, asked me not to tell anyone, and… asked me to never come back. So I honored that."

"Wow. That's…"

"Dysfunctional? Yes. The only reason I'm telling you this, is on the off chance that maybe he *is* involved, now that somebody tried to harm Kayla. I… I couldn't live with myself knowing I was holding on to that secret, if something happened to her."

Wick nodded, and then released his hold on my wrists to slip his arms around my waist, pulling me closer. "Well… the fact that Kay factors highly enough to you for you to tell me this means a lot me. It's appreciated. Greatly. Along with the fact that you're trusting me with something you haven't told anyone else… I'll do my very best to preserve your secret."

I relaxed into his arms, glad for the opportunity, but still… "Why do I feel like there's a "but" coming?"

"Because there is," he said, looking down to meet my gaze. "The attempt on Kay… it wasn't related to this madness that's going on with you. One of the other dancers, Anais. She has a fucked-up ex. Ol' boy sent people for her, and when Kay stepped out of the building – similar body type, skin tone, wearing a hoodie, hair in her face… they thought she was Ana. Khalil caught one of the guys, kept him hemmed up until the police got there, while the others ran."

My mouth dropped open. "So… you were never mad at me? Never thought my mess had anything to do with it?"

"Never," he said, leaning to kiss my forehead. "You're the one who started acting guilty. I just let you say what was on your mind."

I put my hands on his chest, giving him a playful shove. "That was *not* very nice. At all. I was thinking you almost let me end up with hypothermia because you were pissed at me!"

"Even if I was pissed, I wouldn't do any shit like that. The bathtub thing... was an honest mistake. I was with Kay, and then I came in here to try to look this guy up, and the time just got away from me. I'm sorry."

Narrowing my eyes at him, I tried to feign annoyance, but I couldn't bring myself to do it. As much as he'd done, as much work as he'd put in for me, certainly I could give him a pass.

"Apology accepted," I told him, then let out a long sigh as I sank back into his arms. "It's been a rough day."

His hands came to my back, starting a gentle circular stroke that if I were a cat, would've had me purring. "I'm starting to notice a trend, of you forgiving me because you're just too tired to be mad."

I laughed. "Lucky you. I *am* too tired to be mad."

"Come on then. Let's go lay down."

I nodded. "Yes. Let's."

He grabbed me by the hand, leading me toward his room. "Probably a good idea to get some rest."

Inside his room, he closed the door behind us. As soon as I heard the click in the doorframe, I turned around, unbolting and dropping my robe.

"You're right. And I know the *perfect* medicine to put us to sleep."

# EIGHTEEN

*You don't have to do this.*

Only… I did.

Even though the thought made me sick to my stomach, even though Wick had stopped just short of forbidding it, even though I knew my skin would be crawling for hours after… yes.

I did.

I had to do it because I needed answers, and Asher wasn't giving them to anyone else. He was just in his cell, refusing to speak to anyone, about anything.

Except me.

So I went.

Because my desire to know what the fuck was going on somehow overrode my complete disgust.

I dressed in jeans, boots, a high-necked sweater, and kept on my coat when I went to sit down in the interrogation room with him. Because he'd insisted on being alone in the room with me, I insisted that he be bound to his chair. I wanted there to be no chance of him touching me.

Maybe I was just a bleeding heart, and gave people more credit than they deserved, but seeing Asher chained, and in prison garb, made my chest hurt. This had been my *friend*.

How the hell had he fallen so far?

Ash was handsome – *fine,* actually – smart, wealthy, charming. There was no reason I could see that he couldn't have found someone he loved, who loved him back, and given them the world. Instead… he'd chosen to make *my* world hell on earth.

"Hello, Asher," I said, when he just sat there staring, saying nothing.

His Adam's apple bobbed as he swallowed. "Hello, Monica. Is your new boyfriend on the other side of the glass?"

"I'm not here to talk about that."

Yes, Wick and Sam were both on the other side of the mirrored glass, but I wasn't about to give Asher the reward of confirming what he already thought.

"What are you here to talk about? You want to know how my pinky is holding up? Whoever put my shit back together... they did a really good job. I'd say thank you, but... you know..."

"I don't know anything about that. I'm here to talk about what you did to Kim. And Amanda. And Sheila. And Kellen. And *me*. That's what I'm here for. For you to look me in my face and tell me why you did these things."

He stared at me with those light grey eyes – now more unnerving than sexy, as they used to be – and then smirked. "Okay. If that's what you want."

"It is."

"I didn't do *shit* to Kim," he started, shaking his head. "Other than scare her. I knew she was up to something because the girl I hired to do Kellen, thinking it would finally bring you to your senses... she told me she overheard Kim and Kellen talking, when they had no reason to be doing that. When you got attacked... I knew about it because... yes... I was watching. I was waiting in the parking lot, for you to come out, and go home... I was going to stop by. But I waited, and waited, and then there was an ambulance, and... I followed. After I saw you, I went to Kim, and I told her she had to come clean, or I was telling you what I knew, and I was calling the police. She got pissed, came at me with a lamp, and we struggled... I slapped her. But that's all. That shit that landed her in the hospital? Not me."

I scoffed. "So you expect me to believe that you went to her house, threatened and slapped her, but that's it? What, somebody else came along and finished the job?"

308

"Yes."

"*No.* The police found your fingerprints all over her place!"

"Because we struggled over the lamp. We... fought, I guess, but I hit her *one* time. I don't know what to tell you about anything else."

"I don't believe you."

"That's unsurprising."

"Whatever," I snapped. I took a deep breath, trying to calm my nerves. "Sheila. And Amanda?"

"More shit I have nothing to do with. Sheila is a damn junkie, and Amanda wasn't much better. I loved her, but she... wasn't all the way wrapped."

"Seriously?" I laughed. "That is *rich*, coming from you."

His eyes narrowed. "Maybe so. Either way, Amanda didn't say shit to me when she decided to leave. We'd broken up. I told her that you were getting ready to leave Kellen, because of Crystal, and I didn't want any impediment to being there for you... and finally taking my rightful place in your life. Apparently, I jumped the gun."

"Yeah, Ash. You did."

"We live and learn," he shrugged, pulling against his shackles. "She and I argued. She left. I didn't see her again after that. Haven't seen her. But I... missed her. I really did love her. That's why the phone bill was still getting paid."

*Liar.*

"If she's alive... where is she, Asher? You said she hated me. Was avoiding *me* specifically. How would you know that if you hadn't spoken?"

"Because I *know* Amanda. Better than you ever did. You robbed her of every man she'd ever wanted, Monica. She hated your guts."

I shook my head. "It's all very convenient, Asher. To blame a woman who has been missing for two years for all of your misdeeds, and put words in her mouth. But understand this – I'm *not* buying it."

"Because you still don't get it. But you will, my dear, sweet friend."

"Friend? Is that don't I get? Hmm? Cause I agree. I do *not* get how you called me a friend, called Kellen a friend, but *paid* someone to disrupt and derail my already troubled marriage? How you knew Kellen was... a whore, and said nothing? Knew he was sleeping with my best friend – if that's not just another one of your lies – and said *nothing*! The *pictures*, Asher! That's how you treat a friend?! Hanging up pictures that were supposed to be private, between me and my *husband*, and then pictures of me through my curtains, stalking me in the streets! Plastering them up, to desensitize yourself! I wasn't a person to you, Ash, just the object of your twisted obsession. A fucking piece of *meat*!"

"*That's all you are!*" he screamed right back at me, matching my volume. "Now, since you let another motherfucker touch you, that is *all* you are to me! Believe whatever the fuck you want to believe now. I never did anything but love and protect you, never acted without your interests at heart. Only for you to reject me, over and over. *Fuck you.*"

"*Right back at you,*" I hissed, standing to storm out of the room. "I hope you rot in here, you sick bastard."

The door was barely closed before Wick was on me, wrapping me up in his arms. In that moment, I didn't bother trying to be strong, had no concerns about looking weak. I sobbed because I was hurt, and because I was disgusted, and because I'd put myself through that only for it to be a waste.

He was lying.

The pictures weren't the only thing they'd found in his apartment.

Asher's family had owned a decently sized share in *Blissful Beauty,* the company that had been overtaken by *Canvas* all those years ago. For whatever reasons, there were still existing accounts there – accounts that Asher, because of his family connection, still had access to.

He'd used that access to make it look like *Canvas* was behind everything.

But the police had found the nail polish bottles from leaving the messages, they'd traced those roses left on my doorstep back to him, plus his lack of alibi for... everything.

*Means, motive, opportunity.*

It was all there.

And I was done being fool enough to not believe what was right in front of my eyes. I was over it.

*Finished.*

And I would be right on time to testify at his trial.

"You know... I'm really starting to think you just don't want to let me out of your sight."

I glanced back at Wick as he followed me into my office, dropping into a seat on the couch in the corner. It was my first day back since my attack, and my new assistant had done a great job of eliminating all memories of it with a small, but impactful, office remodel that I'd been intending to do for a while. A brand-new desk, fresh paint, and plush carpeting I could sink my toes into after a long day, when I kicked my stilettos off at my desk.

Something I planned to do as soon as I sat down.

"Really? What tipped you off?" he asked, grinning as he stretched his arms across the back of the couch, getting comfortable.

Even though the case against Asher had insurmountable evidence that he'd been the culprit behind everything, and he never spoke a word in his own defense to the people who mattered, Wick had still been playing bodyguard for me. Not that I minded, because I enjoyed having him around, but it was starting to seem pointless to me.

Especially after learning yesterday that Ash had hung himself in his cell, and would never even see a trial date.

To me, it felt more like Wick was keeping an eye on my emotional state, versus the physical protection he was using as his ruse. But again – he didn't have to front. I *liked* having him around me, because he was nice to look at, and he was funny, and his warm, masculine energy sent the hell of the last few weeks way, *way* back to the back of my mind.

Not to mention, he was a really good lunch date.

In fact, we were just coming from a trip to my favorite custom salad place, *Poke*, which had led to a trip back to my suite at *Veil* for a quickie. So even though I was teasing him about it, I had exactly zero complaints about him shadowing me for my first official day back at work.

"Too many things to name," I said, answering his question. "But I'll say this – for a former spy, you are *so* not sneaky."

He sucked his teeth. "*That's* a lie."

"No it's not."

"Yes it is."

"It's *really* not though."

"But it *really* is though. And I'll prove it. Open your top right desk drawer."

I frowned at him, suspecting that he was playing with me, trying to get me to look away so he could do something… well, sneaky. But curiosity overwhelmed my suspicion, and I pulled open the desk drawer only to scream and quickly slide it shut again once I saw what was inside.

"Oh my *God!*" I shrieked, blinking hard as I glanced toward the open door to my office to see if anyone was close by. "Are you crazy?! How did you… *When* did you?!"

"But you said I wasn't sneaky. Said I was *"so* not sneaky", to be specific. Which is, in fact, a lie."

I crossed my arms. "This is *not* funny."

"That's a lie."

"But it isn't."

"But it *is*," he shot back, with a devilish smirk I had a hard time not returning. "Not every day you end up with a big black dick in your drawer, but here we are."

312

I rolled my eyes, and covered my mouth with my hand trying my best not to laugh. When a giggle broke free anyway, I tipped my head back, letting loose. "Okay. Maybe it is a little funny."

"See?" he asked, pulling himself away from setting up his laptop on my coffee table to stand. "But, what is *not* funny is the situation brewing in my intestines from you making me eat those damn mystery greens."

"Neither mizuna nor tatsoi are *mystery greens*, sir. Expand your palette, please."

"What I'm about to expand is this toilet. I'll be right back."

"*Ewww!*" I called after him, as he closed the door to my private bathroom behind him. "You make sure you use the spray after! And during!"

I giggled over the faint "*yes ma'am*" I heard him answer with, and shook my head as I powered on my computer. As good of a mood as he had me in, there was still work to do, to fix the damage the sabotage attempt had wrought, both on my business structure and reputation.

It was a challenge I wasn't afraid to undertake.

Wick was still in the bathroom, and I was knee-deep in emails when my intercom buzzed.

"Ms. Stuart?" my new assistant, Tarra said, grabbing my attention.

"Yes, Tarra?"

"Your two o'clock, Ashley Cline is here."

*Oh, shit.*

It was a meeting that had been on my books for months – a beauty blogger, who'd wanted to interview me. I'd meant to look into her blog before I said yes, and then passed the responsibility over to Kim, who must've seen something she liked, because she granted the interview, and put it on my calendar.

Now, I was sitting here looking silly, knowing nothing about Ashley or her blog. But I reminded myself that *she* was interviewing me – not the other way around. All I had to do was be gracious, which could cover a multitude of sins – sins being, lack of research, in this case.

And if nothing else, I would just profusely, desperately, apologize.

"You can send her in," I told Tarra, then moved my laptop to the side of my desk, so that we could talk face to face. I looked up when I felt eyes on me from the doorway, and froze.

And then... *frowned.*

"I... *Amanda*?" I asked, standing up from my chair to... see her better, I guess. The last time I saw Amanda, she'd sported blonde, shoulder length locs, an earring in her nose, and the best of the best in floral maxis and beaded bracelets. Now, standing in my doorway, she... looked like she'd been in *my* closet. Tall, spiked stilettos instead of the braided leather sandals I was used to, coral-toned slacks, floral button-up, and a sleek olive blazer. And her hair... was a mirror image of... *mine* – thick, lush weave that framed her face in soft waves.

"You were given a simple instruction," she said, stepping into the office. "Why couldn't you just follow it? Everything would have been fine, if you just did what you were told."

My face twisted. "What? Amanda... what the hell is going on? Why would give a fake name to make an appointment? You're not Ashley Cline, you're *Amanda Gordon*," I insisted, but then remembered. "Amanda... *Ashley* Gordon."

Right.

*Amanda Ashley Gordon.*

*"Ash... le... no. No, Ash—"*

I shook my head, trying to clear my thoughts as my final conversation with Kim came to mind. But it nagged at me, as inconvenient a moment as this was, before something snapped into place.

*She wasn't saying Asher. She was trying to say Ashley.*

"All you had to do was let me have *something*," Amanda said, and somehow, there was a gun in her hands, the barrel pointed right at my face. "You had Kellen, even though I was *better* than you, he told me. And then you... you pranced around Asher, like a whore, and you took him from me too. You're not taking anyone else. He *loves* me. He

314

just doesn't see it yet. But once you're gone, he'll know how much more worthy I am, and always was. He'll see me the way he sees – *saw* – you. I'll be the one who's perfect."

I didn't – couldn't – ask her what in world, who in the world, she was talking about, because several things happened next, seemingly at once. The bathroom door opened, and Wick was there, and Amanda fired the gun. Then I was on the floor, sinking into that plush, luscious carpet as pain radiated through every single one of my nerves. The gun went off again, one, two, *three* more times, but I was dizzy, and numb, and there was… *God*, why was there so much blood?

"Monica? Monica!"

There were voices all around me, screams and yelling, but I focused on the voice that felt soothing, and comforting. I focused on Wick.

"What… what happened? What's happening?" I asked, when his face finally came into focus, filtering through my blurred vision.

Instead of answering my question, he started touching me all over – checking me. "Monica. *Monica*. Are you hit?"

"Amanda was here. Wick, did you see Amanda?"

*Did I imagine that? Is this a dream?*

"Amanda is dead, Monica." Wick's voice was firm, but not unkind as he grabbed my hand, pulling me up into a seated position. "I took care of it."

"You're bleeding?" I asked, even though it really wasn't a question. I'd gripped his arms as he pulled me up, and now there was blood soaking my hand, and my sleeve, and he was cringing.

"It's nothing," he insisted, at the same time that a paramedic – *When did paramedics get here?* – approached him, telling him that he really should get the gunshot wound looked at. "Man, get off me!" he growled, shooing the paramedic away.

"Sir, you're bleeding very bad—"

"I'm fine. Leave it."

"But—"

"Look, I said *leave it*. The only thing I'm concerned about right now is my... my..."

I blinked. "Your... what?"

He looked at me for what felt like a long time, before something like determination... like *certainty*... spread over his face. "Just... *mine*." He held my gaze, wordlessly asking me to understand what he didn't want to – or maybe, simply couldn't – articulate.

I did.

"I want you to let them look at your... gunshot wound," I said, feeling dizzy as I looked at the blood that had soaked the sleeve of his sweater, and was leaking onto the carpet. "What the hell just happened?"

Wick cringed as the paramedic made quick work of cutting the sleeve of his sweater off, to get to a the ragged-looking hole in his arm. "Well... it appears we found Amanda."

"Where is she?" I asked, struggling to my feet. I realized now that the pain I'd felt had been the impact of hitting the ground, thanks to Wick's quick reflexes.

Apparently, the man had taken a bullet for me.

The answer to my question came in the form of a long look, and I followed his gaze to the ground, just on the other side of my desk. There, on the ground, was Amanda.

Just as I'd seen her in that awful dream – with a jagged hole in the middle of her head. Only now, the hole in her head was accompanied by two in the chest, as well.

Continuing the trend.

Everyone who could give me some answers... died.

Policemen pulled me aside to take my statement, and I was beyond relieved to see Sam Turner's face when he came through the door, with Chloe not far behind. The new assistant, Tarra, was visibly shaken, but still met my eyes as I was led out of the office. She took a break from bossing people around just long enough to give me a comforting nod that said she had it.

Chloe had been the one to recommend her, so I believed it.

316

"Will you just stay still, so they can stitch you up?" I asked, earning myself a scowl. I wasn't surprised, not really, that Wick was a difficult patient, but *damn*.

He was worse than a small child.

"It'll be fine if I just leave it alone. Pour some vodka on it, and bandage the shit. It'll be fine. I used to do the shit all the time back in the day."

My eyes got big. "Okay, well... this is *not* back in the day, so how about you just let the people do their job?"

"Why?"

My eyebrows shot up. "Why? *Why*?!" I repeated, not believing that was a serious question. But since I knew it was, I took a deep breath, recognizing that the logical reasons for properly treating a gunshot wound wouldn't appeal to him right now. I looked him right in his eyes as I spoke, making sure he knew I was serious. "Because *Mine* said so. Got it?"

The scowl he'd been wearing faltered a bit, before he broke into a smile he couldn't help.

"Never going to let me live that down, are you?"

I scoffed. "Are you kidding? Why would I ever?"

Instead of waiting around for the process of them stitching up his arm – which was more involved than I'd expected, and ended up requiring a little sedative for the delicate work of reconnecting veins and nerves – I slipped out. As soon as he was off for his induced trip to la-la-land, I went searching for someone who could tell me what I needed to know.

I found Sam.

"You know he suspected something?" Sam asked me, when I spotted him in the waiting area in the hall. "He knew that Asher was a creep, but he just... had a feeling. He was sure something was off... that something was wrong. That's why he was all over you. He wasn't sure this was really over."

I shook my head. "He didn't tell me."

"Probably didn't want to scare you. But... as wacky as it is for this girl to show up out of the blue after two years, with a fake identity... it makes sense."

"It does?"

Sam nodded, running a hand over his bald head, then raking it through the salt and pepper of his beard. "Yeah. It makes everything fit. Psycho motherfucker with an equally psycho partner."

"Maybe." I pushed out a sigh. "It still just feels so weird, to think of Amanda... like this. It's so far from the girl I knew."

Sam shrugged, then stood. "Maybe you didn't know her like you thought you did."

"I guess not. That's just a hard thing to accept, when it comes to someone I thought of like... a sister. But I guess I have to, right? And I can be grateful that this is over... even if I don't get all the answers."

"Keep the faith, Ms. Stuart. We're looking into her now. And who knows... maybe once we've searched wherever she was staying, dug into her background... maybe it'll give you what you need."

I gave him a dry smile. "Yeah. Maybe. Thank you, Sam. And please – call me Monica."

"Will do, Monica," he said, giving me a little salute. "You've already given your statement, but now I have to go in here and talk to this knucklehead. You good? You need to call someone, need a ride?"

"No, not yet. But a couple of my friends are on the way. One of them will give me a lift. But um... I have a question that may seem a little strange."

Sam eyed me curiously, pushing his hands into his pockets. "I doubt you can surprise, but go for it. Do your worst."

"Where is Amanda's body?"

His eyebrows lifted. "Oh. Uh... it's here. Down in the morgue."

"Could I... could I see it. *Her.* Could I see her?"

Sam's head bowed in a nod. "If that's what you want... I can make it happen."

318

"It's what I want," I said immediately, looking him right in the eyes. "I'm sure."

"Then I'll make it happen. It's down in the basement, on the ground floor. If you want to go now, I'll go ahead and make the call, to let them know to expect you."

"Make the call."


That was how I ended up in the morgue.

It was deathly quiet, once the attendant stepped out of the room, leaving me alone with the body, which hadn't yet been placed in one of the refrigerated drawers. She'd already been undressed, I could tell by her bare shoulders, even though she was mostly covered by a sheet.

Her skin was pale, and... lifeless.

Looking at her now felt the same as when I'd looked at Ash across that interrogation table – I'd wanted to be so much angrier than I was, wanted to want to smash in his face, wanted to *hate* him.

But just like with Kellen... I couldn't make myself do it.

Just like I couldn't force myself to hate Amanda.

Even though she'd pointed that gun, even though she'd pulled the trigger...I just wanted to know *why*.

"*Why, Amanda?*" I whispered.

All through college, she and I had been thick as thieves, but now that felt like a lie. She'd as good as confirmed Asher's revelation that she was sleeping with Kellen with that whole, *took my men from me* thing. If anything, *I* was the one who should've been angry. I was the one who'd been betrayed.

All of this, when I'd never done anything except mine my damned business.

I just... didn't get it.

All those stab wounds on Kellen... it had been personal. The roses smashed at my door, with the – albeit distant - possibility of causing an allergic reaction. Personal. I had a feeling that Amanda was the nurse I'd seen sneaking out of Kim's room to finish the job... had she really given that severe beating that landed Kim there in the first place? And Sheila… the woman who'd raised her… if that wasn't an accidental overdose, what could possibly make Amanda want her dead?

"You just can't take a hint, can you?"

My eyes damn near bucked out of my head at my *ridiculous* first thought, that those words had come from Amanda. But then common sense flared, and I turned to see a woman standing at the door, that I hadn't even heard open.

"Miranda?"

The older woman stepped forward, still as beautiful as the first time I laid eyes on her, nearly twenty years ago. She still held every single note of grace, every bit of refinement, every molecule of… distaste, for me.

Maybe more.

"*Hmph*," she sniffed, circling me as my thoughts ran together, trying to understand. "I see you at least have enough respect to remember my name. What a surprise. It seems you have the capacity for very little else."

"Excuse me?"

"I most certainly will *not*," she practically growled, stepping right in front me. She was wearing heels too, putting us at practically the same height. "I have already excused *quite* enough from you."

I frowned. "Miranda, I have no idea what you're talking about. You wrote that check, and I left it at that. I did what you asked. I left you and… *your husband* alone. I haven't called. I haven't hinted. I've said nothing, at all."

"Young lady, you'd do well to remember that I am not your *peer*, nor am I your *friend*. Do not refer to me by my first name again."

"*Fine,*" I snapped. "Mrs. Cline. I kept the terms of our agreement."

"Oh, but you *didn't*," she hissed. "You just… couldn't help yourself, could you? Walking in your daddy's footsteps, thinking you would build a beauty empire, like he did. Your little nail polish company is cute, I guess."

320

"It's not little. And you know what... maybe the beauty industry *is* in my blood."

She scoffed. "Did you think you were making him proud?"

"I *know* he was proud. Even if he didn't know it was me, he was proud. He said so, when he offered to buy my "little company", that I built on my own, without using his name."

"Oh, bravo, you little *bitch*," she said drily, accenting her words with a half-hearted clap. "Good for you... I guess. Finally got the attention of the daddy who never wanted you to be anything but medical waste on a dirty clinic floor. *Give yourself a hand.*"

I shook my head. "Okay, what the *fuck* is wrong with you? What is your problem?"

"My problem?" she repeated, and then smiled. "*My* problem is that I told you to make yourself invisible. To go scuttle away, like the cockroach you are, back to your *whore* of a mother, since I exterminated you. But *no.* You just had to make yourself noticed. Well... congratulations, Monica. *He noticed.* That's why he wanted to buy your shitty little company. I'll never forget the day... I have Nubia Perry on the TV, and then... lo and behold, there you are, on her arm. I knew you two were friends. It wasn't news to me. But *he*... happens to look at the TV. And he looks right at you, and whispers, like the sniveling, *weak* excuse for a man that he is... *Gloria. My Gloria.*"

I took a step back. "Wait a minute... what? He... thought I was my mother?"

"Of course not. But you look just like his main whore – at the time. So of course he immediately knew who you were. Wanted to reach out to you. Wanted to talk, wanted to know you, wanted you to know how proud he was. He thought you were perfect. His *perfect fucking daughter,* from his *whore.*"

"He never said anything to me about that."

"Because I convinced him not to. And then I set my plan in motion."

"Plan?"

She smirked. "Oh yes. You see, your whore mother was already dead, so I couldn't really take it out on her. But you... oh, you, with your implicit trust, and your idyllic views of the people you love. It was so *easy* to disrupt your perfect little life. Screw your husband's boss, and convince him it was you. Make sure he *never* worked in finance again. Set up a mistress for him, so you could feel my pain."

"Asher did that, I interrupted. "You're a liar."

Miranda laughed. "Oh, honey... who do you think gave Asher the idea? But you... you were so... stupid. You stayed."

"So did you!" I reminded her, but she shook her head.

"Not the same. *My* husband left his indiscretions in the past, and we rebuilt, and moved on. You... let the man make a goddamned fool of you. It was so easy to get him on my side, working against you. And then Glen started talking about buying your little company. He was obsessed with you. I couldn't get him to let it go. So I decided it was time to... ramp things up."

I took a step back. "You... *you* killed Kellen."

She shrugged. "Oh, not at first. First was trying to sabotage your business... take you down a few pegs. But that wasn't working, so then I thought I'd scare you... and that didn't work either. And by that time I was sick of you. Impatient. So... yes, I had Kellen taken care of. He was a pain in more ways than one – so emotional, always ready to confront you about screwing Brad, which of course you would deny. And, Amanda was upset, because *she* wanted Kellen, but the idiot had fallen in love with the mistress, gotten her pregnant. So... he had to go."

"You are... *sick*," I whispered, shaking my head. "All of this... Sheila? And Kim? All because my father wanted to know me?!"

"Because you *existed* in the first place. And yes, because he wanted to know you, *yes* because he *wanted* you at all. How was I supposed to feel?! *Huh*?! The child of the woman he came home smelling like, expecting to be able to crawl on top of me after... the very *sight* of you disgusts me. How dare you get a single *molecule* of emotion, of admiration, of *love* when I got rid of *my* child to please him?!"

322

Those words hit me like a smack in the face. "What?! I have a sibling?!"

An ugly sneer spread across her features. "No child of mine will ever claim *any* relation to you. Glen picked me up… from nothing. Brought me all the way out here. Got me pregnant. Told me to get rid of it. I begged, and pleaded. We were in love. I *wanted* my baby. But he told me we couldn't be together if I kept her. He didn't want kids. He gave me an ultimatum, and he left. Didn't call, didn't write, didn't drop in… for a whole year. And when he did come back… I was as childless as he'd left me. And he… he married me. A week later. And a week after that… he started coming home smelling like *her*. Like *you*."

"You're Amanda's mother."

Nothing had ever been as clear to me as that was, and suddenly it all made sense.

Amanda coming to Blakewood. Amanda being my roommate. Amanda being my "bestie"

She wasn't my friend… she was… keeping an eye on me.

"You killed my baby," Miranda said, her voice thick with emotion.

I shook my head. "No, *Miranda*. That was you. By getting her involved with this, at all. You gave her away, for the love of a man who didn't even respect you. Your love… it was all she wanted. All she craved. And you withheld it. You turned her into a monster, and threw her to the wolves."

"No!" Miranda screamed. "*You* did! She wanted Kellen, but he wanted you. She wanted Asher, but he wanted you. She wanted her *father*… but he… after he asked me to give my baby up, and I sent her away to be with Sheila… to be loved and mothered by another woman… he had the nerve to look me in my face after he saw you on that screen, and express his regrets. Claimed he'd *always wanted a child*, as if he didn't know the "niece" I went to visit with Sheila was his flesh and blood. He *had* to. And he thought he was going to make it right with you. You were going to take *him* from her too."

"I had *nothing* to do with the decisions of the adults who conceived me. That is *not* my fault."

She smirked. "Oh, but… it is. The moment you rang my doorbell to disrupt my home, you traded in your innocence. You were supposed to disappear, and you didn't. And now, because of you… my daughter is gone. You've taken everything from me. And that little nail polish collection, those names? You thought you were slick, huh? Taunting me with it. But I got you back tenfold, didn't I? I'm not done with you though, Monica. If you thought these last few weeks were hell, darling… you haven't seen anything yet."

Thinking about it now, it baffled me that *this* was the Miranda Cline I'd grown up admiring. Her company, *Blissful Beauty* had been a force, until she married Glen Pearson, and *Canvas* had slowly suffocated the smaller company, eventually buying it. I still remembered being in awe of the fact that she kept her own name when she got married, at a time when it wasn't the norm.

I'd thought it showed that she was strong, that she refused to let her marriage define her, refused to give up her identity because of who she was married to.

Now I knew the truth.

Marrying my father – *loving* my father – had consumed and destroyed her. Maybe she'd been a different woman before, but nearly four decades of hurt and anger had redefined her, into something way beyond the "bitter" label Kellen used to fling at me.

She was just flat out ruthless.

She turned to walk off, leaving me with my heart racing and my mind reeling from finally getting the answers I thought I wanted. But… it couldn't end like this, not with her threatening to disrupt my life more than she already had.

I wasn't about to play this game with her.

"Miranda. Miranda, *wait*," I called, only to be completely ignored. I blew out a sigh, then stalked up to her, touching her shoulder to get her attention, but as soon as my hand made contact, she turned and shoved me, which sent me reeling in my stiletto heels.

324

Pain rang through my head as I hit the metal leg of one of the autopsy tables, and I closed my eyes for a second, hoping the sting would be short-lived. But when I opened them again, Miranda was standing over me, her face twisted with rage as she drove downward with a knife she'd pulled from somewhere in her hands.

Reflexively, I kicked her, aiming for the side of her knee instead of the front, just like Wick had taught me. She buckled to the floor, and the knife went skittering across the polished concrete, landing underneath the table. I didn't even give it a second thought – I dove for it.

"*Ahhh!*" I screamed as pain shot up my leg, radiating from my ankle. I looked back to find that Miranda had gotten ahold of one my shoes, using it like some sort of dagger to strike me. I kicked at her again, getting another shot off before she could repeat that same move a second time.

I got my hand on the knife and then scrambled away from her, holding it up in warning. I hoped she would pick up on my nonverbal threat, and keep her distance, but instead, she dove at me again, fingernails bared, as if she were some sort of wild animal, so I did what I had to do.

The only thing I *could* do.

Putting all the force behind it that I could, I shoved the knife forward, into her chest as she lunged. The penetration stopped her cold, and I let the knife go, moving away from her as she toppled forward, falling face-first onto the frigid concrete floor.

I got the hell away from her, kicking off my other shoe and moving backward to the door, keeping my eyes on her as I went. She had turned herself over, and was writhing on the floor, clutching at the knife in her chest as her mouth moved, searching for the air to produce words.

None came.

I was on ultra-high-alert, ready to take down anybody else that came at me when the autopsy attendant came back to the door, almost getting his nose broken when he caught me by surprise pulling it open.

He stepped in, looking at me in my defensive stance, ready to fight, and then at Miranda, eyes wide open and lifeless on the floor.

"Oh, *shit*, what the fuck is this?!" he asked, then started backing away from me. "Uh… um… *shit*. Stay here!" he demanded, and then shot out of the room.

A few minutes later, Sam came rushing through the door, followed shortly by Wick, with his bandages hanging half off.

Sam went to Miranda, and Wick came to me, closing me up in his arms. "Are you okay?" was the first question out of his mouth. Not *what happened,* or *what's going on.*

*Was I okay?*

I nodded, to answer his question, snuggling closer as I turned to look at Miranda on the floor.

"Yeah," I said. "I'm fine. It's over."

"*Stop*. You're going to make me late," Monica protested, words that were in direct opposition to her hand around my wrist, urging me to keep doing *exactly* what I was doing. I wasn't sure what she'd thought I'd do, upon coming home to find her – unexpected – in my shower, skin all soapy and wet, looking like a good time I wanted to be a part of.

What I'd done was gotten naked and joined her, pressing her back into the shower wall while I hooked her legs around my waist and drove into her. And she'd enjoyed *every* bit of it – especially after I dropped down in front of her, propping her thigh over my shoulder to indulge myself in the wonder between her legs.

But *now* she wanted to complain about the time, while not *letting* me stop, after we'd already finished in the shower and then moved to the closet, trying to choose my attire for the night.

"Does it seem like I give a fuck about that right now?" I asked her, closing my eyes as her hand strokes hit a particularly good pace, and she squeezed around me. Monica must've hit that same threshold, because a moment later, she went stiff as she came, prompting my eruption all over her hands.

"You *should*," she scolded, once she'd rested for a moment, and then untangled herself from me on the closet floor where we'd fallen after losing the battle to keep our hands to ourselves.

We were *always* fighting that battle.

I followed her back to the bathroom. She didn't know I was watching, but I caught the little smile Monica gave herself in the mirror before she turned the faucet on to wash her hands. After the hell she'd been through, I was just happy to see her smile at all.

I almost couldn't.

Nearly a month had passed now, since that altercation with her father's wife in that morgue. She'd been shaken up about it for weeks – finally getting her answers hadn't brought the peace she'd expected. Instead, she just felt unsettled, and the frenzied media scandal in the aftermath hadn't helped.

Most of her month had been spent holed up here, with me, while Chloe fought the onslaught of people wanting to hear from Monica about her role in a scandal that rocked the beauty industry. People wanting to know how she felt about the fact that Glen Pearson had suffered a heart attack over the stress of the breaking news, especially once other mistresses, other children he'd fathered and abandoned, starting coming out of the woodwork. Monica never even got to speak to him, confront him, talk to him face to face.

But she wasn't bothered by it, she claimed, and I believed her when she said it.

*I already met him. Him and Kellen, those last two years at least… I believe they were one in the same.*

She was coming out of it though. More and more, I was seeing her smile, especially now that the media had moved on to something else, and that new assistant of hers, Tarra, had been phenomenal at helping get *Vivid Vixen* back on track.

I hadn't really expected her to move out though.

I mean… I knew it was only a matter of time before we'd have to discuss living arrangements, but I was still enjoying the hell out of having her under me at all times when she announced she was going

328

back to her place. We hadn't defined anything other than her status as *"mine"*, so there wasn't much arguing I could do – not to mention that it was too soon to do any arguing about that anyway.

Plus, there was that whole, *let it go, if it comes back it's really yours* thing, so… we would see. I was a patient enough man to let it ride, and do what made her happy, including overseeing the installation of the latest in home security systems, and doing the same on a corporate level for the *Vivid Vixen* offices – I was *still* pissed that Amanda had gotten past security with a gun.

"What is Kay going to say if we're late? This is a big night for her," Monica said as I stepped past her into the bathroom to clean myself up.

I raised an eyebrow. "She isn't even going to notice. They do twenty minutes worth of special announcements and making sure the orchestra is right and all that bullshit before the show starts. We'll be fine. Why are you being uptight?"

"I'm not being uptight," she said, pulling the – apparently – super secure shower cap from her head, making way for her head full of natural curls to spill out. "I just… she wants this night to be perfect, and if we can help with that by being on time…"

That made me grin. "Awww. Look at you being a good future-stepmama," I said, not considering the implication of those words before they spilled out. I found myself doing a *lot* of that shit with Monica, letting all my CIA training to do more listening than talking fly right out of the window.

Still though, there was no missing the… *delight,* in Monica's eyes at my words – emotion that she quickly blinked away, always trying to play it cool. I didn't mind it. She'd just left a relationship with a pure asshole, in a pretty ugly manner. She deserved to keep herself a bit reserved about her feelings if she wanted to.

"You know… I did her manicure for tonight, and uh… she hugged me, and it was… nice. It feels good that she's accepted me so easily."

I shrugged. "It helps that I apparently talked about you as Sandy constantly, and she was a fan of yours before all of the… drama. She doesn't feel like you're a stranger invading her life. And I say all that, but… Kay is notoriously mean to women I've dated in the past, no matter how casually. So it says a lot – means a lot – to me too, that she *really* likes you."

"She said that?" Monica asked, her eyes lighting up before she could suppress it.

"Yes," I laughed. "She did."

Monica gave a deep nod, training her expression back to neutral. "Oh. Cool."

I smacked her on the ass I left the bathroom to get myself dressed while Monica did her makeup and whatever else she needed to do. Thirty minutes later, she was dragging me out the door before I dragged her out of the black catsuit she'd donned underneath a white and black pinstriped blazer.

Her ass was begging me to, but the woman herself wasn't having it.

"I'll see you there," she said, blowing me a kiss before she opened the door to her Mercedes. She'd insisted on separate vehicles because after Kay's performance, she was going to dinner with her homegirls, and planned on going home after.

*"Stay over tonight"* was on the tip of my tongue, but I cooled it. After having her life in danger, being confined to the house, and everything else, she *needed* this. And damn if I was going to get in the way of it.

"Yeah, gorgeous," I said, coming to close her door for her. "I'll see you there."

*Damn… it's getting pretty late.*

330

Almost as soon as that thought crossed my mind, I shook my head, telling myself to relax. What the hell was I doing checking the time every few minutes, clocking Monica like she wasn't a grown ass woman with no curfew?

*Who would have thought...*

I sat back from my computer, and chuckled. Two months ago, I would've called anyone claiming that I was the type to be missing the woman who was supposed to be in my bed a lie. Hell, just the idea that *supposed to be in my bed* was something that would ever cross my mind, would've been met with derision. I swore that I wasn't an "attachments" kind of guy.

But here I was, attached as *fuck*, wondering why Monica hadn't checked in or something to let me know she'd made it home. I knew she was going to be out with her girls for a while, but it was coming up on one in the morning, and I'd never known her to hang *that* tough, even back when I knew her as Sandy.

I wasn't *worried* about her though.

My gut still hadn't led me wrong when it came to that. Even after Asher was arrested, something hadn't felt right. Even after shooting Amanda, something hadn't felt right. But with Miranda Cline gone, the inkling that something else was lurking just out of sight had gone away. Aside from the usual things to be on alert about, I was confident that Monica was safe, so it wasn't that.

I just flat out missed her, even though I'd already seen her today.

And... I really didn't give a fuck about it being plain as day.

When I met up with the guys after Kay's performance, it must've been on my face when they asked, because I ended up getting thoroughly roasted. Especially by Quentin, who I'd talked to about Monica in the beginning of this ordeal. He remembered my attitude about it then, my belief that things between Monica and I could never be the same. And really... I was right. They couldn't.

There was no turning back from here.

I was just getting ready to send her a text, when my computer pinged, alerting me of an incoming video call. I dropped my phone to my desktop when I saw that it was from Monica, who I'd set up with a more secure, direct access line to me. My mouth went dry as soon as I answered the call.

She was dressed in white – a simple, skimpy ass gown that her nipples showed right through. Her face was scrubbed clean of the makeup she'd worn earlier, hair tied up in a silky, leopard print scarf. And she looked *damn* good.

"What is this about?" I asked, grinning as I adjusted my camera so that my face was visible now too. It was damn near nostalgic, seeing her on my screen, in her office. A sight I'd seen hundreds of times before, only now, there was no element of anonymity, no need – or desire – to hide anything.

"I… can't sleep," she said, propping her elbow on the arm of her chair, and dropping her chin down to her closed fist. "You told me once that I could *always* call you when I couldn't sleep, so that's what I decided to do."

"You could've just come to me, once you were done with your girls."

She frowned a bit as she dipped her head. "I could've. But, I called myself being respectful, by not coming to your place smelling, and probably tasting, like alcohol. We may have had one or five drinks."

The corners of my lips turned up. "I… appreciate that," I told her. "Thank you for considering me."

"You're very welcome."

"I'd still rather have you here though. Sobriety be damned."

She laughed. "Uh, *no*. But, I will be liquor free for you to have me all day tomorrow."

"I *guess* that'll do," I said, making her laugh again. "If that's the case though, I probably need to get some sleep too."

"What are you doing up anyway?" she asked.

"Working, since Renata reminded me that I do still have a business to run, even though were fine during my absence. And, of course… waiting to hear from you. I'm glad you called. I wouldn't have been able to sleep either. Hell… I still may not."

332

Monica shook her head. "Uh-uh. I have a cure for you."

I raised an eyebrow. "What's that?"

A mischievous grin spread across her face as she reached down, and I heard the sliding sound of her desk drawer. She winked at the camera when she came up again, holding a small bottle of my *Creed* cologne.

"Wow," I said, shaking my head as she sprayed it in the air, then inhaled. "No fair. You know I never did replace your perfume?"

She smiled. "Check your bottom drawer."

I narrowed my eyes as I reached for it, to pull it open. And sure enough, a brand new bottle of her signature Tom Ford perfume was there, just begging to be sprayed. I was already hard from seeing her, but I got harder just thinking about it.

"What are you waiting for?" she asked, pulling my attention back to the screen.

*"Goddamn,"* I groaned. While I'd been looking in the drawer, she'd been hiking her legs over the arms of her office chair, spreading herself wide open for me to see.

"Wick," she said, in that sexy, husky voice, looking sinfully angelic in that gown as her hands moved to grope her breasts, showcasing her deep red nails. "Show me yours. And then tell me what you want me to do."

My dick was already straining against my boxers and sweat pants, so I did as she asked, and set it free. I wrapped my hand around it, and then sat back, admiring the perfection of the woman on my screen.

"Get some of that sweetness on your fingers so you can play with it for me."

If you'd like to learn more about Marcus, Mimi, Quentin, Renata, or any other from the *Five Star* crew, you can check out my *If You Can* series – my very first romantic suspense babies. 😊

## *Catch Me If You Can*
## *Release Me If You Can*
## *Save Me If You Can*

*Special thanks to Love B, Alex, Jeanette, Nasi, and Phyllis and BIG thanks to my betas, for the valuable feedback that made this project possible –Carolyn, Doris, Jemeka, Jill, and Roslyn.*
*Thank you <3*

I hope you enjoyed Monica and Wick's story! Please consider leaving a review. You can also reach me via my website (www.beingmrsjones.com) on facebook (www.facebook.com/beingmrsjones) on twitter (www.twitter.com/beingmrsjones) or instagram (www.instagram.com/beingmrsjones) For notifications about new releases, sales, events, or other announcements, you can subscribe to my mailing list.

*Christina C. Jones is a modern romance novelist who has penned more than 30 love stories. She has earned a reputation as a storyteller who seamlessly weaves the complexities of modern life into captivating tales of black romance.*

**Other titles by Christina Jones**
*Love and Other Things*
*Haunted (paranormal)*
*Mine Tonight (erotica)*
**More Than a Hashtag**
*Relationship Goals*
**High Stakes**
*Ante Up*
**Sweet Heat**
*Hints of Spice (Highlight Reel spinoff)*
*A Dash of Heat*
**Truth, Lies, and Consequences**
*The Truth – His Side, Her Side, And the Truth About Falling In Love*
*The Lies – The Lies We Tell About Life, Love, and Everything in Between*
**Friends & Lovers:**
*Finding Forever*
*Chasing Commitment*
**Strictly Professional:**
*Strictly Professional*
*Unfinished Business*
**Serendipitous Love:**